"SULU! TAKE OFF! *NOW!*"
CHEKOV SHOUTED . . .

. . . just as the shuttle lifted off in a cloud of powder-fine ash. He caught the edges of the doorway, unbalanced on his knees just inside the hatch, and heard the first phaser fire from below as the Elasians turned their stolen weapons against them.

Uhura jerked around at the shrill report, and a deflected bolt skated past the hatchway to splatter against the wall behind her. Chekov meant to yell at her, to warn her to keep down and away from the line of fire.

Instead, he felt his whole body arch in a single unexpected seizure, and his grip on the hatchway went suddenly numb and strengthless. They'd hit him, he realized dully. Damn.

Chekov didn't actually feel it when he let go of the shuttle, but from the horrified sound of Uhura's cry he knew he'd fallen . . .

Look for STAR TREK Fiction from Pocket Books

Star Trek: The Original Series

Star Trek: The Next Generation

Star Trek: Deep Space Nine

STAR TREK®

FIRESTORM

L. A. GRAF

POCKET BOOKS

New York   London   Toronto   Sydney   Tokyo   Singapore

An *Original* Publication of POCKET BOOKS

POCKET BOOKS, a division of Simon & Schuster Inc.
1230 Avenue of the Americas, New York, NY 10020

This book is published by Pocket Books, a division of Simon & Schuster Inc., under exclusive license from Paramount Pictures.

ISBN: 0-671-86588-9

First Pocket Books printing January 1994

10 9 8 7 6 5 4 3 2 1

POCKET and colophon are registered trademarks of Simon & Schuster Inc.

Printed in the U.S.A.

To Rusty

and the Star Trek Widows Support Group.
We'll try to get you a second member soon.

Historian's Note

This adventure takes place shortly after the events of *Star Trek: The Motion Picture,* during the second five-year mission of the *U.S.S. Enterprise.*

FIRESTORM

Chapter One

CAPTAIN JAMES KIRK paused by one of the Johnston Observatory's sloping walls. He pressed both hands to the transparent aluminum as he stood on tiptoe to see a little farther across the horizon. Skaftar wasn't the strangest moon Kirk had ever been on, but long-dead volcanoes and kilometer-wide basalt basins certainly made it one of the least inviting. Some Lunar natives he'd met claimed that moonscapes from any system were more beautiful than planets, once you knew how to look at them. Kirk had been trying to learn how for years. He had yet to find anything to like about fractured rock, changeless dust, and a day-night terminus that sliced across the landscape like a phaser cut.

Someone came up close on his right, and Kirk knew it was Uhura even before she stepped into his peripheral vision to add her own handprints to the much touched and leaned-upon window. Kirk had long ago accepted the fact that he kept track of his landing parties' movements without consciously realizing it. McCoy said it was what made him a good commander. Kirk had a feeling it just made him tense.

"Not much like home, is it?" Uhura rose up on her toes to

peer across the moonscape after Kirk. The motion only brought her head as high as the captain's shoulder, though, and she sank flat-footed again with a little sigh.

"Don't worry, Commander," Kirk reassured her with a smile. "There isn't that much to see."

She shrugged, but didn't turn away from the bleakness outside. "Not here, anyway." She drew Kirk's attention to the planet, huge and blue, just rising above Skaftar's broken horizon. "At least Rakatan has an atmosphere."

Kirk couldn't help laughing a little. Uhura raised a questioning eyebrow, and he amended, "Such as it is." As clear and crystalline as Rakatan's oceans looked from here, word from the observatory was that they were chilly and empty of life above the microscopic, the atmosphere that blanketed them high in carbon dioxide and natural volcanic pollution. Even as they watched, one of the planet's tiny landmasses seemed to bleed like wet ink into the water all around it, billowing gray in all directions. A readout farther down the transparent wall from Uhura came to life and caught the captain's attention: VOLCANIC ERUPTION IN PROGRESS.

Kirk shook his head in wonderment, turning back toward where the roiling black mass was quickly obscuring a large swath of the planet's dayside. *From orbit,* he thought, incredulous. *We're seeing it in this much detail from here!* "That must be Rakatan Mons."

A woman's crusty old voice startled Kirk. "Not quite, Captain."

Kirk turned a bit more abruptly than he'd intended, nearly running into the wizened, white-haired geologist behind him. She elbowed past him, oblivious of his surprise, and squinted up at Rakatan—as Spock, following her, took his place at Kirk's shoulder with arms folded. "Rakatan Mons isn't the only volcano on this planet, you know," she said.

Kirk cocked an amused look at his first officer. "Dr. Bascomb, I presume?" he asked the Vulcan.

Spock nodded once, unperturbed. "Indeed."

Indeed. Then Spock and Bascomb must be finished reviewing the geologists' records; for all that work, it hadn't taken very long.

"That's Mazama Mons," Bascomb announced, tapping one gnarled finger on the window. "Six thousand meters high and one hundred and twenty kilometers in diameter at her base." As Uhura adjusted her position, Bascomb took hold of Uhura's wrist and unceremoniously pulled the lieutenant commander to stand in front of her, the way a teacher would handle a first grader who'd complained about not having a perfect view. Bascomb continued without a pause, "Mazama's active almost continually, with a cataclysmic eruption every"—the geologist shrugged—"oh, six months or so. One of the most frequent patterns on the planet, really. In comparison, Rakatan Mons hasn't done more than rumble for the last fifteen thousand years."

Far from resentful of the scientist's audacity, Uhura seemed charmed by the older woman. She tipped her head back, dark brows curiously knit. "You know all that just by watching these volcanoes from orbit for the last twenty years?"

Bascomb glanced down and seemed to really notice the small officer for the first time. "Not entirely from orbit," she allowed, releasing Uhura and stepping a little away. "We make shuttle trips to the surface every now and again, for samples or to repair monitoring equipment. Rakatan is one of the most geologically active environments in the Federation." She tossed a frown back at Spock. "A lot like Vulcan four or five billion years ago, as I recall. Anyway, we can't stay planetside for very long."

A deep note, like the song of a starship's impulse engines, interrupted, and Bascomb's weathered face brightened. It took Kirk a moment to realize that the sound came from the observatory's own intercom system. By then, the geologist had snatched the shoulder of his jacket and pulled him around to face the planet again. "Dr. Bascomb, I—"

"There, Captain," she said, taking his chin to direct his gaze to the left. "Coming up on morningside now." The

3

pride and pleasure in her voice were unmistakable. *"That's Rakatan Mons."*

Kirk almost forgave her irreverent handling when the snow-mantled peak slipped from night into morning and burst into sun-splashed brilliance. "My God . . ." All he could think of was how much damage Rakatan Mons could do if it ever decided to be active. "That's almost the size of a small continent!"

"Five-eighths the base surface of Australia," Spock confirmed politely.

"And the quietest mountain on the planet," Bascomb added. She gave a little snort of amusement and shrugged. "Go figure."

Kirk tried to imagine Mount Everest on Earth as a volcano, its flanks burning with ash and steaming mud. Or Mount Selaya on Vulcan on the day ten thousand years ago when it destroyed its peak with such force that it cratered moons several light-minutes away. He was suddenly very appreciative of Iowa, with its occasional tornadoes and a tendency toward seasonal floods.

"Dr. Bascomb . . ." Uhura turned to lean her shoulder against the window, frowning thoughtfully upward at the older scientist. "Are you sure the intelligent signals you're receiving—"

"Allegedly intelligent, Commander."

She acknowledged Spock's correction with a little nod, but didn't take her attention away from Bascomb. "Are you sure they're coming from the volcano itself?" She waved a graceful hand toward the planet. "Surely there's enough landmass around the base to support a small civilization."

Bascomb turned her back on the distant volcano and motioned for them to follow when she started into the main observatory. "So far, Commander, the highest form of life we've found on Rakatan is a colonial slime mold that turns a lovely pink when exposed to too much sunlight." She pressed her hand against a print lock outside a windowless door. "There isn't even grass or algae on the planet, much less anything with a nervous system."

The door irised open onto a small, rock-strewn lab littered with workstations and sample slides. A young blond woman—just the right age to be a graduate student or a new Ph.D.—glanced away from her microscopy work long enough to flick blue eyes across their uniforms and frown with worry. Kirk tried smiling to make her feel at ease, but only gained a startled blush in reply. Her eyes flashed to Spock as the first officer continued his conversation with Uhura.

"All of the records Dr. Bascomb has shown me have been taken from the seismic stations located on Rakatan Mons." Spock shot a keen look at the terminal closest to him without interrupting his speaking. "These seismic devices register earthquake and volcanic activity only, and beam the data directly to the observatory via satellite. It is highly unlikely any surface-dwelling life on a planet as young as Rakatan could possess the capability to alter such a signal."

"Unless that life could actually cause the earthquakes."

Spock lifted a disdainful eyebrow at the blond lab worker, and Kirk gave the girl credit for not flinching beneath the Vulcan's chill stare. It was all Kirk could do to suppress a smile.

Bascomb didn't feel so compelled. "Wendy Metcalfe," she introduced the girl, leaning over Kirk's shoulder with a crooked grin. "One of my students."

"And the one who filed the original report to the Federation." Kirk recognized her name from the files he'd read on their way in the night before. He stepped around a lab table to offer her his hand. "Life inside a volcano."

Metcalfe stood, a little hesitantly, and shook Kirk's hand while still stealing glances at the officers behind him. "The seismic reports are very compelling," she began.

Spock cut her off before she could go on. "On the contrary, Ms. Metcalfe. The records themselves are fragmentary and complicated, the identified periodic anomaly not inconsistent with convective circulation inside a large magma chamber."

"But that could be part of the life-form's behavior,"

Metcalfe jumped in, cheeks pink with excitement. "Any creature living in magma at higher than eight hundred fifty degrees Celsius would have to be made of molten silicate—"

"—and therefore lack the structural integrity necessary to conduct bioelectric or biochemical signals."

"Not necessarily. In magma this viscous, incipient crystal lattices could function as a primitive nervous system—"

"That assumes a residence time sufficient to foster crystal variation and natural selection, which I calculate would require at least—"

"Spock?"

The Vulcan paused in mid-jargon to cock his head at the captain.

"Do we need to know this for our mission?" Kirk asked.

Spock seemed to consider the point for a moment, then blinked and admitted, "In a strictly practical sense, no, Captain, we do not."

Kirk had suspected as much. "Then let's skip to the next question." He offered Metcalfe an apologetic nod, and was disappointed when she pursed her lips and returned stiffly to her work. He knew you never did get used to having your ideas ignored just because you were the graduate student, even if you understood why it had to be that way. "Is there any chance the signals are originating as a malfunction in the seismic system itself? Could it simply be transmitting its data incorrectly?"

Spock lifted both eyebrows—a Vulcan shrug. "That is always a possibility. But I would rather defer to Commander Uhura's greater expertise in such matters."

The communications officer frowned thoughtfully when the others turned to her. "I'll have to look at the specs on the equipment." She glanced a question up at Bascomb. "And it would help if I could examine all the planetside stations, too."

Bascomb snorted and hiked herself onto the nearest lab table. "Well, that is the problem, isn't it?"

Kirk exchanged looks with Uhura, who only lifted one shoulder in confusion. He turned to Bascomb. "Doctor?"

"Listen, Captain," the geologist proclaimed with expansive good humor, "if you can get to the seismic stations, you're welcome to them. But nobody from up here's been able to get close enough to adjust their telemetry, much less verify their readings, for almost two months now."

"Volcanic activity?" Spock asked.

Bascomb looked at him as though he were crazy. "Of course not. Elasians."

"Elasians?" Kirk felt as if he'd walked into a different conversation than the one he thought he'd started. "Where?"

"Here." Bascomb laughed aloud at his expression of blank surprise. "Didn't Starfleet tell you?" Kirk found that a particularly irritating question, considering that they obviously had not. "The Elasians barged in here seven weeks ago and set up a mining camp on the slopes of Rakatan Mons." She leaned back on her elbows and scowled with a pent-up disgust that Kirk could all too well understand. "They're shooting down every probe we send into the area."

Kirk shook his head. "But why?"

"Because they claim they own the planet," Bascomb told him. "And we figured Starfleet had a better chance than we do of telling them otherwise."

As often as Uhura told herself it was an illusion born of heightened adrenaline, she remained secretly convinced that the turbolift doors opened faster when Captain Kirk was in a hurry. It seemed as if the rest of the crew knew that, too—all eyes turned eagerly to meet them as they emerged onto the bridge. Or perhaps, Uhura thought wryly, the crew looked up like that at every turbolift when they knew the captain was due back.

"Reports," Kirk said crisply. He hadn't waited to get back to the ship to begin dealing with the unexpected problem of the Elasians. Orders for priority hailing, planetary scans, background reports, and inquiries to Starfleet Headquarters had volleyed through his communicator before he'd finally given Scott the command to transport them back from the Johnston Observatory. The results greeted them now in a disciplined cascade of information.

"No reply from the Elasians to our priority hail, Captain." Commander Scott willingly surrendered the captain's chair. The ice-crowned bulk of Rakatan Mons sprawled across the main viewscreen behind him, dwarfing the big chief engineer as he crossed back to his normal bridge station. "If you ask me, I think they're ignoring us."

Kirk made an irritated noise. "Keep hailing them, Uhura, until they respond."

"Aye, sir." Uhura took over the communications station, accepting the output monitor from the young ensign she'd left in charge. Ashcraft silently showed her the subspace message he'd sent to Starfleet, and she nodded approval of the code he'd used. With a sigh of relief, he headed for the turbolift, and Uhura turned her attention to the familiar problem of making contact with a proud and stubborn alien race.

Kirk had already gone on to the next problem. "Have we located the Elasian base yet?"

It was Sulu's turn to reply. "Long-range scanners report only one manned installation on the planet, Captain. It's about a third of the way up that big volcano—"

"At an altitude of two thousand, two hundred and thirty-seven meters, to be precise." As usual, Spock had wasted no time in reclaiming his science station from the young ensign who'd held it. Cobalt reflections scrolled across the Vulcan's face as he read through the sensor output at a rate no human could have matched. "The planetary coordinates are—"

"Never mind that, Spock." Kirk swung his chair to face the security station. "Defense status of the Elasian base, Mr. Chekov?"

"Their main defense is a class-two force shield, Captain. Able to disrupt transporter beams, but not strong enough to withstand orbital phaser fire." Chekov keyed in a different output screen, and the light on his face shifted from amber to green. "Our weapons sensors detect no active phaser batteries on the planet. There is one warp-capable flyer at the Elasian base, but it's armed only with light photon weapons."

Kirk's eyebrows gathered in a scowl. "One *warp-capable* flyer?"

"Aye, sir." Chekov slanted the captain an uncertain look. "I can scan again for confirmation."

"No, Mr. Chekov. I don't think the problem's with your sensors." Kirk swung around to face Spock again. "Mr. Spock, do we have that background report on Elas yet?"

"The computer is compiling it now, Captain." The science officer consulted his screen. "Completion expected in nine point four minutes."

"See if you can hurry that up." Kirk sprang from his chair and began restlessly prowling the bridge. As he passed her, Uhura answered his inquiring look with a wordless shake of her head. All frequencies had stayed stubbornly silent, including the ones reserved for Starfleet use.

The turbolift doors whistled open again, at a normal speed this time, and let Dr. McCoy through. One look at the quiet bridge must have told the chief medical officer that nothing urgent was in progress. He gave Uhura a friendly smile as he passed her, then strolled down toward the captain.

"So, Jim," he drawled. "What's this I hear about us running into some Elasians?"

Kirk gave the doctor an exasperated look. "Is there a subspace rumor generator aboard this ship?"

McCoy grinned. "Nope, just a computer that accessed my old medical files while I happened to be in them." McCoy leaned over Spock's shoulder, audaciously reading his input lines. "Why are you looking up Elasian mining technology, Spock? Even Elasians wouldn't be stupid enough to try mining a planet that's barely cool enough to walk on."

Spock straightened and lifted one quelling eyebrow at the doctor. "If Rakatan's crust were as hot as you suggest, Dr.

McCoy, the planet would not possess the extensive oceans you see on the viewscreen behind you. And I would like to point out that humans have settled several far less hospitable worlds—"

"Not any that might blow up under their feet at a moment's notice!" McCoy retorted. "Only Vulcans think of volcanoes as normal backyard scenery."

Whatever response Spock would have made to that comment was cut off by a quick chirp from his science station. "A preliminary version of the Elasian background report has now been compiled, Captain." The science officer took the opportunity to turn his shoulder to McCoy. "Do you wish to read it in its entirety, or do you have specific questions?"

"Questions," Kirk said briefly. "First of all, Mr. Spock, I want to know how the hell the Elasians got here."

Spock frowned. "I believe you will have to be more specific than that, Captain."

Kirk gestured the Vulcan's attention toward the volcanoscape on the viewscreen. "Rakatan and the rest of the Ordover system lie half a quadrant away from the Tellun system, correct?"

Spock nodded. "Fifteen point six nine light-years, to be exact."

"But the last time we saw the Elasians—" Kirk paused briefly, and Uhura wondered if he was remembering the Elasian woman they'd carried on that memorable voyage across the Tellun system all those years ago. In Uhura's opinion, Elaan, the Dohlman of Elas and queen of Troyius, wasn't the kind of person anyone could forget. "—they had fission-powered ships. With that technology, it should have taken them eighty years to get here, and Starfleet would have known about it. How did they do it?"

"The obvious answer," replied Spock calmly, "is that they did not come in fission-powered ships."

Kirk frowned across at him. "Do you know that for sure, or are you just guessing?"

The Vulcan lifted both eyebrows, looking as close to

offended as Uhura had ever seen him. "I am making a *surmise,* Captain—"

"He's guessing," McCoy said.

"—based on all available facts, including Lieutenant Chekov's scan of the planet. Do not forget that the Elasians' sister planet, Troyius, holds one of the richest dilithium deposits in the galaxy. With wealth like that available—"

"—almost anyone would be willing to supply them with black-market warp technology," Kirk acknowledged. "But it would help to know exactly who their supplier was. This is a fringe system, after all."

Spock bowed his head in agreement. "I will consult the background report and endeavor to supply you with that information, Captain."

"Good." Kirk swung away from him and prowled back toward Uhura. "Still no reply from the Elasians?"

"No, sir." Uhura paused; then, prompted more by instinct than thought, she turned off the automatic priority hail. "Captain, may I have your permission to try a different approach?"

Kirk blinked at her in surprise. "What could be more effective than a priority hail?"

"But a priority hail is so—" Uhura paused, searching for the right words. "—so *imperative,* Captain. The Elasians might consider it disrespectful." She guessed from the amused quirk of his mouth that Kirk was remembering the same Elasian temper tantrums she was. "Perhaps if I asked them in person and more politely, they might respond."

Kirk's face lit with an unexpectedly boyish grin. "Well, my mother always told me that it doesn't cost anything to be polite. Give it a try, Commander."

Uhura turned back to her board. It took her only a minute to compose her message and key the universal translator to broadcast on all frequencies. "Planet Rakatan, this is the *Starship Enterprise,*" she said in her most courteous voice. "We respectfully request permission to speak to the leader of your expedition, at her convenience."

From the corner of her eye, when she paused to allow the

Elasians time to respond, Uhura saw Kirk's gesture for silence. She turned her transmitter off, keeping her monitor at her ear. "Is there a problem, sir?"

Kirk lifted an inquiring eyebrow. *"Her* convenience?"

"In case there was a Dohlman with them," Uhura explained. "I didn't want to insult her by assuming their leader was a man."

"A logical precaution, Commander," Spock agreed. Uhura felt her cheeks warm with pleasure at that rare compliment, even though McCoy snorted at it. "However, I must inform you that there is very little probability that an Elasian female warlord would accompany a simple mining expedition."

"I know that, Mr. Spock, but—" Uhura broke off, hearing a dim but familiar buzz in her monitor. "Signal coming through from the planet, Captain."

"Put it on the main screen." Kirk swung around and vaulted down to the lower level of the bridge as Uhura tightened her fix on the wavering signal and fed it to the viewscreen. The icy slopes of Rakatan Mons vanished, replaced by a determined young face. The smooth dark skin and strong jaw could have belonged to either a boy or a girl, but the gold-braided hair and arrogant, dark-eyed stare told Uhura that this teenager belonged to the dominant sex on Elas.

"For once, Spock, probability theory has failed you." Kirk inclined his head politely at the screen. "I presume I'm speaking to a Dohlman of Elas?"

"Not a Dohlman of Elas." The young girl thrust back her gilt-edged cloak to show him the ruby-hilted gold knife she wore strapped to her thigh. *"The* Dohlman of Elas."

Chapter Two

"I WISH TO SPEAK to the commander of your cohort," the Dohlman of Elas said for the third time, her eyes narrowing on the screen. Under the lilting Elasian accent, Uhura recognized the snap of irritation in her voice.

Captain Kirk's voice held almost the same tone when he replied. "I *am* the commander of this cohort. Your Glory." The last two words sounded as if he had to force them out between his teeth. Uhura suspected Kirk had as much trouble as she did believing that this coltish youngster really was the supreme ruler of Elas.

"How can that be, underling?" The young girl lifted a hand to point accusingly at him. "I can see two females in the same room as you. I will speak to the one who is a Dohlman."

Kirk looked down at his quiet female navigator, Lieutenant Bhutto, then back over his shoulder at Uhura. He sighed. "In our society, Your Glory, our Dohlmen do not—"

"Takcas, I am insulted by the unauthorized words of this

13

insect," the Dohlman declared to someone offscreen. "Cut the contact."

"—speak to other Dohlmen to whom they have not been properly introduced," Kirk finished smoothly.

A small hand made an imperious gesture, and the static that had begun to cloud the screen cleared again. From beneath snake-thick black curls, almond-shaped eyes regarded Kirk suspiciously. "Introduced?"

"By their chief underlings." Kirk ignored the muffled sound that burst from McCoy. "If you will not speak to me, put your own chief underling on the screen and I will introduce our Dohlman through him."

A curt nod answered him, and the view shifted to a red-haired Elasian male in a leather-belted tunic that exposed heavily muscled arms. "I am Takcas."

Kirk met his grim stare with one just as unflinching. "Takcas, I am Kirk. Behind me, you see Dohlman Uhura, who did you such great honor by hailing you in person when you refused our previous request for contact."

Takcas grunted, not looking very impressed. "And you, Kirk, were honored by the reply of our Dohlman who is *the* Dohlman, the glorious Israi, twelfth of the line of Kesmeth."

"There." Israi's strongly angled face appeared on the screen again, mouth tight with impatience. "We are introduced now, Kirk-insect. Let me speak to your Dohlman."

Bhutto cast an anxious glance back over her shoulder, and Kirk gave her a reassuring shake of his head. "Dohlman Uhura," he said, turning toward her and deliberately away from the communicator pickup. "Are you willing to speak to Her Glory, the Dohlman Israi?" Unseen by the Elasians, the captain's lips formed the words "Monitor channel to science station."

"Yes, Captain," Uhura said, answering both question and command at once. Her fingers ran across her board, linking her monitor to the speaker pickup at Spock's console. Kirk nodded and moved out of communicator view.

"Dohlman Uhura." Israi sounded a little less certain of herself now that she was confronting another woman, and one older than herself, as well. Uhura wondered how long the girl had actually been *the* Dohlman of Elas. "Why did you contact me?"

Kirk's whisper buzzed in her ear through her communications monitor. "Ask her why they're here."

Uhura judged it best to be a little less blunt than that. "As part of our—I mean my—duty to Starfleet, Dohlman Israi, my ship must check all settlements on uninhabited planets. Would you be kind enough to inform me of the reasons for your presence here?"

The girl lifted her chin, giving it an even more arrogant sweep against her black hair. "We are mining," she announced proudly. "Dilithium, in great quantity."

Uhura heard stifled gasps from around the bridge. When Kirk spoke in her ear this time, his voice was more grim. "Ask her what right she has to mine on this planet."

"Dohlman Israi, this planet does not appear on our ship charts as part of Elasian space. By whose permission do you mine here?"

"No one's permission!" Israi's almond eyes glittered with sudden anger. "This system was charted by Elasian ships in the days of my ancestors. It is ours by right of first landing, as set out in Federation law!"

The youthful indignation in Israi's voice sounded genuine. Uhura slid Kirk a swift glance, and saw him looking thoughtful.

"Ask her if we can examine the charts she refers to," his voice murmured from her monitor.

Uhura conveyed the request, and saw Israi glance questioningly at someone offscreen. A male voice spoke, too softly for the universal translator to catch, and Uhura almost smiled. It seemed she was not the only one being prompted in this conversation.

"The charts are here, with us," said Israi at last. "You may examine them as you please, but we will not surrender them to you. You will come to me. After all, you are only a Dohlman. I am *the* Dohlman."

The last words were spoken with a uniquely Elasian

combination of imperious command and disdain. Through
her monitor, Uhura heard Kirk's teeth click with frustration. Then he muttered, "Agree to visit, Uhura. Tell them to
expect a shuttle in an hour, with you and three guards on
board. And a geologist guide, in case you have to navigate
the terrain."

Uhura took a deep breath. "I agree to your request,
Dohlman Israi. You can expect me and four—uh—
underlings in one hour."

Israi raised her angled brows, looking scornful. "You have
a cohort of only four? You are not such a great Dohlman,
then."

This time, Uhura didn't wait for Kirk to prompt her
reply. "I have a cohort of nearly a thousand," she said,
summoning up a voice of equal scorn. "But since my ship
can easily destroy your outpost from orbit, I don't need to
be put to the trouble of bringing them all."

Kirk's soft whistle in her ear told her he approved of the
retort. Israi's mouth never quivered, but the slight crease
between her brows told Uhura that her point had been
taken. "Come when you please," the Dohlman said, and
gestured dismissively at the screen. With a splatter of static,
the contact cut off.

"Whew." Uhura set down her monitor and swung around
to face the captain. "I would never have guessed that being a
Dohlman was such hard work."

"You took to it like a true tyrant," McCoy assured her
with a grin. "By the end, you even had *me* convinced you
owned the *Enterprise.*"

"Keep up that impression," Kirk advised her. "It may be
the only thing that keeps her talking to you." He bounded
down to his command chair, all energy now that he had a
goal in sight. "Spock, contact the Johnston Observatory and
arrange to have one of their geologists transported over to
guide the landing party. Sulu, I want you to pilot the
shuttle—with all the eruptions in progress down there, the
atmosphere's going to be tricky. Chekov, you're in charge of

security." Both men nodded quick agreement, and Uhura stifled a smile. Astute as he was in the ways of command, Captain Kirk was not above taking advantage of her friends' protectiveness to insure the success of a mission. "Uhura, I want you to transcribe those charts. Take a tricorder down with you to authenticate their age. Let me know the results as soon as possible."

"You mean you're not going down with her, Jim?" McCoy's blue eyes gleamed with mischief. "Remember, you told Dohlman Israi you were Uhura's chief underling."

"Which is exactly why she ordered me to guard her ship while she's gone," Kirk retorted. "Right, Dohlman Uhura?"

Uhura smiled wryly. "Right, Captain."

"Bones, I really don't see why this is necessary."

McCoy made a grumpy noise of disgust, and it occurred to Kirk that he also didn't know why he ever bothered arguing with McCoy. It wasn't as if the doctor ever changed his mind because of anything Kirk said, and God knew it wasn't because Kirk enjoyed seeing how long a disagreement could last, the way Spock did. Maybe somewhere deep inside, Kirk liked having an officer who treated him in an irreverent, disrespectful manner, so that he never forgot that he got out of bed one foot at a time, just like everyone else in the galaxy.

"Jim, if you don't get back on that examining table, I'm gonna suture your butt to it."

Then again, maybe Kirk was just too stubborn to give in to any opponent, even when it was an old friend.

"Dammit, Bones, I'm waiting to hear from the landing party about whether or not they could meet with the Dohlman." But he did sit down—in a chair, with one elbow up on the examining table and his fingers drumming against the end. "I don't need to waste time while you dig up some old inoculation for no good reason."

McCoy recrossed the sickbay, hypospray in one hand, data chip in the other. "It's not an inoculation, it's an antidote. Just like you'd get for a rattlesnake bite—you have to take it after the venom's in your system, not before you get bit."

Kirk thought the doctor's choice of analogy unnecessarily negative, but as usual, McCoy didn't seem to notice his captain's annoyance. He gestured with the hypospray.

"Trust me, if I could prevent the effects of a Dohlman's tears, I would have inoculated Sulu, Chekov, and Murphy before you even sent them planetside. As it is, they've got the antidote in their medikit in case they aren't smart enough to keep away from her when she cries." McCoy squinted at the data chip, then tossed it aside. "Take off your jacket."

Sighing, Kirk rocked forward to plant both feet on the floor as he unlatched the shoulder strap and stripped open the jacket's front. "It's been five years . . ."

"And I don't recall anybody saying the biochemical influence of a Dohlman's tears wears off. You've probably got a load of Elasian hormones still cluttering up your blood."

"I'm fine."

McCoy caught the captain's wrist in wiry fingers and shoved back the white tunic sleeve. "Don't tell me how to do my job, Captain, and I won't lock you away from this Dohlman until we leave."

Kirk frowned a little against the hypospray's sting. "The thought would never occur to me." He sat back in his chair, frowning at the doctor while he tugged his sleeve back into place. "I don't suppose I'm now free to go."

"Not yet." McCoy dismantled the hypospray with easy familiarity, barely glancing at the components as he tossed them into their respective cleaning trays. "You've got to keep me company for at least another twenty minutes, so I can be sure you don't throw some kind of funny reaction."

Kirk heard the outer door whisk open behind him, and allowed himself at least a small grin of satisfaction at the startled glower McCoy shot over the captain's shoulder. "I had a feeling you'd say that. What have you got for me, Spock?"

"Captain, Doctor." Spock's greeting was brisk and to the point, as always.

"No visitors," McCoy began, and Kirk waggled a finger at him.

"If I'm going to sit here for twenty minutes assimilating your Dohlman antidote, Bones, I'm going to get some work done."

Spock laced his hands behind his back, nodding gravely. "I infer Dr. McCoy succeeded in convincing you to take the treatment, then."

Kirk pursed his lips sourly. "I didn't get much choice."

"May I say that I think this was a wise decision, regardless of the circumstances?"

"You may," Kirk said, hoping his irritated expression didn't look too much like McCoy's.

"And thank you." The doctor probably couldn't have sounded more pleased.

"Spock, the Elasians." Kirk stood, retrieving his jacket from the examining table beside him. His arm ached from the shot, which didn't improve his mood. "Let's hear the rest of that background report. Any clues in it about where they got their warp technology?"

"None, Captain." Spock settled himself for what Kirk suspected could be a lengthy discussion. He wondered if it would bother the Vulcan to know that he had body language. "Traffic in the Tellun system has increased since the cessation of violence between Elas and Troyius. Starfleet has records of numerous peaceable visitations by the Klingons to Elas over the past five years, as well as much Orion trading activity between both planets within the Tellun system."

"The Klingons to Elas?" Kirk paused in shouldering into his jacket. The image conjured up by that information was distressing enough without further detail. Still, Kirk had to ask. "What could the Elasians have that the Klingons would want?"

Spock raised a disbelieving eyebrow. "Besides similar cultural ethics and a strong warrior's code?"

"The Elasians married off their warlord to the Troyian king," McCoy reminded Kirk, finally abandoning his clean-up procedures to join the other two. "Maybe the Klingons think getting in good with the Elasians will give them a way to reach all that dilithium on Troyius."

"At this point, that seems unlikely, Doctor."

Kirk frowned at his first officer. "Explain."

"Seventeen months ago, Dohlman Elaan was killed in combat defending the Troyian dilithium deposits from raiders."

Chapter Three

KIRK FELT a dull stab of grief, not as strongly as he would have expected, and rubbed at his arm where McCoy had given him the injection. "Go on."

"While Elaan's death established her as a hero among the common people of the Tellun system, it left King Bejas of Troyius without a bride, and Elas without a direct influence in the workings of the Troyian court."

McCoy tugged Kirk's abandoned chair out from between the examining tables and thumped it down at its original workstation. "Why?" he asked, sitting and propping his feet up on the desk. "Couldn't the Elasian Council just marry off the next Dohlman in line to keep their hand in things?"

"The next Dohlman in line, Doctor, was Dohlman Israi, with whom we spoke this afternoon. According to Federation records, she is not yet a mature female and therefore has not yet been confirmed as the supreme ruler of Elas." Spock lifted the doctor's foot only high enough to retrieve his record tapes from beneath it. "Israi has an older aunt who is acting as her Crown Regent until she matures, but

King Bejas objected to a marriage with her. Apparently he became disenchanted with Elasian Dohlmen after Elaan stabbed him with a kitchen utensil on their wedding night."

McCoy nearly tipped his chair from laughing. Kirk couldn't help smiling somewhat at the memory of the fiery, black-eyed warrior nearly taking his ear off with a dagger throw when he tried to leave her presence.

"I guess her miraculous conversion to dewy-eyed miss was too good to last," the doctor drawled amiably.

Kirk glanced down at him, cheeks growing warm. "I liked her better when she was stabbing people."

The doctor snorted. "You would."

"It seems," Spock continued, "that Bejas of Troyius held different standards. He appointed his wife Elaan admiral of the Troyian space fleet, specifically to insure that they would live in separate dwellings. However, their professional relationship evidently prospered where their marriage did not. Elaan held the post of admiral for years, and upon her death, King Bejas settled a magnificent bequest on her sister and heir, in appreciation of Elaan's services to Troyius."

Kirk scowled at his first officer, quick to see the connections Spock had left undrawn. "Enough of a bequest to allow the Elasians to buy warp technology from the Klingons?"

"And to purchase interplanetary weaponry from them as well," Spock agreed calmly. "If they were so inclined."

With a race as aggressive as the Elasians, Kirk reflected, their inclinations were likely to be unpleasant for anyone their hot tempers chose to fix upon as an enemy. "All right, let's assume the Elasians used King Bejas's bequest to buy Klingon warp technology and weapons." Kirk eyed his senior officers intently. "Now the question is—why are they in such a hurry to mine dilithium on Rakatan that they didn't even notify the Federation they were here?"

"To get a quick shot of disposable wealth, before their claim can be disproven?" McCoy hazarded. "The Klingons gave them a taste of what they could get on the black market, and they want to buy more."

"Thus setting up an arms race in the Tellun system that

would destroy the peace Starfleet created there between Elas and Troyius five years ago." Kirk swung around to angle a sharp look at his science officer. "Spock, have you started checking out the Johnston Observatory's sentience report?"

Spock tipped his head in question, coming dangerously close to expressing surprise. "No, Captain. Given the current political developments—"

Kirk cut him off with a nod. "Get on it."

"Jim . . ." McCoy rotated his chair to more fully face the captain. "What in hell do magma men inside volcanoes have to do with the Elasians mining dilithium on Rakatan?"

Kirk grinned down at the doctor over one shoulder. "The Prime Directive."

McCoy repaid him with a look of dour annoyance. "Excuse me?"

Spock folded his arms in unconscious mimic of Kirk, nodding slowly. "Since Rakatan is a Federation planet, any sentient life-forms on it would be protected under the Prime Directive." He shot a confirming glance at the captain. "The Elasians would not be allowed to mine dilithium there, and so would not be able to build their black-market arms supply further."

Kirk smiled, pleased with himself, and McCoy asked skeptically, "Isn't that a little underhanded?"

Leave it to the doctor to find the downside to everything. "Not if we actually find evidence of sentience," Kirk replied smoothly. He motioned for Spock to follow him as he stood. "Get all of Metcalfe's notes. If there's even a chance of intelligent life in one of those volcanoes, I want to know about it now."

"And if there is?" McCoy pressed.

"Then, mining claim or no mining claim—" He leaned across the desk to tap at the clock mounted next to the doctor's elbow. Twenty minutes, to the second. "—the Elasians, just like me, are out of here."

From her seat aboard the shuttle *Gamow*, Uhura watched Rakatan loom against the velvet dark of space below them.

The planet looked like the ghost of an earlier Earth, its blue oceans laced with familiar white clouds, but unbroken by any brown-green shadow of continents. Sulu's carefully plotted approach had taken them away from the enormous peak of Rakatan Mons and its erupting companion, to a side of the planet where the seas were freckled with small, dormant volcanoes. Uhura noticed that in places they linked into curving island arcs, fragments of continents in the making.

"*Underling.*"

"What?" Uhura glanced across the shuttle's main aisle, surprised by the unexpected word.

Chekov made the kind of face he usually reserved for spicy smoked bean curd or raw mollusc pâté. The muffled thrum of the shuttle's impulse engines couldn't hide his indignant tone. "I don't think I like being called an underling."

"But you are an underling, *Lieutenant.*" Sulu didn't look away from his instrument panel, but mischief danced in his voice. Uhura heard a stifled breath of laughter explode from the young geologist who sat in the copilot's seat. "Starfleet is just too polite to make it an official classification."

"But it sounds so . . . disposable," Chekov protested. "Like someone a Dohlman could throw a knife at without anybody noticing."

Uhura smiled. "*I'd* notice if she threw a knife at you."

"We all would," Sulu added lightly. "There wouldn't be anyone gloomy left in the landing party."

Chekov snorted. "You just wait until she throws a knife at *you.* Then tell me how much you like being an underling."

"She's not going to throw knives at any of you," Uhura declared. "You're *my* underlings, not hers. No one's allowed to throw knives at you but me." She caught the amused look Sulu threw over his shoulder at her. "You know what I mean. It's just another way of saying that you're my subordinate officers."

Sulu laughed. "A rose by any other name—"

"—still has thorns," Chekov finished. When Uhura

raised an eyebrow at him, he gave her a shrug and a smile. "That's the Russian version."

The other security guard in the shuttle looked up from the electronic reader he'd been studying, his coffee-dark face alight with interest. "Really, sir?"

Chekov sighed. "No, Murphy, not really. I made it up."

Not being close enough to swat the Russian on the shoulder, Uhura contented herself with practicing what she hoped was a Dohlmanlike scowl. "Don't pay any attention to him, Ensign. He's just trying to tease us."

"I think I'd leave that to Commander Sulu, if I were you, sir." The geologist from Johnston Observatory looked around, speaking unprompted for the first time since he'd transported up from the moonbase. Uhura looked at the young man more closely, seeing the thin, intelligent face beneath his scruff of hair and beard. "He's better at it than you are."

"He's allowed to be," Chekov said curtly. "He's my commanding officer."

The geologist bit his lip and fell back into silence, looking as if he regretted having spoken. Uhura practiced another Dohlman glare on the Russian without any visible effect. She sighed and turned back toward their guide.

"Will there be a lot of ash in the atmosphere down on Rakatan, Doctor—" She paused, trying to remember the name he'd mumbled upon his appearance.

"Mutchler," he supplied, more readily this time. Being asked about his specialty obviously broke through his reticence. "Scott Mutchler. And no, we shouldn't encounter much in the way of volcanic ash, not on the side of Rakatan we're landing on."

"There's some up here in the stratosphere," Sulu said. "You can hear it hitting the shuttle."

Uhura tilted her head, and heard the faint whisper of particles rattling against the shielded windows. She looked out and saw streaks of dark gray fingering through the thin upper atmosphere. Sulu carefully piloted the shuttle through the clearer spaces.

"There's always some ash up at these levels," Mutchler agreed quickly. "We think that's what keeps the planet cool despite all the greenhouse gases in its atmosphere. But Mazama Mons—the volcano that erupted this morning—lies leeward of where we're going. We shouldn't have to wear breathers."

Chekov grunted again and nudged the plastic box sitting in the aisle beside him. "Is that what's in all these boxes you brought? Protective gear?"

"No, that's a focusing device for a ground-motion detector." Mutchler ducked his head, looking reticent again. Uhura began to suspect his quiet manner was due to something other than shyness. "Um—Dr. Bascomb said that as long as I was coming down to guide you guys, I might as well fix Seismic Station Three. That's the one the Elasians messed up when they landed."

Chekov's eyebrows drew together. "Did she clear that with Captain Kirk?"

"Not yet." Mutchler looked up pleadingly. "But we've really got to get the upper caldera site on-line again! If we don't, a year's worth of data collection is going to get wasted. And it'll only take an hour or so—"

"I'll have to check with the captain."

Mutchler opened his mouth, then closed it again when Uhura shook her head at him in warning. She recognized the note of finality in Chekov's voice. Further argument would only annoy him, and she had a question she wanted to ask Mutchler.

"Dr. Mutchler, you must have tried to repair your seismic station before this. What happened?"

The geologist made a wry face. "We got chased away twice, that's what happened. That little Dohlman of theirs took a fit when I tried to explain our research program to her. Those goons she calls her cohort broke my equipment, stuffed me back into my shuttle, and pointed their guns at me until I took off. Which I didn't waste any time doing." He ran a hand through his dark hair in frustration, ruffling it even more. "We tried contacting them by communicator after that, several times, but all the Dohlman would say was that the Crown Regent didn't want her to talk to any of us."

"The Crown Regent?"

Mutchler shrugged. "Some older female relative back home. Dr. Bascomb says she gets the impression that this Crown Regent person actually runs the Elasian government."

Uhura dredged up hazy five-year-old memories of the last Elasian Dohlman she'd met. "I don't remember Dohlman Elaan of Troyius saying anything about a Crown Regent running things for her back home on Elas."

"Was she a mature female?" Mutchler inquired, then flushed at Uhura's lifted eyebrows. "I mean, could she secrete the biochemical compound in her tears, the one that enslaves the Elasian males?"

Uhura exchanged a thoughtful look with Sulu. "I think so," she said at last. Although it had never become public knowledge, the two of them had discussed Captain Kirk's unusual behavior around the Dohlman of Elas, and pieced together some of what must have happened to cause it.

Chekov, obviously, had not. "*Enslave* their males?" he repeated doubtfully.

Mutchler nodded. "We read up on the Elasians after they showed up here. Turns out the Vulcans have done a lot of scientific studies on them lately because of their unusual reproductive adaptations. The females secrete a compound in their tear glands that makes their males"—he flashed a mischievous look at Chekov—"their *underlings,* loyal to the death. They've apparently based their whole governmental system on it."

Chekov frowned at him. "But why would they need to do a thing like that?"

The geologist shrugged. "No one knows for sure. The Vulcans think the adaptation evolved to compensate for the Elasians' pronounced sexual dimorphism."

Uhura saw the Russian's puzzled look and translated. "The big difference in size between the sexes. You remember that, don't you, Pavel?"

27

"I remember that the Elasian men were very big," he agreed readily. "Were the females very small?"

Sulu tossed a quizzical look over his shoulder while he brought the shuttle skimming down toward the sparkling surface of the sea. "You don't remember the Dohlman coming up on the bridge?"

Chekov shook his head, looking baffled. "How could I? We were busy fighting the Klingons."

Uhura and Sulu exchanged smiles, but said nothing in reply.

The shuttle leveled off, the whistle of its descent through the atmosphere easing into a comfortable cruising hiss. Sunlight slanted golden through the windows, and for a moment Uhura closed her eyes and enjoyed the welcome feel of it on her face. It was the one thing she missed in space—the radiant warmth of a nearby star.

After a too-brief moment, however, the sunlight went away. Uhura opened her eyes, noticing that the shuttle had stayed on its arrow-straight path across the ocean. "Are we under a cloud?"

"Not exactly." Sulu's voice held an odd note, part amusement, part awe. "Come up here and see for yourself."

She gave Chekov an inquiring look and got a shrug in reply. Evidently, whatever it was, he couldn't see it either. Sighing again, Uhura threaded between seats and leaned into the small, open cockpit. "All right," she said. "What's so strange that you couldn't—"

She broke off, struck as wordless as Sulu by the view through the shuttle's windshield. Far to the west of them, the sunlit horizon rose up into the massive blue-white peak of an enormous volcano, blurred with distance but still big enough to cast a long, ominous shadow hundreds of kilometers out to sea. The shuttle had just entered into that shadow.

"The biggest stratovolcano in the galaxy," said Scott Mutchler with almost possessive pride. "Rakatan Mons."

Chapter Four

"C<small>APTAIN</small>'<small>S LOG</small>, <small>STARDATE</small> 4372.5.

"On a top-secret diplomatic mission, the *Enterprise* has entered the Tellun star system. Maintaining communications blackout, we have taken aboard Petri, the ambassador from Troyius, the outer planet, and are now approaching the inner planet, Elas."

Duty jacket thrown across the crisply made bed behind him, feet propped beside the terminal on his work desk, Kirk smiled wryly as he turned the small stiletto over and over in his hands and listened to his captain's logs from half a decade before. Light whisked up the oiled blade in his hands like tiny shots of lightning, sparking off the ruby in the dagger's hilt with such depth and clarity that it made the stone glow like a dollop of polished blood. Kirk remembered the first time he'd really noticed the graceful knife— buried for half its length in the Troyian ambassador's back—and marveled at how young and innocent these five-year-old log entries sounded compared to the very real dangers his older self could sense in the situation surrounding them now.

"Captain's log, supplemental.

"Ambassador Petri has just granted me the dubious honor of receiving Her Glory Elaan, the Dohlman of Elas, on board the *Enterprise* for transportation to Troyius. According to the ambassador, Elas and Troyius have only recently ended their bitter interplanetary war by negotiating a symbolic marriage between the female warlord of Elas and the king of Troyius. Petri tells me that the *Enterprise*'s role in this mission should be simple: escorting the reluctant bride to her new home on Troyius. Petri himself has been assigned the more difficult task: making sure Elaan doesn't kill the bridegroom once she gets there."

Kirk ducked his head, pressing the knife handle against the bridge of his nose and wincing at the note of condescending laughter in his younger voice. He'd recorded this entry less than two hours after the first, within minutes of Petri's first whining explanation of the unpleasant duties he faced as Dohlman Elaan's etiquette instructor. Kirk had barely met Elaan at that point, hadn't yet realized how fiercely and easily the Dohlman's temper could flare. Without the option of throwing her into a security cell, Kirk's only choice had been to treat the Elasian warlord as playfully as he would a child, hoping to teach her that the arrogance her culture expected of her would not serve her in the larger world of the Federation. She'd learned her lesson all too well. In turn, she had taught Kirk never to underestimate an opponent. Kirk had often wondered which between the two had been the more valuable lesson.

"Captain's log, stardate 4373.9."

This entry was quiet, the young voice dictating it noticeably stiffer and more grim.

"Her Glory the Dohlman has just hospitalized the Troyian ambassador sent to reconcile her to her upcoming marriage. McCoy assures me that Ambassador Petri will recover, but the Federation High Commissioner has made it clear that completing the ambassador's mission is now my personal responsibility. The prospects of a successful outcome are not promising. Mr. Spock reports that our long-range sensors have detected a sensor ghost—most likely a ship of unknown affiliation—shadowing the *Enterprise* at—"

"Bridge to Captain Kirk."

Memories of the past swarmed over Kirk with startling immediacy. For a moment, he expected Spock to tell him that their sensor ghost was really a Klingon cruiser, that the *Enterprise*'s warp matrix was fused beyond repairing. Then the relative calmness of his darkened quarters registered on his distracted mind, and he remembered that he was waiting for news on his landing party, five years later and more than seven parsecs away.

He pulled his feet off the desk and sat up to punch the intercom stud. "Kirk here."

"Spock here, Captain." The gentle machine chatter of the second-shift bridge tatted a soothing web of sound behind the first officer's voice. "We have just received word from Commander Uhura that the landing party has been denied access to the Elasians' astrogational charts."

Of course they had. Kirk rubbed his eyes with a sigh. "On what grounds? I thought we had agreed—"

"Evidently," Spock interrupted with dry aplomb, "we have somehow managed to offend the Elasians in the time since that agreement was made."

Why didn't that surprise him? "All right, Spock, I'll be there in a minute. Kirk out."

The turbolift whisked open onto a bridge quietly busy with its own efficiency. Kirk trotted down the small flight of stairs leading to the command level, noting the faces of those manning each station with a quick, perfunctory glance. It didn't seem strange yet that Sulu, Uhura, and Chekov were gone—it was evening shift, when they would have been off duty anyway. Kirk would notice their absence most keenly tomorrow, he knew.

Kirk trained his thoughts on the present, trying not to

drum his fingers on the arm of the command chair while Spock rose to relinquish it. "Updated status of the landing party?"

"Commander Uhura reports that they have been allowed to land their shuttle outside the Elasian mining camp," the Vulcan reported, stepping aside to let Kirk round the chair and sit with restless impatience. "However, they have not yet been permitted to enter. The Dohlman's chief underling has indicated that they will be detained until we agree to stop spying on them."

"Spying on them?" Kirk frowned at the aqua-and-turquoise planet on the viewscreen. It was frustrating to see only oceans and the occasional smudge of volcanic ash. "What does he mean? Using our sensors?"

Spock lifted his eyebrows in an eloquent, very Vulcan shrug. "The exact nature of our 'spying' was unclear, Captain. Commander Uhura is attempting to obtain clarification on that point."

Kirk couldn't help wondering if she actually had any hope of getting it. "Have we started any new sensor scans of the planet since we sent out the landing party?" he asked, trying to think what sort of behavior could be construed as subversive by a culture so aggressively paranoid as the Elasians. "Or launched any remote probes into the volcano?"

Spock shook his head. "Neither, Captain. Our scanning systems have continued to monitor the planet at the same level as when we first arrived. If the Elasians can detect our sensor activity at all—" A note of unexpected dryness entered the Vulcan's tone. "—which I doubt—" Kirk suppressed a smile. "—they must have been aware of our scanning before they agreed to allow the landing party access to their camp."

True. "Then it's not us causing the problem." He watched a patch of sharp shadow slice its way across Rakatan's bright disk, realizing it was the edge of the planet's moon, Skaftar, only when he caught sight of a faint string of lights outlining the edge of one otherwise invisible building. "How about the geologists on the Johnston moonbase? Any new scanning activity from them?"

Spock removed himself to his science station without giving any other sign that he had heard the captain's question. Long fingers coaxed a series of unseen readings from the panel. "Negative. At present, the Johnston Observatory is monitoring the satellite uplink from their network of seismic stations, nothing more."

"Uh, sir?"

Kirk turned to face the ensign at the security station. "Yes, Mr. Howard?"

"They may not be scanning from the moonbase, sir," Howard told him, trading uncertain glances between the captain and his own boards, "but the observatory *did* launch a shuttle into orbit about thirty minutes ago."

Kirk felt a little sting of apprehension. "Was that after the landing party left the hangar, Mr. Howard?"

Howard nodded. "Aye, sir."

"Did the geologists on board that shuttle say why they were going out?"

"No, sir." Howard's hands curled into nervous fists, a trace of embarrassed color darkening his bearded cheeks. "I didn't query them, sir. Since the shuttle never tried to approach the planet, I assumed it was a routine data-gathering mission."

"Let that be your first lesson, Ensign—never make assumptions." Kirk found it more than just a little ironic to consider who had taught him that lesson on board this very same ship all those years ago. He put Elaan out of his mind with more ease than he'd ever known and turned to Ashcraft at communications. "Mr. Ashcraft, contact that geology shuttle."

"Aye-aye, sir." Ashcraft's eyes grew distracted as he listened to the voices through his ear transceiver. "Coming on screen now."

The image of Rakatan on the viewscreen blurred and rippled, coalescing into a wash of gold-and-black color and a pert bob of sun-lightened hair. "I'm right in the middle of a laser scan, *Enterprise.*" Wendy Metcalfe didn't even glance up from the shuttle's monitors. "Can you wait a minute?"

Kirk resisted an urge to tap his foot. "No, Ms. Metcalfe, we can't."

The young grad student jerked her head up to blink at him with startled blue eyes.

"Would you care to tell me," Kirk asked her coldly, "just what you're doing out there?"

She frowned in confusion, shaking her head ever so slightly. "Using our precision laser to make a topographic scan of Rakatan Mons." She flicked a worried look back at the abandoned monitors, but apparently didn't feel safe in completely turning her attention away from Kirk. "It looks like there's been at least five millimeters of uplift at the volcano's summit since our last—"

Kirk cut her off without waiting to hear what new scientific wonder she'd unearthed about the planet. "Does this survey of yours involve maintaining a stationary orbit over Rakatan Mons?"

Metcalfe offered him a scowl approaching casual disgust. "Well, of course, Captain, how else—"

"And are you shooting laser beams down at the Elasian mining camp?"

"Well, not *at* it"—she shrugged—"but near it, I guess." She waved impatiently at the equipment crowding the shuttle behind her. "They're very low amplitude laser beams!"

Kirk tipped a look back at his first officer. "Mr. Spock, I believe we have found our 'spy.'"

Spock aimed a stare of cool disapproval at the viewscreen. "Indeed."

"Ms. Metcalfe, you're going to have to go back to the moonbase."

"But, Captain!" She closed her hands around the edges of her monitor station as though planning to prevent his taking it by physical force. "We haven't seen this much uplift on Rakatan Mons since we arrived at the planet! I can't go back with an incomplete topographic scan for the most critical data point in my doctoral thesis."

"You also can't disobey a direct order from Starfleet."

She turned resolutely back toward her equipment without even bothering to cut off the channel.

Kirk twisted his mouth in grudging respect for her tenacity. Two could play at this game. He punched the intercom button with his thumb. "Bridge to Engineering."

"Engineering," a familiar brogue replied. "Scott here."

"Scotty, there's a Federation geological shuttle positioned directly over Rakatan Mons." Kirk kept his attention trained on Metcalfe, poised for her response. "Lock on to it with a tractor beam and pull it into the hangar bay."

Metcalfe spun away from her equipment. "Hey!"

"Mr. Ashcraft, contact the Elasians and tell them that the geologist 'spy' is being withdrawn. We apologize for any inconvenience this might have caused them."

"That's not fair!"

Kirk tipped his head in acknowledgment and gave a little shrug. "Fair may be a human and Vulcan concept, Ms. Metcalfe, but it's not an Elasian one." He saw the young geologist stumble as the tractor beam caught her shuttle and rocked it to a thudding halt. "And right now, we're playing by the Elasians' rules."

"'Insert optical aperture control sensor into angle between diffusion resistance meter and polarizing mirrored filter lens . . .'" Sulu's voice droned as he read from the instruction manual.

Chekov listened to Mutchler drop the half-assembled laser sensor into his lap and growl at Sulu with frustration. "There *is* no angle between the resistance meter and the lens! I should never have let you help me with this." The geologist reached across the seat back in front of him to snatch the operations manual away from Sulu. "Are you sure you're reading this in the right language?"

"What kind of question is that?" Sulu climbed to his

knees in the passenger seat he'd claimed since *Gamow's* landing, hanging over the back and bending the booklet in Mutchler's hands so he could read it upside down. "English, Vulcan, Spanish." He pointed to each section in turn. "What I can read of the Spanish agrees with the English, and the Vulcan probably just goes into even more excruciating detail." He let the book snap back into place. "If you can't find space between the components, Doctor, I don't think it's the fault of the translators."

"Is that supposed to be an insult?"

No longer able to just sit and listen to their squabbling, Chekov stood and came down the shuttle's main aisle to pluck the laser out of Mutchler's hands. "Let me see that."

"Careful!" Mutchler yelped, half-standing as though to follow the small focusing device and optical housing. "That's sensitive geologic equipment, Lieutenant!"

Chekov snorted. "A laser is a laser, Dr. Mutchler." He smoothed out the schematic where it spread on top of Mutchler's seismic equipment, and bent to compare the aperture sensor against the fine-print specs. From the front of the shuttle, he could hear Uhura's patient voice reciting assurances to the Elasians on the other side of the communications link. Her dialogue didn't seem to have changed much in the last hour or so. "I've probably assembled more targeting systems and experimental rifles than you have seismic stations in your network."

"Which means what?" the geologist demanded, sitting back. "That you can put together my ground-motion laser so it can kill somebody?"

Chekov scowled at him over the scattered laser components. "Do you want help with this or don't you?"

Mutchler sighed, but didn't answer. After a moment, he rocked forward in his seat to ask, "Do you think they're ever going to let us in?"

Chekov wondered if the scientist was just trying to make conversation, or if he really thought either of them had any answer.

"Probably not." Sulu sighed and dropped his head into

his hands, relinquishing the operations manual by tossing it atop where Chekov was trying to jockey for the appropriate space between the meter and the lens. "I don't even understand why they let us get this far if all they're going to do is keep their defense screens in place and question our intentions."

"To scare us."

Chekov flicked the manual back into Sulu's lap without looking up. "Knowing the Elasians, Dr. Mutchler, I suspect their scare tactics would be somewhat more straightforward."

"I don't know. . . ." Mutchler stood and paced to the rear of the shuttle, then bent down to peer out one of the small viewports with worry glittering in his gray eyes. "The place just gives me the creeps. An old slump site like this, with valley walls so steep . . ." His voice trailed off, and he scrubbed at his temples as though nursing a headache. "I don't know why anybody would set up their base camp here."

Chekov didn't know why anybody would choose to set up on the surface of this planet to begin with, so didn't venture a guess. "Well, they can't keep us here forever."

Sulu gave a little laugh of disbelief and settled lower in his seat. "I wouldn't count on that."

"Mr. Sulu, Mr. Chekov." Uhura's voice from the front of the shuttle sounded fine-edged and alert. A sure sign that something wasn't going as they'd planned. "Would you join me, please?"

"At last." Sulu bounced to his feet with a breath of relief. "Our lives have meaning again." Bending over to the row behind him, he helped Chekov gather the laser's scattered components, carefully keeping internal and external modules separate between both hands without even having to be told. "Do you think the Elasians have had a sudden fit of reasonability?" he asked Chekov in a low voice.

Chekov snorted and deposited the unfinished laser in Murphy's lap on their way past. "I think Ensign Murphy should amuse himself until we get back. Do what you can," he told the younger man, not expecting much from either the Elasians or the ground-motion laser at this point. "Consider it practice for the next time you have to field strip an optic cannon."

Murphy blinked dubiously down at the pile in his lap, and nodded glumly. "Uh, yes, sir . . . I'll try."

Uhura didn't acknowledge their arrival when they entered the cockpit. Forehead in one hand, the other drumming silently on the edge of the panel, she listened with strained patience to the clear tenor voice over the communications board as though she'd heard his complaint a million times before. Beyond the forward viewport, Chekov could barely glimpse the few surface buildings that made up the Elasian mining camp peeking their tops above the horizon. From here he couldn't see anything that could house a full-scale field generator, but he could just discern the watery heat-ripple effect of screen meeting oxygen several meters away from the shuttle. It was the same system they'd picked up from the ship, and it was still holding them away from the Elasians despite an hour or more of discussion.

"*Kessh* Takcas—" Uhura addressed the communications panel as politely as though the Elasian chief underling were standing there with her. "Perhaps if you let me speak with the Dohlman myself—"

"No." The Elasian's hard voice cut her off as sharply as a slap. "She will not speak with deceitful pigs. Our sensors detect an onboard energy source not connected to your shuttle's engines. The very fact that you lie about its presence proves it must be a weapons system."

Chapter Five

CHEKOV PULLED his attention away from the outside view to exchange a startled glance with Sulu. The helmsman paused in slipping into the pilot's seat, eyebrows and shoulders raised in a silent admission of ignorance.

"This is an unarmed passenger transport, Chief Underling Takcas." It never ceased to amaze Chekov that Uhura's voice could convey such calm and friendliness when every micrometer of her body exuded anger. "The only weapons we have on board are personal sidearms, used by my cohort to ensure my safety."

"Then it is Her Glory's command that you dispose of those sidearms," Takcas's icy voice replied. "Throw them clear of your craft and allow us to destroy them."

Chekov captured Uhura's attention with an urgent touch to her arm. *No,* he mouthed silently, frowning. She was nodding before he even finished the word.

"Chief Underling Takcas," she all but sighed, "I could not debase my cohort so by allowing you to endanger their purpose. Please tell Dohlman Israi that this arrangement is unacceptable."

There was a long moment of dead time on the radio, during which Chekov imagined a brawny Elasian male scurrying to the other end of the mining camp to grovel before his mistress with Uhura's unhappy news. He reached over the lieutenant commander's shoulder to thumb the audio mute for their side of the transmission. "This is ridiculous," he told her, crossing his arms and leaning back on the panel between the seats. "I thought the captain settled whatever their problem was already."

"That was when they were accusing us of spying on them," Uhura pointed out with a sigh. "As you heard, now we're arguing about hidden weaponry."

Chekov made a disgusted noise. "Nonsense. Even counting the power signatures from things like our hand phasers and Mutchler's laser ground-motion detector, there's no way the Elasians could mistake anything we have on board for a shipwide system. The readings are completely different."

Uhura sighed and sat back in her chair. "*You* would know that," she agreed wearily. "But would the Elasians?"

Chekov snorted. "If they're going to use black-market technology," he complained, "they should spend the extra money to learn *how* to use it."

Sulu smiled indulgently and leaned forward to give the lieutenant's arm a sympathetic pat. "Well, it's a nice sentiment, at least."

"Dohlman Uhura!"

They all jumped at Takcas's imperious summons from the radio. Uhura shot a hand out to answer with a speed that could only have been second nature. "I'm still here, Chief Underling Takcas. What is—"

"Her Glory commands that all power sources within your craft be deactivated so that we may scan your craft and verify that you have disarmed all systems."

"No!" Mutchler yelped from the main compartment. The geologist strained forward in his seat, eyes wide and liquid with alarm. "We'll lose the memory in the seismic equipment if we disconnect the power supply. Without it, I can't

40

calibrate the surface equipment and this whole trip will have been for nothing!"

"Then Her Glory commands that you evacuate your shuttle so that we may search your compartments without interference."

Sulu shook his head with slow emphasis. *Sabotage,* he mouthed, and pantomimed an explosion with his hands.

Uhura responded with a hopeless toss of her hands, and Chekov reached across her shoulder to switch off the audio signal before speaking. "Tell him you'll do it."

Uhura stared up at him. "You've got to be joking."

"Tell him that they can search the ship," he continued, waving Sulu into silence when the helmsman would have interrupted, "but that you're leaving the leader of your cohort behind to supervise their behavior."

Uhura chewed her lip, considering. "I don't know how many they'll send."

"It won't matter," Chekov assured her. "They aren't interested in hurting anyone, just in making sure we know that they're serious about protecting their Dohlman." He felt heat come up into his cheeks, but admitted anyway, "I would do the same, if I were them."

"How come you get to be the chief underling of this cohort?" Sulu asked, feigning disappointment.

Chekov scowled at him. "Because it was my idea." He turned back to Uhura. "They'll agree to it. They know you have as much right to be cautious as do they."

"All right." Uhura reached for the comm switch in front of her. "When did you get to be such an expert on Elasian psychology?" she asked with a teasing smile.

"I don't have to be—I know how the cohort's job works, and that means I know how they think." He caught her wrist to stop her just before she reopened the channel. "Give me five minutes to secure our weapons and arm myself before you let them in."

She nodded, but didn't unknit her frown. "You said they wouldn't try to hurt you."

"Most likely," he amended. "But I'm not taking any

chances." He was already running through a mental tally of what they had on board, and what he wanted to do with it all. He tossed a wry smile at Sulu on his way out of the cockpit. "I may not remember what Elasian women looked like, but I certainly remember Elasian men."

Uhura took a deep breath as she stepped out of the shuttle, trying to summon a Dohlman-imperious look for the squad of Elasian males waiting for them. The thin, cold air of Rakatan bit at her throat, dry with dust and sharp with ozone from the defense shield shimmering over the camp. She heard Ensign Murphy cough behind her.

"Dohlman Uhura." The familiar red-haired figure of the Dohlman's chief underling stepped away from the rest of the pack and gave her an almost imperceptible nod. "Her Glory, the Dohlman Israi, is no longer sure she wishes to speak to you. She has been insulted by your delay in arriving."

"*Our* delay?" Uhura allowed some of her annoyance with the Elasians to surface at last. "There wouldn't have been a delay, Chief Underling Takcas, if you had been willing to negotiate a reasonable landing agreement with us when we first arrived. You have not served your Dohlman well."

As a reprimand, it had been a shot in the dark, but it made the Elasian's young face darken with anger. His wordless growl brought both Sulu and Ensign Murphy a protective step closer, but Uhura refused to let herself be intimidated. She reached out and slapped a small hand against Takcas's broad chest, trying to mimic the fearlessly scornful manner she remembered from Dohlman Elaan of Troyius.

"Out of my way," she ordered. "I wish to see the Dohlman Israi at once."

The lash of her voice had the desired effect. Takcas scowled but backed away from her with instinctive obedience. He snapped his fingers, and a bearded older male stepped out from the rest of the guards.

"Oben, bring them to the doors of Her Glory's compound." Takcas's voice was sharp, as if he could take out on his subordinate the resentment he didn't dare show to Uhura. "Her Glory can decide then if she will allow them in."

"Yes, *Kessh.*" Oben's pale green eyes swept over Uhura and her three companions, with an emotion that could have been either suspicion or scorn. "Follow," he said shortly, and turned away without looking to see if Uhura was behind him.

Stifling a sigh of relief at the success of her first confrontation, Uhura followed the older male toward the small, arched portal that pierced the shimmering defense shield. Sulu kept pace beside her, with Murphy alert and watchful an arm's length away. The geologist lagged several steps behind, casting a worried look back at the shuttle that contained his seismic equipment. The thud of booted feet told Uhura that Takcas and the remaining Elasians had boarded it for inspection.

"Lieutenant Chekov won't let them damage any of our equipment, will he?" Mutchler's hushed voice was anxious.

Sulu shook his head. "Not unless they damage him first." He quirked an eyebrow at Uhura while Oben exchanged salutes with the guards at the portal. "I don't remember the Elasians being this obnoxious the last time we met them."

"That's because their Dohlman didn't destroy *your* quarters," Uhura retorted. "*I* remember them being exactly this obnoxious."

Sulu grinned in rueful acknowledgment, but said nothing as the burly Elasian led them through the portal and into the mining compound.

Contrary to Uhura's expectations, it was not a luxurious settlement. A brief straggle of metal buildings crammed into the angle formed by a ridge of dark gray rock and the dusty gravel of a dry streambed, leaving just enough room for a furrowed track of road and scattered piles of rock. Away from the shuttle and the defense shield, Uhura noticed the bleak silence of Rakatan for the first time. There was no vegetation on this planet to rustle in the breeze, no small animals to chirp or whistle or hum. All she could hear, very far away and indistinct, was the rhythmic drumming of machinery.

Oben turned onto the equipment track, and they followed him up the dry streambed. From the upper part of the gully, Uhura could see barren mountain slopes converging into a distant, snowcapped peak. She glanced over her shoulder at Scott Mutchler. "Is that the top of Rakatan Mons?"

The geologist smiled and shook his head. "Just one of the parasitic volcanoes on the upper slope. The main crater's hidden behind those clouds." He pointed at the enormous stack of cumulus clouds towering far above the visible peak, almost halfway across the steel blue bowl of sky. Uhura blinked in astonishment. "You hardly ever see Rakatan Mons from the ground. It's so big, it makes its own weather."

Oben paused outside a metal building as raw and spartan as all the rest. "Wait here, until Her Glory decides whether she will see you." He disappeared inside the plasfoam door without pausing for their acknowledgment.

"Judging from his voice, this could be another long wait." Sulu eyed the big gray boulders outside the door, then settled cross-legged on the least jagged one. Uhura perched beside him, knowing that would make Ensign Murphy's job easier. The dark-skinned security guard prowled an invisible perimeter around the two of them, making it just wide enough to include Mutchler, as well. The geologist crouched beside another boulder, peering at it with a small glass hand lens.

"What are you looking at, Dr. Mutchler?" Uhura ran her fingers over the pale pink tracery of some primitive plant embroidered on the rock's sun-baked surface. "The lichen?"

"It's a slime mold," he said absently. "And I've seen it before." He dropped the hand lens into his pocket and swung around, slouching back against the rock with a frustrated sigh. "Dammit, I wish I could figure out exactly what it is they're mining here."

Uhura exchanged considering glances with Sulu. Because she was the commanding officer of the landing party, the decision to share classified information with non-Starfleet personnel was hers to make. She made it. "The Elasians say they're mining dilithium."

"Dilithium!" Mutchler jerked his head up to stare at her with wide gray eyes. After a moment, his astonishment melted into utter indignation. "No way!"

Uhura blinked at the old-fashioned phrase. "Excuse me?"

Mutchler slapped the rock beside him. "There is *no way* the Elasians or anybody else could be mining dilithium out of these rocks." He saw her doubtful look and bent down, scrabbling a broken shard from the smaller rocks at his feet and tossing it at Sulu. "Here, look at this. What do you see?"

The helmsman caught the rock fragment and held it up to the sunlight so it glittered. Close up, Uhura could see that it wasn't truly gray, but a fine-grained mesh of white and black. "Um—some little white crystals?"

Mutchler nodded approval. "Phenocrysts of plagioclase feldspar. What else?"

Sulu's dark eyes crinkled with amusement. "Some little dark crystals."

"Right. That's amphibole. Now do you see anything in there that looks clear, like quartz?" Both of them shook their heads, puzzled. "That's because there *isn't* any quartz, not in this kind of rock."

"So?" Sulu asked.

The geologist gave him a surprised look. "No quartz, no dilithium," he said simply. "I thought everybody knew that. One of the reasons we didn't discover dilithium until the twenty-second century was that it's crystallographically identical to quartz." He went on, obviously warming to his subject. "Not only does it have exactly the same lattice and spacing, dilithium forms in the exactly the same kinds of rocks as quartz. Pegmatite veins, mostly, in association with the true lithium minerals such as spodumene and—"

"Dr. Mutchler." Long experience with Spock had taught Uhura to recognize extraneous information when she heard it. "Are you saying that there are no rocks anywhere around here that could contain dilithium?"

The geologist hesitated, frowning. "I wouldn't go that far, I guess. After all, this is a supernova-remnant star system, just like Earth's, so there should be *some* dilithium in the crust. And Rakatan Mons is the closest thing this planet has to continental crust. If there are dilithium-bearing pegmatite veins anywhere—which I doubt—they're probably underneath it. But even if they were, they'd be buried way too deep to mine. At least five kilometers down, if not more." He sat up, his young face brightening with excitement. "Unless one got carried to the surface as a xenolith!"

"What's a xenolith?" Uhura demanded, surprised by his sudden flare of enthusiasm.

"A foreign rock that gets taken hostage by a volcanic eruption." Mutchler saw the dubious look Sulu slanted him and waved his arms in the air. "No, really, it can happen! The magma that erupts from Rakatan's volcanoes comes from deep in the mantle. All it has to do is break off a chunk of pegmatite from some underground vein it passes on its way up, then carry it up to the surface without melting it. When the magma hardens, you get a blob of dilithium-bearing pegmatite frozen inside."

Sulu cocked his head. "So you really think that the Elasians could be mining dilithium here?"

"No," Mutchler said flatly. "The odds are a thousand to one against there being dilithium pegmatites under Rakatan Mons to begin with. The odds against one of them getting picked up as a xenolith are probably astronomical." A quick grin split his scruff of beard. "But then, so are the odds against there being a volcano as big as Rakatan Mons in this kind of tectonic setting. If there's one thing I've learned about geology on this planet, it's not to play by the odds." He scrambled to his feet and looked around the mining camp. "Now, if I were a dilithium pegmatite ore, what building would I be hiding in?"

Ensign Murphy spun around from the far end of the circle he was pacing. "Sir, I'd rather you didn't—"

It was too late. Mutchler's long strides had taken him out into the road and down toward the last and largest of the metal buildings before the security guard's belated rush could catch him. Ducking around a corner, the geologist disappeared from view.

"Sir?" Quivering like a dog on a leash, Murphy looked over his shoulder at Uhura. "Should I go and bring him back?"

She glanced at the silent door of the Dohlman's residence, and nodded. "Hurry, before anyone else—"

A distant growl and thump interrupted her. Uhura gasped and sprang to her feet, hearing Mutchler's voice break off in midyelp. "Go!" she ordered Murphy, but the security guard was already in motion.

She sprang to her feet and bolted after him with Sulu at her heels. They rounded the corner of the large warehouse together, then nearly slammed into Murphy from behind. The security guard had come to an abrupt stop. Half-hidden as she was behind his broad shoulder, it took Uhura a moment to see why.

Scott Mutchler lay sprawled and groaning outside a doorway guarded by two grim Elasian males. Both of them were large, bare-armed and prodigiously muscled, but it wasn't their size or their scowls that had stopped Ensign Murphy in his tracks.

It was the Klingon disruptors they had leveled at the *Enterprise* crewman.

Chapter Six

"YOU ARE CHIEF UNDERLING of this cohort?" The big Elasian male paused just inside the shuttle's hatch, scowling with rank disapproval as he looked Chekov up and down. Chekov had a feeling he was going to thoroughly loathe the word *underling* by the time this mission was over. "Your Dohlman thinks to make fun of us." The accusation in his voice was bitter.

Chekov crossed his arms and returned the Elasian's flinty stare with a thin smile. "You must be Takcas." In fact, he remembered the red-haired Elasian from the viewscreen on the *Enterprise*'s bridge, when both Takcas and his Dohlman had spoken to Kirk in the most shamefully disrespectful manner. No doubt his comments now were as civilized as Chekov should have expected. "Welcome aboard the shuttle *Gamow*. I am—"

"I have no care for who you are." Takcas ducked the rest of the way inside, his head brushing the ceiling when he straightened to stand upright. He raked his gaze across the shuttle's stark interior, and his aquiline nose wrinkled as though smelling something sharp and unpleasant.

Chekov was suddenly glad he'd opted to wait for Takcas in here, instead of extending the Terran courtesy of greeting the Elasian outside. Not only was it familiar ground, but the human-proportioned shuttle also granted Chekov a distinct advantage in mobility and comfort when it came to dealing with these seven-foot-tall behemoths. And he had to admit that he wasn't sorry the rest of Takcas's cohort didn't have room to follow their leader inside.

"Chief Underling Takcas—"

"No!" The Elasian swung about with a fierce scowl, his voice as sharp and hard as though he were disciplining a dog. "You will *not* call me that execrable word, little underling. I tolerate such foul language from your Dohlman only because my Dohlman tells me to. *You* will call me 'Kessh,' and you will treat me accordingly."

Chekov had almost forgotten the Universal Translator on his belt until the alien word pricked it into action. It responded to the guttural bark—*kessh*—with the apologetic chime that meant it had no direct translation for the concept. Three words were offered in an attempt at explanation: sergeant, guardian, alpha male. Chekov had to admit that any of those was better than *underling*, no matter what language you spoke it in.

"Is there anything in particular you would like to examine, *Kessh* Takcas?" he asked. The sooner they completed this inspection, the sooner Chekov could rejoin the rest of the landing party. "Your Dohlman expressed concern over our weapons system."

Angular face still drawn into a frown, Takcas paced negligently forward, apparently oblivious of Chekov blocking his path. "This pitiful transport shuttle doesn't have a weapons system." He stopped just short of colliding with the lieutenant, and leaned to peer at the pile of seismic equipment near the rear of the shuttle. "But it has other equally distasteful things. You will move those boxes outside."

"No, I won't." Chekov craned his neck to meet the gaze a half-meter above him, but refused to take the step backward

49

that would have made their conversational distance more comfortable. He had agreed to call this man by whatever title his culture preferred—he hadn't agreed to back down from him. "My Dohlman left very specific instructions regarding those crates." Actually, it had been Mutchler, fretting aloud the whole time he stacked them in the corner as Chekov had ordered. "They contain delicate scientific equipment—"

"I know what they contain." Takcas cut him off with a snort and a dismissive wave. "I have destroyed two such shipments of equipment already."

So Mutchler had remarked. "Then you don't need to see this shipment, do you?"

The Elasian surprised him by turning sideways to try and elbow his way past, and Chekov had to step sternly to his right to impose himself between the *kessh* and his target. They collided briefly—hard enough for Takcas to make clear he wanted access, and long enough for Chekov to shove back at him and make clear he wasn't moving. "I told you, *Kessh* Takcas, my Dohlman doesn't want anyone to touch this equipment."

"Your Dohlman." The Elasian slapped backhanded at the lieutenant's shoulder, a disgustingly patronizing gesture. "I already know that your Dohlman would not even be here if those hairless geologists hadn't gone crying to the government. You take orders from them, not from her."

"If my Dohlman's orders are to safeguard equipment owned by the geologists, then that's what I'll do." He lost a single step against Takcas's pushing, but planted a foot against the seats behind him to keep from going farther. "I don't question her orders—ever. I obey them." He threw his whole weight into the shove, and stumbled Takcas back a step and a half.

"You obey a Dohlman who values the wants of geologists?" the Elasian sneered. But he didn't come closer again. "They only covet this planet because we have found dilithium here."

"The geologists were on Rakatan first—"

"Then they should have protected their claim! Stationed guard ships, formed an armada!" Takcas's hands came down to his sides, and one fist curled possessively around the dagger at his belt. "They are thieving maggots not fit to steal Elasian refuse, and your Dohlman is no better for having been with them." He stabbed a finger at the waiting boxes. "Move those useless machines outside, or I will move them for you!"

Chekov placed a hand on the seat backs to either side of him and clenched the fabric to try and hide his tension. "I'll stop you."

"Will you?" The question was almost a laugh. Takcas spread his arms as if to draw attention to the difference in their sizes. All Chekov focused on was the long, narrow dagger he'd freed with the motion. "How?"

No matter how belligerent the opposition, Chekov knew Kirk would hold him responsible for any insult he paid an alien dignitary—or her staff. That no doubt included foul language, and it certainly included stabbing. So, gritting his teeth against the rush of impolite things his heart wanted to say, he locked eyes with Takcas and repeated only, "I'll stop you," as though the outcome were never in question.

The Elasian's eyes narrowed; then his face melted into a faint smile that made him look younger than Chekov had originally thought. "You talk bigger than you stand."

Unsure how to respond, Chekov kept silent as Takcas slipped his knife back into its sheath and turned to bellow something in Elasian to the group outside the door. Their laughter rolled into the shuttle like a tumble of rough-hewn stones. A single voice broke free of the babble to rattle off a lengthy chain of language. Takcas nodded casually in response before turning back to Chekov. "What is your name, little *kessh?*"

He didn't hide his disgust for Takcas's labeling. "Chekov."

"Chekov." It sounded different, somehow, in the blunted Elasian accent, but seemed to please the alien male all the same. "That's a good name." He smiled hugely, crossing his

51

arms. "You know, Chekov, on my world a male no larger than you would have been killed in adolescence."

It occurred to Chekov then that whatever this was about, it had nothing to do with the shuttle, or security, or anything else he could understand. "As far as human males go," he said noncommittally, "I'm not so small."

"I've seen human males." Takcas cocked his head in cool amusement. "You're not so large, either." He waved toward the open hatchway without giving Chekov a chance to reply. "Now come. My men say we must hurry back to the compound. There's been a problem between our peoples, and if we aren't quick, we'll miss all the fighting before my Dohlman has your Dohlman's precious geologist put to death."

Kirk knew Spock would have told him that impatience was illogical at a time like this. After all, the transporter worked as quickly—or slowly—as it worked, and no amount of irritation or frustration would change the laws of physics. If he felt as if the rematerialization process was taking longer than normal, it was only his flawed human perception misinterpreting invariant reality. Kirk reminded himself sternly of that while he waited for the transporter effect to release him and Metcalfe to the Johnston Observatory's central operations room, but he still felt as if he'd been staring at the same patch of rounded wall for untold minutes before the last energized tingle left his skin and set him free.

"If you'll excuse me . . ." Metcalfe jerked her elbow out of his grip with ill-concealed resentment, then had to fumble to catch the sliding trail of disks she'd dislodged from the stack in her arms.

Kirk didn't try to hold her, and guessed that moving to help her right now would be as big a mistake. He hadn't meant to herd her into the transporter room like a nanny with a stubborn child, but she'd persisted in poring over every piece of data he'd let her take from the shuttle's computer before leaving, even after Kirk explained that they had a limited window in which to return her to the moonbase before the Elasians took offense. In the end, he'd had to drag her to the transporter room by careful force, listening to her wailing protestations all the way.

Now Metcalfe dumped her pile of data disks atop one of the many workstations. Kirk left her to her doctoral thesis, and stalked across the circular ops to vault up the steps leading to Bascomb's private office. She scowled at him without surprise when he keyed open her door and came to stand before her desk.

"Where's my shuttle, Kirk?"

He appreciated the white-haired geologist's directness. "Being held hostage." He jerked a nod toward the central chamber and Metcalfe at her busy station. "To make sure none of your geologists pulls a stupid stunt like that again."

"That wasn't a stupid stunt!" Bascomb slapped shut the data notebook in front of her on the desk, anger flashing in her dark eyes. "That was a normal data-gathering run, and you know it. We can't monitor the whole planet from this moon—we can't even keep Rakatan Mons in view for more than six hours from up here! We make over thirty of those runs every day—something I can't do with only the three shuttles you've left me."

"Dr. Bascomb," Kirk told her tightly, "you can't do it at all." The honest frustration in her wordless snort touched him. It was an emotion he felt rather often when dealing with the Elasians. "I'm sorry," he said, more calmly, "but you know that Starfleet missions always take precedence over the normal scientific operations of Federation observatories. Until we've settled the problem with the Elasians—"

Bascomb waved him into silence. "The problem with the Elasians, Captain, is that they're interfering with the work of our observatory! Your *mission* here was to restore normal scientific operations by getting those people out of our way. Grounding all our shuttles doesn't help—"

"Our mission," he interrupted smoothly, "was to investigate the possible presence of a sentient race inside that volcano. Or had you forgotten?"

Bascomb's only response was a streak of red climbing up her weathered cheeks, and Kirk had to clench his teeth to keep from saying anything he'd regret. Apparently, Metcalfe's sincere obsession with the possibility of native Rakatan sentience had been nothing more than the lure used to pull in a starship to evict the Elasians. Knowing he'd been used in such a ploy didn't improve Kirk's already thinly stretched tolerance.

"In any case . . ." He knew his voice sounded clipped, but didn't entirely mind when Bascomb winced a little at his sharpness. "It doesn't matter what our original mission was, Dr. Bascomb. Right now, my top priority is to establish whether or not the Elasians have a valid claim to this planet and the dilithium they say they're mining here."

Bascomb pulled back slightly in her seat, startlement jerking her eyebrows toward her hairline.

"Until my landing party gets full access to the Elasians' astral charts—" Kirk reached for his beeping communicator without even slowing his train of thought. "—you're going to have to keep your geologists from causing any trouble." He flipped the small grid open. "Kirk here."

"Dilithium?" Bascomb didn't seem to have heard the last half of what he said. "Who said there was dilithium?"

"Spock here, Captain." The Vulcan's deep voice cut across the geologist's disbelieving protest. "We have received a Priority One hail from Lieutenant Chekov on the planet's surface."

Kirk wondered if Spock could derive him an equation for how rapidly problems with the Elasians seemed to develop the longer the *Enterprise* stayed near them. "All right, Spock. Patch him through to me."

Kirk didn't even hear the changeover when Spock cut in the planet-based channel.

"Captain?" Chekov sounded breathless, his words broken by gasps that seemed to come in the rhythm of rapid walking. Kirk didn't envy the lieutenant the chore of trying to travel and talk at the same time in Rakatan's oxygen-poor atmosphere. "I'm outside—the mining camp—near the—

shuttle landing site." He paused for a moment, only his breathing sounding through the link. "The Elasians—" he finally gasped, "say—there's been a—conflict with our landing party. I'm on my way now—"

"A conflict?" Kirk flashed through the last few hours, trying to think of any insult to the Elasians he might have missed. He was beginning to lose count even with the ones he knew of. "Over what?"

Even through his ragged breathing, Chekov's annoyance was easy to hear. "I'm—not sure, sir—but whatever it was—Dr. Mutchler did it."

Chapter Seven

CONSIDERING HOW the Elasians had reacted to everything else so far, Kirk's next question seemed the only practical one. "Chekov, is Dr. Mutchler still alive?"

"I think so," Chekov gasped. Kirk thought he heard other voices through the communicator link, but if they were real, Chekov ignored them. "The Dohlman—is going to—decide on that—" Whether his breath finally gave out or he simply had nothing else to say, Chekov didn't try to go on.

Kirk frowned a keen glare at Bascomb. "See how much trouble your normal scientific observations can make?"

"You don't even know what Scott Mutchler was doing when this happened," Bascomb countered, unimpressed. "Those Elasians get mad at the drop of a rock hammer. Anything can set them off."

Kirk nodded. "My point exactly, Dr. Bascomb. Anything—including normal scientific observations." He raised his communicator between them so that Chekov could hear everything both he and Bascomb said. "By my authority as the ranking Starfleet officer in the quadrant," the captain announced, firmly and loudly for the sake of the communicator, "all Federation Geological Survey personnel are hereby confined to this moonbase. Lieutenant Chekov?"

"Sir?" It was good to know he had enough breath to be paying strict attention.

"Dr. Mutchler is remanded to your custody. I want you to keep him from carrying out any scientific operations—" At Bascomb's piteous groan of dismay, the captain smiled ruefully and amended, "Any *gratuitous* scientific operations that could offend the Elasians. Is that clear?"

"I'll do—my best, Captain." The security chief didn't sound particularly happy with the assignment, but Kirk knew it wasn't in the lieutenant to question a direct instruction. "Chekov out."

"The same goes double for you," Kirk told Bascomb as he snapped shut his communicator. "No overflights of the planet. No launching of remote probes. *Nothing* that could put Her Glory the Dohlman in a bad mood." He'd had enough of the young despot's moods already.

Apparently, so had Bascomb. She slapped both hands down on the desk and swore. "You're putting the demands of a spoiled fourteen-year-old brat ahead of one of the most significant scientific studies in the galaxy?"

"No, Doctor. I'm putting the lives of my people—and yours—ahead of a few hours of lost data." Kirk caught up her scowl in his own gaze of hard resolve, and watched her anger bleed into something closer to disgruntled shame. "Do you have a problem with that?"

Bascomb looked away, lips pursed, and snorted toward a pile of data charts on the edge of the desk. "I suppose not." Her finger made a rigid stuttering sound when she dragged it up the side of one of the piles. "But what are we supposed to do while your landing party verifies those star charts? Play tiddlywinks?"

The image alone nearly made Kirk smile. "If that would make you happy." Bascomb didn't share his amusement. She shot him an angry look in return for his light response.

Kirk strove for a more sober expression in deference to her feelings about the lost work time. "Would you like some advice?"

Bascomb scowled without looking up at him. "You've seemed pretty free with it so far."

"Keep Metcalfe looking for sentient voices in your seismic data." He offered a harmless shrug when the old geologist glanced up in surprise. "If the Elasian claim to Rakatan is validated, Dr. Bascomb, those magma men might be the only ones who can save you."

"Liar!"

The sullen crack of a backhanded slap echoed through the Dohlman's quarters, followed by the thud of a body hitting the floor. Uhura winced and flung out her hands—to restrain Ensign Murphy's instinctive lunge, and to stop Sulu from reaching for his phaser. As she was the "Dohlman" of the landing party, this crisis was hers to resolve. And the first step was obvious.

"Dr. Mutchler," she said between her teeth. "Please don't say anything else."

The geologist squinted up at her, blood trickling down his chin from his split lip. His left eye was already reddish purple and swollen shut from the blow that had knocked him away from the Elasians' warehouse, but his face stiffened with indignation.

"All I was trying to do was explain—" Mutchler broke off when Oben leaned over him and grabbed a handful of his shirt, jerking him roughly to his feet. If the geologist hadn't been so tall, Uhura suspected he would have ended up dangling in the air. "Um—maybe you'd better explain for me, Commander Uhura."

"I intend to." Uhura turned to face the young ruler of Elas, tense as a lioness atop the pile of silk tapestry pillows that served as her throne. "Dohlman Israi, give me leave to speak for this underling."

Israi frowned at Uhura through snake coils of black hair.

She hadn't moved since Oben and the other guards had dragged the landing party into her quarters, although the occasional ripple of muscle in her bare, jeweled arms told Uhura that she wanted to.

"Why should I let you speak for him? Is he your underling?" Her eyes narrowed in suspicion. "Was he acting on your orders when he tried to steal our dilithium?"

"No."

Israi flicked the fingers of one hand dismissively, in what must have been the Elasian equivalent of a shrug. "Then there is nothing for you to say in the matter." She turned toward Oben. "Take him down to the punishment cells."

"Wait." Uhura flung the command out as loudly as she could, but it was drowned under the unexpected thundering of booted feet outside the Dohlman's quarters. Ensign Murphy swung around to face the noise, taking a protective step forward that shielded Uhura even as it frustrated her view. It wasn't until the muscled bulk of Takcas moved out into the room and bent his knee in a deep, respectful bow to his Dohlman that the security guard relaxed and stepped back.

"Your Glory." Takcas straightened, his face sober but something close to laughter moving in his eyes. Behind the Dohlman's chief underling, Uhura saw a flash of Starfleet red almost hidden among the brown leather and brown skin of the Elasians. "Your cohort stands ready to avenge whatever crimes this maggot of a geologist has committed against you."

Israi dipped her head to acknowledge his presence. "He was caught stealing dilithium from our warehouse," she informed him.

"No, Dohlman Israi." Uhura pitched her voice to carry through the mutter and shifting of the cohort, so Chekov would know she was safe and still in command. "Dr. Mutchler was caught before he even entered your dilithium warehouse. Your own guards can testify that he made no attempt to steal anything."

The young Dohlman swung around to glare at her. "I didn't give you permission to speak for him! You told me he was not your underling."

"He isn't my underling, but he *is* my responsibility. His own Dohlman entrusted him to me as a guide for this trip." Uhura searched her memories of past Elasian encounters, trying to find words that Israi would understand. "It would dishonor me to return without him, especially when he has committed no crime."

Israi ran a thumbnail along her lower lip, her scowl fading into a more thoughtful frown. "The Federation geologists want to take our mining claim away from us. They have said so many times." She glanced over at Mutchler, still held taut in Oben's choking grip. "They must want to steal our dilithium."

"We didn't even *know* about your dilithium." Mutchler sounded hoarse but indignant. "All we want is for you to go away and quit messing up our seismic readings!"

The young Dohlman pointed a finger at him shrewdly. "Which amounts to the same thing. Whatever the reason, you are our enemies. We will deal with you accordingly."

Movement skirled among the massed bodies of the cohort, a ripple of moving red accompanied by a scatter of grunts and curses. Chekov broke free with a last determined shove and took a step toward the Dohlman, then paused when Takcas swung around and slid between them.

"Dohlman." The security chief's words were addressed to Israi, but Uhura noticed that his gaze never wavered from the leader of her cohort. "Do you know how many geologists are stationed on the moonbase?"

The unexpected question made the Dohlman's eyes narrow in surprise. "No," she said, with arrogant unconcern. "Why should I?"

"Do you know, *Kessh* Takcas?"

"Twelve," Takcas said. "Five females, seven workers, no cohort."

"Twelve." Chekov paused deliberately, then spoke to Israi

again. "Dholman, is your cohort so small or so poorly trained that they can be defeated in a fight by a dozen human scientists?"

A ripple of outrage ran through the gathered Elasian males, and they closed in around Chekov like a clenching fist. Uhura heard Sulu take in a quick breath, and felt more than saw Murphy poise himself for action beside her. Except for the tightening of the muscles in his jaw, however, Chekov never moved. After a moment, Takcas himself waved the other males away.

"You insult me!" Israi jerked upright on her cushions, shoving her thick black curls aside to glare at the Russian. "Only an idiot could think such a thing! How dare you suggest it?" She pointed an imperious finger at Uhura. "I demand that you reprimand your underling!"

Chekov turned his head, one brow lifted questioningly. Uhura gave him a quick flash of smile to show she had understood his tactics, then deliberately turned her amused look on the Dohlman of Elas.

"How can I reprimand him, Your Glory? You yourself claimed these geologists as your enemies."

Caught in a trap of her own words, Israi scowled and struggled for a moment, then narrowed her eyes at Uhura. "They might wish to be our enemies," she amended scornfully. "But since my cohort has no need to fear them——"

The older male, Oben, interrupted her, his bearded face dark with anger. "Not to fear, Your Glory, but to swat like the biting insects they are! Remember, this isn't the first time these so-called geologists have tried to sabotage our mining operation."

"Sabotage!" Mutchler's head jerked up, his gray eyes wide and startled. "How could I——"

"Dr. Mutchler, shut up!" snapped Uhura. Israi watched her intently as she turned her frown from the silenced geologist to the burly Elasian holding him. "Underling, what evidence do you have that this man was trying to commit sabotage? He didn't bring a single weapon into your camp."

Oben's thick brows drew into a stubborn line. "His weapons he left back at your ship, thanks to our scanners—"

"I've told you before, those are *seismometers!*" Mutchler burst out, despite Uhura's warning look. "Lieutenant Chekov, you can tell them those aren't weapons!"

Uhura saw the Russian give Takcas an oddly measuring glance. "I don't think they need me to tell them."

Takcas grunted. "The scanners say they are high-energy devices. With no offensive capability."

"But they could be rigged to explode," Oben reminded his *kessh.* "And the geologist could have hidden a remote device inside his clothes to trigger them from inside the camp."

"So they could blow up *outside* the camp?" The knife edge of Sulu's voice told Uhura what a strain it had been for him to keep silent until then. "Why would he want to destroy our own shuttle?"

"And why would he have needed to go into a guarded warehouse to do it?" Uhura added tartly. "We could have triggered a dozen remote devices in the time you left us sitting outside the Dohlman's quarters." The startled lift of Israi's chin inspired her to add, "In fact, if you had brought us in immediately as the Dohlman had ordered, Dr. Mutchler wouldn't have had time to become curious about the geological nature of your dilithium ore. Or have had time to try and examine it."

Israi scrambled to her feet, as if the effort of sitting still had just become intolerable. *"Oben!"* She crossed the room with short, restless strides and scowled up at him, affronted pride vibrating through every inch of her coltish frame. "Did you disobey me?"

A growl rose from the cohort at her words, and Takcas came to stand beside her, all laughter gone from his eyes now. Oben released Mutchler and dropped to one knee before the Dohlman, but Uhura noticed that his bearded face harbored resentment instead of remorse.

"Your Glory, I did it because you gave these Federation insect droppings too much honor!" he argued. "They have no right to bring these interfering geologists into our camp, no right to demand to see our charter here—"

"They have the right," Israi said between her teeth, "because they have a *starship*." She startled Uhura with a fierce backhand slap of her own, one that made Oben rock back on his heels and blink at her. "Only a fool refuses to negotiate with a better-armed cohort."

"Yes, Your Glory. You are right, of course." The middle-aged Elasian lowered his face to the floor, his cheek branded coppery red where she had struck him. "I kiss the shadow of your presence."

Israi snorted and spun away, leaving Takcas glaring down at his subordinate. Uhura met the Dohlman's gaze steadily, their eyes nearly level across the pile of cushions between them. "You say you are responsible for this geologist," Israi challenged her. "Will you swear on your honor as a Dohlman that he will not sabotage our camp with his *seismometers?*"

A quick gesture by Chekov caught Uhura's eye before she could answer. The security chief held up his communicator, then pointed from Mutchler to himself and circled one hand around his wrist significantly. Uhura nodded acknowledgment. "I'll do better than that," she assured the Dohlman. "If you permit me to examine your charts as we agreed, Dohlman Israi, I'll make my *kessh* take the geologist into his custody. He will see to it that Dr. Mutchler takes his seismometers up to the top of the volcano and leaves them there." She gave Mutchler a warning look when he opened his mouth. "Is that suitable?"

The Dohlman cocked her head, regarding them with astute dark eyes; then her face lit with a completely unexpected smile. The expression warmed her arrogant mouth into something approaching charm. "Very suitable," Israi agreed calmly. "Even a geologist could not be stupid enough to try and sabotage Rakatan Mons."

Mutchler snorted, still irrepressible despite their combined glares. "Never fear," he told the Dohlman. "I'm the *only* one here who knows just how stupid that would be."

Chapter Eight

"OH, NO!"

Uhura stifled her groan of dismay as she scanned the Elasian astral charts. She knew that Israi had left the door open between her rooms and this outer annex where the mining camp's records were kept, and suspected that the Dohlman wasn't above listening in on her comments as she translated. The utterly lifeless quiet of Rakatan, however, carried Uhura's soft voice all too well. Ensign Murphy looked around from his post at the threshold.

"Sir?" His concerned glance fell to the yellowing sheets of ancient plastic spread under Uhura's fingers. "Is something wrong with the charts?"

"Not wrong, just unexpected." She let the Elasian charts curl back into their age-old roll and reached for her communicator. "Uhura to *Enterprise*. Come in, please."

"This is *Enterprise*." Spock's voice startled her, answering in place of her junior communications officer. The long time it had taken them to be admitted into the Elasian camp must have raised suspicions on the ship. "Is the landing party in danger, Commander Uhura?"

"No, Mr. Spock."

"Then hold for Captain Kirk. Spock out."

Thumbing off the communicator, Uhura rolled the Elasian charts open again in the hope of seeing something she recognized. Star systems freckled the oxidized plastic, stretched out of recognition by the perspective of an unfamiliar planet. Uhura drummed frustrated fingers on a bright star that she would have guessed to be Spica if it hadn't been too close to one even brighter. Maybe Sulu, with his uncanny knack for navigation, could have identified it, but Sulu wasn't here. Why had she let him go gallivanting off with Chekov?

"Dohlman Uhura." Captain Kirk's voice crackled with a mixture of impatience and suspicion, but his words were neutral, obviously chosen for the benefit of possible Elasian listeners. "What's the status of your mission?"

Uhura decided to give him the good news first. "The Elasians were a little suspicious of us at first, but they've agreed to permit Dr. Mutchler to repair his seismometers on the volcano. Sulu and Chekov are helping him do that now."

"And the star charts? Do they support their mining claim?"

Uhura frowned down at the yellowing sheets under her hands. "I'm having a little trouble determining that, Captain. The charts are written completely in Elasian."

Silence answered her for a moment, the hissing silence of an open subspace channel. Then Spock's voice replaced the captain's. "Commander, I believe you learned the rudiments of the Elasian language when we ferried Dohlman Elaan to Troyius, did you not?"

Uhura repressed an urge to tell him exactly how many years ago that had been. She knew that to the Vulcan, the correlation of time and memory meant nothing. "I learned to speak it, not to read it, Mr. Spock. The Elasians have no alphabet, only abstract pictographs."

Kirk snorted. "Not those things that look like someone pasted dead insects to the page?"

"I'm afraid so." Uhura ran her fingers across the faint line of black smudges that labeled the star she thought was Spica. "When Sulu gets back, I might be able to get some of these star systems identified, but that still won't let us judge the dates of their discovery."

Another pause, this time punctuated by the click of a closing channel. Uhura guessed that the captain and the first officer were conferring with each other. Then the contact clicked open again.

"Commander Uhura." Spock seemed to be using her title with even more than his usual politeness. Uhura suppressed a smile as she realized that was as close as the Vulcan could come to misleading the Elasians about her importance on the ship. "I suggest that you persuade one of the Elasians to read their charts into the Universal Translator so you can transcribe them into English."

Uhura glanced at Ensign Murphy, wondering if she would see her own doubts mirrored in his dark eyes. The security guard refused to meet her gaze, his shoulders tense beneath his uniform jacket. She took a deep breath. "But, Mr. Spock, can we be sure that will give us an *accurate* translation?"

"It doesn't matter," Kirk pointed out. "Accurate or not, a translation will give us something to check against our own computer records. And if their claim doesn't hold up—"

"It will hold up." The arrogant Elasian voice at her shoulder didn't startle Uhura. She'd guessed from the direction and intensity of Murphy's gaze that the Dohlman had entered the room behind her. What did startle her were the young ruler's next words.

"I will read the charts myself, and I will read them accurately for your translator." Israi's voice dripped scorn as only the very young could do. "I would not stoop to deceive a Dohlman served by such an inferior cohort as you command, Kirk-insect."

Kirk answered with a strangled sound that could have been either a stifled curse or choked-off laughter. Whatever it was, his first officer clearly judged it better that they didn't hear more. "Spock out," he said and slashed the subspace connection.

Uhura put her communicator away, then gave Israi a considering glance. "When do you wish to start reading the charts for me, Your Glory?"

"Now." The young Elasian pushed back her heavy sheath of gold-braided hair, eyes oddly bright as she leaned over the plastic charts. "Do you have ready this translator your cohort spoke of?"

"Yes, it's on." Uhura hurried to pull a small computer pad and light pen from her jacket pocket, so she could record the English versions of each star's label. Later, she could use the tricorder to duplicate the entire chart, but she would have to trust her memory to match the translations with the correct stars.

"Good." Israi pointed at the first line of dusky smudges on the plastic. "That says, 'Originally recorded during the eighth year of the reign of Dohlman Skuah, of blessed memory.'" She looked up, the expression on her angular face so unfamiliar that it took Uhura aback. "Do you know when that was?"

"Um—no." Uhura jotted a quick note, then glanced up again at the young Dohlman. This time, the eager way Israi met her gaze allowed her to recognize an emotion she would have known at once if she'd seen it in any human teenager. Uhura bit her lower lip and asked gravely, "Do you?"

"Of course." Israi lifted a proud chin. "Dohlman Skuah reigned first in the line of Kesmeth, founded after the rebellion of the Snake Clans. She ruled for nine years. After her came Dohlman Alais, who ruled for twelve years. Then came Dohlman Wywras—"

Uhura recorded the cascade of information, bending her head over her computer pad to hide her smile. There could be no doubt about it. Dohlman Israi, the absolute and sovereign ruler of her planet, was showing off.

"I swear!" Mutchler stopped walking so abruptly that Chekov had to plant himself and let the gravsled bump into him to keep from running the scientist over. "Seismic Station Three should be *right here.*" He stared down at the ashy ground between his feet as though willing the obstinate instrument to appear.

If they hadn't been scouring every inch of Rakatan Mons's flanks in search of a one-meter-high square of geology equipment, Chekov might almost have appreciated this chance to experience the planet's relative charms. Although several kilometers up the same ravine that housed the Elasian mining camp, they were still comparatively low on the mountain—or so Mutchler assured them. Anywhere Chekov looked, the horizons ran too far into the distance to see. Water, a bright, reflective emerald, smeared into turquoise where it mingled with sky far, far below, and wild, exotic sweeps of land thrust cones of barren rock into the bellies of low-hanging clouds.

Or maybe not so low-hanging. Having the rest of a mountain towering out of sight above his head tended to distort Chekov's concept of distance and height. So did the slightly muggy quality of the local air—he kept thinking it shouldn't be so thick and warm at this altitude, even though the depth and speed of his breathing served as a reminder of how little oxygen was really reaching his lungs. He forcibly took his attention away from the landscape, and concentrated instead on getting his breathing under control before they started walking again.

"Are you *sure* you landed the shuttle at the coordinates I gave you?" Appropriately enough, Mutchler seemed the only one not affected by the oxygen-poor environment.

Sulu, hands clasped behind his back so that only Chekov could see the fists he clenched, nodded very calmly. "Yes, Dr. Mutchler. I'm sure." An edge unrelated to his labored breathing crept into the helmsman's voice.

Mutchler seemed to hear it, too. His young face flushed with embarrassment. "Yes . . . Yes, of course you are." He winced a little, and rubbed his cheek when an apologetic smile tugged at his swollen eye. "I'm sorry, Commander. I really didn't mean it like that."

Sulu nodded an acceptance, but Mutchler didn't wait to

see it. Scrambling nimbly up a pile of what looked like blocks of shattered glass, the geologist craned to look toward the horizon with no apparent concern for the dirt and rips suffered by his black and gold clothing. "When we lost contact with this station four months ago, it didn't occur to me that something cataclysmic might have happened. But now I wonder if Rakatan Mons might have experienced some unexpected crustal movement along this gully." He scaled the top of the pile and jumped down the other side, only his tousled head showing above the jumble. "Or—God help me—a slump. I wish I'd thought to compare the last quarter's satellite maps before we came. . . ."

Mutchler's voice faded as he hiked another dozen meters up the ravine, and Chekov thumbed off the gravsled's repulsors to let the device settle gently to the ground. It sighed up a fine puff of ashy sand as it sank. "Does he ever shut up?"

Sulu shrugged, sitting down on the end of the sled and unfastening the clasp on his jacket. "Not that I've noticed." He motioned after Mutchler, but showed no inclination to rise and follow him. "Do you really think it's safe to let him wander off all alone like that?"

Between the warmth, the stuffiness, and the two hundred kilos' worth of seismic equipment he'd been dragging since they landed, Chekov wasn't interested in following Mutchler anywhere. "There's nothing on Rakatan but the Elasians and us," he sighed, scooting one of the crates catercorner so he could take a seat on the other end. "Given Dr. Mutchler's record so far, it's probably *safest* to let him wander off alone." He leaned back to rest his elbows on the crate behind him, but resisted stripping open the front of his own duty jacket against the heat. It would look too undignified, and they were still technically on duty. "Scientists," he grumbled.

Sulu angled a reproving look down the length of boxes at his friend. "And just what is that supposed to mean?"

Chekov glanced aside at him, then back after Mutchler

69

with a shrug. "Just that scientists sometimes don't seem to have the sense God gave lemmings." He allowed himself the minor discretion of tugging at his tunic collar with a finger to let some air under the fabric. "Mutchler hasn't been planetside for five hours, and he's already nearly started a war. It makes me think we should confine scientists to universities and labs until they pass some sort of social competency test."

Sulu snorted, not quite an honest laugh, and kicked sand across Chekov's boot. "That's a very open-minded attitude for someone who spent his first year on the *Enterprise* chin-deep in astrophysics texts."

"That was different," Chekov countered. He shook his foot clean and moved it out of Sulu's reach. "I was a navigator then."

"And now you're a security chief, so you have to think like a football player."

It seemed a strange brand of insult, coming from Sulu. Chekov turned to scowl at him, and felt an unexpected stab of discomfort when he saw that Sulu wasn't smiling. He released his collar and sat straighter, not liking this turn in their discussion. "I don't even know what that means."

Eyes very serious, the commander studied his friend with an intensity that made Chekov's face feel warm. "I don't think I like what's going on between you and the Elasians."

The lieutenant pushed to his feet, suddenly unwilling to sit any longer, but not knowing why. "Nothing's going on."

"Oh?" Sulu stood as well, moving firmly in front of Chekov before he could even get started pacing. "Then what happened back at the mining camp?" he pressed. "A square dance? I thought they were going to kill you!"

"They're not going to kill me." Chekov stepped around him with an irritable wave. "We have an understanding."

Sulu fell into step beside him. "What kind of understanding?"

"I'm . . . not sure." Chekov glared at Sulu when the helmsman barked a laugh. "I mean I can't explain it. But I know I'm right, and I know . . ." The more he talked, the worse it sounded, so he just turned away with a frustrated growl. "Oh, it's complicated."

"It's hormones." Sulu caught his arm, and Chekov stopped himself from pulling away when he saw the worried line between his friend's eyes. "Everything about the Elasians is," Sulu said soberly. "Takcas and his men sweat enough testosterone to choke a Deltan, and just being around them has you so uptight I want to scream."

"I found it!" Mutchler's call from somewhere out of sight beyond the rock pile gave Chekov the excuse he needed to break eye contact with Sulu and turn away.

He was surprised, then, when the helmsman didn't let him go immediately, and he had to reach up and detach his friend's hand before returning to the waiting gravsled. "It's not what you think," he said in an effort to reassure him.

The helmsman grudgingly released him, but didn't look any happier. "I don't think it's what you think, either. Just be careful around them. Okay?"

Chekov couldn't help being amused by the unnecessary warning. "Always."

By the time they'd maneuvered the gravsled around the broken terrain to join the geologist, Mutchler had already pulled off the seismic station's door and disappeared halfway inside on hands and knees. The station itself looked something like a high-tech doghouse, with Mutchler's rump sticking out of the cramped crawlway entrance like the narrow end of some alien house pet.

Chekov eased the sled into position as close to the entrance as he dared without crowding the geologist, and Sulu moved to the other side of the small station to wait, sealing up the front of his uniform jacket as he walked.

"Ack!" Mutchler had been talking since before they were even in earshot, most of his words drowned by his tricorder's hum. "I expected the telemetry to be off—this station hasn't beamed data up to our satellites for months. But look at this!" He didn't even squirm out of the hole, just thrust some unidentifiable piece of machinery out past his shoulder as though the very sight of it explained everything. "This is going to take a lot longer than I thought."

Sulu leaned over the station roof to examine the little piece. "What's wrong with it?"

"Dust damage. It's supposed to look just like the laser we assembled on the shuttle." Mutchler took the piece inside again, then reached out with his other hand. "Lieutenant Chekov, could you open that crate on the bottom and hand me the red attaché with the new laser sensor? And the cleaning supplies?"

Parking the sled, Chekov slipped an antigrav from along one side and fixed it to the box on the top of the pile. "If you didn't plan on cleaning the stations, Dr. Mutchler, why do you have cleaning equipment?"

Inside the housing, the geologist went very still. "Oh . . . well . . ." He became a flurry of activity again, moving things around inside with much bumping and clanging. "I wanted to be prepared, Lieutenant. You never know what you might find when you check up on some of these stations."

He was a worse liar than he was a diplomat.

As if hearing Chekov's thought, Mutchler pulled himself out of the housing so quickly he thumped his head on the doorway. "Please, don't be angry." He talked just as quickly despite the hand clapped on top of his head. "We just haven't had access to the stations for so long, and God only knows what the Elasians have done to them. We were afraid if we told you how long it might take to service them, your Captain Kirk might not let us use you for transportation."

Chekov handed down the laser with a weary sigh. "We're on the same side, Dr. Mutchler," he said as the geologist accepted the small device. "You'd be better off telling us the truth and saving your lies for the Elasians."

Mutchler jerked his head up from sorting out the power leads on the back of the laser's housing. "I haven't lied to the Elasians! Those neckless grunts just think everything's related to their alleged supplies of dilithium." He squirmed back into the housing with the laser clutched in one fist. "No one at the Johnston Observatory cares one whit about their stupid mining operations, so long as they keep away from our equipment and they don't interfere with our seismic data." He clicked something together inside, and grunted with satisfaction. "All right, that ought to have us running, at least . . ."

When the first thrum of movement shivered through the ground at his feet, Chekov thought the station must utilize some much larger power source than he'd originally assumed. Then he heard the gentle rattle of metal on metal from the crates behind him, and looked up to meet Sulu's startled gaze across the station housing as a fine patter of dust began to hiss down the slope around them.

Then, like a giant that's rolled over in his sleep and gone on dreaming, the rumbling died away into silence.

Heart pounding, hands clenched on the towbar of the gravsled, Chekov scowled accusingly down at Mutchler's feet. "Did you do that?"

The echo of the geologist's laughter inside the housing didn't improve his temperament. "Are you kidding?"

"Calm down," Sulu said, reaching across to slap at his arm. "It was just an earthquake."

Chekov's stomach lurched in alarm. *"Just* an earthquake?"

"Volcanoes throw them off all the time," Mutchler added.

"This is supposed to make me feel *better?"*

"Pavel . . ." Sulu rounded the housing to pry his friend's hands loose one at a time. "It's nothing—really. I've slept through worse tremors than that. This was only—" He glanced back at Mutchler as the geologist wormed himself free of the housing door. "—three point nine?"

"Four point one," Mutchler reported. Then he broke into a grin of obvious pride and pleasure. "That's very good, though. Are you from Japan?"

Sulu returned his smile. "San Francisco."

"Ah." Mutchler looked up at Chekov in that sad, pitying way the lieutenant always associated with sincere bureaucrats who thought they knew more about your welfare than you did yourself. "And you're from someplace tectonically very boring, aren't you?"

Not interested in satisfying the annoying geologist's scientific curiosity, Chekov reached into the attaché and pulled free a shiny piece of scrap metal from among the strange collection of repair tools. "We never did manage to get the focusing device on your laser to aim correctly. Try using this to redirect the beam where you need it." He pressed the piece into Mutchler's palm with a tightly held smile. "Now, why don't you go put that laser in place before somebody out here gets hurt with it?"

Chapter Nine

"—AND IT SAYS HERE that this system, containing the planet that you humans call Rakatan, was discovered by Elasian scouts in the third year of the reign of the Dohlman Kiyaan." Israi cast Uhura a triumphant glance. "Long before any of your Starfleet vessels ever came here."

"Mmm." Uhura paged back through her computer-recorded notes, scanning the royal genealogy Israi had recited for her. They were sitting side by side at the table now, formality abated a little by the long afternoon of reading and transcribing the charts. Her computer held many pages of notes, since Israi had saved the reading of Rakatan's label for last. Uhura was no longer so sure what the young Dohlman's motives were. At first, she had almost certainly wanted just to demonstrate her knowledge of her ancestors and her ability to read. That did not explain why she'd deliberately drawn the afternoon out so long, though.

Perhaps Uhura had been given a hint when Israi had sent Ensign Murphy outside to join her own cohort guardsmen shortly after work on the charts had begun. "This is business between Dohlmen," Israi had snapped when the security guard had quietly corrected her pronunciation of a Federation planet's name. "We don't need underlings here with us." Her lip curled. "We see you often enough already."

Uhura had seconded the order, hearing a note in Israi's voice that warned her any insistence on Murphy's presence would have cut the Dohlman's cooperation short. She wondered now if it had been the sheer novelty of spending time with someone not an "underling" that had made Israi so willing to translate for her. Aside from the Dohlman and herself, Uhura had seen no other females of any species at this mining camp since she'd arrived. It couldn't have been an easy life for a youngster, even one trained as Israi must have been.

"Why do you just say, 'um'? What are you looking at?" Israi leaned over the computer pad, her eyes narrowing in quick suspicion. "What are these marks in here? They all look alike, like scratches made by lizards in the dirt."

Uhura's lips twitched as she recalled Captain Kirk's description of Elasian pictographs. "These are the marks that record my language." She pointed to the entry she'd been looking at. "This says that the Dohlman Kiyaan reigned fourteenth of the line of Sevuth, and that she reigned for only three years before the Snake Clans revolted. That made their Dohlman Skuah *the* Dohlman, first of the line of Kesmeth."

Israi tipped her head slightly sideways in what looked like a gesture of surprise. "That is not a bad reading, to come from lizard scratches."

"Thank you," said Uhura, smiling. The young Dohlman gave her a puzzled look, as if the polite words held no meaning for her, and Uhura's smile faded. She looked back at the computer pad. "According to my lizard scratches, the third year of Kiyaan's reign was one hundred and ninety-four Elasian years ago."

Israi nodded slowly. "That is so."

"Which is the same as one hundred and five Standard years." Which was indeed a long time before the first Starfleet vessels had entered this quadrant of the galaxy,

Uhura thought, but did not say aloud. She reached out for the tricorder she'd set down on one edge of the plastic sheet and aimed it at the chart. A quick whistle told her it had begun its spectral analysis. "Now, we'll see if this chart was really made during Skuah's reign. If so, it should be at least one hundred Standard years old."

"This machine will tell you that it is," Israi said with arrogant assurance. And a moment later the numbers scrolling across the tricorder's readout did verify the age: the plastic had been made one hundred and two Standard years ago. The Dohlman read the confirmation in Uhura's face and pointed a triumphant finger at her.

"I told you—" she began.

The low rumble of what sounded like machinery stopped her, growing ominously louder as it neared the Dohlman's quarters. Israi scowled and swung toward the open door. "What fool is driving—"

Plastic whispered beneath them. Glancing down, Uhura saw the Elasian charts shiver across the table, moving without being touched. Her breath caught in her throat. Once before, when she'd been studying for an exam at Starfleet Academy, she'd seen tapes crawl across a library table in that same inexplicable way, responding to vibrations too tenuous for human fingers to feel. A moment later, a magnitude-six earthquake had knocked her to the floor in a rain of falling books.

"*Up!*" She shoved back the bench they sat on and yanked the Dohlman to her feet. "We have to get out of here! It's an earthquake!"

Israi shrugged free of her grasp, contempt leaping into her almond eyes. "We have earthquakes here always. They have never caused us damage."

"Well, this one's going to." Ignoring Israi's gasp of affronted fury, Uhura pushed the small Elasian female toward the door. The corrugated metal floor swayed under them, gently at first, then with increasing force.

"The charts—we can't leave them!" Muscles rippled in Israi's bare shoulders, and she tore out of Uhura's grasp with unexpected strength, rounding back to the table. Uhura gritted her teeth and went after her, her run becoming a stagger as the floor pitched beneath her feet in jagged, unbalancing spasms.

Israi grabbed up the rolls of yellowed plastic and turned back toward the door, but it was too late. The growl of tearing earth exploded into a roar so deep Uhura could feel the vibrations in her bones. She barely had time to knock the Dohlman beneath the table before a cascade of broken roof tiles began drumming on the metal surface above their heads. Something larger fell with a crash out in the hallway.

"What is falling?" Israi's voice was barely audible over the din, but the Universal Translator on Uhura's belt picked it up and amplified it. Uhura turned her head, blinking through the dust-choked light at the young Elasian. "Was it the roof?"

"A wall, I think. Out in the outer hallway." The screech of ripping metal preceded a second crash, this one so loud it made Uhura's ears ring. The reverberating echoes told Uhura what had happened, even before the dust cleared and let her see the slab of crushed metal blocking the exit. "We're trapped."

The Dohlman's dark face had gone stiff and taut, but it was the tension of blind anger, not fear. Even in the chaos of the quake, Uhura felt a twist of pity for the youngster lying beside her. Raised to expect utter obedience from her subjects and surroundings, Israi could respond only with rage to events she hadn't ordered to happen.

"How could this happen?" The Dohlman's voice shook with frustrated fury. "Where was my cohort that they let this happen to me?"

"They're outside, where you sent them," Uhura said dryly. She felt the last ripples of floor motion damp out, and wriggled cautiously out from under the table. Silenced, Israi followed her out, scowling into the ruins of what had been her private quarters. The roof overhead had split in several places, and the roof beams looked as if they had all shifted sideways.

Now that the noise of the earthquake was fading, Uhura finally heard voices past the crumpled section of hall, deep Elasian shouts of alarm and despair as the cohort discovered the collapsed hall. The words were too muffled for even the Universal Translator to catch, until her communicator beeped and a voice spoke breathless but recognizable English out of it.

"Commander Uhura?" Murphy said between gasps. "Commander Uhura, are you there?"

Uhura grabbed up the communicator and thumbed it on. "I'm here, Murphy. Tell the cohort that the Dohlman is alive and unhurt."

"Aye, sir." Murphy relayed the information without bothering to turn off the communicator, and Uhura heard the cohort's howls of despair become a joyous shout of relief. She picked a careful path through fallen roof tiles to the jumble of shattered metal that had been the doorframe, Israi following at her heels. The sound of muffled thuds told Uhura that someone was already attacking the other side.

"Murphy," she said into the communicator. "Look up at the roof beams out in the hall. How close are they to falling?"

There was a grim pause. "Pretty close, sir. How about your side?"

Uhura glanced up at the nearest beam and saw Israi do the same. Both of them immediately scrambled back from the doorway to the table they'd sheltered under. Only one corner of the first beam still kept a toehold on the supporting wall below, its silica resin quivering with the strain of its dislodged position. The others near it were almost as badly damaged.

"At least one's ready to come down, maybe more," Uhura reported to Murphy. The thudding increased in intensity, and she frowned, pulling Israi farther back with her into the Dohlman's private quarters. "Murphy, can't you cut through the door with your phaser? The cohort are shaking it much too hard."

Another pause, this one with the communicator off. When

79

it clicked back on again, Murphy sounded both breathless and angry. "Oben won't listen to me, sir, and the rest of them won't move away from the door long enough to let me fire at it. Should I stun them?"

"No, I've got a better idea." It was the click of the communicator that had given it to her, reminding her of the conversation with Spock and Kirk. "If you can get the camp's defense screen turned off, Ensign, I'll call the *Enterprise* and tell them to beam us out of here."

"But the screen generator is beside the landing pad, sir," Murphy objected. "The way these guys are shoving the door—"

"I know." Even in the inner room of the building, Uhura could see how the walls swayed under the determined attack. "Just get going, Ensign. Call me the instant that screen's down."

"Aye, sir."

Uhura lowered the communicator, then saw Israi's suspicious frown. "What's wrong, Your Glory?" she asked, hoping the Elasian wouldn't refuse to be transported to a Federation ship. "I assure you, we'll only stay on board my ship for a moment or two, just long enough for them to beam us down outside this building."

The Dohlman ignored that entirely. "Your underling *argued* with you," she accused Uhura. "What kind of cohort do you lead?"

"One that can think for itself," Uhura retorted promptly. "And offer suggestions for me to consider, before I issue them orders." She was thankful she had heard Kirk giving the same lecture about his crew to a Starfleet admiral only a few weeks ago. If it had impressed Cartwright, it ought to impress the Dohlman of Elas.

Then again, maybe not. "A true Dohlman does not need the suggestions of underlings to know which decision to make," Israi declared scornfully. "I spit on the suggestions of underlings."

Uhura's mouth twitched with repressed amusement. "Yes, I've noticed. Maybe if you—"

She broke off, alerted by a change in the noise from the outer annex. The rhythmic thudding had broken off, replaced by the furious shouting of Elasian voices. It wasn't that sound that bothered Uhura, though. It was the slow tick-by-tick cracking of silica resin as it splintered under stress.

She looked up at the ceiling over the Dohlman's quarters and saw it bulge as stress transferred from the buckling beams in the next room. "Hurry, Murphy." Uhura shook the stubbornly silent communicator. "Hurry!"

Israi made an enraged sound. "The roof is going to fall on us," she said indignantly.

"I know."

Cracks were beginning to show in the centers of the beams, opening wider as they watched. The ticking sound grew louder, accompanied by a groan of bending metal. Uhura watched the roof sag deeper, watched the cracks become open fractures—then thumbed her communicator with sudden decision.

"Uhura to *Enterprise*. Come in please. This is an emergency."

The response was as immediate as she'd expected. "Spock here. What do you need, Commander?"

"Two to beam up, Mr. Spock, from these coordinates." Uhura prayed that Murphy had managed to get the screen down in time. If not, she and Israi would encounter a far worse fate than being crushed by a falling roof beam. "Immediately."

There was a brief pause in transmission. "Commander, I'm afraid that it is impossible to comply with your request. Our sensors detect a class-two defense screen over your present coordinates. Beaming you though that would be fatal."

Oh, Murphy, where are you? "Mr. Spock, the Dohlman of Elas is in imminent danger." Uhura heard a beam splinter again, this time from the end of the room they were in. She pushed Israi back against the far wall, hoping it would offer some sort of protection from the collapsing roof. "Ensign

81

Murphy is trying to disable the screen. As soon as it's gone, you must beam us up immediately." A second roof beam splintered, closer to them. "Mr. Spock, do you understand?"

"The transporter is locked on to your coordinates and ready to beam you up." Through the communicator, Uhura could hear the sound of the Vulcan's fingers flying over his station controls. "I am linking sensor controls to transporter controls, to eliminate reaction time—" Another roof beam splintered and a sheet of roof metal crashed down, its sharp edge cleaving through plasfoam furniture as though it were made of butter. If Spock said anything after that, it was drowned out by Israi's shriek of impotent rage.

"This *cannot* happen!" The Dohlman whirled on Uhura as if she were responsible for the destruction looming over them. "I am the Dohlman of Elas! *This cannot happen!*"

Uhura caught the flailing fists as yet another roof beam splintered overhead. "Hold still. We still have a chance of rescue, if you just stay close to me—"

The scream of falling metal filled the air, much too loud and much too close. Uhura gasped and threw herself at Israi, trying to flatten both of them against the wall. There was a crash as the roof metal hit beside them, splattering them with torn plasfoam and broken roof tiles. The huge slab teetered on its edge for an endless unbalanced moment, then made its decision and came slamming down toward them.

The last thing Uhura saw before it hit was the sparkle of the transporter beam.

"There! It's doing it again!" Mutchler leaned over the shuttle's twinned console to rap a finger against the viewscreen.

Chekov wasn't sure what ground feature had excited the geologist this time, but he'd learned through fifteen earlier attempts that telling Mutchler to get back to his seat and strap in didn't have very much effect. "Dr. Mutchler, please don't touch the viewscreen while we're flying."

"Oh. Sorry." It was an automatic apology, though, and

didn't carry much of the geologist's attention. He did bring his hands around to the small of his back, locking his fingers together as if to remind himself not to reach out again. Chekov had to squelch an urge to handcuff him in that position. "Wow! That was great—at least a six point six!"

Sulu tossed a startled look across the geologist's back at Chekov, and the security chief felt a sick twist in his stomach. "You mean another earthquake?"

Mutchler nodded, grinning beatifically. "Isn't it neat?"

Oh, yeah, just terrific. "How can you tell what it's doing from all the way up here?" He didn't even have any of his equipment set up, as if he'd been anywhere near it since lift off.

"By the ground waves." Apparently having forgotten earlier admonitions yet again, Mutchler stretched across the console to trace a wavy line with his finger on the distant floor of the long ravine below them. "All our laser-equipped seismometers measure, really, is the amplitude of the waves caused by earth movement during a quake."

"Waves?" The more he heard about this earthquake nonsense, the less Chekov liked the individual details. "You mean waves like on water?"

Mutchler bobbed his head enthusiastically. "Yes, exactly like that. They're hard to see when you're standing in the middle of them—"

"I can imagine."

"—but really pretty spectacular from up here." He turned to grin at Sulu, who was busy looking worried as he guided *Gamow* through a patch of icy clouds. "Did you ever have a chance to watch a quake from up in the San Francisco hills?"

Sulu made a little sound that Chekov thought might be a laugh, although not a terribly amused one. "Only once," he admitted. "And I didn't like it at all—it was kind of scary, really."

"Oh, that's all a matter of attitude." Mutchler squiggled his finger against the viewscreen again, and Chekov realized abruptly that he was demonstrating the rise and fall of the seismic surf. "The waves I saw just a moment ago were spectacular! At least half a meter in amplitude. You can bet there's going to be some wonderful realignment of the local features before the day is out."

Chekov wondered why it was that people always felt the need to find neutral words for the horrible things in which they were involved. Polar bears that wandered into villages and ate the local dogs became "nuisance animals," people blown up by careless military fire became "acceptable civilian losses," and avalanches and cave-ins became "realignment of the local features." Scrubbing his hands against the leg of his trousers, he asked, "Do these earthquakes mean anything?"

Mutchler glanced over at him. "Like what?"

"Well . . ."

"I think what he's asking," Sulu picked up with a somewhat evil grin, "is whether or not this volcano is getting ready to explode." Chekov felt his cheeks warm with embarrassment, and Sulu shook his head in that wise-older-brother fashion that could be so damned annoying. "I can't believe you made it through four years at the Academy without ever getting caught in a tremor even once."

Well, there'd been twice when half the class swore there'd been some shaking—especially the group in the aquatics class. Chekov had been asleep once and practicing takeoff and landing maneuvers the second time. He never felt even the slightest rumble. "I suppose my life is charmed."

Sulu snorted, but didn't make a verbal comment. His snort was answer enough.

"I don't think you have to worry about the volcano," Mutchler assured him, blissfully oblivious of any snide comments Sulu had—or hadn't—made. "Rakatan Mons doesn't have much of a history of cataclysmic eruptions. The magma moves around a lot inside the chamber, but for some reason it tends to erupt along small flanking rifts. That takes the pressure off, so the volcano doesn't need to blow its top to make more room. It's the magma movement that makes the crust expand and contract to cause the earthquakes." A fond smile flashed across his face, and his eyes focused elsewhere for just the barest instant. "It also causes Wendy Metcalfe to dream she hears aliens talking in the seismographs."

Chekov studied the barren landscape below them, and thought about all the different forms of life they'd found in places even less hospitable than this. "Sometimes alien life-forms are harder to recognize than you'd realize." At least Rakatan had an atmosphere, and an ocean not covered in ice. "Dr. Metcalfe is wise not to discount anything."

Mutchler shrugged one shoulder, his mouth twisted into a skeptical grimace.

"You don't believe her?"

Mutchler shrugged again. "Do you?"

Chekov was saved from having to answer by a shrill whistle from *Gamow*'s communication board. Sulu reached for the reply stud without lifting his eyes from his controls. *"Gamow,* Sulu here. Go ahead."

"Underling Sulu." The coarse, deep voice shocked Chekov when he'd been expecting Uhura's softer tones. He straightened in his seat and pushed Mutchler back toward the door to the passenger compartment. "This is Oben."

"Oben," he said, leaning toward the pickup, "this is Chekov. Where is Dohlman Uhura?"

Voices clamored at the back of the channel, and somewhere beneath them Chekov heard the ring of metal on broken metal and something that sounded like crying. "You must come back now." The cold stillness of Oben's voice spoke of pain beyond the simply physical. "There is a terrible thing has happened here at the campsite. I . . . I must say that your Dohlman is dead."

Chapter Ten

THE WALLS OF THE *Enterprise*'s main transporter room
materialized around Uhura, blessedly solid and motionless.
Her hearing returned, as always, just in time to catch the last
chiming note of the transporter. Then the stasis field faded,
and she slammed to the floor. She heard Israi yelp in
mingled pain and outrage beside her.

"Lass!" Montgomery Scott rounded the control console
and leapt up onto the pad, Transporter Chief Kyle on his
heels. The chief engineer bent over Uhura, his craggy face
concerned. "Are you all right?"

Uhura accepted his outstretched hand, wincing as she
rose to her feet. "A little bruised, Mr. Scott, that's all." She
turned toward the Dohlman, then dropped to her knees
again in quick concern. "Israi, you're hurt!"

The Dohlman scowled and raised a hand as if to slap her,
then gasped and cradled it against her chest. Pale,
cinnamon-colored blood trickled down her bare left arm
where one of her bracelets had been caught and driven into
her flesh by the falling sheet metal. Her other hand still
clutched the Elasian charts, the muscles white with strain.

"I did not give you permission to use my name!" Israi's voice was hoarse but still fiercely arrogant. "And don't touch me!"

"I apologize, Your Glory." Uhura drew her hand back, recognizing the irrational anger of shock. She looked up at Kyle. "Call Dr. McCoy and tell him we have a medical emergency in the main transporter room."

"Aye, sir." The transporter chief retreated back to his console as if he had been chased there by Israi's glare.

"No! I will not be treated by any of your incompetent human physicians!" The Dohlman turned her scowl on Uhura again as Kyle spoke urgently into the intercom. "Return me to my camp at once."

Uhura sat back on her heels, anticipating another angry slap. "We can't do that, Your Glory. It's against Starfleet law to transport anyone with an untreated injury, except in an emergency."

"*Starfleet* law?" Israi repeated. Her almond eyes flared with contempt. "If you are Dohlman here, Uhura, you make the law. Now tell your underling to send me back."

"Not until you've seen a doctor," Uhura said flatly. "I *am* the Dohlman here, and that's my decision."

Israi hissed with rage and scrambled to her feet, clutching her injured arm against her ribs and swaying slightly. Uhura rose with her, careful to stay within arm's reach in case she fell. The Dohlman ignored her, swinging around to glare at the chief engineer instead.

"Scott-reptile, beam me down to my planet at once."

Scott winced under the scorching look, but didn't move toward the console. "I canna do that, lass," he said, his rich voice apologetic but firm. "I must obey my Dohlman."

An almost comical look of surprise blossomed on Israi's dark young face. Before she could reply, however, the whistle of opening doors interrupted them.

"Uhura." Captain Kirk came to a sudden stop, eyebrows sliding upward when he saw her companion. Behind him, McCoy's astounded look more than made up for the sudden lack of expression on the captain's face. Then the doctor noticed the blood on Israi's arm, and his eyes sharpened with professional concern. He pushed past Kirk and into the room.

"Dammit, I don't have my medical kit—"

"Dr. Chapel's bringing one, sir," Kyle told him. "She said she'd be here in just a minute."

"Good." Uhura saw McCoy's eyes slide sideways toward Kirk, watching him with curious intensity.

Some emotion stirred in the captain's hazel eyes, so deeply hidden that Uhura couldn't put a name to it. Then Kirk startled her with a quick, graceful bow. "Your Glory. Welcome to the *Enterprise.*"

Israi made a spitting noise that wouldn't have disgraced a cat. "I do not wish to be on the *Enterprise,* welcome or otherwise, Kirk-insect," the young Dohlman snapped. "You are the spineless underling of a dishonorable Dohlman. I command that you send me back to my planet immediately!"

To Israi's evident surprise, this passionate tirade provoked nothing more than a quick flash of smile from the captain. "You know," Kirk said reminiscently, "you sound exactly like your sister."

"Jim . . ." McCoy warned, taking a step forward to stand between the Dohlman and Kirk. Kirk glanced at the doctor, and McCoy stepped back again, sighing in relief. Even from where she stood, half-hidden behind Israi's swaying figure, Uhura could see that it was quiet amusement that lit Kirk's face, nothing more.

"Your Glory." Kirk met the Dohlman's simmering almond eyes, his smile fading into a look of smooth politeness. "Forgive me for not obeying you, but we have not yet established that Rakatan is indeed *your* planet. And I may be a spineless underling, but I will not endanger my Dohlman or the rest of my people by sending you back to your cohort with an injury they could blame on us." Kirk glanced at McCoy. "Take her down to sickbay, Bones, and get her treated for that cut."

"I will not be so insulted!" Israi flung her charts onto the floor and used her good hand to grab for her knife. Only Uhura, standing behind her, could see the effort it took her to draw the blade from its sheath. Kirk must have guessed at it. He made a restraining gesture at Scott when the engineer would have lunged forward. "I warn you, Kirk-insect, I will gut your doctor like a flopping fish if he touches me!"

The doors whistled open again to admit Christine Chapel with a medical kit slung over her shoulder. She paused beside McCoy, eyeing the blood-streaked and infuriated alien on the transporter pad with her usual calm gaze. "You're going to need a pressure sleeve for that cut."

McCoy snorted. "That shows what you know, Doctor. What I *really* need is a tranquilizer dart." He glanced from Israi's scowl to Kirk's equally determined frown and back again. "Give me the antiseptic spray first. At least I can get that on her from a safe distance."

"Wait." Israi lowered her knife a little, her fierce look fraying at the edges. "Why did you call this female 'Doctor'?"

"Because she is a doctor." McCoy climbed onto the transporter pad and edged toward her, antiseptic clutched like a phaser in one nervous hand. "Now, just hold still a minute—"

"No!" Israi jerked back from him, swaying. Uhura put a hand out to steady her, and the Dohlman reluctantly accepted her support. The bare skin of her shoulder was startlingly cold under Uhura's fingers. She hoped that was the Elasian's natural temperature, and not the effects of shock. "Not you, underling. I will let the female doctor treat me." Israi's hand shook as she pointed at Chapel with her knife. "Only her, so there is no insult."

Kirk's eyebrows went up in quick understanding. "As you wish, Your Glory. Doctor Chapel?"

"Of course, sir." Chapel took the antiseptic spray from McCoy and climbed onto the transporter pad without hesitation. Israi made a soft sound of relief when the antiseptic spray hissed out over her arm, then slowly closed her eyes and collapsed backward. Ignoring the protest from her bruised shoulders, Uhura braced the Dohlman's slight weight against hers and kept her from hitting the floor. The complete lack of tension in the sprawled frame told her Israi was unconscious.

"She passed out?" Kirk vaulted up beside Uhura and helped her ease Israi to the floor while his chief medical officer dove for the medical kit Chapel had brought. "Is her wound that bad, Bones?"

"I wouldn't have thought so." McCoy passed a medical sensor briefly across the Dohlman's face and chest, then turned a startled look on his associate. "Christine, when the hell did you find time to put tranquilizer in that antiseptic?"

"Before I left sickbay," said Chapel calmly. "When Kyle told me who my patient was, I thought it might be helpful."

McCoy grunted with laughter even as he bent to clean the metal shards out of Israi's torn arm. "You remembered how much trouble we got from the last Dohlman we had on board?"

Chapel was careful not to glance at Kirk. "No. I could just hear how much trouble this one was making." She handed McCoy a pressure bandage while he finished spraying synthetic skin over the ragged slash. Seeing that Israi was in no danger, Kirk turned his attention to Uhura.

"Spock says his long-range sensors detected an earthquake near the Elasian camp just before you called him." Kirk spoke quickly, one eye on the Dohlman to make sure she hadn't awakened. "What happened?"

"The Dohlman's building collapsed, sir." Uhura answered his next question before he could ask it. "We were the only ones inside."

Kirk's eyes narrowed. "No security guard?"

"Ensign Murphy. But the Dohlman sent him out to stand guard with her cohort. Chekov and Sulu were still out—" Uhura's eyes widened suddenly. "Captain! The rest of the landing party is going to think we're still trapped inside that building. And if the Elasians think Israi's dead and decide to blame Starfleet for it—there's no telling what could happen!"

Kirk shot to his feet, slamming one fist against the nearest communications panel. "Kirk to bridge."

"Spock here, Captain."

"Mr. Spock, contact the landing party and tell them that we have Uhura and the Dohlman safe aboard the *Enterprise*." Kirk released the communicator button and swung around. "That takes care of our side. Now we need to get the news to the Elasians." He turned a sharp look on McCoy. "Bones, are you done yet?"

McCoy looked up, startled by the urgency in the captain's voice. "Well, I'd like to take the Dohlman down to sickbay and run her through the tissue regenerator—"

"No time. I want to get her back to her cohort, before they murder someone to avenge her." Kirk glanced at Chapel. "How soon will that tranquilizer wear off, Doctor?"

She was already loading a hypospray with another capsule. "I've got the antidote right here, Captain. It'll only take a few minutes to kick in."

"Good." The captain swung toward the transporter console. "Scotty, contact the bridge and make sure that Elasian defense screen is still down. Kyle, I want you to beam the Dohlman back into her camp. Get her as close to the previous coordinates as you can manage."

"Aye, sir." Scott began to speak into the intercom while Kyle bent over his board.

Uhura helped maneuver Israi's sprawled body over a transporter locus, then picked up the fallen star charts and deliberately stepped onto the locus beside her. Kirk gave her a questioning look, and she answered it with a sigh. "I have to go back, too, Captain. I left my tricorder and the pad down in the Dohlman's quarters. And all of Israi's translations from the charts are stored there and nowhere else. Seeing the way she objected to our medical treatment, I suspect—"

"—that she won't be in the mood to translate the charts over again for you," Kirk acknowledged wryly. "Very well,

Commander." He stepped off the transporter pad, drawing McCoy and Chapel with him. "Energize."

Chekov keyed open the shuttle's hatch before Sulu had even shut the engines down. Ash gray dust swirled like smoke through the disrupted mining camp, pattering down on the prefab roofs in a slithering, shushing rattle. Two of the storage buildings canted in against each other, standing only because neither would let the other fall, but nothing else had caved in under the earthquake's stress.

Nothing, at least, but the Dohlman's quarters. It was tumbled so completely, Chekov didn't realize at first that the flattened pile of scrap used to be a building. His hands tightened on either side of the doorway, useless and angry.

"Oh, my God . . ." Mutchler pressed up close behind him to peek out over his shoulder. He murmured something else, his voice too thin to hear.

Chekov jumped down from the hatch just to get away from him. "This is your lovely earthquake, Dr. Mutchler," he said bitterly. He knew it was unfair to lash out at the geologist, but he couldn't help it. "It looked better from the air."

Mutchler backed away from the open hatch, his young face pale and full of regret. "I'll see if there's a medikit," he said as he disappeared into the shuttle.

Chekov didn't wait to see if he found one. It was already too late to matter.

Thick Elasian voices clattered against the walls still standing, and only Oben's deep roar stood out above the other wailing and shouting. Chekov pushed through the first line of Israi's cohort, craning his neck for Takcas or the Dohlman. But he saw no flash of red hair among the sea of dark-skinned men, and no female voice rose up to cut across their shouting. He couldn't even see Murphy in the turmoil, and his heart clenched with dread to think how many other lives might be lost beneath that pile of ruined prefab. "Who's missing?"

Oben turned in a dark blur, and his backhanded blow

caught Chekov across the face before he even realized the guardsman intended to hit him.

"Outworld vermin!"

The ground smelled like burned cinders, and slipped like silk beneath him as he rolled to regain his footing.

"Worthless maggot!" Oben surged forward, fists clenched, and Chekov scrabbled back to put more distance between them. His cheek already felt hot and swollen clear through to his sinuses—he didn't want to find out what a full-fisted blow could do. "Your Dohlman has brought nothing but misery upon us!"

Chekov climbed slowly to his feet, blinking against the wash of dizziness that rose up with him. "You said our Dohlman was dead."

"She is!" Oben spat on the ground between them, and the rest of the cohort cinched tighter around them. "She died protecting her foolish machines, and she held our Dohlman prisoner so that she would die as well!"

Chekov scowled despite the knot of pain in his cheek. "That's a lie."

One of the other guardsmen swung at him, but he expected it this time, and danced aside before the fist made contact. A roar of frustration went up all around him. "Uhura wouldn't do that!" he shouted, turning quickly to take inventory of their positions in the hope of finding some escape. Instead, his eyes caught on Sulu and Mutchler hurrying across from the wide-open shuttle, and panic shot through him. "Get back inside! That's an order!"

"No!" Oben's voice cracked out. Sulu had already skidded to a stop, dragging on Mutchler's arm to slow him. "Bring them all! Make them pay for their Dohlman's crimes!"

The cohort broke apart with frightful precision, and Chekov reminded himself with a sting of fear that they had to be better trained than their primitive gear suggested. Ducking around the arm that lashed out to grab him, he dropped to the ground just inside Oben's grasp and cut out the guardsman's knee with a sweep kick that almost got him pinned when Oben fell. The old Elasian was fast, stopping his tumble with one elbow and pushing to all fours with his damaged leg splayed awkwardly out beside him. Chekov caught him in that position, and locked his elbow beneath the Elasian's chin to jerk his head back so Oben could feel the point of his own knife against the base of his skull.

"Don't do it," he warned Oben softly.

The guardsman froze. Chekov couldn't see his face, but he recognized the trembling stillness of fear in Oben's rigid muscles. "Call the cohort back, and we'll search the wreckage for the bodies."

Oben swallowed, took a shuddering breath. "No."

Chekov swore silently, but didn't release him. "Do you know what I'll do to you?"

"I don't care," the guardsman answered hoarsely. "You are only a man, not my Dohlman. You can only kill me."

In most cultures, that would have been enough.

"Lieutenant!"

"Oben!"

Chekov jerked at Uhura's startled shout, pulling back from Oben and earning an elbow in the stomach for his inattention. It was more a practical strike than a vengeful one—they rolled apart without further violence, and Chekov made sure to keep a firm grip on the knife in his hand. Just in case.

Uhura picked her way around the edge of the ruined building, one hand gripping the roll of astral charts, the other hovering near Israi's elbow without quite touching her. The Dohlman's angular face was drawn and pale, but she carried herself with stiff indignation. Even the shiny patch of bandage on her upper arm looked more like a warrior's badge than an inconvenience. She was trying to keep her expression haughty, Chekov suspected, but the flush of girlish anger that leapt into her cheeks when Uhura drew alongside her betrayed more than he thought she realized. Wherever they'd been, the women had been fighting.

As though called by some smell or sound with which only they were in tune, the cohort converged on their Dohlman like bees around a flower. Sulu and Mutchler—dusty and fussing, but apparently unhurt—were swept along with them, then abandoned when the guardsmen realized there was no more need for revenge. Chekov grabbed the geologist's tunic and pulled him off to one side; Sulu he gave credit for extracting himself from the swarm.

"Sorry," the helmsman whispered breathlessly, sidling up close beside Chekov. "Spock called to tell us Uhura and the Dohlman were safe right after you left." He sounded truly apologetic. "I was coming out to tell you."

"Your Glory . . ." Oben stumbled to his knees as though stunned. Perhaps Elasians believed in apparitions, and he thought she'd come back from the dead. Chekov couldn't be sure. "How . . ." he stammered. "How could you . . . ?"

Israi scowled and looked past his head as though he were below contempt. "Can I not leave you alone? You squabble like monkeys the minute you are out of my sight!"

"We thought to avenge you!" one of the cohort shouted. He looked around for support from his fellows, but Chekov noticed most of them were focused on their Dohlman, eyes respectfully downcast. "This worthless human Dohlman— she held you in the falling building so as to murder you!"

Uhura's eyes flew wide with surprise, but Israi motioned her into silence with a single upraised hand. She raked chilly eyes across her cohort. "Who told you this?"

No one answered. Chekov fingered Oben's knife, studying its handle to keep from seeing if Uhura looked to him. He returned Sulu's coaxing elbow with an irritable jab of his own, but said nothing.

At last, Oben stretched himself face-first into the sand, his fingers stopping just before they brushed the Dohlman's feet. "It was I, Your Glory. I . . . I feared for you. . . ."

Her mouth twisted, and for a moment, Chekov thought she would kick the prostrate guard. Then something more childlike and delicate played across her features, and she

95

stepped away from him. "The shaking earth tried to murder me," she said, very stiffly. "It was this Dohlman who saved my life."

The silence that fell across them burned with tension. Chekov frowned a question beyond the Dohlman to Uhura, still not understanding what exactly had gone on. The commander pointed upward, mouthing, *Enterprise*, and fluttered her fingers to mimic the transporter. That explained how Spock knew what had happened with the women. Then Uhura rubbed at her cheek and raised her eyebrows in a question of her own. Chekov shrugged, embarrassed, but didn't try to answer. *Next time*, he thought, wishing there was some way she could hear him, *tell me you're beaming out* before *I get beat up for it*.

"Where is Takcas?" Israi asked. It seemed to soothe her to have imperious questions to ask and orders to give.

"He left with the dark human male," someone answered contritely. "They ran to the other side of the compound, and have not yet returned."

Israi nodded, and stepped away from them in an obvious air of dismissal. Her feet only barely missed treading on Oben's hands, but the guardsman stayed immobile, hardly even breathing. "When Takcas returns, tell him to beat Oben until sundown."

Uhura hurried after her, hand outstretched as if to stop her. "Your Glory—"

"Say nothing," Israi instructed her without turning. "Or I will have your cohort beaten, as well." She pointed at Oben, and the rest of the cohort obediently looked where she aimed. "His is the punishment for any who try to choose my enemies for me." She glanced at Uhura as though she wanted to say something more, but her resolve seemed to fail at the very last instant. Squaring her shoulders, she turned away with regal indifference and waved the commander aside. "As for you—you may go until I need you . . . Your Glory."

Chapter Eleven

THE LAST fire-gold sliver of Rakatan's sun slipped below the flank of the volcano, leaving a deep rose afterglow huddled in the western sky. A hand fell on Uhura's shoulder, warm against the sudden high-altitude chill.

"It's over," Sulu said.

Uhura lifted her head from her arms, but it took her a moment to be able to listen for the sound she'd blocked out of her mind an hour before. The distant lash of a whip rising and falling no longer echoed off the rock wall behind the Elasian mining camp. She heard nothing else in its place, neither groans nor whimpers nor curses.

"Do you think he passed out?" Uhura asked, looking across her shoulder at Chekov. No matter how annoyed she had been at Oben, she couldn't believe that any sentient being deserved this much punishment for a simple error in judgment. The fact that the Elasians accepted it without question made her aware of how truly alien they were, despite their superficially similar appearance.

"I doubt it." Chekov's face was half-hidden by the cold

pack he kept pressed to his swollen cheek, making his expression unreadable. "A direct hit with a photon torpedo might make an Elasian pass out, but not much else would."

Uhura shivered. "But he hasn't made a sound since they started. . . ."

"That's because he'd rather die than cry out," Chekov said matter-of-factly.

Sulu looked up from the remains of the tricorder they had salvaged from the Dohlman's quarters. He'd been tinkering with it all evening, substituting spare components from his shuttle repair kit in a vain attempt to make it work. "And you *like* these people?"

"I never said I liked them." Chekov dropped the cold pack, showing them his scowl as well as the spreading bruise across his cheekbone. "I said I understood them."

"Well, I'm glad someone around here does. I can't decide whether Israi is a psychopathic monster or just a royally spoiled brat." Uhura paused, then shook her head, annoyed with herself for the comment. "No, that's not fair. She's only what her culture made her."

"And it made her to be an absolute despot," Sulu said soberly.

"That doesn't matter." Despite—or perhaps because of—his bruised cheek, Chekov's gaze had lost none of its Slavic intensity. "Commander, our mission here isn't to understand the Elasians or to like them. It's to find out whether or not they have a valid claim to this planet. Have we done that yet?"

"I'm not sure." Uhura flung an exasperated look at the dead tricorder. "I had just gotten the last translation from Israi when the earthquake hit. I haven't had a chance to correlate her information with the original astral chart."

Silence fell, strained and tense with frustration. From the open shuttle behind them, Uhura could hear the clatter of plates and the hum of the food synthesizer as Murphy constructed their evening meal. As the junior member of the landing party, the task of making supper had fallen to him.

Uhura looked up when the dark-skinned security guard emerged from the shuttle at last, more than willing to be distracted from her worries.

"So, Ensign, what have you persuaded the synthesizer to give us this time?"

"Vegetable soup and cheese sandwiches, sir." Murphy slanted a doubtful look at his tray of steaming bowls. "At least, I think it's vegetable soup. It has some little green things floating around in it."

Sulu groaned and fell over backward, clutching the broken tricorder against his chest. "Little green things? I have to eat little green things for supper?"

Chekov snorted, taking the bowl Murphy apologetically offered him. "Why not? You do it all the time on shore leave."

"That's different," the helmsman informed him, sitting up to take his own bowl. "Those are *real* green things, not synthesized green things."

Murphy cleared his throat. "Should I take some supper out to Dr. Mutchler, sir?"

Uhura glanced around, only now noticing the geologist's absence. He'd been so uncharacteristically quiet since they'd left the Dohlman's ruined quarters that she'd forgotten about him. "Where *is* Dr. Mutchler?"

"On the other side of the shuttle. I've been keeping an eye on him from inside." Murphy pointed under *Gamow*'s stubby nose, and Uhura finally saw the geologist, prowling restlessly back and forth across the dry streambed that was their new landing site. "I asked him about supper before I went in, but he said he was busy taking atmospheric measurements and didn't have time to eat."

"Well, take him some anyway," Uhura ordered. "And make sure he eats it."

"Yeah, that way we can all suffer together." Sulu poked one of the green chunks in his soup with a suspicious spoon, putting it down untasted as soon as Murphy disappeared behind the shuttle. "You know, I can't remember the last time we had good food on a planetary mission. Do you think the synthesizers have been programmed to—hey!"

Uhura looked up from her soup and blinked in surprise. In reaching for a sandwich, Sulu had slid the tricorder from his lap to the ground beside him. It hit with a small thump, rattled briefly, then warbled into glowing life.

"Hey!" Sulu dropped his sandwich and knelt down beside the battered instrument, rubbing red-gray dust off its display screen. "I think it's showing us the Elasians' astral chart!"

A spurt of relief ran through Uhura, easing some of the tension that had coiled in her stomach. "Oh, thank God." She set her soup bowl down and went to join Sulu, pulling her salvaged computer notepad from her trouser pocket. "See if you can get it to download my translations onto the map. The entries are keyed to the number of pictograph symbols in each star's name."

Sulu plugged the notepad into the tricorder's data port and tapped a command into the smaller instrument. It whirred and clicked as it dumped its file of translated Elasian names and dates into the tricorder's memory. Uhura sat cross-legged in front of it, propping her elbows on her knees and her chin in her palms while she watched the spiderweb lines of Elasian pictographs transform into English letters. "Chekov—"

"I'm here." The Russian hunkered down on her other side, squinting at the screen. The copied image of Israi's chart flickered slightly, some bands of pixels refusing to light even when Sulu tapped gingerly on the display. "Maybe we should take this into the shuttle and transfer it to a bigger screen."

Sulu made a wry face. "I'd rather not. Whatever circuit connection's loose in there, it's not one I can replace. Better not to move it while it feels like working." The helmsman studied the tricorder, his face hushed with concentration. "I recognize most of these systems," he said at last. "But the distances between them don't look right. Is this an old chart, Uhura?"

"One hundred Standard years old, according to the tricorder's spectral analysis."

"Then we're seeing galactic rotational drift. That would explain the change in distances."

"Where did these discovery dates come from?" Chekov demanded. "I can't believe the Elasians recorded their history in Federation Standard years."

"No, they used a dynastic chronology. I translated the dates using Israi's royal genealogy." Uhura pointed at the star system at the center of the chart. "The oldest discovery date she gave me was for their neighbor, Troyius: twentieth year of the reign of Teslah, ninth Dohlman in the line of Sevuth. According to my calculations, that works out to about two hundred and thirty-five Standard years ago."

Chekov drummed his fingers on his cold pack thoughtfully. "That sounds about right. According to the military history of this quadrant, the Elasians launched their earliest nuclear-powered spaceships about two hundred and fifty years ago."

"And it makes sense that they would discover Troyius first," Sulu agreed. "It's in the system of their home star. Even those old Elasian fission-powered ships could have made that journey fast enough. What could they do, Chekov, about two-tenths of light-speed?"

"Maximum," his former navigator agreed. He gnawed on his lower lip, a habit he had when he was calculating something in his head. "At that speed, it would have taken them four years round trip to Troyius. Not much worse than Earth's first mission to Mars."

"Well, what about Rakatan?" Uhura leaned across Sulu to tap the five-planet system in the far corner of the astral chart. The line of English text displayed under it flickered, then steadied again. "It's got the latest discovery date on the chart—only one hundred and five Standard years ago."

"Ouch!" Sulu made another face. "That's fifty years before the Vulcans ran across it."

"I know." Uhura looked up at her companions, frowning.

"But something about that doesn't sound right to me. I just can't put my finger on it. . . ."

Silence fell again as they peered at the flickering screen, but this time it was the comfortable working silence of a crew used to solving problems together. Sulu broke it with a single triumphant word.

"Time."

Uhura blinked at him, unsure of what he meant, but Chekov's indrawn breath told her he understood. He dropped his cold pack again, this time to stare at her. "You said this chart was one hundred Standard years old, yes?"

She nodded, still puzzled. "That's how old the tricorder said the plastic was."

"So only five years elapsed between the Elasians discovering the Ordover system and making the chart." Sulu shook his head. "That's not enough time."

Chekov grunted. "Not a hundred years ago, not for the Elasians. They were still using fission-powered ships when they came under Federation control."

Uhura felt her breath catch in her throat when she saw where they were going. "So one hundred years ago, they couldn't travel faster than light!" She darted a look at Sulu. "How far away is Elas from Rakatan?"

"Fifteen and a half light-years," the helmsman answered. "At sublight speeds, it should have taken the Elasians at least eighty Standard years to get home and report their discovery."

"*Not* five." Chekov scowled, then winced and brought the cold pack up to his cheek again as the expression tugged at his bruises. "Commander, this chart is a forgery."

"Or at least this entry on it is." Uhura took in a deep breath, the vague sense of unease that had been plaguing her finally put to rest. "I thought the Ordover system looked a little sharper than the others on the chart."

"Added later to an authentic map," Sulu suggested. "That way the tricorder wouldn't detect it unless you specifically told it to analyze the age of the ink it was drawn with." He glanced at Uhura, his smooth Asian face barely visible in the darkness. They had been so intent on the tricorder screen, Uhura hadn't noticed Rakatan's day-night terminus creeping over them. "Do you think the Dohlman would agree to that test?"

Uhura surprised herself with a snort. "I don't think Israi would agree to breathe right now if I told her to." She saw her teammates' perplexed looks and sighed. "She's feeling a little put upon because Dr. Chapel tranquilized her on board the *Enterprise*. I think she's holding me personally responsible for the insult since I'm the Dohlman of the ship."

"So what do we do?" Chekov asked irritably. "Wait for Her Glory to get over her temper tantrum while buildings fall down on our heads?"

Uhura tapped a finger against her lips, considering their options. "I think we already have enough information for the captain to act on. Let's call him." She reached for her communicator. "Maybe he can put some pressure on—"

A strangled choke from the darkness interrupted her. Sulu and Chekov sprang to their feet, closing in on either side of Uhura, but it was too late. Without so much as a foot scrape of warning, a wall of Elasians materialized out of the night. Momentarily blinded by her focus on the bright tricorder screen, Uhura couldn't make out their expressions, but she saw the shivering glints of starlight that marked Klingon disruptors. She didn't need the fierce grip of Chekov's hand on her wrist to warn her against activating her communicator.

Something hit the ground, the solid thud of a body falling. After a moment, Uhura's night vision cleared enough to show her Murphy's unconscious body sprawled before them. Behind him, a large chunk disengaged from the solid wall of cohort and resolved into their leader. With one hand, Takcas held Scott Mutchler pinioned in a taut arc of pain. With the other, the *kessh* held his own disruptor steady against the geologist's throat.

"Thieves and liars." Takcas's voice sounded deeper than usual, as if he spoke through fiercely clenched teeth. "Throw down your communication devices or you will die in howling agony."

Uhura believed him. Carefully maneuvering her communicator up from belt level, she tossed it into the open space between them. Reluctantly, Chekov and Sulu followed her example.

"Weapons, too."

In the lifeless night silence of Rakatan, Uhura could hear the tense breathing of the man beside her. She reached back and gripped Chekov's forearm, squeezing it as hard as she could. She might not understand male Elasians the way the security chief seemed to, but even she could sense that this was no hormone-driven confrontation. If Chekov didn't obey them, he would be killed.

Uhura heard the small but unmistakable rasp of gritted teeth, then Chekov's phaser followed the communicators onto the pile. "Are you going to tell us what this is all about?" the Russian asked evenly.

"Do you tell a worm his crimes before you crush him?" Takcas stepped back and motioned at his cohort. Four of them circled around to drag Sulu and Chekov away from Uhura while a fifth burly shadow stooped slowly and painfully to pick up the equipment. Uhura stared at Oben, barely able to believe that anybody bruised as badly as he was on chest, arms, and back could still walk, much less want to obey the *kessh* who had beaten him for hours. Chekov had been right about Elasian pride and endurance.

Uhura tore her gaze away, forcing herself to meet Takcas's narrow-eyed stare with one just as steady. "And am I a worm, too, *kessh* Takcas?" she demanded, fighting to keep the softness of shock out of her voice. *Arrogance is all these people respect,* she reminded herself, but it was hard to be arrogant in front of twenty Klingon disruptors. "The Dohlman Israi owes her life to us. Is this how she thanks people?"

Takcas shook Mutchler and the geologist choked again, his narrow face pale against the darkness. "Another of this crawling reptile's tricks! We have learned from the Crown Regent how his machines made that earthquake."

"But we rescued—"

"All part of your plan to rob us of this planet. The Crown Regent even told us how you would twist Her Glory's words to make our claim invalid—just as we heard you do tonight!"

Uhura opened her mouth to argue further, but a grunt of pain stopped her. Looking over her shoulder, she saw Sulu double over as one of his guards clubbed him for a second time in the stomach. There was a small flurry of motion to the right as Chekov struggled briefly and was subdued.

This time Uhura didn't have to counterfeit the fury in her voice. "What was *that* for?"

"That was for you." Takcas handed his prisoner to Oben and strode toward Uhura, stopping a respectful pace away. "You are a Dohlman, Your Glory, and our Dohlman says we must not touch you or do you any insult. But if you do not come quietly down to the punishment cells with us, we will crush your cohort one by one until their screams reach all the way to your ship."

"Spock, report."

Kirk knew that all the lighting and environments on the *Enterprise* were artificially created, but the bridge still looked different to him in the middle of third-shift night from the way it did during his normal first-shift day. Some of it, he knew, was the faces—people he could recognize in passing, but whose work styles and speeds he didn't know inside and out. The rest of the difference could be attributed to adrenaline, pumped into his bloodstream whenever the intercom awoke him in the middle of the night for any emergency that couldn't be handled without him.

He took the steps to his command chair quickly, pausing by the arm as his first officer turned to face him.

"Captain, we are being approached by a fleet of three hundred unidentified vessels. They have not responded to repeated hails, nor have they altered their course."

He turned the chair and sat. "Are our shields up?"

Spock nodded once. "Shields were activated when the lead vessel entered firing range, Captain. The fleet has activated its own defense array, but has taken no other hostile action."

"Hmm." Rakatan's blue-gray profile bisected the viewscreen, hanging against a sprinkle of stars and the flat black circle that was Rakatan's shadowed moon. "Can you get the ships on visual?"

The pilot glanced down at the helm scanner, then shook her head. "No, sir. They've taken up a fixed position just outside visual scanning range."

Damn.

"Captain." Spock's distracted tone told Kirk the Vulcan was bent over his science station. "I may be able to enhance scanner sensitivity by temporarily converting it to make use of the unusually high ultraviolet output of the Ordover system." He lifted his head. "That should give us a higher-frequency signal, but there will be no visual color."

Kirk would take what he could and be grateful for that. "Give me what you can, Mr. Spock."

"Aye, Captain."

"Captain?" The navigator glanced over his shoulder, hands poised above his console. "Shall I maintain standard orbit, sir? It will take us out of sensor range of the fleet in approximately ten minutes."

Kirk leaned forward to squint at the empty screen. No matter how many years he spent in space, he would never learn to like facing an enemy he couldn't see. "Hold on for now, Lieutenant," he said at last. "Once we've passed over Rakatan's horizon, bring us back on a steep polar loop. I want to be out of their sight for at least five minutes." Maybe they could catch the mice playing if they thought the cat was on the other side of the planet.

"Mr. Howard?"

The guard at the security station glanced up. "Aye, sir?"

"What sort of reading can you get on their weapons?"

Dark eyes flicked across scanner readouts. Kirk watched the light on the young ensign's face shift from amber, to green, to amber again. "Most of the ships are single-person close-quarter fighters, sir. They carry light phasers, but no torpedo banks. The lead ship's a lot bigger, though, and carries both." He paused again, leaning to his left to check another screen. "The flagship is just under Soyuz-size, but the ionic output from the power source looks like . . ." Eyebrows rose, and he shot a startled look at Kirk. " . . . like a Klingon cruiser, sir."

Kirk tightened his hands on the arms of his command chair. "Keep our phasers trained on that flagship, Ensign."

"Aye-aye, sir!"

"Spock, any luck with that conversion yet?"

"Coming on-screen now, Captain."

Rakatan's horizon line broke and rippled, and all color washed out of the screen like sand sliding between two plates of glass. A ghostly black-and-white image fluttered into focus, barely detailed enough for the viewer to pick out individual vessels from the shifting blur. The flagship stood out most clearly, smooth and sinister as a snake, with sharp, well-tooled edges and the sweeping arc of a warp pylon jutting out to either side. The myriad smaller ships were more primitive, bullet-shaped, their outlines blurred into harsh checkerboard patterns wherever the ultraviolet was absorbed by weld seams and converted into heat. Kirk chewed his thumbnail as he studied the motley armada.

"The big one looks like it used to be a Klingon heavy frigate," Howard remarked to no one in particular. He sounded hesitant, and a little confused.

"Yes . . ." Kirk pulled his gaze away from the viewscreen long enough to reward the ensign with a grim nod. "They've made quite an industry out of retooling their older vessels for sale to non-allied systems. But those smaller ships . . ."

He glanced a question back at Spock, and the Vulcan raised both eyebrows as though surprised the captain had to ask.

"I believe we are in the presence of the Crown Regent," he said, quite formally. When Kirk only frowned, Spock nodded toward the viewscreen. "Captain, what we are seeing is the Royal Armada of Elas."

Chapter Twelve

THE MOUTH OF the dilithium mine yawned before them in the night, indigo black against the dusky cliffs that walled the Elasian mining camp. Uhura only glanced at it briefly while they approached. She was too busy watching her footing on the rough dirt track and trying to keep up with Takcas. The pace set by the cohort leader made her leg muscles hurt and her throat burn with the effort of breathing Rakatan's oxygen-poor air.

"In here." Takcas stepped aside, gesturing for Uhura to enter the mine before him. The pale amber light of Rakatan's moon sparked reflections from crystal flecks in the carved rock doorway, but no light showed inside. Uhura paused involuntarily on the brink of utter blackness, then remembered what had happened to Sulu when she'd argued with Takcas before. Digging her teeth into her lower lip, she forced herself into the mine.

The first shock was the temperature. Instead of the dank earthen chill she expected, the air inside the mine was dry and summer-hot. At first, Uhura assumed it was waste heat from the machinery she could hear thumping somewhere below. But when she put out a hand to guide herself into the tunnel, she felt the rock warm her palm like a live beast. Despite the underground darkness, the walls of the mine were hot as sun-baked brick.

Takcas caught her shoulder when she took another blind step. "No, Your Glory. This way." A hand-lamp flared into life behind her, chasing Uhura's shadow down a short length of entrance tunnel until it fetched up against a solid rock wall. The rest of the cohort followed Takcas as he led her toward that seeming dead end. It wasn't until they were a meter away that Uhura realized the rock wall was just the far side of another, more natural-looking tunnel, which the mine intersected. Takcas ducked into it and turned left, following the downward slope.

"Hey!" Despite a new hoarseness, Mutchler's whisper still managed to sound young and excited. "This isn't a mine shaft, it's a lava tube!"

"Dr. Mutchler, shut—" The sound of a blow interrupted Chekov's curt command. Uhura winced when she heard the geologist's cry of pain, but she didn't try to turn around. Knowing the Elasians, she guessed that any protest on her part would just get more of her landing party hurt.

"Down here." Takcas's hand-lamp glittered off a thick metal door, set into an equally thick metal bulkhead. He swung it open to reveal another section of snake-shaped corridor, this time lit with sullen yellow lights down the center of the roof. The thumping of machinery grew louder as they stepped in, and the air temperature went from summery to skin-prickling hot.

Uhura eyed the smooth rock walls on either side, seeing no signs of gouging or pits for mineral extraction. Wherever the Elasians were finding their dilithium, it wasn't here. The big machine must be some kind of air-cooling unit for the lower levels, she decided as they edged their way past its pounding roar. Otherwise, the miners would have needed environmental suits to work in this kind of heat.

"Stop." Just past the machinery, Takcas motioned Uhura to one side of the passage. The other side, she could see now, had been dug out in three neat cubical cells, each fitted around the edges with the familiar metal collar of a forcefield generator. The spiderweb of wiring that ran across the rough rock ceiling from the pounding machinery showed where the generators got their power.

"You go in this one, Dohlman, with the *kessh* of your cohort." Takcas steered Chekov toward the first and largest cell. Uhura darted a quick look at the security chief, waiting to see his nod of acceptance before she followed him in. The rock-cut room was deep enough that both of them could stand well away from the forcefield, but the ceiling hung so low that even Uhura had to stoop under it. For a male Elasian, the room's dimensions would have been torture.

"You, underling-pilot, go in here with the dark man." There was a thud as the cohort unceremoniously tossed Murphy into the center cell. Sulu ducked in after him, aiming a quiet but remarkably profane Orion curse at his captors. For his sake, Uhura hoped the Universal Translator hadn't caught it.

"And you, spineless scientific worm, you go in the small-est cell of all." Another choke from Mutchler preceded a second, louder thump. "Oben, turn on the field power."

A shimmer of force prismed inside the collared space when the burly older Elasian—still hunched and swollen from Takcas's cruel beating—flipped switches on the thrumming power source. After a moment, the forcefields steadied into their usual invisibility. Takcas pushed Oben unceremoniously away from the field generator to verify its settings himself, his strong-boned face carved with harsh lines in the overhead yellow light.

"Her Glory the Dohlman has not yet decided what to do to you for attempting to murder her." His lips curled in what looked more like a snarl than a grin. "But never fear. If she takes too long to decide on the method of your execu-tion, you will simply sweat yourselves to death in here."

Chekov scowled but wisely said nothing while the cohort retraced their steps past the pulsing power generator and back up to the surface, Takcas leaving last of all. From the soft scuffing noises in the next cell, Uhura guessed that Sulu was moving Murphy's unconscious body to a more comfortable position. She stepped as close as she could to the corner without triggering the forcefield.

"How is Ensign Murphy?"

"Coming around." Sulu's voice echoed oddly off the flat rock walls, as if it were coming from across the corridor instead of from the next cell.

Chekov grunted, squirming out of his uniform jacket. Even as Uhura watched, a trickle of sweat carved a path through the dust on his bruised cheek. "Take his jacket off, so he doesn't get too hot," he advised Sulu as he rolled up his own sleeves.

"Coming down here was not a good idea."

Uhura paused in opening the flap of her own jacket, startled by the bleak despair in Mutchler's voice. Even the blistering heat couldn't account for it. It was uncomfortable, certainly, but not life-threatening. At least, not yet.

"We didn't have a lot of choice, Dr. Mutchler." Chekov sat and leaned wearily back against the rock wall. "Trust me, you don't argue with Klingon disruptors."

Sulu chuckled. "I don't think Dr. Mutchler means coming down to the mine, Chekov. I think he means coming down to the planet."

"I mean both." A frustrated pounding echoed down the passage. Uhura frowned, knowing the geologist couldn't pace inside his tiny cell. He must have been kicking the wall. "You guys don't want to know what my last argon isotope reading was before those idiots grabbed us."

Chekov snorted. "You're right, we don't."

"Yes, we do." Uhura shrugged her jacket off and pillowed it beneath her. "What was it, Dr. Mutchler?"

"It was—well, let's just say it was higher than any reading I've seen anywhere on Rakatan, much less on Rakatan Mons."

Uhura frowned. Even through the doubled thickness of her uniform, she could feel heat pouring out from the volcanic rock beneath her. She felt her stomach tighten nervously. "What does that mean? Is the volcano going to erupt?"

"Not necessarily."

Chekov shook his head, eyes closing in frustration. "I told you we didn't want to know about the argon levels."

The thumping noise stopped. "Hey, it's not my fault that I don't know how Rakatan Mons likes to erupt! Some volcanic eruptions are preceded by lots of tectonic activity. Others go up all at once, without any warning at all."

"And what does that have to do with your atmospheric measurements?" Sulu inquired reasonably.

Mutchler sighed. "Well, when dilational stress levels rise, microfractures open in the diorite and release trace levels of radiogenic argon from feldspars into the atmosphere."

Chekov groaned. "Could you repeat that in normal English, please?"

"We're going to have another big earthquake," the geologist said bluntly. "Probably within the next twenty-seven hours. Conceivably any minute now."

The mingled sounds of Chekov cursing in Russian and Sulu in Orion completely overwhelmed the hiss of Uhura's indrawn breath. Of the three of them, though, she was the first to recover.

"Dr. Mutchler, what chance do we have of surviving an earthquake inside this mine?"

"Some," he admitted. "The fact that the Elasians have incorporated some of the natural lava tubes in the volcano helps. Circular cross sections are always stronger than cubic ones, and given the intrinsic compressibility of andesite—"

Uhura ruthlessly cut across the geologist's incomprehensible scientific explanation. "Do we have as good a chance down here as we would on the surface?"

"Probably not."

The rhythmic drumming of the generator filled the silence that fell between them. After a moment, Chekov sighed and stirred from his sitting position.

"Well, that leaves us no choice," he said gloomily. "We're going to have to escape."

Sulu's chuckle was joined, although weakly, by one from Ensign Murphy. Uhura gave Chekov a concerned look. "You don't sound very enthusiastic about it. Is it going to be incredibly hard to do?"

"No, it's going to be incredibly easy." Chekov squatted next to the forcefield and stuck his arm through it. Instead of the fierce crackle Uhura expected, there was only a sizzle that barely rocked the security chief back on his heels. He grunted, then looked over his shoulder at Uhura. There was more sweat on his face now, and not all of it, she guessed, from the heat.

"Slip through the field now." Chekov spoke between clenched teeth. "You can get out while I'm drawing off—"

Uhura dove through the spitting field before he finished speaking, then ran for the power generator. It was easy to guess which way to push the switches, since they were positioned at the lower end of their range already. She glanced at the high end of the scale and suppressed a shiver, seeing how much power the Elasians thought was necessary to confine one of their own males.

"Good work, you guys." Sulu emerged from his cell first, then turned to help a swaying Murphy to his feet. "How the hell did you break through your field?"

"We didn't." Chekov scrubbed sweat off his face for a moment, then slowly levered himself to his feet. "Takcas set it on partial power—enough to be painful but not enough to knock both of us out." He waved Uhura off when she would have come to support him, pointing instead to Mutchler, who was trying to extricate himself from the pretzel he'd become inside his tiny cell.

"How did you know Takcas did that?" Sulu demanded curiously.

Chekov held out one forearm, bare beneath the rolled-up tunic sleeve. "A full-power field should have made the hair on my arm shiver. This one didn't." He reached back in the cell for his and Uhura's discarded jackets. "Takcas wanted us to escape."

"Well, that wasn't done out of the goodness of his heart."

114

Uhura hauled Mutchler to his feet with slightly more force than necessary. "Why did he do it?"

Chekov scowled, handing over her jacket. "If I had to guess, I'd say Takcas isn't so sure that Israi will order us executed. This way, if we're shot trying to escape—"

"He gets us killed without disobeying his Dohlman's orders," Sulu finished. By now, the helmsman was frowning, too. "So the minute we step past that metal door, we're going to get every cell in our bodies disrupted."

"That's my guess." With a sigh, Chekov turned back to the forcefield collars around the punishment cells. "We'd better see what kind of weapons we can jury-rig out of these generators. If we can take out some of the guards waiting at the door—"

"Why do we need to do that?" Mutchler looked up from the cracks he was examining in the ceiling of the lava tube. "Won't it be dangerous?"

"Very." Uhura could see muscles clench in Chekov's jaw when he faced the geologist. "But you're the one who told us we'd be better off outside when this earthquake hits."

"We would," Mutchler agreed. "But we don't have to go past that stupid door to get there." He jerked a thumb at the tunnel. "Lava tubes have two ends, you know. It may be a bit of a walk back to the camp, but we can get out going downhill as easily as we can get out going up."

Uhura exchanged a considering look with her security chief. "Will the Elasians think to guard the other end of the tunnel?"

"Only if they know about it," Chekov said grimly. "And there's only one way to find out if they do."

"Captain!" Spock looked up from his sensors, dark eyes locking with Kirk's as the captain turned the command chair to face him. "The Elasian flagship is arming phasers."

Kirk's blood raced with sudden alarm. "Red alert! All crews to battle stations!"

Bloody light throbbed across the bridge, and Kirk heard the echo of alert sirens from the lower decks of the ship behind status reports. The ripple of raising deflector screens, like heat waves above a desert, distorted the frigate-turned-warship's lines for only an instant. When the image cleared, the flagship had peeled away from the backdrop of smaller ships behind her, bright streaks of phaser fire stabbing across the black of space. Kirk braced himself against the back of his chair, waiting for the impact. And it never came.

Howard gave a cry of surprise from the security station. "They're firing on the Johnston Observatory!"

"But . . ." The navigator looked up in shock from his console. "That's an unarmed station—they don't even have defense screens!"

Kirk was already out of his chair, leaning over the helm and snapping orders. "Break orbit! Get us between that flagship and the observatory."

"Aye-aye, sir!"

The ship surged beneath Kirk's feet, and he felt his own heartbeat quicken as they picked up speed. "Mr. Howard, ready torpedoes for launch on my mark."

"Torpedoes armed and ready, sir."

"Captain." The science-station sensors painted Spock's face in pale contrast to the red emergency lighting. "I am reading extensive damage to the observatory's surface facilities, and loss of atmosphere in at least one inhabited lab."

Kirk paced back to his command chair, teeth clenched. "Communications—get me that armada's commander." The alien flagship filled the viewscreen now, slewing nose-up as they silently braked to avoid collision with the starship now squarely in their path.

Ashcraft jerked his head up in surprise. "They're hailing us, sir."

Kirk smiled grimly. He'd been counting on that—they just took a little longer than he would have.

"Coming on screen now, sir."

"This is Captain James T. Kirk of the *United Starship Enterprise*—"

The dark, elegant woman who materialized on the screen

didn't even wait for Kirk to finish his introduction. "Starfleet vessel *Enterprise*," she spat in a voice both deep and thickly accented. "You are trespassing in Elasian territory. You will remove yourselves from this quadrant immediately."

Judging her against the stockade fence of Elasian men behind her, Kirk guessed that she was taller than Elaan of Troyius, and broader through the shoulders and arms. But she and the late Dohlman were without doubt related. This one had the same magnificent cheekbones and piercing black eyes, the same disdainful downcast to her generous mouth. With her inky hair cropped close to her skull and only a topknot's worth of braids left to cascade past her armored shoulders, she looked like some sort of wild samurai, caught without her sword.

Kirk met her gaze steadily. "You are the Dohlman of this fleet?"

One of the tall, flat-faced men behind her announced in a booming voice, "You are in the presence of Her Grandeur, the Crown Regent of Elas, Heir and Guardian to the glorious Dohlman Israi."

"Ah." Kirk tipped her a formal, if stiff, little bow. "Your Grandeur," he said, quite carefully, "I'm afraid I can't act on your command without the permission of my own Dohlman. As she is—"

"Don't patronize me," the Crown Regent snapped. "Starfleet has no Dohlmen."

It wasn't quite the response Kirk had expected, and he straightened slowly, considering.

"You call yourself captain. That means you command this vessel. You will deal with me yourself."

"Very well." He paced down the few steps of the command chair's dais to round the dual helm console. "As the Federation authority in this quadrant, I'm ordering you to deactivate your weapons and withdraw to a distance of fifty thousand kilometers from Rakatan."

"No!" She slashed the air with both hands, giving her head a braid-whipping shake. "I will *not* negotiate terms

117

with the spineless pink eunuchs who sought to murder my glorious Dohlman!"

Kirk caught himself just before showing his surprise. "No one has harmed Dohlman Israi."

"She has told me differently!" The Crown Regent came closer to her own screen. Kirk could hear the heavy sound of footsteps against her flagship's decking. "Those rock-grabbing worms the Federation claims as scientists used their machines to start an earth tremor near our mining camp; then your own false 'Dohlman' tore my neice from her cohort when that attempt to murder her failed." She dropped her hand to the knife hilt on her hip. "Either of these deeds could be considered a despicable act of war against the government of Elas!"

Kirk shook his head, keeping his own hands still at his sides. "I promise you, Your Grandeur, no one from the *Enterprise* or the Johnston Observatory has made any such attempt against Dohlman Israi. But you—" He gestured offscreen at where the engineering station still labored over distress calls from the observatory. "You have opened fire on an unarmed Geological Survey outpost. That violates every treaty Elas has with the United Federation of Planets."

"I spit on your Federation." She followed word with action, then ground her foot against the wet floor. "You are lying dogs who use your own laws to steal what rightfully belongs to Elas. We use Elasian laws to defend what is ours." The men behind her broke formation with no apparent direction from her. She flicked only the briefest glance after them as they dispersed out of sight all around her. "Our first shot was but a warning," she said, nodding to something obviously said to her by someone Kirk couldn't see. "You will remove all Federation pigs from Rakatan and its satellites, or I will crush this outpost like a rodent's skull."

Kirk stared at her coldly. "And you will start a war."

She tossed her chin as though utterly unconcerned. "The Federation is not the only government in the galaxy. And I have powerful allies."

Kirk thought about the distinctively Klingon construction of the flagship in which the Crown Regent rode, and clenched his hands around the knowledge of exactly which allies the Crown Regent could call upon. Turning his back on the viewscreen, Kirk caught the young communications officer's eyes with his own and pressed a finger to his lips. He waited until Ashcraft had dampened the audio signal, then looked at Spock and sighed. "How long will our screens have to be down in order to evacuate the observatory?"

The Vulcan raised an eyebrow in what could almost have been human surprise. "Captain, withdrawal of Federation personnel could be construed as acceptance of Elas's claim to Rakatan."

"The Crown Regent has three hundred single-pilot fighters with her, Spock." He knew his voice rang sharp with annoyance, but trusted his first officer to know it wasn't aimed at him. "Unless we're willing to shoot them all out of the sky, we can't guarantee the observatory's safety under these conditions. We can always return the geologists to the moonbase once we've settled everything up here."

Spock glanced aside to consult some reading on his board. "With a transporter room standing by, we will only require a window of one minute sixteen seconds." He lifted dark eyes to Kirk. "Dr. Bascomb is not likely to approve."

"I didn't intend to ask her permission." He nodded Spock back to his science console. "Have Transporter Room Two standing by, then contact Bascomb via a closed circuit. Tell her she's got five minutes to get her people and her data together, then we're pulling them out of there." At the Vulcan's tacit nod, Kirk bent to the arm of his command chair and thumbed open the intercom. "Transporter Room One."

"Scott here," the engineer's familiar voice replied.

"Scotty, have you got a fix on the landing party's communicators?"

There was a brief pause as the Scotsman consulted whatever readings his transporter console gave him. "Aye, sir," he said at last. "That Elasian defense screen has been down since we brought up Commander Uhura this afternoon."

Kirk nodded shortly. "Good." At least something was still going in their favor. "Lock on and beam them out of there as soon as I get our own shields down."

The engineer hesitated for only a moment. "Sir?"

"All of them," Kirk told him. "I don't care what they're doing or where they are, I want them back on this ship *now*."

"Aye-aye, Captain." Scott's voice was crisp with determination. "I'm on it."

"Kirk." The Crown Regent broke across the last of his conversation in a cruel, waspish tone. "Speak to me, Kirk, or I will open fire."

She'd already been remarkably patient, compared to the Elasians Kirk had known. He couldn't help smiling somewhat at that thought. Turning, he seated himself as casually as possible while Ashcraft reopened their channel. "I wouldn't be too trigger-happy, if I were you, Your Grandeur," he offered, sitting back. Before her scowl could grow into a new string of insults, he continued, "In the spirit of cooperation, I'm removing all personnel from the Skaftar moonbase. I trust you will allow me to drop my screens long enough to effect a safe transfer."

She studied him for what seemed a very long time before stepping back from her own viewscreen and crossing her arms. "My neice Elaan warned me of your many wiles," she said with no small amount of disdain. "Make no attempt to deceive me."

Kirk couldn't help feeling that any deception on his part would be the least of the untruths floating around this coveted planet. Nodding to Howard, he stated formally, "Mr. Howard, lower shields."

The guard's face looked positively grim with apprehension as he threw the chain of simple switches. "Shields down," he finally announced, not looking up from his panel.

Kirk nodded again, and opened the intercom. "Transporter Room Two. Are you ready to beam up the geologists?"

"Aye, sir. Dr. Bascomb and crew report ready."

"Energize."

Only a moment later, the technician's voice came back, more subdued than before. "Beam-up complete, sir. We've got seven geologists safely aboard."

Four fewer than they should have had. Kirk thought of the breached lab in the Crown Regent's first phaser volley, and anger pushed dully against his chest.

"Your business here is finished," the Crown Regent announced. She waved in haughty dismissal. "You may now withdraw with your tail between your legs and leave us to our mining."

Kirk shook his head, clenching his hands on the arms of his command chair. "Not so fast, Your Grandeur." The flash of bitter fury in her eyes came nowhere near making up for what she'd done to those geologists. "I still have my orders, and those orders require me to secure proof that you have the rights you claim to this planet. I'm not going anywhere until I've got that."

"Impudent dog! I should unleash my cohort on you for such presumption!"

"And if you do," Kirk returned, "I will be forced to return fire, endangering you, your armada, and the Dohlman Israi." He leaned forward to lace his hands between his knees. "Face it, Your Grandeur. No matter who ends up with rightful claim to this planet, the *Enterprise* still has you outgunned. And neither of us wants this to come down to a fight."

But, as an Elasian, she would probably die before admitting that. Kirk matched stares with her for a long, hard minute; then she swung away with a brutal curse and the scene flicked again to the darkness of space and the waiting armada. Kirk sat back with a sigh.

"We take round one." He slapped open the intercom with the side of his hand. "Scotty, what's the status on our landing party?"

"I . . . I don't know, sir."

The nearness of the engineer's voice startled Kirk. He

jumped to his feet, turning, and found himself facing the burly Scotsman as he exited the turbolift. "What's the matter?" Kirk frowned at the collection of equipment in Scott's cupped hands. "You didn't bring them up?"

"I tried, sir." Scott held out his hand to display four Starfleet-issue communicators and one Geological Survey comm band. "All I got was these."

Chapter Thirteen

"So—DO YOU THINK they know we're gone?" Sulu's voice, barely louder than a breath, floated across the darkness between them.

Aided only slightly by the pale Rakatan moon, Chekov watched Elasian men disappear from one slab of floodlighting and rematerialize in the next as they made their unhurried passages between the prefab mining buildings. "I don't think so." He raised up slightly on one elbow and pointed past Sulu's nose. *Gamow* waited where they'd left her, just inside the edge of the encampment with her fine, reflective carapace stained amber in the tiny moon's light. "No guards," he whispered when the helmsman turned his head to look.

"Isn't that good?" Sulu asked.

Chekov crawled back away from the chain of rubble they'd chosen as their blind, tugging on Sulu's jacket for him to follow. "Not necessarily." Ashy dirt hissed in a dry river down the volcano flanks below them, and Chekov felt every muscle in his neck and shoulders knot as he willed the billow of dust to continue downhill, out of reach of the lights from the Elasian mining camp. He wished for a moon as large and white as Earth's Luna, so he could see where he was going and not just feel his way through the breathless alien darkness. Then he considered how much a full Earth moon would aid the Elasians in hunting them down, and was sorry he'd even had the thought.

Sulu caught up to him, for whatever reason moving more easily among the loosened stones. Crawling up the face of Rakatan Mons had stained both their hands and trousers an iron red to rival their uniform jackets. In the fullness of the night, the dust conspired to make both of them nearly invisible, even when they stood side by side.

"So why is it not good that they haven't missed us?" Sulu asked, pointing Chekov toward a clearer passage just a little to their left. "You just in the mood to argue with these guys, or what?"

"No." Chekov slid carefully to the lower edge of the slope, then let himself drop to what he remembered as a stretch of more even ground that he couldn't actually see. "The farther along we get in our escape, the more justification they'll have for killing us on sight."

Sulu landed beside his friend with a grunt. "You do have a talent for looking at the bright side of things. Come on—this way."

They hiked the rest of the distance to the landing party in silence. Chekov tried to listen for sounds of pursuit as they scrambled down the dirty mountain, tried to watch for some sign of Israi's cohort circling around from the sides. But vast, unbroken night made everything look unnaturally distant and two-dimensional, and even the slightest whisper of wind on rock traveled through the dry atmosphere like thunder. Every nerve in his body felt alert and overextended, and trying to walk without losing track of Sulu's dim outline didn't help. Chekov wondered how much longer it would take to exhaust himself beyond the point of being useful with worry over what to do when the Elasians caught up to them.

"We're back." Sulu's quiet greeting to the others was Chekov's first clue that they were nearly on top of the landing party's hideout.

Bodies just inside the mouth of the narrow hollow jostled further back into the blackness, giving Sulu and Chekov room to slip in away from even the most anemic touch of moonlight. The sudden blind pressure of total sightlessness sent a weak shiver through Chekov's insides. He found a wall to lean back against for the sake of keeping track of up and down, then folded his arms and blinked into the darkness in the hopes his eyes would adjust and he'd be able to see.

"Did you have any problems?" Uhura asked. She sounded both disembodied and impossibly near, and Chekov almost jumped at the loudness of her voice.

"No, we're fine," Sulu answered for both of them. "They don't even know we're gone."

Mutchler's sigh was just as overwhelming, but Chekov was ready for it this time. "Well, so far so good."

Chekov decided not to bother reexplaining the disadvantages attached to their current run of luck. "Dr. Mutchler was right," he said, nominally meaning the report for Uhura. "The shuttle's only about three hundred meters west of here."

"And straight up," Sulu added sourly. "The climb is not fun."

Uhura made a small, thoughtful noise. "What are our chances of being able to board the shuttle without attracting attention?"

"Fairly good." Chekov mentally pictured the mining-camp layout, complete with the few guards they'd spotted in their reconnaissance. "Most of their lighting is concentrated around where the Dohlman's quarters used to be, and there's no one assigned to watch the shuttle itself." He turned to face where instinct said Uhura should be. "There's always the possibility they've already disabled the shuttle, though, so they know we can't make use of it."

"Mr. Cheerful strikes again."

If Chekov had been sure which body he could feel beside him was Sulu, he'd have kicked the helmsman.

"Then why are we doing this?" Mutchler moved aimlessly from somewhere deeper back in the cut, and everyone ahead of him jostled a step in response to whoever he first bumped into. "Why are we all going into this if we aren't even sure we'll be able to get out of it again?"

"You would rather wait for your earthquake in the Elasian punishment cells?" Chekov asked testily. But Uhura spoke over him calmly, and he assumed it was her hand that landed warningly on his arm.

"Even if *Gamow* won't fly," she explained, "we can still use her subspace radio. Once we've made contact with the *Enterprise,* they can beam us out of here."

"But only if we're all together," Sulu added. "Without our communicators, there's no way to determine coordinates for the rest of the landing party if we get separated."

Mutchler sighed with obvious unhappiness, and Chekov heard what sounded like the scuff of a boot against the ridged basalt floor. "So all we have to do is climb up there and get inside your shuttle? How hard do you think that will be?"

The honest innocence of the question made Chekov smile. "Have you ever tried to sneak past an entire camp filled with seven-foot-tall, armed warriors, Dr. Mutchler?"

"No."

"Then this is going to be harder than you can possibly imagine."

Chekov crouched with his back to a volcano-spawned boulder, and waited while Sulu scrubbed dirt on his face and hands to minimize the contrast with his own darkened clothing. The security chief had smudged himself with swift efficiency upon first reaching the crest of the incline. He didn't feel as if he was moving quickly, but he knew Sulu wasn't the sort to dawdle and it seemed as though the helmsman were taking four times as long as necessary to do everything. It was an effect Chekov recognized from a dozen other planetary missions, so he merely fidgeted in silence and tried to concentrate on counting the stars while he waited.

"You ready?" Sulu whispered at last.

Chekov only nodded. He'd been ready since halfway up the slope, when all the nerves and adrenaline and borderline terror inside him finally caught up to his conscious awareness of what they were doing. Now even his thoughts seemed to tumble past at an accelerated speed, until the time between his nod and their move into the open felt like agonizing minutes. He suspected their hesitation had lasted less than a second.

The powerful floodlights near the center of camp carved a great wedge of light out of the night sky. Everything between the lights and the two officers was pressed flat and black by the stark brilliance, including *Gamow,* whose normally subdued paleness had been crushed by the backlighting to a pearly dark gray. Chekov tried to remind himself that those same bright lights worked drastically in their favor, too— anyone with his back to the camp looking outward would see the night as one uniform plane of flat blackness. But seeing every movement of the cohort so clearly exaggerated by their monstrous shadows left Chekov feeling hopelessly defenseless and exposed.

Sulu crawled around to Chekov's side of the rock, his eyes locked on the waiting shuttle. "Okay." It was less a comment and more a bracing sigh. "The maintenance access is about two-thirds of the way from the stern, underneath. It works on maintenance codes, so I won't need any special tools to get the panel off. Opening it should only take me about a minute, then another couple minutes to clear a crawlspace into the passenger compartment. Once I'm inside, I'll signal you."

And until then, he would stand out painfully in the slice of bright yellow that burned its way under the shuttle's raised belly. It would have made things so much easier if they'd parked the shuttle with the hatch facing away from the camp, instead of opening onto it.

"Just be careful," Chekov heard himself say in a grim whisper.

Sulu reached across to squeeze his shoulder. "Always." Then he lifted himself into a runner's crouch, and was gone.

The helmsman's speed was remarkable. He covered the open distance without a sound, dropping into invisibility alongside the nearest warp nacelle without appearing even to break his stride. Only the topmost curve of his head showed above that meager cover when he boosted himself to peek past the shuttle toward camp.

After what seemed a slow eternity, Sulu rose in a swell of shadow that seemed to pour over the lip of the nacelle and under *Gamow*'s bottom. Chekov waited until he saw the helmsman reach up to begin work on the maintenance panel, then crept back around the boulder to rejoin the rest of the party.

Uhura had already moved her trio up from their place a stone's throw farther downslope. She looked a silent question at Chekov through the darkness, and the whites of her eyes shone above dark mahogany cheeks. He wished there were something they could do to lessen that effect, but couldn't think of anything in their present position. At least she'd exercised her usual quiet foresight and removed her bracelets and earrings without having to be told.

Chekov glanced down the row of tense faces to make sure everyone was ready. "He's in place," he whispered. "You all know what to do?"

Uhura nodded and held up a single finger. Murphy followed suit by holding up two, and Mutchler, behind him, three. The geologist looked particularly pale and thin in the darkness.

"As soon as I'm gone, move up," Chekov told Uhura. "The rest of you follow one at a time on my signal. And whatever you do, don't make a sound."

Even Mutchler didn't feel the need to comment on those orders. Flashing them an "O.K." for reassurance and luck, Chekov slipped away again to wait for Sulu's signal.

Sulu must have managed to pry free the access panel. The helmsman's slender shadow knelt almost upright under *Gamow*'s belly, and even as Chekov watched, Sulu pulled himself through some unseen portal to disappear completely. Taking two slow, deep breaths to ready himself, Chekov padded away from his shelter and into the twelve meters of open night between the sheltering rocks and the shuttle.

Backlighting from the camp stretched *Gamow*'s shadow into a long, unnatural parallelogram. Chekov stayed carefully within the shuttle's darkness. He knew he wasn't as limber as Sulu—that he couldn't crouch as low or cross the distance as quickly—so he concentrated instead on stealth. Keep to the shadow, avoid jerky movements, breathe in as much of the surrounding environment as his senses could give him. He was only halfway across, trotting lightly, when a flicker of movement disturbed the corona of light around the shuttle's edges. Nerve-heightened instincts dropped him into a ground-hugging crouch before his civilized mind even realized what he'd seen.

A tall, thick Elasian silhouette pulled away from the shuttle's greater darkness to stand as a separate feature a few meters off *Gamow*'s stern. Chekov's fingers dug into the ashy ground between his knees, but he allowed himself no other movement, not even the releasing of his in-held breath. His thoughts raced ahead to fifty different permutations of what he must do should the Elasian see him, see the others, hear Sulu, open the shuttle, signal the cohort, bring up the lights. The answers flashed through his mind with emotionless clarity all in the few seconds it took the faceless entity to stand in the bracket of floodlight, look to left and right, then turn and walk away.

He could see the flash-black-flash of the Elasian's legs in the stream of light shining under the shuttle. Only after that ghost movement narrowed with distance, then vanished, did he rise up on cramped, shaking legs and dash the last distance to the shuttle.

Lying flat along the outside of the warp nacelle, he

breathed into his hands to hide the sound of his gasping and told himself that "almost caught" didn't count. They still had three more lives to go.

Sulu's voice floated out to him on the faintest of whispers. "So much for them not posting any guards."

Even that tiny sound made Chekov's heart seize with fear. "Shut up and start your preflight sequence!" he hissed in reply. Then he lifted his hand into the light under the shuttle and raised a single finger for Uhura to see.

She slipped into the covering darkness, as lithe and graceful as a cat. Her small, dark figure barely disturbed the night's black fabric, and she followed the sweep of shadow just as Chekov had done. He never heard a sound from her, not even when she reached out to clasp his hand before slipping past him to disappear up the access panel after Sulu.

Turning back to the waiting darkness, Chekov lifted two fingers in the second signal.

Equally dark, but taller and less lissome, Murphy moved away from their hiding place to follow Uhura. Mutchler's pale face hovered like the faintest smudge of moonlight among the rocks a dozen meters from the shuttle. He was too lost in darkness to have any readable expression, but the preternatural stillness in his lanky frame spoke eloquently of his quiet terror. Chekov felt suddenly very sorry for the scientist, and for all the years of study that couldn't have prepared him for fieldwork quite like this.

A column of startling shadow blinded Chekov on the left. He registered a grunt of Elasian surprise, and saw Mutchler jerk to his feet with his mouth open as if to shout something. Then the blow Chekov aimed at the Elasian's knee contacted, and the scream of the Elasian's disruptor drowned out even the sound of breaking bone.

Someone barked a hoarse cry of anguish—Mutchler? Murphy? he couldn't tell—and Chekov shouted, "Go! Get into the shuttle!" at whichever of them hadn't been shot as he clipped an elbow across the Elasian's chin to take the warrior down. All hope of subtlety was gone. Wrenching the

130

disruptor pistol out of the guard's vicious grip, Chekov jammed the muzzle into the throat joint on his breastplate and fired before looking up to see who was running for the shuttle, and who wasn't.

Mutchler was already squirming under the shuttle and into the access hatch, shouting frantically at Uhura and Sulu inside. Oblivious of the growing roar of voices from deeper in the camp, Murphy, wounded by the disruptor blast, writhed weakly on the ground only a few short meters away. They had minutes—moments, really—before the rest of the cohort recognized what they'd heard and descended on the shuttle like feral dogs. Knowing that speed was his only ally, Chekov bolted back for the young ensign with the disruptor still clenched in one hand.

Murphy had pulled himself almost to all fours—he'd made it to his knees, but collapsed forward over his arms in a fit of fluid, broken coughing. Chekov caught him from behind. "I've got you," he said, locking his arms around the ensign's chest and hauling him to his feet. "I'm not going to leave you. . . ."

Murphy gasped, stiffening, and reached up to clutch at Chekov's arm as his chief dragged him back toward the *Gamow*. A spasm of fierce protectiveness tightened Chekov's throat, and he breathed again, "I'm not going to leave you!" as the boil of angry voices behind him swelled nearer.

"Pavel! Here!" Uhura appeared around the rear of the shuttle, grabbing at his jacket to redirect him. "I opened the hatch—bring him here!"

They rounded the shuttle into the fearful exposure of light. Uhura raced ahead while Chekov, thighs burning, tried to run the last few meters backward with the security guard in tow. He could see the Elasians now, a swarm of distorted shadows coalescing near the source of the distant lights. Slinging the disruptor into the open shuttle door, he twisted sideways to pass Murphy to Uhura and Mutchler, and shouted, "Sulu! Take off! *Now!*"

Under *Gamow*'s unflinching interior lights, one side of

Murphy's face and collar looked warped and glossy with
blood. Uhura and Mutchler dragged him away from the
open hatchway, and Chekov climbed in behind them just as
the shuttle lifted off in a cloud of pale and powder-fine ash.
He caught the edges of the doorway, unbalanced on his
knees just inside the hatch, and heard the first phaser fire
from below as the Elasians turned their stolen weapons
against them.

Uhura jerked around at the shrill report, and a deflected
bolt skated past the hatchway to splatter against the wall
behind her. Chekov meant to yell at her, to warn her to keep
down and away from the line of fire. Instead, he felt his
whole body arch in a single unexpected seizure, and his grip
on the hatchway went suddenly numb and strengthless.
They'd hit him, he realized dully. Damn.

"Chekov!"

He knew he'd fallen from the horrified sound of Uhura's
cry. But he didn't actually feel it when he let go of the
shuttle, and he never knew when he hit the ground.

Chapter Fourteen

THE SHUTTLE LURCHED into the cold night sky, its empty
hatch gaping like a mouth opened to scream. The fear that
had been drumming through Uhura unnoticed in the rush of
crisis suddenly clawed at her throat until it tore her breath
away. She thrust the shuddering security guard she held into
Mutchler's startled arms, and flung herself across the shuttle, flat against the floor to avoid phaser fire, intent on
finding Chekov's fallen body below. All she could see
through the darkness was a wind-lashed flag of dust marking
the place where he had fallen. A dozen big shadows were
converging on it.

"Sulu!" Uhura locked both hands on the vibrating edge of
the hatch and craned her head back toward the cockpit.
From this angle, all she could see was the swift red flicker of
the instrument panel as it responded to the pilot's stabbing
fingers. "We have to go back! We lost Chekov!"

The baying sound of a disruptor splintered the night
before the pilot could reply, and *Gamow* jolted sideways.
Compressed nitrogen screamed as it escaped from the

cracked nacelle below, blasting a surge of cold air through the hatch. With a jerk that made Uhura's stomach reel, the shuttle began to skid sideways.

"*Starboard nacelle!*" she shouted at the cockpit, then rolled away from the hatch and scrabbled up the steeply sloping floor toward Mutchler. Sulu needed all their weight over the good port nacelle to have any hope of controlling the shuttle's downward plunge. Uhura shoved the geologist toward the far wall, stooping to help him drag Murphy with them. The injured security guard's shudders had become outright convulsions now. His face was a gray-brown mask of pain, and his juddering torso felt rock-hard beneath the blood-drenched uniform.

"Internal bleeding." Mutchler's voice over the laboring roar of the shuttle's remaining nacelle sounded ragged in her ear. With their balance readjusted, Sulu was slowly bringing them up again. "I think he's dying."

Another disruptor burst bayed through the outside dark, this time shearing harmlessly through *Gamow*'s roof. Fragments of shredded metal drifted down on Uhura like ash. "I'll call the *Enterprise*, they can beam us straight to sickbay—" She struggled out from under the sprawl of Murphy's body and ran for the communicator panel in the cockpit.

"Hurry." Sulu's hands were steady on his helm controls, but the bare edge of a quiver in his voice told Uhura how close they'd come to crashing when the starboard nacelle blew. The lights of the Elasian camp were quilted bright across the ground below them, startlingly close. "We're still only four hundred meters off the ground. If they turn their defense shield back on before we make the perimeter, it'll fry us."

Uhura slammed the hailing signal, waiting only the bare second she knew it took the *Enterprise*'s computer to acknowledge before she started to speak. "Uhura to *Enterprise*. Four to beam up immediately, from these—"

It was too late. As if Sulu's words had summoned it, the iridescent glitter of the defense shield flared on the edges of the shuttle's viewscreen. It began to close, its wavering fingers reaching toward the shuttle.

"Hurry, we can make it—" Uhura resisted an urge to shake Sulu to make him fly faster. With one nacelle gone, it was a miracle they were flying at all.

"Higher," Sulu said to the shuttle between his teeth, as the field swam through the night toward them. "Get us just a little higher—"

As if it had heard him, the shuttle bucked upward. For a moment, Uhura thought they had made it through. Then the *Gamow* jerked back like a fish caught at the end of a line—and the thundering crash of explosive decompression rolled over them.

"Port nacelle exploded—" Uhura could barely hear Sulu's voice over the scream of fusing metal. Her communications panel erupted into an inferno of sparks as the electrical surge of the explosion burned through its circuits, scorching the hand she had reached out to transmit their coordinates. Yellow smoke swirled off the blasted equipment, acrid with the smell of melted plastic and singed metal.

"We've lost all power." Oddly enough, Sulu's voice had steadied with the inevitability of disaster. Ignoring sparks, he pounded at the smoldering flight panel, trying to find a flight control that still worked. Uhura looked up from her own lifeless communication controls and saw the horizon vanish into a sky full of cold stars. The Elasian forcefield had spit the *Gamow* out like a lobbed rock, tossing it up and outward into the night. Right now, they were traveling faster than they could have done under their own power, but as soon as the momentum of collision faded, the shuttle would fall like a rock, too. And they had no way to stop her.

Sulu made one last stab at resuscitating the darkened flight board, then gave up with a quiet sigh. The sound was almost lost in the rushing wind of their unpowered flight. "We're starting down. I'm going to engage the shock webbing—"

"Wait." Uhura spun and pushed herself out of her chair,

barely feeling the bite of her burned fingers. "Mutchler and Murphy aren't strapped in."

"Uhura, *no!*" Sulu's grab caught her just before she ducked through the cockpit door. "There's not enough time—"

"Make time." She shook off his hand and ran for the huddled pair at the back of the shuttle. The sickening dizziness of free fall tangled her feet, but Uhura stubbornly fought her way through it. She made it almost to the back before an explosion shook the shuttle and reversed their downward motion briefly.

Uhura blinked in surprise, then realized that Sulu had manually jettisoned their port nacelle. The force of the blast momentarily buoyed them, giving Uhura time to throw two safety straps across the fallen men. Then free fall dragged at her again, harder this time, as she turned to skid back toward the cockpit.

Not enough time, Uhura thought, hearing the scream of approaching ground outside the shuttle even as she ran for the safety of Sulu's outstretched hand. *Not enough time, not enough time, not enough—*

Noise and activity swarmed over Kirk when he stepped through the sickbay doors. Quick eyes flicked over the instrument trays scattered on top of diagnostic beds and counters, noting what was in use, what was left untouched. Judging from the array of supplies and the number of geologists sitting up and arguing with their nurses, Kirk guessed that most of the injuries sustained by observatory personnel had been minor. He pushed past one knot of gesticulating researchers, and aimed a supportive smile at Christine Chapel when she turned to see who was trying to sneak by.

"You could always sedate them," Kirk suggested.

The doctor didn't return his smile. "Don't think it hasn't occurred to me." She shoved aside a storage cart with her foot, and nodded Kirk toward the back of the sickbay. "Leonard is in ICU. I think he's expecting you."

Kirk nodded his thanks, then hurried out of the press of people to hunt down McCoy in the restricted rooms of intensive care.

The chief surgeon stood with his back to the door, green lab coat hanging loose on his stooped shoulders while he read something off the panel on the bed in front of him. The patient's heartbeat pulsed strong and slow, but what Kirk could understand of the other vital signs on the monitor didn't look promising. He stepped up next to McCoy to study the quiet body.

"You didn't transport these people a minute too soon," the doctor said by way of greeting. He gestured to the patient in front of them, then again at a woman who lay equally still in a bed across the room. "These two were half-dead when they got here. If Spock hadn't warned me to expect some cases of vacuum exposure, I would have lost them both. Why'd you wait so long?"

Kirk couldn't take his eyes from the young man's frostbitten lips, or the spiderweb pattern of vacuum bruises lacing across both cheeks and eyes. "A Dohlman got in my way." When McCoy shot an anxious glare at him, Kirk made himself look up and smile thinly. "A Dohlman in a Klingon heavy frigate, Bones. Don't worry."

The doctor grunted. "It's my job to worry."

"Where's Dr. Bascomb?"

"In my office." He jerked a thumb over his shoulder without turning, his attention suddenly caught by something he didn't like about the placement of his patient's IV. "She's examining some of her precious seismic records on my medical computer," he grumbled as he fiddled the line back to where he wanted it. "I splinted a bad ankle fracture for her a little bit ago, but she refused to sit and rest until I let her look at her data." He shook his head in grim disapproval. "I should have sedated her."

Thinking of his own flippant comment to Chapel, Kirk chuckled softly and rubbed at his eyes.

"Any word yet from the landing party?"

This time it was the captain's turn to shake his head and

sigh. "Not yet. Spock's trying to raise the shuttle now, but that's about all we can do. I don't want to try and beam anyone else past the Crown Regent until I know for sure what we've got going on down there."

"Well," McCoy drawled, a little too seriously for Kirk's tastes. "Now *that's* an uncommon bit of discretion." He glanced sideways at his captain, but Kirk decided he had more important things to do than let his chief surgeon bait him.

"Thank you for your input," he said dryly. "I'm going to talk with Dr. Bascomb now." But he clapped the doctor on the shoulder before leaving, just to let McCoy know Kirk didn't hold his ill tempers against him.

Bascomb had left McCoy's office door open, but the dimness of the inside light made it clear she wasn't inviting visitors. Kirk paused in the doorway, his hand near the lighting control even though he made no move to touch it. "Dr. Bascomb?"

She glanced up from the terminal screen in front of her. "Captain." McCoy's chair had been scooted back from the desk so she could stand with her injured leg bent, foot draped across the chair's seat. One hand braced against the top of the terminal while the other traced dancing rows of multicolored lines as they snaked and jerked across the screen.

"Doctor . . ." Kirk came farther into the darkened room, stopping just at the edge of the cluttered desk. "I . . . I'd like to apologize." Such words, like always, never came easily. "With the *Enterprise* in the system, that Elasian attack on your observatory should never have happened. I am truly sorry."

Bascomb shrugged off his apology, not even glancing up from her data. "Captain Kirk, maybe you can read the minds of alien female warlords, but *I* sure as hell can't. Who could have guessed that the Crown Regent would want to shoot at us?" She keyed through a sequence of codes on the terminal screen. "Other than disrupting our research, it didn't accomplish a damned thing."

"I think it was the Elasian equivalent of a warning shot." He took a deep breath, trying to decide how best to ask his next question. At last, he had no choice but to settle for his usual frankness. "How many people did you lose?"

"Three." Then she blinked and looked away from the terminal, a little real-time intellect coming back into her eyes. "No, make that four. Park, Dembosky, Poole, and Metcalfe." Her mouth twisted into a sour scowl. "The whole damned geophysical team." She thumped a finger against the squiggle lines on the screen. "Do you know what that means?"

Kirk leaned over next to her to peer at the screen. The horizontal bands of jumping color looked like little more than a collection of erratic alien heartbeats. "No."

Bascomb sighed and dropped her hand. "Neither do I. I'm a petrologist, not a geophysicist! All I'm sure of is that this damn seismic activity is *not* an aftershock from yesterday's earthquake." She sank against the chair back with a frustrated grumble and wrapped her forearm over the top of her head in profound thought. "Finally, after all these months, Rakatan Mons starts to do something interesting, and I've lost all the people who might understand what it means."

Kirk knew from years of dealing with Spock that what a scientist considered "interesting" wasn't always what a layperson meant by the term. "Dr. Bascomb, are you saying Rakatan Mons might erupt?"

She snorted. "Captain, eruption is what volcanoes do. And with all the earthquake activity we've had lately—well, let me just say that if I were you, I'd keep an eye on my orbit from now on." Kirk frowned at her, and she added, smiling, "When Rakatan Mons goes up, it's going to blast a lot of the planet straight up through the atmosphere and out into space. I wouldn't recommend being in the way when it happens."

Kirk's mind immediately fragmented into a dozen different task options. "How long before the eruption starts?"

"I just told you!" Bascomb cried, flinging wide her arms.

139

"I don't know!" She slapped a hand against the terminal as though disciplining a recalcitrant child. "That seismic pattern appeared on our network yesterday, but I don't have a guess what it means. Hell, for all I know, it's Wendy Metcalfe's magma men chattering to each other about the weather!"

"I believe that particular type of harmonic tremor commonly signifies that molten magma is within a kilometer of the surface."

Kirk turned at the sound of his first officer's voice. Spock nodded a succinct acknowledgment of his captain's presence, and Kirk gestured with his hand for Spock to turn up the lights as he entered.

"Are you a geophysicist?" Bascomb hobbled around behind Kirk, gripping his shoulders for support as she beamed hopefully at Spock. "That would be really convenient."

Spock lifted an eyebrow as if surprised. "Not at all, Doctor. I merely reviewed the studies done by your staff while we were en route to Rakatan. According to that data, a swarm of small seismic tremors typically precedes the onset of a phreatomagmatic eruption on this planet." He stepped up next to Kirk to examine the terminal screen. "Unless I am mistaken, the rate at which the magmatic front is rising can be determined from—"

"Spock . . ." Kirk tried to keep the impatience out of his tone, but guessed from the cool look of reproach on his first officer's face that he hadn't been entirely successful. "You can play geophysicist later. Did you manage to locate the landing party's shuttle?"

"Unfortunately, Captain, yes."

Kirk lifted his own brows in surprise. "Unfortunately?"

"Just a few moments ago, Ensign Ashcraft intercepted a subspace communication from Commander Uhura on the *Gamow*. We do not yet know the circumstances surrounding the contact, but before an accurate fix on the shuttle's coordinates could be determined, *Gamow*'s transponder signal ceased."

Kirk chewed his lower lip. "Deliberately disengaged?" He didn't know whether it would occur to Chekov to disable the transponder to keep the Elasians from tracking *Gamow,* or even whether the lieutenant would do such a thing when he must know it meant the *Enterprise* wouldn't be able to find them, either.

Spock's answer erased what little hope he might have had in that scenario. "Unlikely, Captain. The transponder's final signal was the automatic distress call sent when a shuttle's engines are too heavily damaged to allow her to fly."

Kirk clenched his teeth, not wanting to admit that a distress call followed so closely by total transponder failure could only mean one thing.

"Captain," Spock said evenly for both of them, "I am forced to conclude that the shuttle *Gamow* has crashed."

Chapter Fifteen

CONSCIOUSNESS crawled over Chekov, tasting like vomit and dirty prefab floor.

He pushed weakly up to his elbows, and a spasm of nausea cut his arms out from under him and dropped him straight back down again. He lay very still after that. Sensation gnawed its way back into his limbs and spine in burning tremors, and a hoarse, distant howling roared inside his skull. For a man who thought he'd wake up dead beneath the boots of an Elasian cohort, he knew he should be grateful to suffer only the system shock associated with a heavy phaser stun. Instead, he was just grateful that he'd never gotten around to eating any of the food Murphy prepared for them just before their capture—it meant he had nothing more in his stomach to throw up, even if he'd found the strength to do it.

Pulling his arms beneath him one hand at a time, he struggled stiffly to all fours. Simple dizziness swept over him this time, and he was able to rock slowly back onto his heels with his hands pressed flat to the dirt-strewn flooring. His cheek still throbbed from Oben's earlier blow, and his hand trembled when he lifted it to comb through his hair and rub at the back of his neck. Then, as he straightened gingerly into a back-arching stretch, the wail of sound he'd taken for tormented nerves in his own ears heaved a racking breath and howled with renewed vigor. A man, Chekov realized with a jolt. He was hearing a man's voice—screaming.

He flashed his eyes open on a half-lit storage room, encircled by grim Elasian men.

Israi's cohort squatted shoulder-to-shoulder in an arc that started more than two meters beyond Chekov's reach and extended to either side until it disappeared out of sight behind him. He opted not to bother turning to see if the circle continued. Their eyes bored into him like phaser burns, black and angry, and he realized with a horrible twisting in his belly that they had let him live this long only because they had plans other than simply killing him.

He took a deep breath and scrubbed his sleeve across his face to wipe off dirt and sweat. He winced as his arm passed over his still-tender cheekbone. The cohort watched him with the dispassionate interest of wolves around food when they're not yet hungry. Even the ragged screams from somewhere outside failed to reflect in their alien eyes. Chekov wanted to throw himself on them, beat the chill superiority from their faces until they were forced to take him down quickly and kill him where he fought. *At least Uhura and Sulu aren't here,* he found himself thinking with painful desperation. *At least they've taken the shuttle and gone.* After all their years together, he didn't want Sulu to know that he'd died so helpless and frightened, and the thought of Uhura seeing his body when the Elasians were finally done with it was enough to clog his throat with tears.

He clenched his hands into angry fists and tried to speak over the distant, horrid screaming. "Well?" His voice was hoarse, the words broken with dryness. "What are you waiting for?"

The answer came from somewhere behind him and to his left. "Nothing."

Chekov twisted to look over his shoulder. One of the

cohort looked up from where he crouched beside his fellows, black hair feathering his eyes until everything above his nose was lost in tattered shadow. He was the smallest of the Elasian men—still easily two meters tall, but lithe and whipcordlike compared to the rest of the hulking cohort. He lifted his chin to meet Chekov's gaze as the security chief turned slowly to face him.

"If you don't stay where you are, some of us may be forced to kill ourselves."

Chekov froze with one hand on the floor. That wasn't exactly what he'd expected to hear. "Have you been ordered to confine me?"

"We've been ordered not to touch you." The Elasian shifted his weight and looped his arms around his knees. "Takcas said to keep a man's-length distance from you at all times, but the walls only go back so far." He waved a weary hand back over his shoulder, and the metal prefab wall behind him gonged. "If you want to see us dead, so be it. But as *kessh* of your own cohort, we hoped you'd let us seek more honorable ends than death for disobedience."

Chekov glanced left and right among them, but still couldn't read their stony faces well enough to guess what lay behind them. "Where is Takcas?" he asked, settling crosslegged on the plascrete floor in an effort to prove he wanted no trouble.

The black-haired Elasian simply tipped his head toward the door. Outside, the screaming continued.

Chekov shook his head, frowning. "I . . . don't understand."

"Neither do we," the Elasian admitted. He sounded despondent, and infinitely worn. "Last night, the Crown Regent's men beamed down to tell us how the Federation planned to use its spineless scientists to murder our Dohlman with earthquakes and mountain slides."

"That isn't true."

The guardsman's angry black eyes burned with distrust, but he didn't answer Chekov's claim. "After we had taken you to the punishment cells," he went on as though the lieutenant had never interrupted, "Takcas told us to do nothing to interfere with your escape. And we obeyed. We did nothing when we heard the shooting as your airship took flight, then . . ." He shrugged, his expression hollow. "Then the Crown Regent's men brought us here and left us with your lifeless body. Our Dohlman did nothing to stop them or save us."

Chekov waited for him to continue. When he didn't, the lieutenant asked, "And Takcas?"

The Elasian's eyes flicked away toward the floor. The entire cohort fell into a terrible silence, and it occurred to Chekov for the first time that Takcas was the one being tortured, not the one administering it. His heart thundered hard against the base of his throat.

Outside, the soul-rending screaming had stopped.

"Why did he let us escape?" The question fell out of Chekov with desperate innocence. "He must have known that he'd be punished if we succeeded."

Invulnerable hauteur flared in the Elasian's dark face. "Our *kessh* is not afraid of any punishment!"

From the sound of what had gone on out there, he should have been. "He could have killed us in the punishment cells," Chekov said dully. "I just don't understand what he gained by letting us go."

Light dashed across the flooring, bright and sharp, and raced in a long, pale rectangle up the opposite wall. Chekov scrambled to his knees, turning, just as four Elasians he didn't recognize pushed their way through the open doorway with a fifth rigid figure suspended between them. They threw a shuddering Takcas to the feet of his waiting cohort, then left again without closing the entrance behind them.

The Elasian who'd spoken to Chekov silently broke formation. Approaching the *kessh* on hands and knees, he studied Takcas with grim intensity for a long moment before finally reaching out to brush a startlingly tender hand against the other man's face.

Takcas convulsed once, and the other guardsman jerked his hand away at the sound of his *kessh*'s rasping scream. A crash of horrid memories raced like pain through Chekov's nerves, and he croaked a breathless, "Don't!"

The Elasian shot him a suspicious glare, but didn't move again toward Takcas.

Chekov crawled forward to join them, trying to pretend that movement could give him strength to beat back years-old terrors. "Don't touch him," he whispered.

"Why?" The Elasian's voice was hard and angry, even though he skittered back out of Chekov's reach. "I told you—don't come close to us!"

"I don't care what Takcas ordered you to do." He stopped just short of making contact with the *kessh,* not sure how to proceed. Shuddering, his breath jerking out of him in uneven gasps, Takcas stared straight upward with eyes too wide and dark to see. His pupils showed only as pinpricks of black inside a ring of duller amber. "He certainly isn't going to punish you himself."

Chekov gently probed behind the *kessh*'s jawline, gritting his teeth instead of jerking back from the explosion of anguished movement that answered his touch. The nearby guardsman lunged in a blur of motion, then his hand clamped with stinging force around Chekov's wrist. Chekov gave in to the Elasian's wrenching pull for the sake of his human bones, but not before he'd found the soft, bruised patch of skin just under Takcas's hairline.

The Elasian drew back a fist to hit him, and Chekov said, very quietly, "You buy black-market equipment from the Klingons."

The alien hesitated, arm still cocked over his shoulder. "What does it matter to you with whom Elas trades?"

"It matters to all of us now." Chekov twisted his hand free from the Elasian's grip and aimed somber brown eyes down at Takcas. "He's been tortured with a Klingon-made agonizer. That burn behind his ear is where they accessed his nervous system. The agonizer . . . it . . . ." The ware-house seemed suddenly frigid, and he hugged himself against a soul-deep chill. "His nerves are overloaded," he made himself say slowly. "After all that time with the agonizer, they don't know how to feel anything but pain. Sometimes, if you keep the victim quiet and free from stimulus, his body will learn how to recover. More often, the victim simply dies."

"Don't underestimate the strength of an Elasian man." Oben's deep voice clamored off the corrugated prefab walls. "Takcas will survive, just as I survived his beating. We have many other things to talk about yet, he and I. Doing the bidding of Her Grandeur the Crown Regent is my most sacred task in this life, but I did not enjoy pretending to be Takcas's inferior just for the sake of winning trust within the Dohlman's cohort. He will pay dearly for each indignity I suffered as his 'underling.'"

Chekov raised his head to scowl at the dark figures in the doorway, but made no effort to come up from his knees. Bracketed among the four guards who had returned Takcas, Oben smiled thinly and paced beyond the doorway to stand just inside the captive cohort. "Takcas says he wrought his treachery with your help, little Starfleet *kessh.*" His smug expression looked distorted and bitter with the marks of Takcas's beating still so livid on his face. "Is that **true**?"

Did it matter? Would Oben believe him, even if it did? Chekov sat back on his heels and wished like hell he could stop shivering. "I don't think I have anything to say to you," he whispered hoarsely.

Oben only nodded as though he'd expected that answer from the beginning. "Maybe so." He pulled a disruptor from the hand of the guard closest to him, then motioned the others to encircle the waiting lieutenant. "We'll see if we can't change that soon enough."

The persistent sound of banging roused Uhura from something deeper and more painful than sleep. She woke with her face pressed into a tangle of shock webbing, one arm numb beneath her chest, and her mouth thick with the taste of smoke. The afterglow of burnt circuitry shed a faint reddish light over the cockpit, but the rest of the shuttle lay shrouded in predawn darkness.

The banging sound echoed through the metal walls again, angrily insistent. Something stirred and groaned under Uhura's outstretched hand. With an effort, she turned her head against her ropy cushion and saw Sulu peering back at her through the ruby-veined darkness.

"You all right?" The pilot's voice was hoarse.

Uhura nodded, not sure she could speak past the dry rasp of her own throat. She pushed herself up to her knees and promptly bumped her head on a crumpled sheet of metal that had punched its way through the cockpit door above her.

"We have—" Uhura heard the ragged whisper that came out as her voice, swallowed, and tried again. "We have to check on Murphy and Mutchler."

Sulu groaned again, but hauled himself up by means of the broken instrument panel. "What happened to Chekov? He told me to take off—I assumed that meant he was on board."

"He was, almost." Uhura scrubbed her hands over her eyes, trying to shake off her persistent muzziness. Lack of sleep gnawed at her, worsening the ache of abused bones and muscles. Her last glimpse of Chekov's face gnawed at her, too, a pale blur of remembered shock against the darkness. "I heard phaser fire just before he fell. I think they must have shot him."

"Damn." Sulu stood in dismayed silence for a moment, then staggered past her, slithering down on his knees to duck below the obstruction in the door. From somewhere farther back in the shuttle, the pounding had started again. "All right, we're coming—"

Uhura didn't bother getting to her feet. She simply crawled below the crumpled sheet metal, then crouched on the threshold of the shuttle's main cabin, trying to make her eyes resolve shapes out of the vague darkness. After a moment, she thought she could see the charcoal outline of a sprawled body against the far wall. She scuttled in that direction, carefully feeling for shrapnel on the floor. After a moment, her searching fingers hit warm flesh instead of cold metal.

"Wha—?" Mutchler's voice was a startled croak, as if her touch had jogged him awake. "What happened?"

"We hit the defense shield and crashed." Uhura slid her fingers down his arm, hunting for the safety strap she'd thrown over him. She found it jammed tight under his shoulder and worried the clip free to unhook it from around him. "Are you hurt?"

The geologist's bark of pain as he tried to sit up answered her. Uhura reached out to hold him still. "Don't move. Where are you hurt?"

"Leg. Left leg." Mutchler's fingers clamped vise-tight on her wrist, and he gasped brokenly. "Don't touch it! I think—I think it's broken."

Patiently, Uhura waited until he caught his breath and let her go. "There must be an intact medical kit in here somewhere. I'll get you some analgesics for the pain." She turned back to the dark interior of the shuttle and saw a familiar slender shadow move toward her. "Sulu, did you find Murphy?"

"Yes." The bleak tone of the helmsman's voice told her without words that the security guard was dead. Uhura couldn't answer, newly aware of the raw ache in her throat. "Here. I found you a medical kit for Mutchler."

She reached out with a wordless murmur of thanks to take it from him, but froze before their hands touched. The metal walls around them had begun to vibrate again with the echo of muffled pounding, and it certainly wasn't coming from Mutchler. Instead, it sounded as if it was coming from the back end of the shuttle.

"Good Lord!" Uhura spun around so fast she nearly fell over a dislodged seat. "Sulu, do you hear—"

"Yes. Don't go near it." Sulu scrabbled over debris to the far wall of the shuttle. Uhura heard the crisp pop of a locker door unsealing; then her eyes burned with the sudden light of an emergency lamp. When she managed to squint them open again, it was to see shadows chasing themselves up the back wall as Sulu approached it.

"Be careful," she said when he paused and cocked his head to listen. "It might be a trap."

Sulu shook his head, a torn scrap of his uniform collar fluttering with the motion. "No. I can hear someone crying." He leaned forward and dragged at a tortured metal panel whose red and white stripes identified it as the access to the warp core. "I think—" He grunted with the effort of pulling. "—that someone's stuck inside here."

"But who—" Uhura broke off as the metal panel sheared free of its splintered brackets. Light from Sulu's emergency lamp shot into the empty space behind it, striking golden sparks from heavily jeweled arms. Slowly, a dark head lifted from those cradling arms, showing them a sharply angled and familiar face.

"Israi!" Uhura blinked in utter astonishment. "What are you doing here?"

This time, the Dohlman of Elas did not flare up in instant fury at the use of her name. "My *kessh* hid me here, Uhura. He thought I would be safe." Tears brimmed from her almond eyes, sliding down to join the trickle of cinnamon brown blood spilling from her split lip. "I've been pounding on that door for hours. I couldn't make it open from inside, and I thought you were all dead—"

"Hey, it's all right." Sulu reached down to pull her out. "Where are you hurt?"

"Just here, from the torn metal." Israi brushed her snake-thick curls back as simply as a child, to show him a brownish line of drying blood across her shoulder. "And my face. It's nothing."

Despite herself, Uhura smiled at the Dohlman's tone of quavering bravado. "It may be nothing," she agreed, reaching for the medical kit Sulu had dropped beside her. "But we still don't have to ignore it. Just wait until Sulu and I have splinted Dr. Mutchler's leg, and we'll bandage you up." She paused, waiting for the pilot to join her. She was surprised when he didn't move. "Sulu, did you hear me?" Another, longer pause. "Sulu?"

Slowly, the helmsman turned his head to look at her. There was an odd rigidity to his expression, an unnatural stiffness around the mouth that usually smiled so easily. The wooden look clashed with the fierce leap of panic in his dark eyes. "I—Uhura, I can't—unless the Dohlman orders me—"

"Oh, my God." Uhura's appalled gaze went from Sulu's wet fingers to the equally wet smudge of tears on Israi's bare arms. The Dohlman gasped in comprehension, then reached up and touched the moisture on her face. She transferred her fingers to her mouth and tasted them in amazement.

"The tears." Her voice shivered, torn between apprehension and delight. "Finally, I am mature. I have the tears of a Dohlman." After a moment, she lifted her head and laid one hand proudly on Sulu's shoulder. "And you, Starfleet pilot, are the first true bondsman of my cohort."

Chapter Sixteen

"HAVE WE GOTTEN sensor readings on the shuttle's location yet?"

At the security station, Ensign Howard looked up as Kirk and his first officer exited the turbolift behind him. Faint dark smudges underlined eyes already glossy with fatigue, and it occurred to Kirk that he couldn't say for certain when Howard had last been off the bridge. Just counting back quickly in his mind, Kirk could place the young ensign here for at least the last two shifts.

"No, sir." Exhaustion made the ensign's voice uncharacteristically despondent. "We're having trouble getting clear readings from the surface past the Elasian armada."

Kirk frowned, trotting down the short flight of stairs. "Are they jamming us?"

Howard sighed. "Not exactly, sir. The Crown Regent has positioned her flagship in firing range in orbit above the Elasian mining camp. The single-man fighters in her armada have, well . . ." Howard waved in frustration at whatever played across his security screens. "Dispersed! They're scattering all over the outer atmosphere, shooting their phasers at random and exciting the ionosphere until it's impossible to get any kind of coherent signal through."

"Firing at random?" Kirk glanced curiously at Spock, then slipped behind Howard's shoulder to look where the ensign pointed. "I doubt that." He felt Spock move up beside him.

A three-dimensional globe representing Rakatan inched around on its axis as the *Enterprise* circled it in real time. Bright scarlet blips marked each of the three hundred Elasian gunships, speckled all throughout the upper atmosphere like mites on a sun-warmed log. Between them, flashes of white and yellow displayed the path of their phaser bursts as they fired across the ozone at each other. Shot answered shot, beam met beam until each and every salvo was contacted by another ship's phaser blast and stopped in midflight, rendered useless. Kirk watched the intricate net they wove between themselves for almost a full minute before he recognized the antiquated pattern they made.

"Not random, Mr. Howard," he announced, leaning over the ensign's shoulder to tap a finger on his screen. "Very carefully planned. Haven't you ever seen a geodesic defensive array?"

Howard's eyes danced all over the display as he tried to retrace his captain's reasoning. "Uh . . . no, sir . . ."

"Understandable, Ensign." Spock came to his defense with a reproving sideways look at Kirk. "It is an outdated battle tactic developed in the twenty-second century, primarily to thwart ground-based missile fire."

"But, sir . . ." Howard craned a frown back at Kirk. "Why would the Elasians be defending against ground missiles on an uninhabited planet?"

"Because," Kirk sighed, motioning for Spock to step aside so he could slip from behind the security console and back out onto the bridge, "a geodesic defensive array has exactly the side effect you've already noted. It disrupts everything from radio signals to transporter beams." He crossed his arms and scowled at the planet hanging before him on the viewscreen. "For some reason, our friend the Crown Regent doesn't want anyone beaming off Rakatan."

"Or escaping it by shuttlecraft." Spock answered Kirk's questioning glance by pointing at the Klingon frigate hanging motionless against the glare of the rising sun. "In her current position, the Crown Regent can easily intercept any shuttle attempting to dock with the *Enterprise*."

"You know, Spock—if the Elasians really do want Rakatan for its dilithium resources, cutting off everyone's access to the planet isn't exactly winning them any favors."

Spock dipped a small, acknowledging nod. "And yet, judging by our experience with her, the Crown Regent is efficient to the point of ruthlessness." He cocked his head and followed Kirk's gaze to the viewscreen. "The only logical explanation is that she has some other goal in mind."

"And it isn't very hard to guess what that goal is."

"Captain?"

Kirk turned to face his first officer, drumming a fist on the arm of his command chair as his mind raced ahead of his words. "Think about it, Spock—as Israi's guardian, the Crown Regent is the de facto ruler of Elas. As her aunt, she's also the heir to the Dohlmanyi." He waved toward silent, sea blue Rakatan. "All she has to do is get Israi killed on some dangerous, unsettled planet, and she'll rule Elas permanently."

Spock considered for a heartbeat, eyebrows raised. "Given the ties the Crown Regent appears to have established with the Klingons, Captain, such an outcome could prove disruptive to peace in that quadrant of the Federation." He flicked dark eyes back to Kirk. "However, if the Elasian claim to Rakatan is proven valid, and if there are, indeed, significant dilithium deposits here—"

Kirk waved that line of thought aside. "I'm starting to doubt there's any dilithium at all on Rakatan. You've talked to Bascomb—it must just have been an excuse to get Israi here." Suddenly decisive, Kirk bounded up to the turbolift.

"Mr. Howard—have Mr. Scott called up to the bridge, then relieve yourself of duty." He shook a stern finger at the ensign, but smiled to lessen the sting. "Take a full shift off, or I'll report you to your boss. Mr. Spock, you're coming with me. We're going to see if we can't rescue a certain young Dohlman from her aunt's tender loving care."

Spock followed him to the turbolift at a more appropriately dignified pace. "You have a plan by which to bypass the Crown Regent's defenses?"

"The simplest one in the world, Spock." Kirk ducked into the 'lift when the doors were barely open, then paused to hold them wide so his first officer could enter. "We're going to come at her from the direction she least expects us—from below."

The silence inside the wrecked shuttle seemed endless to Uhura. Israi was smiling at Sulu, not her usual flash of amusement, but a slow radiant smile like a sunrise. Sulu stood pinioned by her dark gaze, suspended between fascination and terror like an insect transfixed by a stalking reptile. The shuttle's medical kit, containing their only supply of antidote to Israi's tears, dangled forgotten in his hands.

"Your Glory," Uhura said quietly. "Would you please tell Sulu to bring me the medical kit for Dr. Mutchler?"

The Dohlman swung to face her, almond eyes alight. "So! You acknowledge my bonding of this male from your cohort?"

Uhura didn't have time to wonder if that had been a tactical mistake. "Dr. Mutchler needs painkillers and a cold pack for his leg," she said, trying as hard as she could to keep her voice calm. "Can I have the medical kit?"

"Of course." Israi's chin lifted with a more confident arrogance, despite her blood-streaked shoulder and bandaged arm. "But I cannot let your former bondsman run to your bidding now that he is mine. Come and get from him what you need."

Uhura gritted her teeth in dismay. Israi's pride in her newfound maturity was going to make what she had to do a hundred times harder. And Sulu wasn't helping. He stood with his back to Uhura, unable even to hold the medical kit out toward her without Israi's authorizing command.

Taking a deep breath, Uhura slipped Mutchler's hand out of hers and tried to give him a reassuring pat. The geologist's gray eyes had fixed on Israi with all of the fear and none of the fascination that Sulu showed. "Don't worry," Uhura told him on the merest thread of a whisper. "I won't let her cry on you."

Mutchler's gaze darted toward her. "But him—can't you do anything—"

Uhura laid a shushing finger across his lips, afraid that Rakatan's intense silence would carry his hoarse whisper to Israi. The geologist's eyes narrowed and he fell silent.

The canted floor of the shuttle shifted as Uhura crossed it, settling with an odd groan as if the ground beneath it were not entirely solid. Uhura slipped and caught her balance with a gasp, figuring it couldn't hurt to make Israi think she was scared. She *was* scared. Her heartbeat thundered in her ears, driven by the knowledge that she only had one shot at this.

"Sulu." Uhura tugged at the medical kit, but couldn't force it from his frozen grip. She swung around to frown at Israi, who watched her with an odd mixture of triumph and teenage mischief in her almond eyes. Uhura had to force words out through her teeth to keep her anger from showing. "Israi, please tell Sulu to give me the medical kit."

The Dohlman smiled again. "Give your former Dohlman her medical kit, bondsman."

Without a sound, Sulu relinquished the medical kit to Uhura, and she slipped a hand inside to rummage among its contents. Tiny ampules of inhalants and cans of spray bandage tumbled together beneath her fingers, but she didn't dare look down to separate them, knowing that would attract Israi's attention.

"We'll need a splint for Mutchler's leg too," she said, talking at random to cover her lack of movement toward the geologist. She found the hyposprays and fingered her way along them, knowing from McCoy's briefing that the antidote to Israi's tears was stored in the last of the five side pockets. "You'll have to tell Sulu to open the locker for me, Your Glory." Uhura fumbled with the pocket flap, her fingers sliding in at last to reach for the reassuring coolness of a hypospray. "With the power gone in the shuttle, I can't—"

It happened almost too fast for Uhura to follow. With all her strength, she yanked the hypospray of antidote out of the medical kit and stabbed it toward Sulu's shoulder. At the same moment, a dark hand snapped out and caught at her wrist with steel-wire strength. Uhura stopped as if she'd run into a forcefield, the hypospray held quivering only a few centimeters away from its target.

"What," Israi asked coldly, "is in that medicine dispenser?"

Uhura bit her lip to moisten a mouth gone dry with failure and fear. Her life rode now on how well she could judge Elasian psychology. If she made another mistake—

"It's a chemical antidote to your tears," she told Israi bluntly. "Because I don't want to give my bondsman up to you."

"Ah." Israi stared at her for a long measuring moment, then reached up with her free hand to wrench the hypospray out of Uhura's fingers. Its automatic trigger released a useless spray of mist when she slammed it against the wall beside her. Uhura tried to swing the medical kit out of her reach, but the Dohlman was too quick for her again. She yanked it free and sent it hurtling out the shuttle door into darkness, with one negligently powerful snap of her slender arm.

"The painkillers—!" Uhura protested.

"You had other doses of antidote in there," Israi said, turning calmly to face her. Sulu stood at their shoulders, face rigid with his inability to intervene in the confrontation. "If not, you would have thrown the kit away when you tried to free your bondsman."

Uhura flinched at the accuracy of the Dohlman's interpretation of her actions. *Just because she's young and arrogant,* Uhura reminded herself, *doesn't mean she's stupid.*

"Dohlman Uhura." Israi reached a hand out to close around her wrist again, gently this time. "I do not blame you for trying to retain your cohort. It is what an honorable Dohlman should do." A frown crept onto her face and her grip tightened. "Although you should not have used such a craven method as an *antidote*. You should have challenged me, tears against tears, to see which of us is the stronger."

Uhura took a deep breath. "Since I am not of Elas, Your Glory, that would not be—" She paused, searching for the best word. "—diplomatic."

Israi snorted and released her. "Diplomacy is for the spineless. From now on, Uhura, you and I will settle our differences without it. Agreed?"

Uhura considered how well her gamble of being honest about the antidote had served her, and nodded. "Agreed."

"Good." The Dohlman pointed a slim, imperious finger at Mutchler, who was watching them in gasping silence from the other side of the shuttle. "Now, go and tend that idiot geologist with the medications you carry on your belt. And tell him he is safe from me." Israi stood back, resting one hand proudly on Sulu's stiff shoulder. "A Dohlman is measured by the strength of her cohort, and I would scorn to have a scientist among mine."

Years ago—when he was still a young ensign, and hadn't yet figured out that he was destructible—Chekov had felt the agonizer's kiss rip him open and tear him inside out. It had lasted for only a minute, maybe not even that long. But it had been enough to father nightmares for more than a year, and to make him awkwardly excuse himself from a class at the Security Academy during a lecture on what the agonizer did to a victim's nervous system. Only a year ago, the prospect of being face-to-face with Klingons during border negotiations had kept him sleepless for three awful nights, praying that nothing went wrong enough to allow the capture and torture of hostages.

And now, on a planet half a galaxy away, here he was.

They all but carried him across the mining compound. If they had let him walk he could have attempted escape, and possibly been killed in the process. As it was, he didn't even have the leverage to fight effectively. He made one attempt to plant his feet against the doorjambs to keep from entering their destination building, but Oben only shoved his legs aside with one shoulder and barked at the others to bring him along.

Chekov's eyes caught on the row of portable control stations lined up against one wall as someone slammed the door behind them. A power-frame manager butted up beside a field communications panel, with the security monitor for the camp defense screen tucked into the corner away from them both. A dozen armor-clad Elasians milled around the equipment, pointedly taking no notice of Oben's arrival or the delivery of his prisoner to the briefing table on the other side of the room. For some reason, Chekov had thought they'd drag him somewhere dark and sterile to do their interrogation, not a place so grossly public as the base of camp operations. Humiliation mingled with the flutters of terror in his chest, and he closed his eyes against the crowd of faces as they pushed him flat atop the narrow table and pinned him there.

"On Elas, kidnapping is punishable by the loss of both your legs."

He opened his eyes to find Oben at his shoulder, hands resting lightly on the edge of the table.

"Kidnapping a member of the Dohlmanyi, punishable by death."

An anger more comfortable and familiar than fear pushed at Chekov in an effort to break to the surface. "We've done nothing to your Dohlman."

"Prove it." Oben's face was still, and unconvinced. "Tell me where she is."

"I don't know."

The older Elasian shrugged, his gaze drifting to one side as he reached for something Chekov couldn't see. "Not according to Takcas. He placed her on board your shuttle, knowing that you would escape and take her far from here." He straightened again and turned over the small device in his palm as though marveling at its simple construction. "Now we have you, and we don't have her." Frosty green eyes flicked to Chekov. "I would like to rectify that."

The dry overhead lights stitched silver sparks along the agonizer's edges. "I don't know what you're talking about. . . ."

Oben didn't ask again.

Chekov tried to steel himself—tried to believe that knowing what to expect this time would at least help preserve his dignity while they used this Klingon technology to winnow him down to a shuddering scrap. Instead, primitive fear took over the instant cold metal brushed his skin. He exploded away from Oben's touch, twisting, kicking, wrenching himself to the edge of the table with no thoughts in his mind but to run. He somehow missed the actual moment when he tore free, but he knew when he hit the floor, and scrabbled for the outside door without looking behind. Shouts of anger and alarm boiled up from all over the room. The men who before had minded their panels with such studied disinterest suddenly broke away from their stations in a pack and rushed for him. Chekov knew he couldn't really fight his way through the wall of them, but he had to try. He landed a dozen blows before their combined weight overpowered him and toppled him to the floor in a tangle of violent struggle.

"So . . ." Oben's laughter, surprisingly soft and amused, lit his battered face with delight. He leaned forward to brace hands on knees, and smile. "This isn't your first exposure to the agonizer, is it?" Whatever he saw in Chekov's eyes made him laugh again, and he straightened. "Isn't that intriguing."

Chekov clenched his hands, unable to move in any other way. "We had no idea your Dohlman was on board—"

"I know that."

"We were only trying to reach our ship." The truth rushed out of him, too harmless to matter, even to him. "If Israi was somewhere on board, she was taken to the *Enterprise* along with the others." Surely Oben would realize there was nothing either of them could do. Chekov couldn't bear the thought of being tortured to death for simply knowing nothing.

"Your shuttle never reached the *Enterprise*," Oben stated with deliberate slowness. He knelt, first on one knee, then on both, and Chekov's heart thundered breathlessly against his rib cage. "It couldn't have, we know that. Which means the Dohlman is still somewhere on Rakatan, and you're going to tell me where." He displayed the agonizer between two fingers, and waited.

Chekov hated the thin, frightened sliver of voice that crept out of him. ". . . I don't know where she is . . ."

This time, he could only buck once against the bodies holding him when Oben put the agonizer in place. Its slick, alien contours moved against his temple, and he squeezed his eyes shut in anticipation of agony. "I don't know where she is!" he cried, helpless. Then inspiration sliced through him on the memories of long-ago pain. "But I can show you how to find her . . ."

Oben answered with a silence so long, Chekov felt the first hope he'd known since waking up in the Elasian warehouse. He dared, very slowly, to open his eyes.

"You know what will happen if you've lied to us," Oben warned him darkly.

Chekov nodded, never taking his eyes away from Oben's. No belief flowered in the grim Elasian face, but the agonizer's threatening touch lifted. Chekov found himself suddenly able to breathe again, dizzy with the prospect of freedom. "I would do anything to avoid that," he promised hoarsely. "Believe me."

Chapter Seventeen

RAKATAN'S SUN rose grudgingly out of charcoal clouds, its sullen fire picking fragments of twisted wreckage out of an encircling sea of red-gray mud. Even as Uhura watched, braced on her elbows in the crumpled hatch, a shard of nacelle housing shifted and disappeared. She made a wordless sound of dismay as her last hope of freeing Sulu sank with it. There was no way she could find the lost medical kit in this swamp.

"Any luck fixing the communicator?" Already mud-stained to the thighs, Sulu clung to the outside of the shuttle with both hands to keep from sinking in the ooze that had saved them. Although he spoke to Uhura, his gaze slid inevitably behind her, drawn like iron to Israi's silent magnet.

"No," Uhura answered, in a voice almost as toneless as his. "All the circuits are burned out."

Sulu grunted. "Then we're going to have to walk out of here. The mud is only bad around the shuttle. Away from it, there's a hard crust we can walk on, and a sort of shoreline not too far away."

Uhura pulled herself through the hatch, balancing carefully on what remained of the starboard nacelle. *Gamow* canted steeply beneath her, its blunt nose buried in a mud-softened impact crater. The shuttle's main cabin was buoyed up by the nacelle beneath her feet, but the other side, from which Sulu had jettisoned the port nacelle, had sunk deep into the churned-up mud. From the occasional bubbling noises that swam up through the metal hull, Uhura suspected the ship was still slowly sinking.

She stood on tiptoe to peer across the top of the shuttle, but from this angle all she could see was the shredded metallic lacing of the disruptor blast in the roof. "How far is the shore from here?"

"Less than a hundred meters." Sulu stepped up on the nacelle behind her and pointed to the right, where a pale gray bluff of volcanic rock ended the sprawl of mud. Thunderheads loomed in the sky beyond it, shrouding the crest of Rakatan Mons in a dark cloak of clouds. "The mudflat is long, but not very wide."

"That's because it's really an abandoned river channel." Mutchler wriggled his head out of the empty hatch beside them and eyed the surrounding mudscape with professional interest. "Probably left over from the last ice age, when Rakatan got a lot more rain than it does now." He leaned down and scraped a drying curl of clay from the mud-splashed shuttle, rubbing it to reddish dust between his fingers. "Hmm. Smectite and montmorillonite. About what you'd expect from weathered volcanic ash."

Uhura exchanged amused looks with Sulu, relieved to see a glint of his usual humor beneath the somber mask Israi had made of his face. If there was anything short of impending disaster that could distract a scientist from making scientific observations, Uhura had yet to find it. "Are you ready to go, Dr. Mutchler?"

"Oh, no. I want to salvage my seismic monitor first." He wriggled back into the shuttle before they could haul him out. "Don't worry, it's portable."

Something bulky and Starfleet red tumbled out of the hatch as soon as he was gone. With a gasp, Uhura recognized it as the bundle of survival packs she'd put together while waiting for the sun to rise. She snatched at it, spurred by a horrid vision of all their food sinking under the mud, and managed to catch it by one strap just before it hit the clay.

"Uhura, why do you allow that rock-grubbing insect even to speak?" Israi's voice demanded from somewhere inside the shuttle. Another bundle of blankets slid out the hatch before Uhura could drop the one she held. Fortunately, Sulu caught that one. "He has been witless beyond helping since first we met him."

Uhura frowned, finding a dry place on the nacelle for the survival kits. "How do you know that?"

"Because he babbles in words that make no sense." Uhura heard an indignant yelp from inside, and then a third package sailed out the hatch. This time it consisted of Scott Mutchler's field pack, belted with hammers, sledges, and a specialized tricorder.

Uhura sighed. "Israi, all that means is that your language has no equivalents for the scientific words he uses."

"Humph." Israi appeared in the collapsed hatch and dropped the last piece of salvageable equipment—Chekov's Klingon disruptor—into Uhura's hands. The Dohlman regarded the expanse of red-gray mud around them, then turned her intent gaze on Sulu. The pilot let out a quiet sigh, then pulled in another breath and held it tight, as if her nearness both calmed and disturbed him. *Oh, Chekov,* Uhura thought, *I wish you were here to help me cope with this.*

"You can get me out of here, bondsman?" the Dohlman demanded.

"Yes."

Israi nodded and swung herself through the hatch without another word. Her angular face had lost much of its aggressive uncertainty, Uhura saw. Instead, her almond eyes

165

glittered with a new and serene confidence, born of knowing that men would now die for her. The expression made her look intensely like her older sister, Elaan.

In matching silence, Sulu slung the bundle of blankets over his shoulder and stepped forward to lift the small Dohlman in his arms. It apparently never occurred to him, Uhura thought wryly, that Uhura might not be the best one to support Mutchler's lurching steps through the mud.

An unfamiliar alarm went off inside the wrecked shuttle, a thin rising whine like a wasp's warning buzz. Uhura threw a bewildered glance at Sulu and saw his equally baffled head-shake. Then Mutchler cursed in a voice that barely sounded like his own. Uhura could hear him scrabbling frantically across the floor toward them, his splinted leg dragging behind him.

"We've got to get out of here, *now!*" The geologist wrestled himself through what was left of the hatch, his resin-epoxy splint catching painfully against one edge. Pain crashed white across his narrow face, but Mutchler hauled himself free despite it, half-falling and half-vaulting down to a mercifully soft landing in the mud. Uhura leaned out to steady him when he swayed, and he slewed around to catch her by the shoulder, his thin fingers digging hard through her uniform jacket. "There's been an earthquake near the summit! If we get caught in this damned thixotropic mud when the surface waves get here—"

The panic in the geologist's voice told Uhura more than the unfamiliar words. She slapped his field pack into his hands and shrugged the bundle of survival kits over her own shoulders, then plunged into the mud beside him so he could use her as a crutch. The wet clay dragged at her feet, sludge-thick and determined to cling to her boots. In minutes, she had sunk so deep that each step became a battle.

"*Hurry!*" Mutchler groaned, as if she and not he were the one lagging behind. The thin air of Rakatan had already broken Uhura's breath into ragged gasps that burned against her ribs. Mercifully, the geologist seemed to be less affected by the lack of oxygen. Perhaps he was used to it. "We don't have much time!"

They labored through the mud at a heartbreakingly slow pace. Sulu had already rounded the shuttle ahead of them, grimly determined to see his Dohlman safe at all costs. Israi, however, had not lost track of them. She cast a frowning look back at Uhura over the helmsman's shoulder.

"Have you forgotten the one of your cohort you gave death to in the shuttle?" she demanded. "You wouldn't leave his unburned body for the crows?"

Mutchler saved Uhura from having to answer that. "There *are* no crows on this damned planet!" he snarled. "Get it through your empty Elasian head—if we don't get out of this mud in the next two minutes, we're going to die!" The geologist groaned as his splinted leg caught on some snag beneath the mud. "And all because you don't want to get your glorious feet muddy," he added, soft but vehement enough for her to hear.

Israi spat at him in wordless fury, then shocked Uhura by twisting out of Sulu's grip to land in a staggering splash of mud. "No!" She shoved the pilot back when he would have picked her up again. "Go back and help that idiot geologist. I *order* you!"

Sulu scowled and picked her up anyway, but only to toss her a meter toward the shore, out of the shuttle's impact crater. She landed on a stiff scum of drier clay that cracked and grumbled beneath her weight, but held firm. The helmsman didn't wait to see if she stayed or went on. He turned back and helped Uhura tug Mutchler's leg free of the sucking clay that now engulfed them to their knees.

"I'll drag him by the shoulders," Sulu said curtly. "You hold up his broken leg."

Uhura nodded, too winded to bother with words, and bent to her task. Despite their rough handling, Mutchler seemed impervious to pain. "Hurry!" he urged again, his voice cracking with desperation. Uhura heard the now-familiar roar of tearing earth, far away but getting closer. Memories of the Dohlman's collapsing quarters crashed over her, and lent her aching legs new strength. *"Hurry!"*

With one last, lung-tearing effort, Uhura helped heave the geologist up onto the drier crust of the mud. It broke beneath their combined weight, like the thin edge of newly frozen ice. Mutchler's breath hissed in pain as part of Uhura's weight fell on his broken leg. Cursing, Sulu shoved the younger man up onto the hard surface again. This time, it held him.

"Thank the Lord—" Uhura moved a careful meter away before hauling herself out. Sulu did the same thing on the other side.

Mutchler struggled up onto his elbows stubbornly. "We're not safe, not until we're up on those rocks. Help me up."

She groaned, but went to help Sulu hoist him to his feet. Surprisingly, Israi had waited for them. Without a word, the Dohlman of Elas pulled the geologist's field pack from his shoulder, then turned and started running for the ridge. The rest of them followed at the best pace they could manage.

The first shock waves hit while they were still on the crusted mud. Uhura felt the swaying, sealike motion of the clay and heard it sigh beneath them as it shifted. Instinctive panic thundered through her at the thought of being stuck in the engulfing morass again. She forgot her burning lungs and aching legs, forgot the heavy, clinging jackets of mud on her boots. With a gasp of utter terror, she grabbed at Mutchler and dragged him toward the shoreline ridge.

They made it with only moments to spare. Uhura collapsed against the blessedly gritty and solid rock face, barely feeling the tug when Israi pulled her up to safety. More shock waves chased across the mud crust after them, but they dampened out when they hit the ridge, giving them only a slight shaking. Cracks followed the crests of each wave, twining and intertwining until, with a vast, moaning grumble, the entire lake of mud bubbled and turned itself liquidly over.

"Oh, my God—" In the center, the shuttle pitched and

sank beneath the mud with a breathtaking suddenness. Uhura blinked, barely able to believe what she had seen. A last set of shock waves shivered through the red-gray clay, this time slapping foamy wavelets against their ridge. There could be no doubt. The mud that had cushioned and supported them a few minutes ago now sloshed like water beneath their feet.

"Thixotropic clay." Mutchler's voice may have been shredded with shock and pain, but it remained stubbornly pedantic. "Solid under long-term stress, liquid under a sudden shock. It always causes the most damage in an earthquake."

"I know," Sulu said bleakly. Uhura felt him shudder where his shoulder pressed against hers, and wondered if it was the nearness of death or the memory of how he'd first responded to the threat of it that bothered him. Even now, the pilot had one arm wrapped around Israi's bare shoulders in an unwilling but fiercely protective embrace.

The Dohlman took a deep breath and lifted her head, scrubbing at her cheeks with muddy hands. "Idiot geologist, you were right about the earthquake coming," she admitted with immense reluctance. "I—I wish I hadn't called you witless."

As close as a Dohlman could ever come to an apology, Uhura guessed in half-hysterical amusement. She glanced over her shoulder to see if Mutchler appreciated Israi's grand gesture, only to see the geologist staring transfixed up at the crest of Rakatan Mons. If he'd heard Israi, he gave no sign of it.

"What is it?" Uhura demanded, alarmed by his odd silence. "Dr. Mutchler, what's the matter?" And then, as she saw the way the muscles clenched in his bloodless cheeks, "Is it your leg?"

Mutchler made a painful sound, something between a bitter laugh and a gasp. "My leg is the least of our problems. Look there. The earthquake must have set it off."

Uhura followed his shakily pointing finger and blinked, unable at first to take in what she was seeing. Above the liquid expanse of shivering mud, dark clouds had congealed around the distant crest of Rakatan Mons. Lightning spit faint flashes through them, but they looked too thick and wrinkled to be thunderclouds. Even as Uhura watched, another ruffled wall of black curled up from behind the rest, and this time she saw the telltale glint of volcanic fire exposed for one brief moment in its heart.

"Oh, my God." The realization kicked inside her stomach like an exploding rocket. "The volcano's erupting."

"Only spineless human worms would think up a plan so inefficient and crude."

Chekov kept his eyes locked on the turbulent scenery outside the flyer window, and willed his face to stay impassive. Considering he'd only made up this plan a few hours ago, with the threat of a Klingon agonizer hanging over his face, the efficiency of it seemed nothing short of miraculous. *It was good enough to get you this far,* he thought at Oben bitterly. And the plan only had to work a short while longer.

"It isn't inefficient." Chekov tried to sound brusquely disdainful, but had a feeling he only sounded scared. "We took the geologist to this seismic station in the first place so that we could establish the details of our rendezvous plan."

Oben made a face and lounged in his seat near the front of the flyer's passenger cabin. "The Mutchler geologist said he was doing repairs."

"He lied." *Just like I'm lying now.* "We left a recording device there so that we could leave messages for each other if we became separated. If my Dohlman hasn't already gone there to contact me, then I will at least be able to leave instructions for her to find when she reaches the station later. I can tell her to meet me anywhere you say. Or lead you to wherever she is waiting for me."

"You would do this?" Oben asked, eyes narrowed. "Betray your Dohlman and your cohort?"

Chekov swallowed hard against a shiver of remembered fear, and turned back to the flyer window. "All my Dohlman can do is kill me," he said softly, intentionally echoing Oben's words from the night before.

The guardsman laughed darkly, but asked him nothing further.

Outside the flyer's window, clouds the color of smoke smeared the landscape to a minimalist blur. Chekov had watched the first rolling thunderhead sweep down on them when they were barely north of the mining complex, only to realize it wasn't rain pattering against his window when a dark layer of ash caught and built up in a crescent along the trailing edge. He'd wondered then if Rakatan Mons normally spit up such volumes of burnt material, but didn't think Oben would be predisposed toward answering his questions. For the first time since separating from the rest of the party, Chekov found himself wishing Dr. Mutchler were here.

"You are worse than the scientist maggots who feed off the corpse of this planet."

Takcas's voice startled Chekov. It was the first time the *kessh* had spoken to him since they were herded into the flyer's passenger compartment more than an hour ago. Coming out of his long silence after Chekov's supposed display of treachery, the big Elasian's words burned through him like fire.

"The science-maggots are honest in their weakness. They slink behind our backs to steal their rocks and readings— they make no attempt to curry our acceptance or walk upright among us."

It doesn't matter what you think of me, Chekov told Takcas silently, still staring out his window. *Your understanding was never part of this plan.* But his hands clenched within the manacles behind his back, and he couldn't stop a swell of frustrated anger from twisting his stomach full of acid.

"I am ashamed that we are both called *kessh*. Even a soft-bellied carrion crab would not betray its own for a few more moments of pitiful living." Seat leather creaked and hard Elasian boots struck decking as Takcas shifted and moved to stand. "I should do your Dohlman the favor of killing you, little tick, since you obviously haven't the dignity needed to kill yourself."

A crash of noise behind him jerked Chekov around, and he ended up facing the seats along the flyer's other wall just as Takcas slammed back against the bulkhead and sat down heavily. Oben stood over the *kessh* with one hand cocked back as though to strike again, the other poised on his disruptor while he waited to see if Takcas would fight. Takcas glowered hatefully up at the other Elasian, but didn't try to stand again. Chekov had to grip the cushion of his own seat to keep himself from leaping up to interfere.

"What a brave dog you are," Oben commented acidly. He kicked Takcas's feet out of the narrow aisle, then went back to his own seat at the front of the compartment. "You bark loudly for someone who is only here to flush out Israi if she refuses to come when I call for her."

"So you claim." Takcas rolled to his knees with surprising grace considering his hands were manacled behind his back just like Chekov's. "But I am not like you and this gutless parasite—I will not betray my sworn mistress."

"You do not have to choose to betray anyone. Under the right inducement, you scream as well as any parasite." Oben propped his feet up on a sliver of window frame and smiled evilly. "You forget, *Kessh* Takcas—I know."

What could only have been deep humiliation darkened Takcas's face to the color of tea. Chekov leaned across the seat back in front of him, suddenly unable to sit in brooding silence any longer. "Why don't you use that agonizer on yourself?" he snarled, nodding at the tiny device hanging in wait on Oben's belt. "Show us how bravely you don't scream while it strips you down to nothing."

"Stop it!" Takcas lunged across the aisle, face still red, and came to his knees on the floor next to Chekov to meet his startled gaze eye-to-eye. This time, Oben only sighed with weary disinterest and made no move to separate them. "I want no words from you in my defense! You sit here in silence, unable to explain away even your own filthy cowardice, then you wish for me to be grateful when you rise up to strike at my enemies! No! I vomit on your sympathy! I spit on your deceit!"

Chekov could only stare at Takcas while his own face burned. *Lying,* he thought in an agony of frustration. *If only I were a better liar, I could think of something—anything!— to say.* Instead, he clenched his jaw around his silence and remained painfully aware of just how much he would despise anyone who did what Takcas believed he was doing right now.

Beneath them, the flyer began its swift, even descent, and ash hissed like rain against the outside bulkhead.

"Go ahead," Chekov told Takcas dully. He just wished it didn't hurt so much to see the fierce disgust on the Elasian's face. "I would do the same, if I were you."

Gold eyes met brown ones with such force that Chekov nearly looked away, ashamed of the scaffolding of lies he'd erected between them. Then, the instant before his resolve broke, he saw something move in those Elasian eyes like water under ice.

"Human!"

Breath catching in startlement, Chekov snapped his attention back to the front of the flyer. They'd opened the door between the passenger cabin and the cockpit, and another of his captors leaned through the narrow hatch to scowl across the craft at him.

"We are at the top of the cleft. Say if this is where you meant to take us."

He turned away from Takcas, just as glad for the distraction, and peered through the ash-fogged window to study the ground as it approached below them. "Yes." Drifting ash had obscured the FGS identifiers on the sides and roof of the tiny seismic station, but a tall stake with a placard reading NO. 3 at its top still canted awkwardly just off to one side. Chekov had tried righting that sign while he and Sulu waited for Mutchler to install the laser sensor yesterday, but it had stubbornly resisted fixing. Now it seemed to stand there in effigy of all the other things around him that might be past the point of repair. "You'll find a landing area one hundred meters east of the station."

Then something struck him hard from behind, catching him at waist level and throwing him to the deck between the seats. Chekov tried to turn himself, but the space was too short and narrow, the sudden weight on top of him too heavy for him to displace without anything to brace himself or hands to help him. He met the deck facedown, and felt the heavy thump of the flyer touching down just as a growl of warm breath hissed next to his ear.

"Forgive my ignorance and my violence, *Kessh* Chekov," Takcas whispered, almost too quickly and softly to be understood. "But I can't let Oben know that I speak to you now in friendship." Chekov felt the *kessh* wedge himself more firmly between the passenger seats as other Elasian voices tumbled frantically over them. "Whatever your plan is to free yourself—if it fails, I hope you may die bravely."

Chekov struggled onto his back while a half-dozen of the Elasian guards wrestled Takcas back and tackled him out of sight. "If you try to kill the human maggot again," Oben snarled from the front of the flyer, "there will be nothing left for your Dohlman to claim except your ravaged corpse!"

The snap of the agonizer's activation cells echoed through the little flyer. Chekov closed his eyes, shuddering, and waited breathlessly for the screaming to stop. Fighting would only make this worse, he told himself, and it wouldn't help Takcas, it wouldn't get them any closer to freedom. He wanted desperately to believe that lying here motionless was the best thing he could do for either of them.

But he wondered if Takcas appreciated how much Chekov hoped that, if his plan failed, he would simply be able to die—bravely or otherwise.

Chapter Eighteen

"WHAT IN GOD'S NAME is this stunt supposed to accomplish?"

Kirk looked up from behind the transporter console, his finger pausing on the readout he'd been going over with Kyle. "Can I do something for you, Bones?" He knew perfectly well what McCoy was here for, but didn't have the patience to put up with it just now. "We've got a lot of work to do."

"Scotty says you're planning to fly a shuttle down to Rakatan." McCoy halted next to Spock on the other side of the console, arms crossed accusingly as he glared over the panel at Kirk. "Is that true?"

The captain tried to keep his voice neutral. "It's true."

"Dammit, Jim—!"

Sighing, Kirk tapped the room on the schematics where he wanted Kyle to set them, then retrieved the gloves of his environmental suit from the console. "Bones, I really don't have time to argue about this."

"Why? In too much of a hurry to get yourself killed?" The

doctor turned on Spock as Kirk rounded the console to join them. "And what about you?" McCoy demanded, knocking on the faceplate of the Vulcan's suit helmet. "Don't tell me *you* think this is a good idea!"

Spock stepped neatly out of McCoy's reach to retest the seals on his helmet. "Given the extent of hull damage to the Johnston Observatory, Doctor, I find the captain's decision to beam over in environmental suits an extremely logical precaution."

"Why, thank you, Mr. Spock." Kirk wiggled his fingers to seat his glove in its joint, and returned McCoy's furious scowl with a warning look of his own. "But I don't think the doctor is critiquing our choice of duty attire."

"Damn right I'm not! Jim, I may only understand half of what Florence—" The doctor flushed abruptly and interrupted himself. "—I mean, Dr. Bascomb tells me, but even a security guard could tell that volcano is nothing but a goddamned time bomb!"

"And I have a landing party sitting right on top of it." Kirk took his helmet from Kyle a bit more brusquely than he'd intended. "We haven't been able to locate them past that geodesic defense net the Elasians set up, and I'm *not* going to leave them down there."

"Jim . . ." McCoy caught the edge of Kirk's helmet with one hand, and the captain looked up to find himself pinned by the doctor's steady sympathy. "Has it occurred to you that they might already be dead? And the Dohlman dead along with them?"

Yes, of course it had occurred to him. Every time he thought about it, it made his stomach ache. "The fact that they were separated from their communicators means *somebody* took them captive, Bones, and that somebody had to be our friend the Crown Regent. But if there was the slightest chance of escaping her cohort, I'm betting Chekov found it. I'm also betting Uhura had Her Glory the Dohlman tucked under one arm on their way out the door." He tugged the helmet away from McCoy with a grim smile. "I know my people, Doctor."

"And I know you!" McCoy threw his arms up in exasperation. "The minute you get anywhere near that planet, the Crown Regent's going to blast you right out of the sky!"

Kirk pursed his lips in irritation and flipped his helmet to lift it over his shoulders. "Have some faith, Bones. The Crown Regent can't blast us if she doesn't see us coming." He settled the lock ring until it caught. "That's why we're taking one of the observatory shuttles, and not one of ours."

"Bridge to Captain Kirk."

He hadn't expected a call over the suit comm so quickly. Glancing across at Spock, he waited for the Vulcan's nod to verify that both of their units were working, then punched his reply button with his chin. "Go ahead, Scotty."

"We're all set up here," the engineer reported. With Scott's voice made so artificially distant by the communicator channel, Kirk felt suddenly as though the bridge and ship were already a dozen light-years away, and not still humming beneath his booted feet. "I've got the screens rigged to flicker a wee bit, then drop when Mr. Kyle activates the transporter. Unless the Elasians' sensors are a sight better than the Klingons usually build 'em, it should read as nothing more than an energy fluctuation in our warp core."

Kirk flashed a thumbs-up to Kyle, who nodded. "Good work, Scotty. I don't want the Crown Regent to get even the slightest hint of what we're up to."

"Then you'll not be maintaining contact while you're at the observatory, sir?"

"No." Kirk turned to face the transporter pad so he wouldn't have to watch the medley of disapproving expressions march across McCoy's face. "We probably won't be able to get a communicator signal through that geodesic net once we're below it anyway. If we manage to find a working shuttle, we'll trigger a remote message from the moonbase after we've taken off. If you don't hear from us within six hours, that means we're still at the observatory. Drop the screens then and beam us back aboard, no questions asked."

"Aye-aye, sir. Good luck. Scott out."

McCoy lingered near the transporter console as Kirk waved Spock up onto the pad. "I don't suppose it would do any good to tell you this wild-goose chase of yours only has one chance in a thousand of succeeding."

Kirk scooped their phasers off the edge of the console. "If I want to hear depressing statistics, Bones, I'll ask Spock for them. At least his are accurate." He stepped onto the platform to hand the first officer his weapon, then pulled the gun back out of reach when he saw the Vulcan's mouth open behind his visor. "I said, 'if,' Mr. Spock, not 'when.'"

Spock raised an indignant eyebrow, but accepted his phaser in silence.

Kirk grinned to take the edge off his very human sarcasm, then stepped into place beside his first officer. "Bones, we don't even have that one chance in a thousand if we can't get a shuttle below that geodesic net. I don't care what the odds are, I'm going after my people." He looked up and met Kyle's waiting gaze. "All right, Mr. Kyle—energize."

Ash swept around the edges of Seismic Station Three in a breathy, silent roar. The square metal seismic housing looked smaller and more frail than when Chekov had been here before with Mutchler and Sulu, its roof frosted with volcanic debris, its sides obscured by drifts of ash and reddish sand. Showers of cinder had apparently been falling here for some time, sheeting down on the broken landscape as if someone in the heavens were shaking out a huge dusty blanket, or upending an impossibly mammoth container of soot. The cloud roiled down the slopes to engulf them, like smoke rushing ahead of some phantom fire they couldn't see.

Chekov ducked his face against his shoulder to avoid taking in a mouthful of soot, then still had to turn his back to the onrushing cloud when the additional grit stirred up by the four Elasians made its way into his eyes and breathing. Damn them for shackling his hands behind his back when he could hear them so clearly coughing into their own. He tried to keep his head bent and his breathing short, but there was only so much of his own reflexes that he could deny—he was coughing just as hoarsely as the rest of them by the time the billow of ash rushed past them to disappear farther down the volcano's slopes.

"It has been raining dirt all morning," one of the Elasians complained to the guardsman next to him. "What a great mess these humans have made of the planet!"

Mutchler might have considered Moscow someplace very tectonically boring, but at least Chekov knew that nothing done by man or machine could cause volcanic reactions like this.

"All right, human . . ."

Someone behind him caught his elbow and jerked him about to face the seismic station as though the ash cloud had never interfered. Planting his feet, Chekov tried to wrench himself out of the Elasian's grasp, just as a matter of principle. He gained a scowl and a vicious shake for his effort, but that was all. Oben, now as pasted with filth as the rest of them, commented amiably, "He sometimes needs reminding who among us wears the weapons."

Chekov's first instinct was to spit at him, but he decided that wouldn't be wise, considering how quick to make use of his agonizer Oben seemed. He hadn't cared for Oben as an underling; he liked him even less now that Oben considered himself in some position of command.

"This is the place my Dohlman and I agreed upon," Chekov said aloud, hoping to deflect the discussion from whatever inducements he might require. "If our party became separated, we were to come back here."

"They must not care for you very much." The guard gripping his elbow peered around suspiciously. "I see no one."

"We aren't stupid enough to wait out in the open. Whoever arrived first was to have left instructions so that the others could later find him." Chekov threw a sharp look at Oben. "Or her." He jerked a nod at the grit-scarred seismic housing. "The message should be inside somewhere."

Oben walked slowly around the squat metal station. Pausing again on the side nearest Chekov, he kicked the maintenance access plate with visible disgust. "Is this the only means by which to enter?"

For the first time since lying to them on the floor of the control center, Chekov felt a scream of panicked adrenaline through his bloodstream as it occurred to him that this might not work after all. "Yes."

"Which means only a small, worthless human like you can fit inside." The guard glared across at him coldly.

Chekov nodded. "Yes."

Tossing the manacle release keys to the guard at Chekov's elbow, Oben snorted disdainfully and sat on the top of the station. "It seems you humans are not so stupid as our Crown Regent would have me believe."

If all went well, he would be a lot more impressed with human intelligence by the time Chekov left this station.

Chekov's shoulders ached from being wrenched behind his back all morning, and he paused a moment to rub at his neck muscles before one of the Elasians butted him with a disruptor from behind and he stumbled forward a step. Chekov stopped himself from whirling to curse at the alien, then turned and glared anyway for the sake of locating all three of the Elasians still standing between him and the waiting flyer. They weren't clustered, and they weren't nearby. This was going to be so goddamned hard.

Moving slowly to the front of the seismic station, the lieutenant exchanged a furtive glance with Oben, still sitting on top of the housing. Chekov hated kneeling in front of the Elasian as though paying homage to his languid posture and smug grin. Bad enough that Oben thought selling out his own Dohlman made him somehow superior to the men who'd remained her loyal guards. The access panel only stood a bare one meter high, though, and Chekov couldn't crawl into it without first getting down on the ground, no matter where Oben was sitting. Gritting his teeth and staring resolutely in front of him, Chekov sank into a squat and attacked the first set of bolts with his fingers.

The panel came off in a shower and puff of grimy ash. Chekov coughed against his sleeve this time, trying to maneuver the panel off to the side one-handed without letting it fall and kick up an even bigger plume. Above them, curdling across the primrose sky, another smudgy veil of ash burped up above the mountain's crater, then began its silent slide away from them down another part of the summit. Rakatan Mons's thunderous rumble shivered through the ground beneath Chekov just a few moments later.

"Hurry up, human." Oben poked him irritably with one foot. "I want to be gone before it drops dust on us again."

Chekov only nodded stiffly, not trusting his voice with an answer.

He had to go down on his elbows to slither in through the narrow entrance. A dim, watery light blinked into being somewhere on the station's ceiling, and Chekov's shadow splayed out suddenly dark and swollen beneath him, filling the floor of the tiny chamber. He wished he'd had a chance to follow Mutchler in here earlier, to see what things looked like once they were all assembled and in their final place. Instead, he had to squint at every dark component and try to guess at its function while ash eddied past his hips to settle into feather patterns on the floor.

"Well?" Oben called after a moment. His heavy voice echoed from beyond the narrow doorway.

"I'm looking."

"What is there to look for? Either your Dohlman has left you a message, or you have wasted our time just so we can kill you out-of-doors."

Squirming over onto his back, Chekov pulled himself a few inches farther into the station. "I told you—I'm not certain what kind of message she would leave me. She wouldn't have wanted just anyone to access it."

The top of the seismic station *ponged* loudly as the Elasian hopped down and let it spring back into shape. "I think you are nothing but a lying root-worm," Oben grumbled. "I tire of this. Come out of there!"

"Wait!" Chekov glimpsed his own reflection in the strip of

polished metal he'd given Mutchler for refocusing the misfit laser. "I found it! Give me just a moment to pull it free."

"One moment." As if that were some measurable period of time he intended to hold Chekov to. The lieutenant scooted under the laser fixture without bothering to reply.

Ash twinkled like bits of broken glass in the laser's steady light. Careful to avoid the forward optic projector, Chekov felt along the back of the laser device until his fingers ran over the tiny hole that served as access to the laser's emergency shutoff switch. He marked the spot with one finger, then brought his left sleeve up to his mouth and tugged at one of the service pins there with his teeth. It came off cleanly enough. He spat it into his palm, rolled it between thumb and forefinger, and lifted it gently into place against the back of the laser box. He needed both hands to guide the pin into the tiny hole, but once through the casing it clicked easily home. The dancing fiber of light above him vanished.

"Your moment is over."

Chekov held the pin in place with his thumb and started working the laser free of the station's ceiling. "I'm coming!" Beyond the doorway, Oben's feet straddled his—a silent warning.

Thin, spider-silk cables connected the laser to the seismic station's power source. Tracing them with one hand, cradling the laser with the other, Chekov ripped loose each point where the cables had been stapled out of the way, always careful to keep the conduits alive and intact. Then, with his pulse hammering thickly in his throat and a coil of cable tangled up in his lap, Chekov turned the laser over in his hand and snapped off the charge-buildup governor.

As if in response to his action, Rakatan Mons gave a great, gunshot report that made the walls of the seismic station ring like thunder.

"All right, human—*out!*"

A wave of earth shock followed almost immediately. Chekov saw Oben's feet stagger as pebbles and shimmers of ash danced up from the ground all around him.

"Oben, hurry!" someone else shouted from closer to the flyer. "Here comes another cloud!"

Cursing, Oben bent to grab Chekov's ankles. Chekov waited until their eyes met—until he was sure Oben was committed and couldn't jerk away at the last moment—then aimed the laser through the doorway and flicked the service pin out with his thumb.

Emergency shutoff now lifted, the laser released its overcharge in a single, silent blast. Chekov saw Oben stumble backward a step, then recoiled from a deafening disruptor shriek that shattered the roof of the station and kicked him back against the floor as it tore through him. Shock slammed over him, ripping away breath and pain together, and he saw Oben topple backward, face toward the sky, as if through a long watery tunnel. By then, it was too late to regret not being farther over to his right, not being more respectful of the speed of Elasian reflexes—a wave of soot crashed over the little seismic station and turned the world outside into a tumbling mass of gray.

Coughing and strangled cries of alarm marked the locations of the three Elasians still waiting outside for him. Chekov reached down to catch either side of the maintenance access doorway, trying to ignore the uneven tugging across the left side of his jacket as he dragged himself out into the swirling ash. He'd never been hit with a disruptor before—he didn't know how long he had before shocked tissue recovered enough to graphically explain the extent of his injuries. His only hope was to get as far away from the station as possible before that happened, and hope somebody found him there in time to make it matter.

Oben's disruptor lay, a milky gray outline beneath the carpet of fallen ash, still gripped tightly in the Elasian's lifeless hand. Chekov stumbled to his knees long enough to grab the pistol by the muzzle, perversely amused at the thought of fighting his way free with the very same gun that might have killed him. The muzzle cone was still warm, and tingled to his touch. He'd hadn't even tugged it free, though, before another disruptor called out from the gloom and ripped a corner off the top of the seismic station.

Chekov jerked the gun loose to return fire, then scrabbled away from the station's entrance as pain began its first deadly crawl across his middle. Behind him, another segment of the station housing disintegrated in a wail of disruptor fire. He wondered how many shots these guns were good for, and how many a human had any hope of surviving. Judging from the warm sheen of blood he could feel collecting beneath his left elbow, he had a feeling the answer would depress him.

Ash and dust and sand tore at him with stinging fingers. Unable to keep his eyes open against the blowing cinders, Chekov let himself drop full-length to the ground and buried his face in the crook of his arm. A blossom of anguish, deep and hard, made him gasp, and he choked for air against his filthy jacket sleeve as he waited for the pain to subside. It didn't. When he finally felt the sting of sunlight against his cheek that told him the ash cloud had settled, Chekov knew that if he wanted to escape the Crown Regent's cohort, he wasn't going to do it by running.

One of the Elasians shouted in excited anger, and Chekov jerked his head up, leading with the disruptor in time to catch a glimpse of quick, deliberate movement at the extreme right of his pain-blurred vision. There wasn't time to question the guard's intent. Firing blindly, Chekov rolled tight against the seismic station and took in a great gulp of ash when a disruptor bolt vaporized a patch of ground right in front of him. He shot again toward the sound of the disruptor's report, this time squeezing the trigger and sweeping as wide an arc as he could reach until the gun went dead and silent in his hand—drained of charge.

Chekov let the useless disruptor drop into his lap, and leaned wearily across the top of the station. Two more of the Elasians sprawled in the dusty rigor of startled death, making an uneven triangle with Oben's corpse near the station's access door. The last of the four Elasians who had escorted Chekov out of the flyer now lurched back to the craft with one twisted, bloody arm clutched rigidly against his side. Whatever he shouted, the two guards inside obviously heard him—the hatch whisked open to admit him, and a covering spray of combined phaser and disruptor fire drove Chekov back behind the station as the remaining pair dragged their wounded comrade inside.

Almost before the doors could have skated closed, the flyer's engines howled into life and sprayed a sheet of ashy dust over the seismic station and the bodies. Chekov closed his eyes and huddled down against the station, the heel of one hand dug into his side as if that pointless effort could somehow stop either the blood or the pain. There was no way he could outrun them now—they could blind him endlessly with flying dust and ash, then shoot at him from above while he was helpless to seek out better cover. *Six to one are just bad odds,* he decided dismally. He laughed weakly, but a fierce bolt of pain cut it short. If he actually managed to survive both the Elasians and the volcano, he promised himself he would never, ever try something this stupid again.

Boulders from some rock face farther up the slope formed a jumble at the mouth of the station's ravine. It seemed an impossible run in this ashy, oxygen-poor air, but Chekov saw nowhere else in the barren terrain that offered even a hope of shelter. Maybe if he avoided them long enough, they'd be forced to abandon the chase and take their wounded friend back for medical treatment. Or maybe expecting Elasians to care whether or not their companion died was giving them credit for too much compassion. After all, they could exercise exactly the same tactic on him, if they chose to. Seeing the flyer carve a graceful loop out of the sooty sky to come back at him, though, Chekov struggled to his feet in the bed of loose cinders. He might not be able to run either fast or far, but he couldn't just sit here and wait for the Elasians to kill him.

Blood darkened the pale dust on his jacket to a fearfully dark, sticky red, and ash slipped like oil beneath his feet. Dizziness crashed into him almost immediately, twisting tight in his stomach and lungs as a warning against trying to run too far in this improper air. He fought to keep his breathing deep and steady, struggled to stay upright and running despite the pain that ate at his resolve, and despite the rocks and crevices hidden beneath the blanket of ash. When the flyer's crisp black shadow swept over him and swallowed the light, he didn't even have strength to spare on grief or regret. When they told their Crown Regent how they'd caught him, they'd at least have a lot of explaining to do.

The force of the flyer's passage slammed into him as a wall of disturbed air. Wrapped in a blinding swirl of flying cinder, he dropped, gasping, to his knees and let the flyer scream by. It hitched nose upward as though starting into a sudden climb, then held in that position as the ship's rear thrusters roared and kicked it forward. Chekov realized it was going to slam the ravine's far wall only an instant before the undercarriage ripped open on the broken stone. He hit the ground just ahead of the warp core's dying pulse.

Only the faintest wisp of heat licked over him at this distance. Chekov shivered with horror, knowing what that unshielded blast would have done to him if it hadn't died out before spanning the high-walled ravine. Waiting for his heart to stop pounding and his spinning head to clear, he looked up carefully for what was left of the wreckage on the slope high above him.

The flyer itself was mostly intact. A long scar of shattered rock marked the course of its impact, and one slender warp nacelle had been wrenched almost upright underneath the passenger cabin, tilting the whole craft grotesquely sideways. There were no fires staining the ground around it with red, though—no squeal of freezing metal from the kiss of compressed nitrogen. Only the liquid heat shimmer of excited atoms dancing above the twisted nacelle betrayed how deadly a place that crash site must be. What could the pilot possibly have been thinking when he cut in those rear thrusters? Surely even an Elasian knew they would never have time to pull out of such a . . .

Chekov climbed slowly to his knees, resting with his head bowed almost to the sand when he found he couldn't straighten beyond that point. Light from the glowing flyer picked out his blood against the ash as hard little specks of flatly shining black. Takcas, he realized as he watched the splatters slowly fill in to a puddle beneath him. It had to have been Takcas. Knowing that the Crown Regent would just have him killed when the flyer returned to the mining camp, Takcas had taken command of his own destiny and exacted the only bit of revenge in his reach. The Crown Regent might only have lost six members of her cohort and a single human prisoner, but for Takcas that had apparently been damage enough.

"I just hope this volcano doesn't make everything you died for pointless." Chekov's voice sounded impossibly tiny against the high, distant rumbling of Rakatan Mons. Right now, he didn't know how he was going to rescue himself, much less Israi, Uhura, and the others.

But whatever he did, he wasn't going to do it here.

Straightening, he thrust out a hand to keep himself from swaying, and bid Takcas a silent, respectful farewell. He was afraid to think about how soon he and the Elasian *kessh* might yet see each other again. Now, in the shaky, adrenaline aftermath of the firefight, he peeled aside his tattered jacket and stole his first look at what Oben had done to him.

Jacket, belt, and tunic had all been blasted raggedly away along the side of his waist, taking enough of him along to leave a bloody patch wider even than the hand he had clamped over it. This probably wasn't a good time to know too much about disruptor damage, Chekov reflected dryly. Without a sickbay, or at least a well-equipped medikit, there wasn't much he could do to stop the bleeding—direct pressure would only work for so long, and he was too inconveniently hit to allow for a tourniquet. He crawled to his feet, hissing against the pain that rose with him, and turned awkwardly to look down the long, rugged length of ash-clogged ravine.

The three dead Elasians were dusted with ash, barely

visible now against the monochrome ground. They could be a source of rags for bandages, but that was all they would be good for now. What really mattered lay beyond them, a frightening distance away.

Past the ruined seismic station, past the crude landing pad, past even what Chekov could see now as the horizon, lay the only subspace communications console within a million kilometers. If he could reach it, he might still have some chance of contacting the ship and getting them all pulled out of here in time.

Considering that he wasn't certain he could live long enough to find it, the fact that both the console and Israi's captive cohort were well guarded by the Crown Regent's men inside the Elasian mining camp was, at this point, a technicality.

Chapter Nineteen

MULTIFORKED LIGHTNING lit the ash cloud over Rakatan Mons to the color of blood. It was followed by a sound too long and enormously explosive to be thunder—the blast from another volcanic eruption. Uhura felt her eyes wince shut in automatic reflex despite the hundreds of kilometers that separated them from the distant crater. She slipped on an unseen patch of loose cinder and would have fallen if a strong hand hadn't caught at her elbow and managed to steady her.

"You all right?" Sulu's voice demanded, barely audible over the volcanic roar.

"Yes." Uhura forced her eyes open again and scanned the towering ash cloud overhead. By now she knew that each thunderous outburst of the volcano launched a dark rooster-tail of ash out from the central column, feathering the sky with falling cinders and bombs. So far, they'd been lucky—prevailing winds pushed most of the ash trails toward the far side of Rakatan Mons. But each smoky curtain that swept across their path kept them halted for a frustrating length of time, heads huddled into arms to keep from choking on the gritty ash.

"*No!*" Feet braced on the steep talus pile beneath them, Israi tilted her head back and scowled up at the erupting volcano. The Dohlman's face was filthy with crusted mud and ash, but her almond eyes blazed out of the dirt with youthful indignation. "Turn your cursed evil ash away from us, you vile mountain! You will *not* spit at me again!"

Uhura heard a muffled choke of laughter from Scott Mutchler. The geologist had taken advantage of the pause to sink down and rest his splinted leg, leaning his head back against a fallen boulder. Pain had drawn his skin down tight over jutting cheekbones, but his eyes still managed to glint with amusement.

"You can't order a volcano not to erupt at you, Your Glory," he said dryly.

"No?" Israi pointed in triumph to the dark ash trail hurtling east and away from them. "What do you call *that*, idiot geologist?"

"Luck." Mutchler turned his shadowed gaze toward Uhura, his flicker of amusement fading back into strain. "Can you still get a reading from Seismic Station Three?"

"Let me check." She sat back on her heels and unstrapped the portable seismic monitor from her belt, wiping off the display screen as she turned it on. Volcanic ash gritted under her fingers, adding more scratches to the screen's transparent shielding. Uhura squinted past the fretwork of fine lines, setting the output to STATION SWEEP the way Mutchler had shown her when he'd first handed the monitor over.

Five circles appeared on a map display, glowing into life one by one as the monitor picked up the signal being broadcast from each seismic installation on the volcano. The last time Uhura had checked, there'd been six of the small circles; originally there'd been eight. One by one, they were losing seismometers on the far side of the volcano, where the ash fall was greatest. But the station labeled THREE was still on the map, its neon green halo far larger than the rest.

"It's there." Uhura laid a fingertip over the scale at the bottom of the screen, then slid it up to measure the diameter of the glowing circle. "I think we're about two kilometers away now."

"Two thousand meters." Mutchler dropped his head into his hands, groaning. "God, I'd hoped we'd be closer than that."

Uhura eyed him worriedly. "We can give you another painkiller. I have one more left in my emergency pack, and it's been an hour since the last one."

The geologist nodded and began to roll up his muddy sleeve. Israi slid down the slope in a sputter of loose cinders and held a dirty hand out to Uhura.

"I'll do it this time."

Uhura looked up from her emergency medical kit in surprise. It might have been a delusion born of exhaustion and stress, but she thought she could read concern in those slanted almond eyes. "You don't have to—"

"We must both care for him." Israi kept her voice carefully lowered, so it wouldn't carry past the dwindling volcanic roar. "His own Dohlman is not here to give him the death he needs."

Uhura gritted her teeth against a surge of anger, knowing that it was mostly born of frustration with her own helplessness. "He's not going to die!" she hissed back. "As soon as we reach the seismic station, he's going to use the transmitter to send our coordinates up to the moonbase. That's all Captain Kirk will need to beam us up to our ship."

"So you say." Israi made an odd noise, something between her usual snort of disdain and a wholly unaccustomed laugh. "Forgive my doubting, Uhura. But from all I can see, nothing done on this planet has ever gone as smoothly as you say this will."

Uhura felt a reluctant smile crumble the dried mud from her cheeks. "Well, I can't argue with that." She dug out her last blue-green hypospray of painkiller and handed it to the Dohlman. "You know how this works?"

Israi nodded. "Hold against the skin and press the button down. Do I give him all of it?"

"Yes." It was Sulu who answered. "Otherwise, he's going to pass out before we ever get to this station of his." The pilot rummaged in his own belt kit, coming up with a bright yellow hypospray. Uhura frowned, recognizing it as a mixture of adrenaline and natural endorphins.

"Activity stimulant?" She darted a glance past Israi at the hunched figure of the geologist, seeing the lines of pain carved deep into his face. "Sulu, do you think his system can handle it?"

"No, but mine can." Sulu began to roll up his own jacket sleeve. "There's no way Mutchler can take another two kilometers of hiking. I'll have to carry him."

"Bondsman." Israi's sharp voice arrested Sulu's hands and brought his gaze rocketing toward her. She pointed at the yellow hypospray. "Will this not harm you?"

"No—" Uhura saw Sulu's throat muscles ripple, as if the Dohlman's scowl had arrested the lie before he could finish it.

"Not much," Sulu said. "Not enough to matter."

"It will let him work past his usual threshold of exhaustion," Uhura explained quietly. "And he won't feel the pain until it wears off. We only take it in extreme emergencies."

"But this idiot geologist—he is not even of your own cohort." Israi put her free hand out to clench on Sulu's shoulder when he shrugged. "Why do you care so much about him, bondsman?"

"The same reason that I care so much about *you,* Israi." Uhura reached out and pulled the Dohlman's hand away, freeing Sulu. "Because you're a sentient life-form and you're in danger. It's called compassion."

Israi frowned at her for a moment, as baffled as a student faced with an unfamiliar equation. "You care about me whether or not you are of my bond or bloodline? Whether or not you even know me?"

"Yes."

"That is crazy." Despite her negative words, however,

Israi's hand turned and tightened for a moment around Uhura's before she let go. "Very well, bondsman," she said to Sulu with a resigned sigh. "I permit you to carry the idiot geologist to this seismic station we seek."

A ghost of Sulu's usual smile tugged at his lips. "Thanks so much, Your Glory."

An answering smile curved Israi's mouth, surprising Uhura once again. "The favor costs me nothing," she said dryly, then scrambled up to give Mutchler his shot.

"Is this really a good idea?" Uhura asked quietly once the Dohlman was gone.

"Probably not, but I don't think we have any choice." Sulu positioned the hypospray against his forearm and pressed. "Did you get a good look at that last spurt of ash?"

"Not really." Uhura turned to peer through the storm-dark afternoon, but the brief volcanic spasm was already over. The noise of the eruption had dropped to a distant low thunder as Rakatan Mons pumped out more wrinkled, billowing folds of ash cloud. "What was wrong with it?"

"It glowed red, even on the outside." Sulu rolled his sleeve back down.

"So the next time it hits us, it will burn." Uhura was amazed her voice could sound so calm when her pulse was thundering in her throat as loudly as the volcano. "We'll have to hurry."

"Yes," Sulu agreed. "And pray the seismic station is working when we get there."

As always, the transporter effect released Kirk a seeming instant after he'd first felt it engage. Habit made him check his air levels, verify his suit integrity, and test his comm circuit before he even glanced up to inspect the room around them. By then, Spock's tricorder warbled strongly beside him, and Kirk knew they at least had atmosphere enough to hear by.

"What's the air like?" he asked, turning in a circle to visually scan the area for rents or signs of leakage. They were in what looked like the observatory's central ops—science panels, equipment, and monitor stations kept him from seeing all the corners and edges.

"I am detecting traces of oxygen depletion, undoubtedly as a result of life-support system shutdown." Spock's voice came to Kirk twice over, through the comm and through outside audio pickup, an eerie imitation of itself. "As we will be the only life-forms present, the depletion should not reach critical levels for another forty-nine point six five hours."

Kirk grinned and reached up to pop the seals on his helmet. "Well, that should give us a good forty-three-hour safety margin."

Chill, dry air blasted up under the collar of the helmet, and Kirk winced against a sudden urge to sneeze when his sinuses tingled with the sharp cold. The air smelled clean, though, and carried no betraying currents to warn of rapid heating nearby, or atmosphere breach somewhere else. He set his helmet on the seat of a chair, then rounded the central console in search of the docking controls. For whatever Vulcan reason, Spock retained his own helmet and drifted away to his tricorder's continued singing.

The control panels were dusty but free of frost. Some still glowed on a trickle of minimal backup power, while others sat as dark and useless as children's toys. Kirk only made two attempts to initiate a wake-up sequence with his gloves on before irritation moved him to yank them off and slap them onto the panel beside him. Across the room, Spock glanced up with a curious lift of his eyebrow, and Kirk pretended not to notice.

If there were docking controls for the observatory's shuttle fleet, Kirk couldn't find them. He didn't want to waste even a few minutes of their six hours looking. Waking up the central command board, he ordered an abbreviated station status report and drummed his fingers impatiently while awaiting the reply.

The first screen of amber type made him sigh. "Looks like Shuttle Bay Two is the only one still on-line," he called to Spock without looking up from the terminal. "Of the other three, one's got first-level contamination from a breached shuttle core, one's unoccupied—" The shuttle they'd dragged into the *Enterprise*'s hangar bay, no doubt. "—and the last is altogether gone. That means . . ." He fell silent, caught by the flow of schematics now flickering across the screen. "Damn!"

Spock paused in his readings and glanced up. "Captain?"

Kirk waved at the traitorous screen. "According to this, the only thing they've got in that bay is a K-117 light transport shuttle." He sat back in his seat with a growl. "I thought they took those old dories out of service years ago."

"The K-117 was once one of the fastest interatmospheric shuttles in Starfleet, Captain."

Kirk snorted. "About a hundred years ago."

"I believe the Federation Geological Survey now utilizes the K-117 as a portable drilling rig. The heavily shielded warp core provides a safe source of power, even with personnel nearby on the ground."

"Shielded or not, Spock, a shuttle that old probably also has the power conversion of a food synthesizer." Which meant unmaneuverable and slow—painfully and dangerously slow. "We're not going to evade those armada gunships by running past them at a dead crawl." He swore again.

"At present, Captain, the efficiency of our chosen transportation is not our most immediate problem." Spock stopped on the opposite side of the control panel and turned his tricorder to face Kirk. The captain studied the chemical readout on the little screen for a moment, then felt a jolt of surprise when he realized what it was telling him.

"An oxygen problem?" He shot a startled frown across the tricorder at Spock. "I thought you said we had fifty hours of air left, even with the life-support gone."

"Forty-nine point six five hours," the Vulcan corrected him. "Indeed, that estimate remains acceptably accurate given the rate of our combined oxygen consumption. Upon compiling additional data, however, I have been forced to revise my estimate to forty-two point eight one hours."

Kirk propped his elbow on the edge of the panel and rubbed tiredly at his eyes. Sometimes, he actually suspected that Vulcans came by their supernatural patience by eating it away from everyone around them. "Mr. Spock, I believe I made it clear we aren't even going to be here for six hours."

Spock straightened his already ramrod posture ever so slightly—a gesture Kirk had learned meant his first officer didn't appreciate being spoken to as though he were dim-witted. "You misunderstand me, Captain. It is not the duration of our oxygen reserves that concerns me. It is the reason for their depletion." He consulted his tricorder again, but this time made no attempt to show the results to his captain. "There is a third life-form sharing our atmosphere in Johnston Observatory."

Kirk shot to his feet and quickly rounded the console. "Human?"

"It would appear so."

"Where?"

"According to the observatory moonbase plans I downloaded before leaving—"

Kirk stopped himself just short of shaking his first officer. *Where,* Spock?"

The Vulcan closed the tricorder and returned it very pointedly to his side. "In the main seismic processing center." He nodded impassively beyond Kirk's shoulder. "Beyond that exit, and twenty-seven meters down the hall."

"Oh, my God!"

Kirk froze just inside the lab doorway, not sure what he'd expected to find, but knowing it hadn't been a tired—yet unhurt—Wendy Metcalfe huddled over a fall of data disks as tall as she. He'd assumed anyone left behind on the moonbase was too critically injured to contact the *Enterprise* for help.

"Captain! Mr. Spock!" Metcalfe sighed dramatically with relief and turned back to the bank of data screens scrolling behind her. "You scared me half to death! I thought you were that horrible Crown Regent woman."

Kirk picked his way through the disk- and coffee-cup-littered lab, trying not to step on anything that looked important without really knowing why he was taking the precaution. "Ms. Metcalfe, what the hell are you doing here? This base was supposed to have been evacuated hours ago."

"You didn't expect me to leave right in the middle of gathering the most crucial data in my doctoral thesis, did you?" She reached up with a light pen to scribble some annotation amid a shimmer of squiggled lines just like the ones Kirk had seen Bascomb grumbling over in McCoy's office. "We've just had a magnitude-six quake near the summit," Metcalfe explained excitedly. "There's been at least one landslide triggered by the event, and satellite reports have confirmed at least six incidents of venting, including two from the central chamber." She scooted a little to one side to give Spock a better view when the Vulcan came to lean over her shoulder. "And look at this, Mr. Spock—I'm even more sure than ever that there's some kind of sentient life inside that magma chamber. If you look at the cyclicity of the harmonic tremor—"

"Wait a minute." Kirk pushed up beside his first officer to separate the two scientists. "You said venting," he told Metcalfe, catching her attention with the keen sharpness of his voice. "Are you saying Rakatan Mons is actually starting to erupt?"

She beamed like a mother over her baby's first tooth. "You betcha! See now why I *couldn't* leave when you told us to? Rakatan Mons is prone to such long periods of dormancy—this may be the only time our species will ever get a chance to see it active!"

"Given those circumstances, Captain," Spock broke in quietly, "I must admit that I would be equally inclined to remain aboard the moonbase."

Kirk thumped a hand against the breastplate of the Vulcan's environmental suit. "Don't even think about it, Spock. I'm not leaving either of you up here while I play hide-and-seek with the Crown Regent. This is the first place she'll take shots at once she realizes I'm gone."

Metcalfe wheeled around in horror. "You mean you're *trying* to get the station destroyed?"

"I'm *trying* to rescue four of my crewmen from your doctoral thesis!" Kirk shot back at her. "How long do we have before there's no chance of setting down on the volcano's slopes?"

Metcalfe blinked at him as though she didn't understand. "You mean you're going down to the planet? *Now?*" When Kirk only nodded, she rose slowly to her feet with one hand braced on the edge of her seismic console as if for support. "You're actually planning to *land* on Rakatan Mons? And you want to take *me* with you?"

Kirk felt a twinge of sympathy for the student, and nodded soberly. "I'm sorry, Ms. Metcalfe. I don't have any choice."

She gave a whoop like a cadet on her first training flight and began slapping at panel controls too fast for Kirk to follow. "Captain, you have just made my thesis committee happier than you can possibly imagine! Getting surface data from Rakatan Mons right in the middle of an eruption—" She stopped with her hands full of portable seismic equipment and tricorders. "My God!" she gasped, grinning. "I could win a Nobel and Z.Magnees Prize in geology for this!"

Kirk ducked out of her way as she shot past him for the nearest suit locker. "That's assuming you survive to write it up," he pointed out dryly.

She shrugged and kicked open the locker door. "If I don't, they can always name the next geological observatory here after me. Because as you'll soon see . . ." She threw both officers an apologetic shrug as she shook an environmental suit off its frame. ". . . the Elasians haven't left us very much of this one."

Uhura was the first to climb down into the narrow ravine that sheltered Seismic Station Three, and thus the first to see the ruin it had become.

Disrupted bodies littered the bare gray rock around the

station, each one ringed in cinnamon brown spatters of dried blood. Uhura's throat tightened in dismay, but she forced herself to scan the silent battlefield, searching for the one corpse she didn't want to find. She saw only the hulking forms of Elasian males, most dressed in unfamiliar steel blue armor. At least one of the bodies had been scored with laser burns as well as disruptor lesions. After a moment, Uhura recognized the short-trimmed beard and burly face as Oben's. The other two she didn't know.

Behind the corpses, the small metal enclosure of the station looked charred and gashed, too, as if it had been used for shelter during the firefight that had obviously erupted here. On the far side of the ravine, the crumpled remains of a small Elasian flyer lay strewn and smoking, the empty husk of its shattered warp core crackling as it cooled.

One by one, the others joined her at the base of the slope, staring wordlessly at the destruction of their hopes. Sulu was the first to break the appalled silence.

"Well, the good news is that Chekov's still alive."

Chapter Twenty

EVEN IN THE ash-dark afternoon, Uhura could tell how badly Chekov's firefight had damaged the inside of Seismic Station Three. From where she squatted outside the access hatch, she could see at least three jagged holes torn into the seismic array by disruptor blasts. One of them had ripped apart the laser sighting device that Mutchler and Sulu had so carefully put together back on the shuttle. The fallen laser itself lay half-buried in ash, a trail of scorched metal leading from it to the satellite uplink module, where it branched into blackened spiderwebs of burnt circuitry.

Uhura forced herself to focus on estimating the extent of damage to the data-link boards and how it could have been repaired if only she had a repair kit. It wasn't a very useful thing to do, but it was easier than trying to watch while Mutchler hauled himself into the station with little spasming grunts of pain, struggling to reach what was left of the data-communications port.

"You should have let me do that." Ash and cinders grated under her palms as Uhura braced herself over the geologist's exposed legs, careful not to touch the splinted one. "I know how to use that kind of transmitter."

"Not the way—I have it wired." Even in the shelter of the ravine, Mutchler's breathless voice was barely audible over the background rumbling from Rakatan Mons. He reached the data-link module at last and tugged out its central transmitting controller, then erupted into cursing.

"What's the matter?"

"The superconducting circuits have all fused back to metal oxide." Mutchler twisted awkwardly in the constricted center aisle of the station to show her the circuit board. Even in the gathering darkness, Uhura could see the telltale rainbow colors prisming beneath the glassy inner surface.

"Oh, no." She grabbed at the sides of the access panel to keep her balance while the ground shook again beneath her. During the last half-hour, while the ash cloud spread like a dark stain across the sky, the volcano had begun to quiver every few minutes with a swarm of small but relentless earthquakes. "Are there any other circuits here we can replace it with?"

"Not a single damned one." The geologist dropped the ruined board, then cursed again when ash spattered him wetly where it fell. "Some lubricant must have leaked in here—oh, God, no. I think it's blood from one of those Elasians—"

Uhura felt him shudder and heard the incipient hysteria in his voice, born of injury, fatigue, and desperation. She leaned down and grabbed at his belt, hauling him out of the station before his useless thrashing did more damage to either him or the equipment.

"It's all right." She caught one flailing hand and held it tight despite its wet stickiness. "It's all right."

Mutchler shook once more, convulsively, then fell still. After a moment, he managed to roll over and look up at her, his eyes more black than gray in the volcanic twilight. "Sorry," he muttered. "It was just—seeing all those dead bodies. And knowing we're going to die too—"

Uhura shook her head with fierce determination. "Don't give up yet. Just because your transmitter doesn't work doesn't mean we're going to die." Footsteps crunched on loose ash and she looked up, recognizing the slightly too-quick step. "Sulu! Did you find any communicators on those dead Elasians?"

"No. Sorry." Three metal wristbands clattered into Uhura's lap, tossed with a little more force than necessary. Sulu's face was shadowed with exhaustion, but his eyes still held the glitter of excess adrenaline. "All they had were short-range Klingon comm bands."

"That low-power rubbish!" Uhura restrained an urge to fling the useless units down into the ravine. "We can't even jury-rig them together to reach the ship."

"But we *can* use them to talk to each other in case we get separated." Sulu nodded significantly at Mutchler, whose ash-encrusted face looked noticeably pasty even in the growing dark.

"That's true." Uhura's glance traveled from the geologist back to the helmsman as she tried to guess which of them would pass out first. After two kilometers under Mutchler's considerable weight, she had half-expected Sulu to collapse when they arrived at the seismic station. Perhaps, she thought wryly, he couldn't do it until Israi gave him permission.

Sulu saw her assessing glance and smiled. "Don't worry, I'm holding out. The volcano keeps giving me booster shots of adrenaline with all these earthquakes."

"That's just harmonic tremor." Mutchler struggled to sit up, then rested his head on folded arms with a sigh. "It means there's magma moving up into the main chamber."

"And that's supposed to be reassuring?" Uhura traded amused glances with Sulu. Their faint smiles died when Mutchler's answering head-shake turned into a sudden, convulsive shiver.

"Nothing about what this volcano is doing is reassuring."

They sat a moment in silence, listening to the distant growl of the eruption. Then Uhura lifted one of the wristbands to eye level, squinting at it resolutely through the dimness.

"I'd better adjust the frequency on these so no one else can listen in to us." She fished one of her earrings out of her pocket and used the thin edge of its backing clip to lever out the tiny access panel inside the band. "You didn't find any Federation equipment at all, Sulu?"

"No. If there was any here, someone got it before us." Sulu half-turned when Israi came to join him, her hands full of gleaming gunmetal weaponry. "We found three Klingon disruptors, though, two of them still with some charge."

Startled, Uhura opened her mouth to ask the helmsman why he'd entrusted the weapons to Israi, but the slight tic of muscle in one thin cheek warned her not to press the issue. She bent her head and concentrated on retuning the transmission settings inside each of the three comm bands, her hands doing the delicate work with automatic precision while her mind worried over alternate ways to contact the ship.

"If we can't contact the *Enterprise* from here, we'll just have to walk to the next seismic station," she decided at last, closing up the last wristband. She handed one of the short-range communicators to Sulu and one to Mutchler, keeping the third one for herself. Israi watched in silence but surprised Uhura by making no sound of protest.

Mutchler snorted weakly while he took the comm band. "That's another ten kilometers away. *I'll* never make it that far." He turned his gaze to catch Sulu's, equally shadowed and equally somber. "Neither will you."

"No, probably not."

"My camp lies just a few kilometers down this dead stream." Israi's intent almond eyes met Uhura's, as if the men's problems didn't really matter to her. The Dohlman hefted one Klingon disruptor, her long fingers closing expertly around its curved stock. Then, abruptly, she held the other out to Uhura. "Here. We will call your ship on our communicator, after we kill all the rest of them."

Uhura didn't hesitate to take the weapon from the young

203

Elasian. She only wished she could get the other one away as easily. "Kill the rest of *who*, Israi?"

"The Crown Regent's cohort." The Dohlman jerked a disdainful chin back toward the three scattered bodies. "These dead belonged to her. There will be more of them alive below."

"Why do you have to kill them?" Exasperation lent Mutchler the strength to lift his head and scowl at her. "Can't you just gloriously order them to let us into camp?"

Israi traded hostile stares with the geologist. "They will not obey me," she said at last, almost reluctantly.

He snorted again. "I thought you were *the* Dohlman of Elas."

"I am!" Loose ash kicked out as Israi whirled to her feet, as tireless as if they hadn't been climbing steep volcanic slopes for the past four hours. She strode three impatient paces away, then turned and came back to scowl at Mutchler. "But my aunt wishes to be Dohlman—and as Crown Regent she is my heir. *Now* do you see why we can't just walk into camp, idiot geologist?"

"Oh." Mutchler dropped his head back onto his arms, his brief spurt of energy obviously fading. "Well, go kill them if you want to. I'll guard the wreckage while you're gone."

"Wreckage!" Uhura shot to her feet. "We haven't checked the wreckage of the flyer for a communicator. If there's one anywhere, it's there."

Sulu glanced at the opposite slope of the ravine, where the smashed flyer still smoldered sullenly. A barely visible heat shimmer trembled over the broken warp core, vanishing against the ash-dark sky above it. "It's not safe, Uhura. There's too much heat coming out of that core, too long after the explosion. You know that means there's subspace leakage."

Uhura tucked her chin into one fisted hand, tapping her thumb against her cheek while she judged safety margins in her head. "Fifteen minutes' exposure to subspace radiation won't kill us."

"And what matter if it did?" A quizzical smile tugged at

Israi's lips. Uhura couldn't remember seeing the expression on the Dohlman's face before, but still it looked oddly familiar. After a moment, she recognized it with a start as a replica of her own rueful smile. "If the idiot geologist has the truth in him about this volcano, we will all be dead soon anyway."

Sulu's eyes narrowed, emotions struggling in his face as he stared at her. "So you want me to go look for a communicator?"

"No." Israi lifted her chin, smile fading into more typical Elasian arrogance. "You have served beyond your strength, bondsman, and will be more hindrance now than help. Stay here. *I* will look for this communicator."

"We'll both look for it." Uhura saw the frustrated way Sulu tried to rise, despite Israi's curt order. "Don't worry, we'll just yank the communicator board as soon as we find it and bring it back to use with the station generator."

Sulu grunted, settling back to the ground under Israi's compelling gaze. "Don't wait to see if it works." His grim voice was aimed at Uhura although his eyes never wavered from his Dohlman. "Just grab it and get out."

"All right." The ground quivered again beneath Uhura's feet as she rose, rippling and twitching like the skin of some huge nervous beast. The motion reminded her of the geologic equipment she still carried and she unstrapped the portable seismic monitor, handing it over to Mutchler. A flicker of scientific interest fought through the weariness in his face as he accepted it. He had the display turned on and was muttering over it even before Uhura and Israi turned away.

"Babbling again," the Dohlman commented, but the scorn in her voice sounded tolerant rather than angry. Becoming mature seemed to have done a lot to improve her personality, Uhura reflected ironically. Or perhaps, like any human adolescent, Israi was molding her behavior on the adults she could observe around her.

They slid down the final slope of the ravine on a steeply piled layer of ash, then began to struggle up the opposite side. The loose volcanic cinders had a nasty habit of holding firm until Uhura put her full weight on them, then cascading out from underfoot. The low-oxygen air of Rakatan tore at her lungs. "When we get to the flyer, I'll look for the communicator," she told Israi, between gasps. "You check the bodies for equipment and—and identity."

Israi gave her a sidelong glance. "You fear your *kessh* is there."

"Yes." Uhura swallowed ash, bitter and choking in her throat. A memory of dust rising over a fallen body filled her mind, fresh knowledge painting steel blue armor on the dark forms converging there. "Your aunt the Crown Regent held the camp when we escaped, didn't she?"

"Yes." Israi broke stride, blinking at the sizzling heat that met them several strides away from the Elasian flyer. Uhura pushed into the shimmering core emission without hesitating, her mind starting the fifteen-minute clock that would get them out before they absorbed too much subspace radiation. She scanned the twisted wreckage quickly, seeing with relief that the front end, where the communicator would be, had survived battered but intact.

"In here." Uhura dropped to her knees to slide through the wrenched-off end of the flyer cabin and heard Israi scramble in behind her. A faint thrumming shivered in the tips of her fingers, telling her how much subspace radiation still laced the flyer's interior. Uhura revised her estimate of their safety margin down to ten minutes.

A faint glimmer of emergency lights illuminated what was left of the murky, ozone-tainted cabin. Uhura scanned the main cabin first, seeing only three Elasian-sized shadows strewn across the floor. Heaving a thin sigh of relief, she turned toward the cockpit, searching for a communicator panel. She found it more by luck than knowledge, catching at the nearest panel to steady herself as she lurched over the last row of seats and only then seeing the unlit frequency display in the dark.

"None of those I searched had communicators," Israi's

voice said from the dark just behind Uhura. "Have you found—" The Dohlman's voice broke off as something stirred in the wreckage of the cockpit. Busy tracing power cables to their unfamiliar sources, Uhura didn't pay much attention, not even when the Dohlman choked in what sounded like wordless horror. There was no ignoring the words that tumbled out of her afterward, though. *"Kessh! You're still alive!"*

Uhura cursed and snapped the communicator cables free with more force than she'd intended. One whipped back to lash across her face while a second tangled itself around a panel support strut. She yanked it free with merciless haste, then turned to where Israi knelt. Only the top of her black head was visible above the twisted pilot's seat, and Uhura couldn't see the man she spoke to.

"Your Glory." The hoarse tenor voice stilled the frantic pounding of Uhura's heart even before she got close enough to see Takcas in the darkness. Only the gold Elasian eyes and red hair allowed her to recognize him. His face was already swollen and glazed hard with subspace damage, blood blisters spattered like rusty brown stains beneath the peeling skin. "I do not deserve the honor of seeing you yet alive."

"Yes, you do, my *kessh.*" Israi bent over him, her eyes fiercely intent on his. Uhura paused at a discreet distance, compassion welling inside her. She should have known that only someone with an Elasian's strength and endurance could have survived in the flyer this long. The subspace radiation would have killed a human many times over.

"But I should have known—" Takcas's throat closed on a strangled cough, then cleared again. "—that legless lizard, Oben, was a traitor. Should have known he was already the Crown Regent's bondsman, before ever he swore his oath to you." His gaze slid to Uhura and then back again, bleakly resigned. "The Starfleet Dohlman has the better *kessh,* Your Glory. He fooled Oben into unleashing him. Now he goes to die like a man against your aunt's cohort while I lie rotting like a gutted fish."

"He is not the better *kessh!*" Israi protested hotly. "It was not he who hid me on the Starfleet shuttle, it was not he who saved me from my aunt's bondsmen."

"When it was too late to fight them." The hand the *kessh* lifted to his Dohlman was bloated to a misshapen, fingerless lump, but Israi took it anyway. "I would have known about Oben in time, if you had cried the tears, Your Glory. I would have known and I would not have betrayed you—"

"You have never betrayed me, Takcas. I say it, who now have the tears of a Dohlman." Her face was wet with them, reflecting back the emergency lights in thin, flickering stripes as she bent to him. Takcas sucked in an astoundingly deep breath as the moisture touched his swollen fingers, then let it out again in a long, almost singing sigh.

"My life in your hands, Dohlman Israi," he whispered, ritually slow and deep. A brown tarnish of blood was beginning to dull the fierce gold shine of his eyes as tiny blood vessels ruptured and leaked.

Israi's voice shook, then steadied again. "My honor in your hands, *Kessh* Takcas. Be my bondsman."

"I am—" He coughed again, more rackingly, then groped blindly up at her. "Your Glory—you have your knife?"

"Yes."

Takcas's rigid face still managed a faint smile. "Then it is a good day to die."

"It is a good day to die," Israi agreed.

The steadiness of her voice left Uhura utterly unprepared for the swift flash of metal in the darkness, the downward plunge and the wet impact of metal on flesh. Blood bubbled around the quivering knife, embedded deep in the swollen throat with Israi's hand still clenched upon the ruby hilt.

Rakatan Mons jumped, bouncing rocks across its broken surface, and snarled a long, heart-stopping peal of thunder. Chekov jerked upright from where he'd been resting against a tall rock outcrop with his head pillowed on his arms. Pain, dulled to nearly nothing beneath the roar of the awakening volcano, kicked him in the side as protest to the sudden movement.

He turned clumsily to put his back to the rocks, then pressed one hand hard to his side to try and keep the pain at bay while he squinted up the slope toward the distant peak of the volcano. Billows of crawling black poured over the clouds already gathered halfway up Rakatan Mons's flanks. Roiling darkness swallowed every shred of white that tried to flee ahead of its burning breath, chewing up the cumulus vapor until not even a glimpse of the sky beyond remained. Below it, Chekov took a shuddering breath as he watched the monster's shapeless shadow flow across the ground around him until it finally ate every feature and detail of the land, as well. Then the volcano rumbled again in satisfaction, and unleashed a single, brutal crack that nearly broke the clouded sky.

How close did this mean they were to the end? Chekov wondered. The mountain had bucked and grumbled almost continuously since he'd left the seismic station—what felt like hours ago now, but he really couldn't be sure—yet this was the first belch of ash that hadn't simply swept across the mountainside like a quickly passing storm. Hanging high above the ground like a filthy slick on top of deep water, this black cloud seemed to grow and darken with every trembling rumble. Chekov looked down the length of ravine still standing between him and the Elasian mining camp, and his heart throbbed painfully with regret.

He couldn't walk in this. It was darker than the night they'd tried escape from the mining camp. The weak air and shifting earth made it hard to stay standing where he was, much less hike another uncounted number of meters. Feathers of what looked like dirty snow floated lazily through the air to pepper the ground all around him. He held out a bloody hand to catch an errant flake, and it stung like fire where it set down on his palm. *Hot ash,* he realized dismally as he jerked his hand back and scrubbed it against the leg of his trousers. *So I either bleed to death or burn to death.* He wasn't fond of either option.

When he first interrupted his hike to rest here, he promised himself he wouldn't stop for long. Walking at all had become a painful matter of stubbornly moving because he refused to fall, of concentrating on breathing deeply enough in the poor atmosphere, of ignoring the heavy limp that had gradually crept into his step over the course of the last long hours. He'd told himself that he could catch his breath while standing up, because he knew if he sat down the chances were good he wouldn't get up again. Waving flecks of burning ash away from his face and hair, he admitted now that he wasn't going onward either.

Only a few limping steps farther down the ravine, some sort of fracture in the rock had dropped a clutter of stones away from the rock face, leaving behind a long indentation that might have been scooped out by some giant's arm. Chekov didn't even have to duck to step under the overhang, but easing himself to the ground against the back wall proved harder than he'd expected. He sat down more heavily than he meant to, and cried out sharply at the pain. It felt good to be sitting, though, to give in to his shivering muscles and lean his head back against the rock with a weary sigh. A whole other man's length beyond his feet, black and scarlet ash drifted randomly in the burning breeze, building little glowing cairns. If the sky cleared and the ash moved on, he could try to stumble farther downslope ahead of the next explosion of darkness. If they didn't . . .

Tucking his elbow tight against his aching side, Chekov watched the rain of luminous ash and waited for the world to end.

Chapter Twenty-one

KIRK FINGERED THE EDGES of the blast-shattered corridor, studying the frozen splash patterns now recorded forever by the debris strewn across Skaftar's dusty surface a hundred meters below. Apparently there had once been a whole other wing of the Johnston Observatory down this direction—complete with a waste-elimination system, judging from the piping that jutted out from the remnants of the wall. Now nothing stood beyond this airless intersection except the flat, matte darkness of space, and the brilliant aqua crescent of Rakatan peeping up over Skaftar's horizon.

"There!"

Kirk turned at Metcalfe's breathless but triumphant shout. She obviously wasn't used to functioning inside an environmental suit, much less talking to her companions only via radio. The captain had given up reminding her that she didn't need to shout to be heard when they were out of sight.

"All clear?" he asked, intentionally pitching his voice softly and calmly.

Wriggling backward out of the narrow cranny Spock held

open for her in the collapsed wreckage, Metcalfe paused as though caught off guard by the nearness of his words. Kirk understood how she felt. "Yeah, it's set," she said more quietly as she crawled free and rotated to sit on her bottom. "I managed to shove the power conduit off to the far side." She scooted to jab a thickly gloved hand awkwardly toward the one wall. "Under that chunk of transparent aluminum."

Kirk nodded, then glanced over to catch the confirming tip of Spock's head when the Vulcan lifted his tricorder in front of his helmet's faceplate. Every time Spock consulted the device in the eerie vacuum silence, the complete lack of sound washed a chill of unreality over Kirk, as though everything around him were part of some unfinished dream. He waited until Spock, still studying his tricorder, reached to take Metcalfe's arm and move her aside; then Kirk checked the charge on his phaser and aimed at the snarl of debris.

A finely calibrated beam splashed silently against the blockage and flashed it an instant, stunning white. The sudden rise in the corridor's ambient temperature registered on the gauge to the right of Kirk's vision, then vanished abruptly as the heated gas cloud puffed away into vacuum on the other side of the wreckage. Kirk cut the beam and waited for the dust to settle.

Even though they'd done almost the same thing at every barricade they'd found for the last four hours, Kirk still held Metcalfe back while Spock inspected the burned-out passage. Only after the Vulcan had declared the edges cool enough to pass and stepped through to the open corridor beyond did Kirk release Metcalfe and start forward as well. It wasn't that the young geologist had made any sort of attempt to hurry forward when she shouldn't; Kirk just wasn't taking any chances. They were running out of time as it was.

Reflected light from Rakatan's watery surface lent the faintest trace of detail to the dark corridor beyond the wreckage. Kirk ducked through the still-warm hole, gritting his teeth in frustration when the light from the lamp on the top of his helmet glanced off another debris wall barely ten meters ahead of them. Spock already stood at the base of it, sweeping his tricorder smoothly left and right as he scanned the pile from top to bottom.

Something thumped the seat of Kirk's environmental suit, and he sidled against the outside wall in response. "Sorry, Captain." Metcalfe crawled clumsily through the opening, then stumbled into Kirk as she regained her footing. She smiled a thanks when he reflexively caught her, but sobered again quickly as soon as her eyes turned to follow the course of his gaze. A groaning little sigh escaped her. "I was *sure* we were almost there. . . ."

"I was hoping so." He only had a few shots' worth left in the phaser. "Clearing battle wreckage isn't exactly what Starfleet designed these things for."

Metcalfe glanced at the pistol in his hand, then let her frown travel upward to the scarred window above his left shoulder. Kirk recognized the bright smear of reflection across the front of her faceplate, but turned to face Rakatan anyway. It looked sharply defined, and very, very distant. "What's this?" he asked, reaching up to trace a smudge of gray trailing off across the water to the east of Rakatan Mons.

Metcalfe scrubbed at the image, as though it were a dirty patch on the transparent aluminum that she could somehow rub away. "Ash from Rakatan Mons. It's thrown up about a cubic kilometer of it so far."

Kirk remembered the inkblot of smoke and lava they'd watched on their first day here. "I thought Dr. Bascomb said that when Rakatan Mons erupted, it would throw debris up into outer space. So far, this eruption doesn't look any worse than that other volcano we saw."

"Mazama Mons," she informed him automatically. He could tell from her grim nod, though, that her mind was on the more serious question. "So far, it *isn't* any worse. I won't know for sure until I get down there and analyze the ash composition, but my guess is that Rakatan Mons is just clearing its throat." She turned her shoulder to the window and looked up at him. "The volcano has to blast out the old welded ash that's clogging the crater before any new magma can get through."

Which meant there was worse yet to come. "How long does that stage usually last?"

"Hard to say." Metcalfe shrugged and shook her head. "Sometimes, months. Other times, hours."

Kirk glared across the kilometers at the volcano, acutely aware of which time frame the damned thing had better be working in.

"Captain . . ."

Over the suit comms, Spock's voice sounded tinny and flat. He slipped his tricorder into its holster on the side of his equipment belt and came back through the darkness to join them. "I detected no active power conduits inside this deadfall, Captain. I believe it will be safe to destroy it all."

Kirk moved as close to the wreckage as he dared and studied the surface for a weak spot. Two shots, he estimated. That's all he had left before they were forced to resort to tearing obstructions apart by hand and hoping they didn't damage any of their suits in the process. He fired low, carving out a deep cleft through the wreckage near the floor and letting the upper layers collapse downward and forward to clear themselves out. It wouldn't make for the best walking environment, Kirk suspected, but it would be better than no passage at all. He actually managed to coax a third weak shot from the weapon before it lapsed into darkness in his hand. "All right . . ." He returned the spent phaser to his belt. "Let's see what we've found."

"Be careful, Captain."

Kirk grinned as he felt for his first toehold in the partially collapsed pile. "Thank you, Mr. Spock. That was my plan."

Debris slipped and settled only slightly beneath his moon-lightened weight. When he reached the top of the pile, he polished dust from his helmet lamp with the palm of his glove and directed the light straight forward in an effort to see how far the jumbled deadfall extended. He pulled back slightly in surprise when a glare of Starfleet white erupted almost directly in front of him, the blocky crest of a scarlet "2" just rising above the junk line.

"Congratulations, everyone. I think we've found the shuttle bay." It was all he could do to keep from shouting the way Metcalfe had.

"Are the doors intact, Captain?"

Kirk had an impression of Spock moving up closer behind him, but couldn't turn around enough to see for sure. "I don't know, Spock—I can't tell. Ms. Metcalfe, is there an airlock on this door?"

"Yes!" she exclaimed. Then, as if the loudness of her own voice in her helmet had startled her, she went on more quietly, "There should be controls about halfway up on the right."

Kirk dug a hand down between the wall and the pile, shifting stray bits of debris until he'd gained a little column of clear space. A keypad and visual display nestled almost out of reach below him. "I found it. What's the access code?"

"Sesame."

"Ah." He started to punch in the letters with some effort. "Very secure."

"Well . . ." Metcalfe sounded embarrassed. "We don't have a lot of problem with intruders around here."

"Not even with your sentient magma men?"

"Very funny, Captain."

Water vapor puffed, white and diaphanous, into a cloud against Kirk's faceplate as the airlock doors ground silently open. Scraping away frost with the fingertips on his gloves, Kirk swept his light around the small room within, looking for damage or contamination. The walls and floor gleamed as clean and even as the day they'd been installed. "Well, it holds an atmosphere. Let's see if it cycles." He leaned over on one elbow to swing his legs around and slide down.

Kirk busied himself kicking and shoving debris away from the doorway as Metcalfe climbed in behind him. She landed with a grunt on the floor of the airlock, then crawled out of the way to give Spock room to enter with a more agile jump. The Vulcan cranked the doors manually shut without having to be told. "I presume you have some plan for exiting this airlock should the atmosphere fail to cycle, Captain."

Kirk leaned a hand against the big red button that should start the flood of breathable air. "None whatsoever, Spock. That's the beauty of it—I can't be disappointed."

He felt the press of invisible weight against his suit, though, and heard the faint sounds of the atmosphere pump gradually rush up on him, louder and louder, as the lock filled with air. He smiled up at his first officer with a suave spread of his hands. "At least something on this station works."

The Vulcan raised an eyebrow. "It would be preferable if that something were the shuttle."

Kirk grimaced, unhappy to be reminded about that century-old bucket. "There is that."

"Don't worry, Captain," Metcalfe assured him from her place on the floor. "John Dembosky was really proud of our ships—he kept them in good working order, even when he had to build the parts himself."

Somehow, that image wasn't very reassuring. "Unfortunately, Ms. Metcalfe, what's considered good working order for a Geological Survey outpost probably isn't what I had in mind for outrunning the Elasians." He cocked his head back to watch the airlock's pressure light darken slowly from amber to green. "We'll just have to make do with whatever we've got." And hope to hell it was enough.

The doors to the shuttle bay opened with a deep, reassuring sigh. Dim emergency lighting painted the domed walls a sick mercury orange, with the four-fold seals for the launch doors running up the framework like scars until they crossed at the top to form a great X. Beneath that X, balanced gracefully on runners that had been swept back for aerodynamic beauty while still allowing room for a warp nacelle, the K-117 looked too fragile and tenderly constructed to have survived for one hundred years beyond her retirement. But every contour of her monopiece hull had been kept polished and calibrated, and even the difficult exhaust manifold on the rear of her nacelle had been cleaned and resealed so recently that the heat bleed-offs still shone. There wasn't even a reentry ripple or debris scar in her brilliant blue-and-white finish.

Kirk shook his head in admiring wonder. "Thank you, Dr. Dembosky."

"Captain?" Spock glanced aside at him curiously.

"Why, Mr. Spock," Kirk said jauntily, "don't you realize that the K-117 was once one of the fastest interatmospheric shuttles in Starfleet?" At his first officer's uncertain frown, Kirk waved Spock forward toward the waiting craft and hurried Metcalfe along beside him. "It looks like it's going to be again. Let's go get our people."

By Uhura's mental clock, they'd spent at least eleven minutes in the brutal subspace radiation of the Elasian flyer. She'd hustled Israi out even before the Dohlman had finished murmuring her ritual chant over Takcas's body, but the spidery shiver of cold in her bones told Uhura it hadn't been soon enough. She clenched her teeth on her instinctive dread, telling herself that there'd be time enough to have the damage treated on board the *Enterprise*. Or else not time enough for it to matter.

The climb back up to the seismic station seemed much steeper than it had coming down—a bad sign, Uhura thought wryly. As they approached the splintered building, she could see Sulu sitting exactly where they'd left him. His gaze tracked them up the ravine slope, precise and fierce as an automated phaser. Behind him, Mutchler huddled under an emergency blanket, engrossed in whatever data were still coming through to his portable seismic monitor. Ironically, the geologist had his back turned to the actual column of volcanic ash looming overhead.

Rakatan Mons had spread more of that gray-black shroud across the sky, Uhura saw, and occasional scatters of it swept across the ravine like thin veils of rain. Unlike the earlier falls, these cinders still glowed ember-bright and left tiny seared places on Uhura's uniform—and on her skin.

Lightning blasted almost constantly through the curdled ash cloud, but the answering roars of volcanic thunder were drowned out by the larger thunder of the eruption itself. Only the western horizon still held light: a thin rim of sunset darkened by ash to the mahogany of Elasian blood.

Uhura hoped the dimness would keep Sulu from noticing her persistent shivers, but he read her face as easily as one of his star charts. "You were inside too long." The pilot half-rose from the ground, his thin face contorted with the effort even that slight disobedience cost him. "What happened?"

"We found my *kessh* and had to comfort him." Israi clicked her teeth in exasperation and went to push Sulu down again with one hand on his shoulder. "I told you to rest, bondsman. Who will carry our idiot geologist if you cannot?"

Sulu's glance up at her somehow managed to combine fierce devotion and equally fierce frustration. Even through the livid volcanic twilight, Uhura could see smudges of exhaustion around his eyes and mouth, dark as bruises beneath the gray volcanic ash. The synthetic adrenaline must finally be wearing off.

"He's not carrying anyone anywhere." Uhura tried to put a Dohlman-sharp edge in her voice, but was afraid it came out sounding more like alarm than anger. "We're going to contact my ship from here as soon as I hook this communicator up to station power."

Israi scowled at her, hefting her Klingon disruptor in one hand. "But my cohort remains captive. We cannot leave them on this smoking mountain."

"Don't worry, we know their coordinates. As soon as we make contact with the *Enterprise,* we'll have them beamed up, too." Uhura headed for the open access panel of the seismic station without waiting for an answer, hugging the Elasian communicator under one elbow while she crouched to peer inside. A nearby flash of volcanic lightning strobed through the cramped interior of the seismic station, but it didn't last long enough for her to find the power source whose reassuring vibration she could feel through the housing. Hot ash hissed and pattered on the metal roof, sounding oddly like rain.

"Israi." This time, Uhura didn't have to fake the impatient snap of her voice. "Bring me one of the lights from our emergency kits."

"Generator's in the far right corner." Mutchler raised his head, cheekbones jutting like dead branches underneath his ash-crusted skin. One volcanic cinder a little brighter than the rest fell onto his blanket, but the fireproof material merely blackened under it until it cooled and faded. "I left the power leads there when I yanked the controller."

"Were they still live?" The volcano groaned and lurched beneath them before the geologist could answer, slamming Uhura headfirst into the station. She fetched up against the array of broken seismometers and banged her shoulder painfully on their concrete dais. When the ground stopped quivering at last, Uhura caught her breath and found the power leads by the simple expedient of putting her hand down on one and feeling it bite at her palm. That answered her question about whether they were live. Then her other hand landed on something damp and sticky, and she yelped in dismay.

"Uhura?" Bright white emergency light stabbed through the darkness of the station, making her shadow skitter across the bloodstained concrete floor. Israi's voice sounded concerned. "Are you hurt?"

"No, I'm all right." Uhura squirmed backward, away from the drying pool of blood. "Point the light over my right shoulder, Israi, so I can see to connect this. A little more— yes, there." It only took her a moment to untangle the coil of wire Mutchler had left dangling and splice it into the Elasian communicator. With Israi's emergency lamp brightening the wires to strands of silver and her fingertips to copper-gold, Uhura even managed to avoid touching the live ends of the circuit.

"That's it." She plugged the last circuit together and sighed in relief when the communicator's antique frequency display flickered into faint blue life. She tried to angle the display up into the beam of Israi's light, but gave up when the power leads stretched so far that the display flickered. "Israi, can you tilt your light a little further down—no, not that way, back—"

Uhura broke off abruptly. The momentary wobble had skated the brilliant emergency light across one of the bloodstains on the floor and kindled it into a dark garnet red glow. Not the mahogany brown of dried Elasian blood, not even the warm cinnamon of Elasian blood when it was fresh. The color of that gummy pool was the unmistakable iron-rich red of human blood.

Chapter Twenty-two

"CHEKOV!" Uhura almost dropped the communicator in her shock. Chekov *had* been here, and he had been wounded. Although Sulu had been certain that this mayhem marked their friend's passage, Uhura realized she hadn't entirely believed it until now. She put down the communicator and scrambled back to the opening, suddenly needing to see how much of his blood the Russian had left here. "Israi, throw me that light!"

It bounced and rolled toward her in a wild spiral of light that showed her more red stains: a few trickles down one side of the station housing, small droplets splattered across the bank of seismometers, a web of smears and handprints around the still-wet pool in the far right corner. It looked like a reassuringly small amount until Uhura shone the light downward. Dark red stains glinted in a long smeared trail across the floor, almost hidden by the thicker layer of volcanic ash that clung to them.

"Oh, my God." She spun around and nearly collided with Sulu outside the station door. Either Uhura hadn't heard the order that freed him, or he'd finally managed to move without Israi's permission. "Sulu, I think Chekov's been shot! Look!"

The helmsman steadied himself with one hand on her shoulder, bending to watch the unsteady path of her light across the bloodstained floor. "He bled a lot."

"I know." Uhura met his gaze unhappily. "He wasn't in the flyer. I looked."

"And he wasn't here." Sulu swung away from her, frowning down the dark gash of the ravine. The hot ashfalls had ended for the moment, but a ghostly red glow of drifted cinders tracked the dry streambed down the slope. "Chekov knew this was the same valley that runs through the mining camp. If he went anywhere—"

"Wait!" Israi reached out to catch at Sulu's arm before he could move. The pilot glanced down at her and froze, pinned by her intent frown. "You say your *kessh* is hurt, but why do you need to go after him?" She turned her scowl on Uhura, ignoring an errant particle of ash that landed in her thick curls and glowed there, ruby bright. "Did you lie when you said we could beam my cohort up with us?"

"No." Uhura reached out to brush the cinder gently away from the Dohlman's smoldering hair. "We can beam them up anytime—now, if you want. But we can't beam up Chekov when we don't know where he is. We have to find him—"

"—before he bleeds to death," Mutchler finished grimly. The geologist had shed his blanket and was dragging himself painfully across the two meters that separated him from the station, seismic monitor cradled carefully against his chest. Guessing at his goal, Uhura went to help him. "You go look for Lieutenant Chekov," he told her unnecessarily, his rasping voice barely audible even this close. "I'll make contact with the *Enterprise* and get the Elasians beamed up."

Israi must have had sharp ears. Despite the thundering roar of the volcano, her startled gaze swung down toward the geologist. "You would do that?"

"Of course." Mutchler set down the seismic monitor and grabbed at the sides of the station access panel, wincing as he prepared to haul himself in. "No one deserves what's going to happen when this volcano finally erupts. Not even your damn Elasians, Israi."

"I did not give you permission to call me Israi, idiot geologist." Despite her sharp words, the Dohlman released Sulu and came over to Mutchler's other side, helping Uhura lift him into the station. After he had wormed himself in far enough to reach the communicator, she carefully handed the seismic monitor in behind him. "Give the idiot geologist your light, Uhura, so he can watch his screen make those stupid worm-lines."

Mutchler accepted the emergency light with an echoing snort that might have been laughter. "Those stupid worm-lines are going to tell me when this volcano decides to blow up, Your Glory."

"And what good will that knowledge do you?" she demanded.

"It'll just make me happy to know."

Israi looked up at Uhura over Mutchler's outstretched legs, baffled. Uhura answered her with a shrug. "All geologists must be idiots," the Dohlman decided, her voice sounding almost affectionate. She reached down to pat at Mutchler's good ankle, scattering crusted ash from his boot. "However, if you save my cohort, I promise never to call you idiot again. Even though you are one." A tremor of delicate emotion crossed her face, and she added suddenly, "Perhaps I should stay behind to pull you out of this punishment cell when you are finished calling the ship."

"No." Mutchler's voice was flat. "If that hot ash starts coming down thicker, I'll be better off inside here. You won't have any other place to shelter if you stay with me, Israi. You'll be safer going with the others to look for the lieutenant."

Israi reached down to Mutchler's boot again, this time to clasp his good ankle with her unseemly strength. "You speak as though you wish to protect me." The geologist didn't answer, but Uhura sensed an uncomfortable stillness from inside the seismic station. "You are not of my cohort, idiot geologist. Why would you think to do such a thing?"

"Because you're a royally spoiled brat . . ." Mutchler squirmed as though trying to dislodge himself from her grip, then gave up and sighed gruffly, "But I like you."

"Like me?" Israi's voice held bafflement and growing wonder. "But you have not tasted my tears."

The qualifer seemed to amuse Mutchler. "You're the one who keeps saying I'm an idiot geologist. Remember?"

"Yes," Israi agreed readily. "One whom I would be proud to have in my cohort."

Mutchler went quiet again inside the station, then asked plaintively, "Israi, please, can we not talk about this right now? We're running out of time as it is."

Uhura cleared her throat to stop Israi when the Dohlman opened her mouth to argue. Israi clenched her teeth with evident concern, but said nothing aloud to Mutchler's booted feet. "As soon as we find Chekov," Uhura suggested, "we'll call you on the Elasian comm bands and relay our coordinates."

Mutchler poked one hand out of the station to flash her an O.K. "Got it."

"You tell the ship to beam us up immediately. *All* of us, including you."

"Of course." The Elasian communicator whined when Mutchler began to dial in a Starfleet frequency. "Don't worry, Commander. You just take care of the Dohlman. I don't plan on claiming the honor of being the first geologist killed on this planet."

Kirk smiled as the little K-117 blasted clear of its moorings and leapt away from the shattered moonbase. Above them, Rakatan smoked like a clouded topaz, painting a provocative trail of dust and ash about her ample middle. The crude bulletships of the Elasian armada were too small and dark to see against the growing black shroud beyond them, but the ionized glow of their geodesic net glittered through the planet's stratosphere, as luminescent as an aurora, but steady, and more deadly.

"Spock, does this old boat have anything approaching a sensor array?" Kirk blinked hard against the sudden swap of subjective up and down as Skaftar disappeared beneath them and Rakatan suddenly dominated the screen. He gently rotated the K-117 until its attitude matched his new perception. "It would be nice to have some warning before one of those one-man fighters comes up to blast us."

The Vulcan interrupted his study of the approaching phaser web to examine the operations panel in front of him. "We do have a crude proximity sensor, Captain," he said at last. "However, its detection range is less than three kilometers. As I suspect no one-man fighter will risk approaching us that closely, the only thing we are likely to detect is an incoming photon torpedo."

Kirk grinned ruefully. "About a millisecond before impact." He edged them as precisely as he could between two of the onrushing lines in the phaser net. "Well, as long as the Crown Regent doesn't know we're here, we won't have to worry about torpedoes." At least, that was the plan.

Kirk felt the faint acceleration in their velocity a bare instant before it registered on his instruments. Accepting that as their entrance into the unyielding pull of Rakatan's inner gravity well, he carefully boosted the K-117's tail until she addressed the planet's surface nose downward. Feathers of atmospheric fire licked at the edges of the viewscreen as the little shuttle built up speed.

"Uh . . . Captain?" Metcalfe called uneasily from the passenger cabin. "I don't think this is the accepted reentry orientation for one of these."

Kirk tried to throw as much warm reassurance into his tone as possible. "Don't worry, Ms. Metcalfe—I know what I'm doing. Minnows slip through the open spaces in fishing nets all the time back on Earth." He flicked the switch for the rear impulse boosters, and threw them into a screaming, high-velocity dive. "Right now, we're the minnow, and the open space we're heading for is between those phaser beams."

Metcalfe fell silent behind him, but Kirk could feel her uncertain gaze follow every command he gave the shuttle's panel.

"Spock, what kind of sensors are those Elasian ships working with?"

"Unless they have been retrofitted with contemporary Klingon equipment, Captain, they should possess no visual scanning capability, and their electromagnetic field sensors should be as poor or worse than ours."

Not as bad as it could have been, then. "So a minimum drop of three kilometers once we're through the net before we can assume we've evaded them."

The little shuttle jolted suddenly, shuddering so roughly that Kirk caught his breath. They whisked too close to one dying phaser strand in the net, taking a surface burn along one pylon while ionic discharge laced electrostatic fire across the viewscreen. Kirk forced himself to ignore the ship's complaints, keeping his eyes and mind on the altimeter reading flashing at his elbow. They'd made it through their open space—all they had to do now was fall.

"Mr. Spock?" Metcalfe called, somewhat tentatively. "What if those little ships *have* been retrofitted with modern equipment?"

The question seemed to intrigue the first officer. "Given a typical Klingon shuttle-based sensory array, their maximum detection range would then extend to fifty kilometers."

"Unfortunately," Kirk sighed, still fixated on the altimeter, "a free fall of fifty kilometers would put us somewhere inside this planet's crust."

"Actually, the upper mantle." Metcalfe released her safety harness with a clatter, and Kirk heard the shuffling stumble of her environmental suit boots on the decking as she came forward to join them. "Look on the bright side, Captain—at least there are no dinosaurs on Rakatan for us to kill off when we hit."

A scientist's version of "the bright side." "I think we'll just assume the Elasian ships have *not* been retrofitted."

A loud *crack!* echoed down the shuttle's frame, and Metcalfe barked a cry of surprise. *Just expansion from atmospheric friction,* Kirk assured himself. But he felt a trickle of sweat down his chest underneath the breastplate of his environmental suit. One kilometer below the geodesic net, and counting.

"Metcalfe, do you know where the troposphere starts on this planet?"

She sighed from behind his right shoulder. "I'm a geophysicist, Captain, not a meteorologist. I *think* it's about the same as Earth's, but I won't swear to it."

"Damn." He would have liked to pull out of their dive where no one was likely to see them. "Another five kilometers, then, before we hit significant cloud cover."

"Atmospheric pressure at two hundred millibars, Captain," Spock reported. Slim Vulcan fingers danced lightly across the monitoring instruments. "Hull temperature, five hundred fifty degrees Kelvin and rising."

Kirk nodded absently. "She ought to be good up to at least nine hundred degrees." The control panel shuddered dully beneath his hands. "Come on, we only have another kilometer. . . ."

Ash began its strident song against the ship's ceramic outside, and Kirk glanced up by reflex. What he took at first to be the edge of a small continent intruded on the shuttle's viewscreen. He realized it was one small part of Rakatan Mons when a white-gray plume of gas and steam slapped water across the vista and crackled against the overheated hull.

"Your landing party's in luck, Captain." Metcalfe leaned between Spock and the captain, tapping at what looked like a billowing cumulus cloud of black ash stretching off to their northeast. Another cluster of smaller clouds clung to the base of the first formation, flashing and winking with strikes of dirty lightning. "The monsoonal winds are blowing most the ash away from the Elasian mining camp."

"Hull temperature, six hundred eighty degrees Kelvin and rising. Atmospheric pressure, three hundred millibars."

"Only another five hundred meters to go," Kirk told his first officer tensely.

Metcalfe's tricorder warbled with excitement as she aimed it toward the view outside. "Ash cloud estimated at four thousand meters in height, with significant development of ground surge at the base." Kirk realized with a twinge of unreality that she was recording her observations for future reference. "The volcano has apparently completed the throat-clearing phase of the eruption and commenced a Vesuvian or sub-Plinean stage of the main eruptive sequence—"

The last five hundred meters vanished in a flash. "Ms. Metcalfe, sit down!"

Kirk couldn't wait to see if she obeyed him. With excruciating slowness, he coaxed the shuttle's nose out of its shuddering plummet, away from the surface, into a parallel streak. Despite his care, G-force slammed him back into his seat like a hammer, and he heard Spock grunt beside him. Blood seemed to rush away from his extremities, clouding his vision with sparkles of dizziness and gray—

Then, abruptly, his blood pressure stabilized sharply enough to make him gasp, and Kirk sat very straight in his pilot's chair. A mountain as tall and wild as the sky nearly filled the horizon ahead of them, its rear flanks carpeted with a rain of falling ash. Gray-violet smoke rolled down the volcano's slopes in long, clinging fingers. Their red-hot interiors were only visible near the leading edges, where the ash clouds devoured the ground before them in forward-springing jets, as powerful as charging lions. Behind the incandescent avalanche, black smoke and ash rose in towering clouds several kilometers high. Lightning split the blackness in vicious, recurrent strikes.

"Hull temperature, six hundred fifty degrees Kelvin and falling. Atmospheric pressure, five hundred millibars and stable." Spock looked up from his instruments at last. "My compliments, Captain."

Kirk, however, couldn't take his eyes away from the orgy of destruction pouring down the broken cliffs in front of them. "Metcalfe," he said softly. "It's too late, isn't it? The volcano has already erupted."

"Oh, Captain . . ." The young geologist reached out to knot her hand on the shoulder of his environmental suit. "You don't understand—Rakatan Mons hasn't even *started* its eruption yet."

Chapter Twenty-three

"CHEKOV?"

A warm hand pressed beneath his jawline, and Chekov came awake quite suddenly, gasping with surprise. He could feel his own pulse, quick and thready, thumping against someone's fingers, but couldn't quite blink enough focus into his eyes to recognize the darkened face bending over him.

Twisting on his knees to shout back at the lip of the overhang, the figure leaned back into his own lantern light. "Uhura! Your Glory!" Beneath layers of sweat and gritty ash, Chekov caught the faintest glimpse of golden skin above a jacket of Starfleet red. "I found him!"

Dark, brittle ash reached crooked fingers across the rock floor, as if the monstrous dark outside were trying to creep its way into the shelter while Chekov slept. He couldn't see anything of the storm or landscape past the mouth of the hollow, but the rocks inside had been lit to a pungent gray by what had to be an emergency lantern out of sight on the floor beyond Sulu. Chekov reached up to grasp at the helmsman's wrist.

"What are you doing here?" he asked miserably. "You were supposed to have escaped!" Fine, sparkling ash made a sheen of the air around them, like dust suspended in some thick and bitter liquid.

"Well, we had some problems." Sulu felt behind him for the lantern, then brought it around in front of him to sweep them both with its light. "The Elasians didn't like our flight plan." Chekov could tell Sulu didn't mean to let him see the shocked frown that tightened his lips and drew his brows together. The helmsman smoothed the fear from his expression quickly, then tried on a thin smile as he leaned across Chekov to deposit the lantern on his other side. "So what have you been up to?" he asked lightly, peeling Chekov's hand away from the bloodied patch along his side. "You were obviously in fine form back at that seismic station."

Chekov laughed faintly as Sulu unlatched his jacket and eased it gingerly aside. "I could have used some help," he admitted.

"Yeah . . ." Sulu prodded at the strip of makeshift bandages bound around Chekov's waist. It didn't hurt much—not really—but Sulu's cheeks twitched against another expression of somber worry before he drew his hand back to dry it against the leg of his pants. "Apparently."

Weak beams of electric lighting slashed a bobbing trail through the darkness. Ash swam and glittered in the approaching lights, then wound into a swirl as first Uhura, then Israi disturbed the windblown piles near the entrance in their scramble under the shelter. They both looked pale and breathless in the murky lantern light, and their clothes and skin were sprinkled with tiny burns from the rain of ash outside. Kneeling, Uhura touched his shoulder as if to verify that he was really there. "Thank God you're all right."

Chekov decided it wasn't worth questioning her usage of "all right" just now. He gripped her hand when she slid it into his. "I really wish that you weren't here," he told them both.

"Don't worry," Sulu assured him. "None of us is going to be here much longer."

He wondered if Sulu realized how well that applied, regardless of whether or not the ship came to rescue them.

Uhura frowned and pressed his hand between both her palms. "Your hands are cold," she said, somehow making it sound slightly accusatory.

All of him was cold. He had been cold forever, it seemed. "It's the least of our worries."

"Sulu . . ." She shot a keen look across at the helmsman as she unlatched her jacket and started to strip it open. "How far are we from Mutchler at the seismic station?"

Pursing his lips, Sulu turned to look out at the violent ashfall, as if studying the invisible horizon would somehow give him the answer. Chekov smiled in tired thanks when Uhura draped her jacket over him and tucked it behind his shoulders.

"About three kilometers south-southwest," Sulu said at last. He looked back at them with an apologetic shrug. "I can't estimate any closer than that."

"It'll have to be enough." Settling back on her heels, Uhura pushed up the sleeve of her blue tunic and punched at the Klingon-made comm band on her wrist. It acknowledged her with a spit of static. "Uhura to Mutchler. Dr. Mutchler? We've found Lieutenant Chekov. Are you there?" Thin strips of high white noise were her only reply. "Dr. Mutchler? Hello?" She looked up at the rest of them with a frustrated sigh.

"Has the geologist been burnt by this fire rain?" It was the first thing Israi had said since joining them in the shelter. Chekov was a little surprised to find out that Mutchler was alive at all.

"Let's hope not." Uhura scowled down at the clumsy radio on her wrist. "These things don't use subspace frequencies, which means these rocks must be interfering with the signal." She sighed and turned an unhappy look over her shoulder at the ashy rain. "I guess I'll be right back."

She climbed to her feet and trudged to the edge of the overhang, eyeing the drifting ash with grim suspicion. Chekov watched her reactivate the comm band from just beneath the lip of rock, then scowl and slip out into the pelting cinders. He wished she hadn't given him her jacket.

"Your exhaustion has made you thoughtless."

Chekov transferred his gaze to Israi, and found her almond eyes studying him in cool, almost clinical curiosity. Maybe she'd never seen a man bleed to death before. He thought about telling her to come closer if she wanted a better view, but found he couldn't even summon the energy for sarcasm.

Her chiding voice, though, was aimed only at Sulu. "Do not sit there as though you are powerless. Take off your jacket and cover him as well."

Sulu's hands leapt to release the seals on his jacket even before the Dohlman finished speaking. "Yes, Your Glory."

Shouldering out of the garment, he carefully overlapped it with Uhura's and offered Chekov a worried smile. The combined weight of the heavy duty jackets felt good, somehow comforting and safe, but didn't do anything to warm him. He doubted anything they could do here would.

"Kessh Chekov." Israi's tone was a clear summons, and he turned his attention back to her simply because there was nothing better to do. "I think that even your breed of human is not meant to be as white as you," she said, obviously passing judgment on his condition from her seat on the other side of the shelter. "You have lost much blood on this walk of yours, yes?"

He didn't want to admit it, but trying to lie and be brave was more than he could do right now. "Yes."

Israi nodded. "Have you enough to await a rescue from your people?"

"I . . ." A sudden shudder trembled through him, and he felt Sulu's hand tighten on his arm. He didn't want to talk about this, didn't want to face the truth out loud. "I don't know," he whispered at last. ". . . I don't think so . . ."

"You're going to be fine—"

"Silence!" The snap of Israi's anger cut off Sulu's words as sharply as any blade. "This *kessh* does not have time for useless comfort."

L. A. Graf

Chekov closed his eyes and leaned his head back against the warm rock face. The Elasians would certainly win no awards for their bedside manner today.

"Your Dohlman," Israi said after what seemed a very long time. Or perhaps Chekov had drifted off again—he couldn't be sure. "She does not cry the tears, does she? She has not bonded you."

The words meant nothing to Chekov, so he was relieved when Sulu said softly, "No," as if he'd expected this question all along.

"And yet you march for her," the Dohlman pressed. Chekov heard her move farther into the outcrop, dislodging small rocks as she came. "You have both fought for her, and she walks all this way that she might find her *kessh*. You *all* refuse to abandon each other. If there is no bond between you, why do these things happen?"

Chekov answered without even opening his eyes. "Duty."

And above him, at the same time, Sulu told her, "Friendship."

In many ways, they were the same thing. Chekov knew that he and Sulu both understood that.

"Among humans," Sulu explained, "no person can bond another without their consent. We have to *choose* to be bonded. When we do, we can form bonds that not even the fear of death can break apart."

Israi was silent for a moment. "Bonds like mine?"

"No, Your Glory." The stiff difficulty with which Sulu forced out the words made Chekov open his eyes and look at his friend in concern. He didn't know how to interpret the hollow tension he could read on the helmsman's thin face. "Not like yours. But just as strong."

"So it seems." As though drawn by the low murmur of Uhura's voice giving their coordinates to Mutchler, the Dohlman glanced behind her and hazarded an understanding smile. "Then she is forgiven for not helping you in the way a Dohlman should her underlings. She does not know the responsibility and pains of being a Dohlman, for all that she has been given the name."

234

Impatient with their talk, Rakatan Mons pealed a crack of thunder so strong and loud it echoed for uncounted minutes afterward. Sulu cried out in alarm, and, outside, Uhura ducked reflexively as though anything she did could protect her from the mountain's fury. Caught off guard by the dull tremor of pain pushed through him by the jerking ground, Chekov clenched his teeth around a hard grimace and fisted a hand against his side beneath the jackets.

"Tell me truthfully, Starfleet *kessh*." Israi was suddenly beside him, her eyes dilated to nearly black despite the lantern light bathing her face, her cheeks flushed and her voice breathless with something more urgent than fear. "Is this a good day to die?"

The mountain around them bucked and rolled again, and Chekov found himself smiling weakly at the desperate question. "It had better be."

The Dohlman wrapped her fingers around the ornate dagger strapped to her thigh. It was a slim and delicate weapon, well fitted to the hand that held it. Israi seemed acutely aware of its beauty as she tried to steady it before her in both shaking fists.

"Israi! No!"

The young Elasian shook her head, not even turning to face Uhura when the older woman hurried back into the shelter to grab at her arm. "He is not your bondsman, Uhura. With no Dohlman to protect him, he must make this decision himself." She locked serious eyes with Chekov, and tried to pull her arm out of Uhura's grip. "Is it a good day to die?"

Something about the bright terror in Uhura's dark eyes broke through his confusion. His breathing stuttered on a sudden spasm of horror. "No," he croaked. "It isn't." He saw Uhura dart a fearful look at the Dohlman.

Israi lowered the knife onto her lap, eyes grave. "You haven't blood enough left to stand, or even breathe," she told him seriously. "You will slip from this world in weakness if you wait—I offer you the chance to die in strength." She leaned forward with surprising concern and

235

laid one small hand against his chest. "There is no dignity in dying as you are."

"There's no dignity in giving up, either. Please . . ." He wanted so badly not to seem afraid in front of her, in front of any of them, but there was nothing he could do to keep the pain and weakness out of his voice. "Whatever life is left me, it's mine. Let me keep it."

The young Dohlman nodded slowly, then slipped her knife back into its scabbard and tied the lace that bound it closed. Chekov noticed that Uhura kept one hand on the girl's arm until the very last knot in the leather had been tied. Even then, the creases of uncertain worry didn't leave the communications officer's brow.

"Very well," Israi said at last, very formally. She gently removed Uhura's hand from her arm, placing it in the lieutenant commander's lap with the same regal precision with which she'd scabbarded her blade. "I have learned that I must respect a different people's beliefs, and so I grant you this freedom. But there is no need for you to suffer any longer." Wiping her fingers through the sweat and ash on her elegant cheeks, Israi startled Chekov by leaning forward to stroke the side of his face with her hand. "You have served your duty well, Starfleet *kessh*," she said soothingly. "Sleep now in peace."

As though her words left him no choice, calmness and trust flowed over him in a delicious wave. Beside him, he heard Sulu groan in quiet sympathy just before sleep eroded the last of his thinking and carried him mercifully away.

Chapter Twenty-four

UHURA STARED DOWN AT Chekov's bruised face, astonished by the expression of smiling peace that curved his bloodless lips and smoothed the perpetual lines from between his eyebrows. His head rolled back into the crook of Sulu's elbow with a long, easy sigh, and his hand at last dropped away from his wounded side.

"Israi." Uhura dropped to her knees, reaching out to catch the young Elasian's hand and turn it upward. Even through the fine glitter of ash that drifted into the overlapping halo of their lights, she could see moisture glistening on the slender gold fingertips. "What did you do to Chekov?"

The Dohlman's fingers turned and tightened reassuringly around Uhura's own. "It is difficult to comfort the unbonded, Uhura. I did not mean to steal your *kessh* from you. I only used the tears to make his pain less." She gestured down at the sleeping Russian. "You see it worked."

"Yes. Thank you." Uhura glanced from Chekov's serene face to the Sulu's fiercely haunted eyes, then pondered the small factory of alien biochemicals responsible for both expressions. "I think."

Sulu tore his own gaze away from the Dohlman. "Why aren't we getting beamed up now? Didn't you manage to contact Mutchler?"

"I gave him our coordinates and he relayed them to the ship, but the *Enterprise* can't beam us up." Uhura clenched her teeth on remembered frustration, crouching down to shield Chekov as more luminous ash swirled under their protective ledge. "The Crown Regent has a whole armada here and she's using it to create an antitransporter screen around this planet."

Israi sprang to her feet with a spitting snarl. "It is not *her* armada, it is *my* armada! Now that I have the tears of a Dohlman, the Crown Regent has no right to command it as my protector." She whirled and began to stride the three-meter length of their shelter, the furious pacing of a caged leopard. "This should not be! I am truly Dohlman now, she is only my heir."

"But she doesn't know that yet, Your Glory," Sulu reminded her.

"Then I will tell her!" Israi skidded to a stop in front of Uhura, kicking enough ash into the gritty air to make both of them cough. Lightning crackled outside and turned the young Dohlman into a slim pillar of darkness, her expression unreadable. "You were right," she said bitterly. "I should have stayed with the idiot geologist. Then I could have used his communicator to tell the armada I have the tears—"

"And your aunt would have blasted you from orbit!" Uhura reached out to catch the girl before she could break free of shelter. "Israi, calm down. I haven't dragged you halfway across this volcano just to lose you now."

The Dohlman hissed in wordless frustration but allowed herself to be tugged down beside Uhura. Sulu squatted protectively beside her, forming a solid shoulder-to-shoulder wall that shielded Chekov from the thickening fall of ash. Uhura could feel the occasional wincing bite of hot cinder against the exposed skin of her neck and hands.

"Captain Kirk must be doing something about that

defense screen," Sulu said at last, his voice almost lost beneath a renewed fusillade of volcanic explosions. "What exactly did he tell Mutchler?"

Uhura gave him a sidelong glance across Israi's dark head. "Mutchler says he talked to Mr. Scott. Evidently, neither the captain nor Mr. Spock were available."

Despite the exhausted shadows painted on his face by their upward-slanting lights, Sulu's head went up alertly. "*Neither* of them? During a red alert situation?" He paused to consider it. "They're up to something."

"I think so, too." Uhura twisted to look out into the ravine, ash spilling from where it had begun to accumulate on her shoulders. Behind the frenetic dance of lightning strikes, a sullen fire-shot glow was building in the ash cloud overhead. "I just hope they manage to pull it off in time."

Israi straightened between them, her neck curving proudly. "If they do not, I can comfort my bondsmen before they die." Her voice sounded all the more fierce for the faint quiver beneath the surface. "We—" She stretched her hand to Uhura again, the quick, childlike clutch of her fingers betraying the fear she refused to show in her voice. "We must be stronger than the males, Uhura. We will die the true death as all Dohlmen do, but this evil smoking mountain will *not* frighten us."

Uhura managed a smile for Israi's steadfast arrogance, even in the face of death. "No, it won't." She tightened her grip on the small hand clenched inside hers. "Even if you did not have the tears, Israi, you would still be truly Dohlman."

Ash blasted fiercely under the ledge before Israi could reply. For one horrible moment, Uhura thought the final spasm of the eruption had finally reached them. But the choking swirl of ash collapsed after a moment as if it had been kicked up by some brief violence of wind. It took a long moment for Uhura to recover enough breath to hear anything past her own coughing. When she finally did, her brain almost refused to acknowledge the rhythmic pulse her ears detected below the volcanic rumble. It took Israi's startled turn of head and Sulu's growing smile to bring belief pouring into Uhura in a warm flood of astonishment.

"It's a ship!" She scrambled up and went to peer eagerly through the red-flecked rain of cinders. A shuttle's familiar dark bulk loomed across the ravine, but the crossed-rock-hammer-and-satellite symbol it wore startled her into a curse.

"Federation Geological Survey!" Uhura ducked as a cascade of hot ash slid off the overhanging rocks above her and sizzled in sinuous drifts around her feet. "Don't tell me those idiot geologists are doing fieldwork *now?*"

"Not unless they're a hell of a lot better pilots than I am." Sulu dragged her back into the safety of their rock shelter. "That's Captain Kirk!"

Floodlights blazed around the shuttle, their sweeping arcs starkly silhouetted by the surrounding blizzard of ash. In the glare, Uhura saw two cumbersome figures detach themselves from the larger shadow of the ship and cross the ravine, arms full of unwieldy bundles. She recognized the first one's fast, dynamic stride and let out a trickling sigh of relief.

"It *is* the captain."

"You were expecting the Crown Regent?" The voice was distorted by suit amplifiers and muffled by ash, but its quiet humor was unmistakably Kirk's. The captain ducked in below the ledge, movements exaggerated to compensate for his clumsy environmental suit. "Sorry we had to drop in unannounced like this, but the fewer people who know what's going on down here, the safer we'll all be. Everyone all right?" Behind the glint of his face shield, the bright hazel gaze raked the shelter and fastened immediately on Chekov. "Spock, get Chekov into the shuttle and see what you can do for him. I'll carry the rest of them over."

The taller suited form bent silently, shaking his bundle out into a fireproof emergency blanket. He wrapped it carefully around the wounded security chief, then used his alien strength to lift Chekov like a sleeping puppy. "I advise

you to hurry, Captain. The volcano is becoming dangerous."

"I'd noticed that, Mr. Spock." Kirk moved aside until the
Vulcan left, then unrolled his own blanket and took a step
toward Uhura and Israi. "Who's first?"

"Sulu," they said in unison.

Kirk's eyebrows shot up behind his visor, and Uhura
wondered if she was getting too good at sounding like a
Dohlman. "All right." He held the blanket out toward the
helmsman. "Ready, Mr. Sulu?"

"But Your Glory—" Sulu met Israi's stern glare and his
protest collapsed stillborn. He wrapped himself obediently
in the emergency blanket, hands shaking hard with exhaustion. "I can walk across myself, Captain."

"Not over the half-meter of hot ash out there, you can't."
Kirk grunted and hefted the pilot over one bulky shoulder,
then swung out into the heavy deluge of glowing red cinders.

Uhura stood on tiptoes to watch them go, almost losing
sight of them in the dust and smoke until their lurching
shadows cut the murky gleam of the floodlights. Someone
much smaller than Spock came out to meet them, steadying
Sulu as Kirk set him down, then handing something to the
captain. Kirk turned and came back to them, somehow
managing a jolting run even in the awkward environmental
suit.

Uhura spoke as soon as the captain ducked into the
shelter, forcing the words out between gasping coughs.
"Take Israi next, Captain."

"No!" Israi grabbed her wrists and swung her forward
with startling Elasian strength. "I am the Dohlman of Elas,
Kirk-insect, and I order you to take Uhura next!"

"That's enough." Kirk tossed a blanket at each of them,
face grim behind his helmet's faceplate. "Wrap yourselves
tight and stand next to each other. I'm taking you both."

Knowing that crisp snap of command, Uhura didn't
waste time arguing. She hooded the flame-proof blanket
over her head and wrapped herself tightly inside it, glancing

out through the folds only long enough to see that Israi had copied her actions. Kirk grunted in satisfaction, then ducked and caught one of them over each wide shoulder of his environmental suit, rising with only a slight stagger under their combined weights.

"No worse than Sulu," he assured them, although the breathless catch of his voice contradicted him. "Hold on!"

Uhura never knew how he did it, but somehow the captain managed to sprint through the thundering ashfall. There was one nightmarish moment when smoky air swirled up into her face and stopped her breath with its heat. Then she heard machinery grate on trapped cinders, and felt herself spilled down to a blessedly ash-free floor.

She struggled free of the smoldering blanket with someone's help and looked up through steady shuttle lights to see a vaguely familiar face regarding her from an unkempt tousle of brown-gold hair. "Are you all right, Commander?"

Uhura nodded and turned toward Israi, but the Dohlman had already scrambled free of her blanket and gone to crouch over Sulu's crumpled body. The woman in the environmental suit caught Uhura's arm when she would have followed.

"It's all right," she assured Uhura. "Mr. Spock said he just passed out from exhaustion."

"And Chekov?" Uhura swung around to see Spock fitting an emergency oxygen mask over the Russian's face. Kirk was already in the cockpit, gloves stripped off and hands busy on the controls. The shuttle's impulse engines rose to a roar, but the science officer must have heard her despite the noise.

"I have rebandaged the lieutenant's wound and given him synthetic plasma and oxygen to compensate for his blood loss," he informed her gravely. "There is little more I can do at this time. For the moment, he seems to be in no pain."

Uhura flicked a glance at Israi, silently thanking her when their eyes met over Sulu. "Let me hold him, Mr. Spock. You go help the captain." The shuttle had lurched off the ground, but seemed to be having difficulty getting any higher.

Spock nodded and reached out to guide her across the slanting shuttle floor. Uhura skidded across to him, gasping as another shuddering jolt slammed all three of them against the wall. Guessing that the protection of her lap wasn't going to be enough for Chekov, Uhura waited until Spock had climbed past her to the cockpit, then slid her hand along the base of the wall until she felt the corrugated mesh of shock webbing. She began to lace it carefully around the security chief's sprawled figure, seeing Israi watch her and then do the same thing for Sulu on the other side of the ship.

The woman in the Federation Geological Survey environmental suit looked up from the blankets she was folding. "Don't forget about Mutchler at the seismic station!" she reminded Kirk anxiously.

"Don't worry, Ms. Metcalfe. That's where we're headed next." Kirk's hands flexed on the controls, deliberately rolling the shuttle from side to side again. Uhura realized he was trying to shake off the heavy cloak of ash that had welded itself to the hull.

"Why didn't you pick Mutchler up first?" Uhura asked Metcalfe quietly, knowing better than to distract the captain from his work. "If you overheard his message to the *Enterprise,* you knew he was at Seismic Station Three."

Metcalfe nodded, gnawing at her lip. "Yes, but when he talked to Commander Scott on the ship, he was very insistent that your party should be rescued first." Her glance slid across Uhura to Chekov and became somber. "Now I see why."

The shuttle shook again, more violently, as it struggled to rise. "Come on," Kirk muttered under his breath. "Don't let that dirt stick to you—ahh!" A splintering crash outside the hull told Uhura that the shell of ash had broken and dropped away. The shuttle promptly hauled itself into the sky. "Mr. Spock, you have the coordinates of that seismic station?"

"Inputting to navigations console now, Captain."

A faint crackle of speech leaped out of the communicator panel, barely audible behind the transmitted thunder of volcanic eruption. Uhura recognized the raspy voice at once, although its tone of frantic excitement startled her. "Seismic Station Three to *Enterprise,* do you read me?"

Neither of the men in the cockpit moved to touch the transmitter controls. Uhura bit her lip as she guessed why. "We're still maintaining communicator silence, Captain?"

"Until we're out from under the geodesic defense screen and within beaming distance of the *Enterprise.*" The shuttle bucked and pitched in a sudden gust of turbulent ash, even under Kirk's expert hands. "Otherwise, we're going to get blasted out of the sky by the Crown Regent's phasers. I don't want her to know we're down here until we're long gone."

Mutchler's voice threaded out of the communicator again, almost lost beneath the roar of the volcanic firestorm behind him. *"Enterprise,* do you read me?" He sounded even more desperately excited, his voice a mixture of terror and pride that tore at Uhura's heart. *"Enterprise,* this is Scott Mutchler, at Seismic Station Three. We've just had an earthquake of magnitude ten, repeat *magnitude ten!"* A thunderous explosion rocked the shuttle, overloading the communicator's circuits an instant before it hit. Mutchler's voice was a distant, drowning scream. *"Enterprise! Enterprise! This is it—!"*

The thunderous impact of what sounded like an avalanche of hot volcanic ash slashed the geologist's voice away abruptly. Before Uhura's shock had time to turn into grief, a hammer blow from what must have been the same ash storm crashed into the shuttle and slammed it toward the ground.

Chapter Twenty-five

ONLY UHURA'S FIERCE GRIP on Chekov's shock webbing saved her. Thrown sideways by the impact of the immense eruption, the shuttle reeled and tumbled like a windblown leaf. Metcalfe collided with Uhura, then was flung helplessly away again to the other side of the ship. Uhura saw Israi catch the geologist with one hand, the other locked into Sulu's restraining straps. Muscles tightened to steel wires in the Dohlman's arms as she fought to hold on to Metcalfe.

"Get the rear impulse boosters back on-line, Spock!" Kirk's shout echoed through the rushing din and fierce stutter of the engines. The Vulcan's reply was inaudible, but after a dizzying plunge and swoop, the shuttle's flight path finally stabilized. The little ship paused like a runner collecting her breath, then slowly began to rise again.

Through the viewscreen, Uhura could see the nonstop glare of lightning through billowing ash. An occasional bolt engulfed the shuttle in its sheeting white glare and made the control panels blink in alarm, but the ship's internal surge protectors held firm. Uhura took a deep breath, barely able to believe they were still alive, then unwrapped her protective arm from around Chekov.

"Damage reports." Kirk's voice sliced through the chaos as sharply as if he stood on his own bridge.

"Rear boosters on auxiliary power, Captain." As usual, Spock sounded much calmer than any organic being had the right to be. "They will continue to function for approximately forty-five minutes. Other impulse systems are operating within minimum tolerance."

Uhura tried to pitch her own shaking voice loud enough to carry to the cockpit. "We've got structural damage to the hull just behind the main doors, Captain. Sulu and Chekov are alive and strapped in against turbulence, but Ms. Metcalfe—"

"I'm all right." The geologist sat beside Israi with both hands pressed to her ribs, but she lifted her tousled head with the determination of a Starfleet cadet. Behind her, a trickle of smoke and ash coiled into the shuttle through a series of rock-torn gashes. "The hull's wide open to atmosphere, Captain. In Rakatan's air, that means we'll drop below minimum breathable oxygen pressure at five thousand meters."

Kirk threw a grim look at his first officer. "See what you can do about making us airtight again, Spock. We need to make at least nine thousand meters to get past the Crown Regent's geodesic net and get beamed aboard the *Enterprise.*"

Spock nodded and reeled back down the shuttle's central aisle, threading his way carefully between Uhura and Israi. Metcalfe staggered to her feet and joined his inspection of the breached hull, still with one arm wrapped around her ribs. Uhura hurried forward to take Spock's vacated seat. Kirk acknowledged her presence with a nod but never took his eyes from the flashing instruments on his panel.

"What's the hull temperature?" he demanded.

Uhura searched the antiquated copilot's board until she found the correct readout. "Six hundred degrees Kelvin, sir."

The captain grunted. "We're all right up to nine hundred." His hands flickered over the controls, responsive to every slight change in wind and air pressure despite their ash-blinded instruments. Uhura watched him in awe. With her command qualifications, she could nominally pilot this kind of shuttle, too, but she knew she couldn't possibly do it so well in this lightning-shattered darkness.

"Thirty-five hundred meters," Kirk read from the altimeter. "How's it going back there, Spock?"

"The damage is not extensive, Captain, but without welding equipment—"

Metcalfe interrupted. "We *do* have welding equipment, Mr. Spock. This is a drilling rig, after all." Uhura glanced back to see the geologist hauling a small plasma torch out of one equipment locker. "But I don't know what you're going to use to weld those holes shut with."

Spock accepted the torch from her with a lift of one eyebrow, then wordlessly began to shrug off his environmental suit. The torch sputtered, eating across the suit's metallic breastplate carapace and cracking it into polygonal chunks. Before the pieces had even cooled, Spock fitted one over the closest rent and began welding it closed. The plasma arc was so bright that Uhura had to look away. She hoped the Vulcan's inner eyelids gave him some protection from the glare, if not from the drifting sparks.

When she turned back, the volcanoscape below them wrung a gasp from Uhura. They had risen into the spreading thunderhead of the ash cloud, and she could see immense fountains of red-hot debris illuminating the darkness.

"Oh, my God." The shallow breathlessness of her own voice told Uhura how near they were getting to the limit of breathable oxygen. "It's—it's beautiful!"

"Yes, it is." Metcalfe had come forward to lean over her, aching ribs obviously forgotten in the thrill of exhilaration. Her wide eyes tracked an enormous spray of incandescent ash as Kirk banked the shuttle around its feathery fire. "It's the inner heart of a Krakatoan-type eruption. And we're probably the only sentient beings that have ever seen it."

"And lived to tell about it." Kirk sounded a little breathless now, too. Black sparkles had begun to dance across Uhura's eyes, making the view outside almost hallucinogenic—roiling clouds, platinum-bright lightning, hot ash glowing like the open gates of hell. "Assuming we *do* live to tell about it. Spock, we're at forty-two hundred meters. Haven't you got those holes sealed up yet?"

"All but one, Captain," the Vulcan reported. "Unfortunately, I have exhausted the charge in this welding device."

Uhura swung around to see the welding torch expire in a burst of spitting sparks. Spock straightened, his olive-dark skin freckled with the flash burns that came from welding without protection. He frowned thoughtfully at the last narrow gash in the hull, then picked up the severed sleeve of his environmental suit and plastered it over the break, using both hands to spread the metallic fabric taut. Uhura knew that only someone with a Vulcan's strength could have held that seal shut against the buffeting volcanic wind. "I believe Ms. Metcalfe may now reactivate the shuttle's oxygen-exchange systems."

"Ms. Metcalfe." Kirk spared a swift glance up from his instruments when the fascinated geologist didn't move. "Wendy." He nudged her gently with one elbow and she turned to look at him with startled eyes. "Hit the oxygen. You can admire the view better if you don't pass out."

"Oh." Quick color chased up her cheeks before she swung around to the life-support panel and dialed the oxygen exchangers to their highest level. After a moment, Uhura drew in a deep breath of oxygen-rich air, feeling its cool comfort pour down her raw throat into weary lungs.

Without warning, the shuttle burst out at the top of the towering column of ash above Rakatan Mons. It wasn't until they lost the screaming rush of volcanic particles past the battered hull that Uhura realized how loud it had been and how loudly they must have all been shouting to be heard over it. She suddenly understood why her throat ached so fiercely.

Kirk let out an almost silent sigh of relief and increased the shuttle's upward velocity. "Closing in on six thousand meters—"

"Vessel approaching, Captain!" Uhura pointed at the silver speck floating over the black mountain ranges of ash below them. She scanned her instrument panel and found its crude energy-field sensor. "I think its shields are up."

"Damn!" Kirk swung the protesting shuttle into a precautionary dive. "We would come up right at one of the nodes in the Crown Regent's geodesic net."

Radiant light blasted past them, fierce as volcanic lightning but arrow straight. "They're firing phasers, Captain," Uhura said unnecessarily.

"I only wish we could fire back." Kirk threw the shuttle into another evasive spiral and a second phaser shot missed. "We're not going to outrun them with our rear impulse boosters on auxiliary power, that's for sure." He sounded as though he was thinking out loud. "We can't turn on the warp drive, we haven't got weapons or shields—"

"We have a weapon." Uhura started to leap to her feet, but found Israi already at her shoulder, pushing a startled Metcalfe back to steady the unconscious men on the floor. Behind them, Spock leaned hard against his unwelded hull patch, straining to hold it against the drag of the stratosphere.

"*My* armada," the Dohlman muttered between her teeth as she watched the little warship chase them. She pointed an imperious finger at the communicator, but Uhura was already tuning it to all known Elasian frequencies. Kirk slammed them into another unexpected bank, then glanced over at Uhura assessingly.

"Cease-fire orders?" he guessed. When she nodded confirmation, his hazel gaze slid up to Israi's intent face. "Can you enforce them, Your Glory?"

Utter Elasian arrogance radiated from every ash- and mud-crusted inch of the Dohlman's body. "Yes." She leaned over the communicator, dropping a hand on Uhura's shoulder to steady herself against the jolting of the shuttle. Uhura made one last frequency adjustment, then switched on the communicator and nodded at Israi to speak.

"Cohort of the Crown Regent and ships of the royal Elasian armada, your Dohlman Israi speaks to you. I have—" The young Elasian paused, throat muscles working while she gathered all the whiplash power of her voice. "—the tears of a Dohlman."

Some wordless noise tore across the static-plagued communicator in response. It might have been a ragged cheer or an equally ragged shout of rage. Israi ignored it and kept speaking.

"I have cried the tears, I have bonded my *kessh* and my cohort. As the true Dohlman of Elas, I command you—stop firing at the Starfleet vessel!"

Another phaser shot screamed past them, so close it rocked the shuttle with its heat corona. Israi's voice rose to a panther-sharp snarl that made even Uhura flinch.

"Worms that ate my dead ancestors, stop firing! *I am aboard!*"

The little gunship veered off, so abruptly it vanished into its own contrail. Kirk heaved a second and louder sigh of relief, banking the shuttle up through the last of the stratosphere and toward outer space. Uhura watched the darkness loom overhead, stars pricking through it one by one as the atmosphere thinned around them. Somewhere up there was the *Enterprise*. . . .

The communicator sang a faint but familiar whistle. Uhura hurriedly brought her gaze down to the instrument panel, dialing the frequency back to Starfleet standard. The signal must have come through most of the planet's ionosphere; it was interference-cracked and barely audible. "—caught the tail end of that signal," Commander Scott's voice said through the surrounding static. "I'm assuming it's you, Captain. We chased the Crown Regent to the far side of the planet, sir, but she gave us the slip and doubled back. We're coming around the other—"

A much clearer voice interrupted him with a shriek of

rage. "It is a lie, all a lie! Dohlman Israi is dead, killed by the Starfleet assassins sent down to that planet. I am her appointed heir!"

"My aunt, the Crown Regent." Israi's voice trembled, but when Uhura glanced up at her, she saw the almond eyes burning with anger, not fear. "It is a good day for *her* to die."

"Males of my cohort," the Crown Regent continued fiercely. "Ships of my intrepid armada, destroy this false Dohlman who speaks to you. I command it, I who have cried the tears for each of you!"

Kirk's breath hissed between his teeth. "How many of them will obey her?"

"Only those of her own cohort, I think." Israi's fingers dug nervously into Uhura's shoulder. "They all know the sound of my voice, but those who are bonded will believe any lies the Crown Regent tells them." One of the tiny white pricks of starlight enlarged and resolved into a bullet-shaped gunship. "Some of them may fly ships of the armada."

"That figures." Kirk flung the shuttle into a steep dive as the second vessel began firing. "Isn't there anything you can say to make your aunt back off?"

"One thing, perhaps." Israi crouched down beside Uhura's seat, giving her a searching look she didn't entirely understand. The Dohlman nodded once, as if satisfied, then motioned her to adjust the communicator to Elasian frequencies again.

"Males of the glorious armada of Elas, all those who are not of my aunt's cohort—listen and remember my words if I am killed." Israi's clear voice deepened to the somber ceremonial tones she'd used when she bonded with Takcas. "Thus speaks Israi, sister of Dohlman Elaan, youngest daughter of Dohlman Kutath, and twelfth of the line of Kesmeth. On this first day of my tears, the first day of my true reign, I say unto you that my heir and Crown Regent shall no longer be Zhirnen, sister of Dohlman Kutath and my nearest of blood."

Another snarl of rage issued from the communicator, but Israi overrode it, her voice rising to a commanding shout.

251

"Hear now and know the voice of your new Crown Regent."
She glanced over at Uhura, and a surprisingly mischievous
smile floated across her mud-stained face. When she spoke,
though, her voice held only that uniquely Elasian kind of
arrogant assurance.

"Dohlman Uhura of the line of *Enterprise.*"

Chapter Twenty-six

KIRK GLANCED AWAY FROM the ancient shuttle's instrument panel only long enough to register Uhura's wide-eyed look of stunned surprise. Behind her, Israi regally placed both hands on the communications officer's shoulders and pronounced grandly, "Welcome to my family, sister of my heart."

Then the ship jolted, bucked almost into a roll, and Kirk flashed his attention back to the helm to fight for control of the spin. "I'm somewhat new to Elasian politics," he remarked through clenched teeth as he used their tumble to buy momentum. One of the armada gunships tore past at the farthest edges of the viewport, skating wildly across the curve of the upper atmosphere with a trail of ionized ozone glowing behind it. "But I suggest you accept the Dohlman's appointment, Commander."

"But, Captain—"

He arced them away from another line of approaching ships. Phaser fire ignited the space nearby. "Just say yes!"

"Crown Regent Uhura does not need to accept." The young Dohlman sounded remarkably unconcerned despite their pitching and slewing. "I have stated it. That makes it so." She patted peremptorily on Uhura's shoulder, motioning at the open comm line. "Speak to them that they may know your voice, my Crown Regent," she said, somewhat more loudly. "Let them know that your words must be heeded as my own."

"They know my voice, evil child!" The Crown Regent—Zhirnen now, Kirk reminded himself—sounded even closer and more angry than before.

"Your voice no longer carries power." Uhura managed to project a hauteur to rival Israi's, even though she sat in worried stillness with her hands clenched tightly on the edge of her panel. "Her Grandeur the Crown Regent does not recognize your existence, nor does Her Glory the Dohlman." She threw a questioning glance over her shoulder at Israi. "Isn't that right, Your Glory?"

The Dohlman nodded, smiling. "Hear the voice of my new Crown Regent, males of the magnificent fleet of Elas! Her words are as mine!"

A great corona of plasmic light swarmed across the nose of the shuttle, scarring the viewscreen and hurting Kirk's eyes. Zhirnen's voice came right behind the explosion. "You will all of you choke on your own lying spittle!"

The captain twisted in his seat, instinctively searching behind him for the source of the shot even as he aimed the shuttle into a screaming plummet. "Oh, hell . . ." Sunlight glinted off brushed gunmetal beyond the starboard portals; then Zhirnen's flagship swept up and away as their vectors crossed and sped apart again. The old K-117 slammed the skin of the atmosphere, creaking with stress.

"Captain!" Scott's voice broke across the open channel, loud with apprehension as he intercepted the Elasians on their own frequency. "Sensors report you're down below their array again!"

"Thank you, Mr. Scott, I know that." They entered the stratosphere badly, and a pocket of superheated air butted up against the small ship from below. Kirk fought to keep his hands on the controls as the first waves of ash darkened the viewscreen and roared like demons against the outer hull. He hoped the spreading mass of particulate matter scrambled Zhirnen's weapons sensors as thoroughly as it blinded their own. "Scotty, give me polar coordinates—where are you?"

"Sixty degrees and twenty-seven seconds—" Lightning strikes and ion buildup in the cloud of ash shredded the comm signal with static. "—heading for south of the equator, counterrotational." A crack of electricity from somewhere very nearby kicked the shuttle like an angry mule.

"Captain," Spock interrupted from his position near the main hatchway, in the rear of the ship out of Kirk's direct sight. "May I remind you that maintaining an adequate atmospheric seal is exceedingly difficult during such turbulent maneuvers."

"Spock—" They were nearly ninety degrees off the *Enterprise*'s position, heading rapidly away through the waves of glowing ash. "Tough." A roll of ash-filled thunder shook them as though in a vicious fist, and Kirk found himself nearly standing in an effort to force the ship into a downward arc instead of out of the atmosphere again. Above the disrupted atmosphere, they could be picked up on Elasian sensors or visually seen—that made them dangerously vulnerable.

"Scotty, keep on that orbit and don't slow down. As soon as we show up on your sensors, beam us out of here." Kirk could try to bring them around circumpolar, but didn't want to voice the plan while Zhirnen was surely listening.

"I'll do my best, sir," the engineer promised gloomily. "But if they've still got that geodesic net in place . . ."

"With all the ships that have been pulled out of alignment to fire at us, that geodesic net can't still be working." At least, Kirk hoped not. "For now, you just concentrate on beaming out anyone still at that mining camp. Once we're in range—"

Light, as white and searing as a warp core, blasted across Kirk's vision. He felt a jolt like a punch to his stomach, then the unmistakable pressure of his safety harness straining against the shoulders of his environmental suit as their downward plunge tried to lift him out of his seat.

"Rear boosters are off-line!" Spock was almost shouting.

They barely had emergency lighting up front, much less useful controls. The communications board and navigations console were dark and shock-cracked, the helm a frightening mixture of unresponsive and sluggishly inactive. Kirk could barely coax life out of the attitude thrusters spaced along the shuttle's bottom edges.

"What has happened?" Israi cried, gripping the back of Uhura's chair for support. "What is wrong?"

Kirk tried to estimate the ship's position relative to the surface. All he could tell was that they were falling. "Lightning. It finally overloaded the systems." He didn't dare fire the thrusters until he knew which way they were headed, but didn't dare wait, either, for fear of delaying too long. "Your Glory," he said, very stiffly and calmly, "I think it would be best if you and the Crown Regent went into the back and strapped down."

Uhura snapped open her safety harness without question and ducked out from under the belts. "Come on, Your Glory." Her voice was firm, her hands steady despite the gaunt look on her burned and ash-smeared face. She turned Israi with no-nonsense force and shoved her toward the back of the shuttle. "I'll tell Mr. Spock to be ready."

Kirk didn't actually hear them break out the shock webbing, or even talk to Spock. The crack and groan of the old shuttle's frame wound together with the crash and roar of the storm outside to devour all other sound. He felt vaguely guilty for the damage he'd done to this faithful old vessel. Then he smiled wryly, considering how little this was likely to matter in just another few minutes.

Ash rolled like boiling mud directly in front of the small ship's muzzle, then dashed aside like a ripped-open curtain to reveal clear, night-black air and the heaving surge of an ash-carpeted ocean. *Downward*, Kirk realized with a fist of shock jamming into his throat. They were headed straight downward. He hauled back on the manual attitude controls and dragged the shuttle into a deep, sweeping climb. At this speed, they'd smash into the ocean surface as if it were solid rock—even clipping the crest of the waves would steal precious momentum they couldn't spare just now. Their only hope of reaching the *Enterprise* was if Kirk could steal enough speed from this plummet to throw them back out of atmosphere when he finally pulled up out of their dive.

Kirk pleaded with the little ship under his breath, watching the horizon creep with agonizing slowness into the top of the viewscreen as the K-117 screamed and shuddered and fought to lift its nose skyward. Rakatan Mons, steep sides now carved into a pulsing webwork of ash rain and lava rivers, crouched beneath the lightning-shot clouds, blasting up ocean waves as tall as mountains with each explosion at its summit. It grew in the shuttle's viewscreen, grudgingly edged downward as Kirk continued to drag the K-117 out of its dive, then plunged suddenly out of sight as the ship's nose finally tipped upward and shot up along the tall flanks, headed back for outer space.

Zhirnen's flagship burst into being just off their port. Kirk shouted a curse, but didn't dare try to alter their upward plunge just for the sake of avoiding an encounter. They had to get out of this ash, away from this volcano, or no amount of evasive maneuvering would save them. The little shuttle screamed past the Klingon frigate at a speed so high that Kirk barely saw the enemy ship as they passed it.

"She's coming around!" Uhura shouted from the rear.

Bless you, Kirk thought to his communications officer. Not that he hadn't expected Zhirnen's move, but it was reassuring to know he wasn't piloting this antique craft without some help from his loyal crew. Killing the damaged engines, he counted aloud as they rocketed upward, estimating the seconds, estimating their speed. When the shriek of storm and cinder against the hull at last began to fade, three stingy blasts from the attitude thrusters boosted the shuttle into an awkward tumble, tail over nose.

Kirk heard a crash, and shouts of alarm from the back,

then the unmistakable roar of atmosphere rushing out into vacuum. He hoped Spock was all right—hoped they'd all be all right—but didn't have time to make sure of it just now. The ash-smothered column of Rakatan Mons rotated slowly into view, the battered Klingon flagship charging upward after the shuttle in a swell of alien smoke. Stabilizing as best he could in this nose-down position, Kirk cut every system still active and poured all their power into the forward thrusters. "Let's see how fast that bucket of yours can go," he growled at Zhirnen. He leaned into the throttle—ready to tear away in reverse with every ounce of speed the old shuttle's forward thrusters could manage—and the world beneath them exploded into a brilliant lake of flame.

A ripple of shock-torn air bucked through the accelerating shuttle, distorting the image on the viewscreen. They broke atmosphere to sudden blackness and terrifying cold. Kirk watched, transfixed, as a great column of fire roared silently up behind the Elasian's pursuing flagship. There was a moment—just the barest of instants—when light consumed the enemy vessel like flame licking over a moth's dry wings. Then the ship just seemed to evaporate without even its own death flash to indicate its passage, and the hungry red-and-black pillar surged up after the shuttle like a roaring god.

Oh, well, Kirk thought, still nursing the controls for every ounce of speed the old ship could give him. *At least it's a damned spectacular way to go.* Then the gout of superheated magma slammed over them, and the familiar tingle of the transporter effect raced along Kirk's frayed nerves before the volcano's first burning breath even touched him.

Chapter Twenty-seven

"GET YOUR BUTT back in that bed!"

Chekov froze with his hands still on the examination table behind him, and peeked a guilty look over his shoulder at McCoy. The doctor stood in the doorway connecting their room to the rest of sickbay, slapping a medical instrument against his palm as though contemplating some use for it the designers never intended. Groaning, Sulu fell flat in his own bed and pulled the covers up over his face. "I told you it wouldn't work," he grumbled from beneath the blanket.

"I wasn't leaving sickbay," Chekov protested. But he hopped back up onto the bed anyway when McCoy took his first determined step into the room. "I was just going to—"

"—check on the Dohlman," the doctor finished sourly, and Chekov felt his face grow hot. McCoy glanced at the readout above the lieutenant's head. "I tell you, I can't wait 'til your blood chemistry settles and I can pump you full of that damned antidote." He punched some notation into the chart at the foot of the bed and turned away with a snort.

L. A. Graf

"Not that it would make you behave. I'd just be confident that it was *you* trying to sneak out of here instead of *her*."

Sulu's laughter trickled from under his bedclothes, only to change into a startled yelp when the doctor slapped at his foot on the way by. "Don't laugh! You're second in line."

"Thank God!" the helmsman exclaimed, but McCoy was already through the door and too far into the main sickbay to hear him.

Sighing, Chekov sat cross-legged on top of his bed and propped his chin in one hand. His side still ached despite McCoy's commendable patch job, and the faint thread of breathlessness fluttering deep in his lungs told him his blood count was probably still way below any acceptable standard. He and McCoy simply differed on what they considered necessary treatment for such disabilities. The doctor insisted on complete bed rest in sickbay until such time as he decided the patient was free to leave; Chekov couldn't see what difference it made if he just went to his quarters to sleep it off, considering how much sickbay time he already spent out of bed trying to sneak past the doctor. The fact that he couldn't stop fidgeting with worry over Israi in the room across the way only made his forced inaction even more unbearable.

He waited until Sulu sat up and let his blankets fall into a puddle on his lap before scowling across the empty distance between them. "What is this about an antidote?" he asked pointedly.

The helmsman's eyebrows raised in a blatant expression of counterfeit innocence. "Hmm?"

"You heard me." Chekov unfolded to come up on hands and knees. "Did something happen in the shuttle that you neglected to mention to me?"

Sulu shrugged glibly. "Not in the shuttle."

"Sulu . . ."

A hush of quiet door movement announced someone's entrance from the direction of the sickbay labs. "Chief?"

Sulu startled at the thin whisper, but Chekov breathed a little prayer of thanks as he slid down off his bed to meet

Howard and Lemieux near the room's rear doors. "The doctor's just outside," he whispered. "Keep your voices down."

Howard nodded, pushing Lemieux past him toward Sulu as he handed Chekov the bundle of clothes he had tucked under one arm. "Sorry we didn't get here earlier, Chief." He clapped one hand over a jaw-stretching yawn. "I only just woke up and got your message."

"Better late than never, Mr. Howard." Chekov slipped his trousers from the bundle and shook them out to step into them. It felt wonderful just to be in clean clothing that didn't belong to a sickbay. "How are things in the department?"

"Quiet," the young ensign admitted softly. "From what I heard, you had all the excitement planetside."

If Sulu's head hadn't been inside the collar of his tunic, his amused snort would have been loud enough to alert the doctor in the next room. "You can say that again." He straightened the seams on his turtleneck, then reached for the jacket Lemieux held out to him. He picked up one sleeve and turned it over in his hand. "Hey!" he exclaimed in a squeaky whisper. "Is this my uniform?"

Chekov shrugged into his own jacket. "No, it's Uhura's," he sighed. "Of *course* it's your uniform."

"Well, where did they get it?"

"From your quarters."

"My quarters?!"

Chekov dashed across the room to clap a hand over Sulu's mouth. "Stop shouting!" he hissed, nodding sharply toward the main sickbay. "Do you want Dr. McCoy to hear you?"

He felt the helmsman's mouth twist grumpily against his palm, and accepted that as some small sign of submission. Taking his hand away, he kept a careful eye on Sulu while he fastened the front of his own jacket.

"I sent them into your quarters on my authority," Chekov explained, latching his shoulder strap. "What's the point of being a friend in a high place if I can't help you sneak out of sickbay? We're less likely to be picked up outside the infirmary doors if we're dressed as though we're going on duty."

"What are you, some kind of expert at this?" Sulu paused in sliding his jacket down his arms, glancing at Chekov. "No, never mind. Forget I asked." He took his boots from Lemieux and stooped to tug on the first one. "So where do we go, noble leader, since we *aren't* really leaving for duty and probably everyone on the ship knows it?"

Chekov sighed. That was probably their biggest problem. "Usually," he admitted, "I go to visit you." He straightened after fastening his boots. "I'm still working on it."

Sulu grinned at him brightly. "We could go visit Uhura."

"No dice, sir," Howard told him, shaking his head. "She's on duty up on the bridge."

"On the bridge?" Sulu intercepted Chekov's hand before the security chief could muffle him again. "How come she gets to go on duty while we're still both stuck down here?"

"Because she has more than two pints of her own blood in her body and she isn't sporting metabolic ratios that would knock down an Orion."

McCoy met the bank of guilty stares that turned to him with a wide-eyed look of sarcastic concern. "What's the matter? Am I interrupting something?" He flashed sharp blue eyes over Chekov's shoulder, and the lieutenant heard both crewmen behind him jump. "Howard! Lemieux! Get out of here before I put you on report!"

Chekov felt them hesitate, but knew from the thin set of McCoy's lips that this wasn't a time to challenge the doctor's authority. Reaching behind him, Chekov waved a dismissal to both ensigns without turning. "Go on."

"Yessir." He wasn't sure which breathless voice answered him. An instant later, two pairs of feet hurried out the laboratory doors just ahead of the doctor's scalpel-edged glare.

"As for *you* two—"

If another word fell from McCoy's lips, Chekov didn't hear it.

Something slim and golden moved in the doorway behind

the doctor's right shoulder, and Chekov glanced back at it for fear of being reprimanded in front of one of the wounded geologists. His eyes locked on the wide, angular face he saw there as though caught by a tractor beam. A sharp, unnamed apprehension had been chewing at him ever since he woke up, shaky from too much synthetic plasma, in the intensive-care unit of the *Enterprise*'s sickbay. Now, without warning, his unease melted away the instant Israi stepped into view around McCoy.

Something in his stomach twisted uncomfortably at the thought that he could grow so painfully fond of the girl in such a short number of days. She was like a precious little sister whose delicacy and beauty fired such a painful protectiveness inside him that he had to clench his hands in Sulu's rucked-up blankets to keep from dashing across the sickbay to join her. It was her age, he decided. Or the fact that she was so tiny, and looked so fragile and slight. He glanced aside at Sulu to see if her appearance instilled the same feelings in him, and was horrified to find the helmsman almost leaning across his hospital bed to stare at her in helpless intensity. Even the six Elasian males trailing her followed the Dohlman's every movement with identical expressions of grim dedication.

Chekov forced his eyes to meet with Israi's, and the animal power of her gaze struck him clear to the soul. "You—you drugged me!"

"I saved your life," she corrected him, as though the hideously wonderful effect her words had on his heart was of little consequence to her. "Just as your people saved mine." She waved her cohort's attention toward the two Starfleet officers. "Behold the first brave men of my cohort. They have served me well, yet they have known me for but a day. You should all strive to be as true and loyal."

"Yes, Your Glory." Each of the Elasians went respectfully to one knee, bowing their heads until their burned and weary faces rested on their hands. Chekov swallowed hard against a storm of embarrassed guilt. He wasn't sure how he was supposed to feel about seeing such humility from a

263

group of men who only the day before had to be ordered by their leader not to murder him.

"Dohlman Israi . . ." McCoy approached her gingerly, coming as close to her side as he could without actually reaching out to take hold of her. "I'm having enough trouble as it is keeping these two idiots in bed. Now, I promised Crown Regent Uhura I'd see to it that you were safe and cared for until—"

"I am *the* Dohlman of Elas," Israi cut him off haughtily. "*I* choose when I go and where I stay." She motioned her cohort to stand without even moving her bright almond gaze from McCoy's exasperated face. "Starfleet Doctor, it is the custom of the Dohlmanyi to bestow gifts upon subjects who have proven worthy. As the Dohlman of Elas, glorious warlord of the planet, daughter of the House of Elasi and twelfth in the line of Kesmeth, I gift you with this sword which my father once wore." She extended one hand behind her to receive a thin, elaborately jeweled saber from the man behind her. "You have pleased me well by treating my own sickness, and by caring for the mortal wounds of these, my bondsmen," she announced. "May this weapon serve as a symbol of your great healing powers, and may you wield it to slay all of the enemies who ever rise up against you."

McCoy took the sword as though not sure how to refuse. "I'm touched," he remarked dryly.

Whatever sarcasm the doctor had intended whisked by Israi completely unnoticed. "Now I must go and bestow gifts upon the other who has served me so well in this conflict." She flung out her hand in summons, and the touch of her flashing eyes stung Chekov like a lash. "Bondsmen—come!"

His body obeyed as though she'd jerked on a cord tied through his nervous system. He hated every movement he made against the screaming of his own will—hated the expression of impotent disgrace so plainly sketched on Sulu's haunted features—hated knowing that his own face no doubt displayed his own mortification just as plainly. But to actually be allowed to stand near her, to feel her heat, to breathe her musky smell—

McCoy grabbed at his arm, mercifully shattering his obsessive attention. "Now, wait just a doggone minute!"

Israi frowned in regal displeasure and knocked the doctor's hand away. "There is nothing you can do to stop them. Not while they are under my command." She smiled up at both of them, something very far removed from anger in her eyes. "They will return to rest and heal presently. But first there is a duty that must be done." Her hand against his cheek felt smooth and warm and strong. "Where is Crown Regent Uhura?"

Chekov leaned into her palm without knowing how to resist her. "On the bridge," he whispered hoarsely.

Beside him, Sulu seemed no less uncomfortable with their situation. "We can show you how to get there."

"Very well." Israi stepped back, at least releasing them physically from her overwhelming touch. "Then let us go together and make this circle complete."

Chapter Twenty-eight

UHURA WATCHED DAWN creep across Rakatan, the bright gold terminus washing quietly over the broad ring of volcanic ash that circled the planet. According to Mr. Spock, the eruption of Rakatan Mons had by now hurled over twenty-five cubic kilometers of ash and debris into the planet's atmosphere, ejecting a few more into outer space for good measure. It made Uhura very glad to be sitting at her normal station on the bridge, helping to route communications from what remained of the geologists' seismic network to their new headquarters in the science lab. The task busied her just enough to take her mind off her half-healed burns and the lingering nausea of the antiradiation treatments Dr. McCoy had run her through the night before.

A different signal chimed on her panel, and Uhura recognized the frequency even before she heard the words spilling through her monitor. "Captain." She spun and caught his quick hazel glance. "There's a message coming through from the Elasian warship *Esar*. The captain says he's ready to beam Her Glory the Dohlman over at her earliest convenience."

Laughter glinted in Kirk's eyes, although his face remained serious. "I hear and obey, Dohlman Uhura." He leaned forward and punched his chair intercom. "Bridge to Dr. McCoy. Is our glorious patient ready to be discharged?"

The doctor's voice was dry. "She's already gone, Jim, along with all those scorched Elasians Scotty beamed up last night. I got the impression she was headed your way."

The turbolift doors hissed open on McCoy's last words and Israi stepped onto the bridge, flanked by Sulu and Chekov and backed by a solid wall of cohort. The helmsman looked acutely aware of the bare-armed Elasian female beside him and mortified by it; the security chief mostly looked pale.

"I want Uhura." Israi subjected the bridge to a scornful stare that made her look strikingly like her sister. Her frown moderated a little when it fell on Captain Kirk, but it wasn't until she found Uhura's station that her almond eyes warmed with a smile.

"My Crown Regent." Israi stepped away from her cohort, keeping them in place with one stern glance. "I have come to bid you farewell."

Uhura saw Kirk's silent nod of permission and left her station to meet the Dohlman halfway, not sure whether or not that was the correct protocol. Israi's flickering smile told her it would do. They clasped hands, the Dohlman's touch alien-cool against Uhura's skin.

"I have bonded my cohort, Uhura, and taken a new *kessh*. It is time for me to return to Elas." Israi's voice seemed to have cloaked itself in the mantle of regal maturity overnight. Uhura blinked down at the angular golden face, almost missing the unpredictable lash of youthful arrogance she'd grown so used to. "But I owe you thanks and to pay it, I wish to bestow a gift on you before I go."

Uhura's hands tightened on hers. "You don't owe me anything, Your Glory."

"I do!" Now the old Israi was back, stubbornly insistent on what she wanted. "My life was in your hands down on that smoking mountain, and you guarded it like a bonds-

man." Her voice changed again, taking on a note of quiet
amusement that was clearly modeled on Uhura's own. *"Not
like a Crown Regent."*

Uhura matched her smile. "Israi, that was only my duty
as a Starfleet officer."

"I know. But I may honor you for it anyway." The
Dohlman turned and beckoned peremptorily at Sulu and
Chekov. Both men went to her at once, tugged by the
invisible chain of her glance. Uhura saw Kirk's eyebrows lift
in startled recognition.

"These two of my bondsmen have served me well," Israi
told Uhura. "But I think they will be of little use to me back
on Elas." She eyed them resignedly. "They will probably
pine for their *chosen* bondings here."

Uhura pretended to give both men a considered stare.
"They probably will," she agreed, trying hard not to smile as
Sulu squirmed and Chekov scowled at her helplessly. "Per-
haps you shouldn't take them with you."

One corner of Israi's mouth quirked up, as if she, too,
knew this was just a formal play of words. "Such was my
decision. And since I must leave them in any case, I thought
I would gift them to you for your own cohort." She leaned
forward, heavy amber earrings clinking against Uhura's
lighter gold ones as she whispered in her ear. "I know you
have none, really, but this will gain you standing as my
Crown Regent. It is a mark of great favor to transfer
bondsmen voluntarily."

Uhura lowered her own voice to an even softer murmur,
trusting the Dohlman's sharp ears to catch it. "You want me
to remain Crown Regent?"

"For a while, yes." Israi stepped back, almond eyes
glinting this time with a malicious and entirely Elasian
amusement. "After all, who will try to overthrow me now
that my designated heir is not even an Elasian? With you as
my Crown Regent, I will be left in peace until I marry and
have heirs of my body to replace you. Depending on how
long it takes my council to arrange a marriage for me, I may
even become the longest-reigning Dohlman of my line!"

Kirk chuckled behind them, a half-strangled sound as if he'd been trying to hold it in and failed. When the Dohlman turned to glare at him, he spread his hands helplessly. "I—um—am pleased to see that you share your sister's intelligence, Israi."

Israi snorted. "I did not give you permission to use my name, Kirk-insect."

"Oh, right. Sorry."

Mollified now that the captain's smile had been properly tucked into hiding again, the Dohlman turned back to Uhura. "You will accept this gift?"

Uhura nodded. "I will."

"Very well." Israi swung around, bringing Sulu and Chekov to attention with one intent glance. "I release you from your bonds to me and to Elas, males of my cohort. You may go free of your own will to accept the bonds of this, my sister and Crown Regent."

Both men started and blinked muzzily, as if they had just woken from some walking dream. Behind them, Uhura saw Kirk's eyes widen in astonishment.

"That's it?" the captain demanded blankly. "That's all there is?"

"Yes." Israi turned a knowing almond gaze on him. "My tears will linger in their blood, of course. I cannot make that bonding vanish with a word. But if I tell them to act and be as if they were not bonded, they must obey me utterly and do so." She smiled. "Of course, if the bonding had become an attachment, it would be much more difficult. And I believe my sister was very attached to you, Captain Kirk."

"Oh." The captain's face tightened in a wince of rueful embarrassment. "I see."

Israi spared him further discomfiture by turning back to Chekov and Sulu. "Do you accept this new bond?" she asked them sternly.

Her former bondsmen stared down at her, looking dazzled with the freedom of having choices again. Naturally, Sulu recovered first. "We accept it gladly, Your Glory." He elbowed Chekov, and the Russian grunted in pain. "Right?"

"Right," Chekov said between his teeth.

"And you," Israi turned to Uhura. "Do you accept these my bondsmen, sister of my heart?"

Uhura nodded, mind leaping ahead to what must follow. "I accept with great honor and pleasure, Your Glory." With an effort, she forced herself to think of the saddest thing she could: Scott Mutchler's last moments on Rakatan Mons.

Israi nodded and motioned the men forward. Uhura took a deep breath and stepped forward to meet them. Mutchler's last words echoed through her head: Enterprise! Enterprise! *This is it—!* The geologist hadn't sounded angry or bitter, Uhura thought poignantly. He had sounded—excited.

One tear stung at her lashes, then another. Uhura caught them carefully as they rolled down her cheek, then reached out to brush her wet fingers first against Sulu's cheek, then against Chekov's. "My honor in your hands, bondsmen."

Israi nodded approval. "Now you say, 'My life in your hands, Dohlman Uhura,'" she prompted the men.

Sulu's mouth twitched, but he managed to keep the rest of his face solemn. "My life in your hands, Dohlman Uhura," he repeated. Chekov snorted, but a stern glance from Israi and another nudge from Sulu dug the ritual words out of him.

"That was performed well." The glint in Israi's almond eyes told Uhura what the words truly meant. "I will now permit you to beam me over to my ship, Kirk-insect." She stepped back, her own bonded cohort closing around her like a jealous cloak.

"My pleasure," the captain said smoothly. He flicked a glance up at Scott, who watched in wide-eyed wonder from the engineering station. "If you would do the honors, Scotty?"

"Oh, aye, Captain." The chief engineer hurried forward to escort the Elasians down to the main transporter room, giving Israi a discreet but definite berth as he passed her. Uhura's mouth quivered with amusement.

Israi waved her bondsmen ahead of her into the turbolift,

then turned to gaze over her bare shoulder at Uhura. "Rule your underlings in strength and glory, Crown Regent Uhura of the line of *Enterprise,"* she said quietly.

Uhura smiled at her. "Rule your planet in peace and wisdom, Dohlman Israi of the line of Kesmeth."

The turbolift hissed shut on the Elasians' barbaric glitter of gold and jewels, then almost immediately slid open again on the gold-and-black uniforms of the Federation Geological Survey. Uhura skipped out of their way, retreating back to the safety of her station as the excited handful of geologists surged out onto the bridge. All of them seemed to be talking at once, although only one word in three was recognizable as English.

"Ladies and gentlemen—" Kirk's entreaty had no discernible effect on the chaos. Uhura could see Wendy Metcalfe at the center of it, her thin face flushed with excitement and her hands full of crumpled seismic profiles. "Professors, if there's something you want—" That plea didn't get their attention, either. *"People!"*

The resounding shout—Starfleet's equivalent of a Dohlman's command, Uhura thought in amusement—finally got the geologists' attention. All five fell silent and turned to regard the captain expectantly. Kirk gave them back an exasperated look.

"Was there some reason you brought this argument up to the bridge?" he inquired with chilly politeness.

"We're not arguing about anything." Florence Bascomb detached herself from the group, white hair ruffled and eyes snapping with excitement. "We're here to tell you what we just found."

Kirk's eyes narrowed. "Don't tell me—"

"It's true, Captain!" Wendy Metcalfe pushed forward to the front. "Our computers on the station weren't powerful enough to resolve it, but when we analyzed our data on the *Enterprise*'s processor, the signals jumped right out at us." She turned and waved her papers happily at Spock. "We've catalogued thousands of calls and replies so far, Mr. Spock. By correlating them with our earthquake and eruption records, we've even begun to translate some of their words. For instance, they use a sort of magma reverberation to say—"

"Whoa, whoa, whoa!" Kirk reached out to catch her madly waving hands. "Are you trying to say that there are actually sentient creatures inside Rakatan Mons?"

"An entire society of them!" Metcalfe beamed up at him. "Built on partially coagulated silicate molecules, just like I suspected."

"Designed to propagate as volcanic crystallites, spreading from cone to cone—" added another young gelogist.

"Maybe even from planet to planet—" a third chimed in.

Metcalfe nodded vigorously. "And they keep their colonies intact as long as possible by repairing cracks in the magma chamber before eruptions get too big. That's why—"

"—Rakatan Mons got so big to begin with!" Bascomb finished excitedly.

That broke the dam and got the technobabble going again. Kirk stepped back from the din, tossing an inquisitive look across at his science officer. "Is it really possible, Mr. Spock?"

The Vulcan lifted one austere eyebrow. "Theoretically, Captain, quantum theory makes anything possible. The actual likelihood of a given event may be vanishingly low, but—"

Kirk cut him off with a scowl that would have done Israi credit. "Spock, just answer my question. Could there be magma creatures down in that volcano?"

"I see no reason why not."

"Huh." The captain eyed Rakatan's image on the screen. The planet's disk lay in full sunlight now, its immense volcano just coming into view below its canopy of ash and smoke. Kirk stepped back into the scientific fray and silenced it by the simple expedient of hauling Metcalfe out from its center. The graduate student blinked up at him in surprise.

"I suppose you're going to want to stay here and study

these creatures for the next few months," Kirk said resign-edly.

"Oh, *no!*" The geologist waved her papers at him. "We'll want to come back eventually, of course, but we have more than enough data from the past year to keep us busy translating for months. Until we know enough to actually talk to them—"

"—it's *much* more important to tell the rest of the scientific community about our discovery here," Florence Bascomb finished firmly.

Kirk looked from one to another of the geologists, seeing agreement on every flushed face. He quirked an eyebrow and turned back to his helm officers.

"You heard the professor," the captain told them blandly. "Set a course for Starbase Seven and take us there at warp five." He slanted Spock one last amused glance. "After all, we don't want to stand in the way of scientific progress."

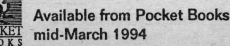

BLAST OFF ON NEW ADVENTURES FOR THE YOUNGER READER!

A new title every other month!

Pocket Books presents two new young adult series based on the hit television shows, STAR TREK®: THE NEXT GENERATION™ and STAR TREK®: DEEP SPACE NINE™.

STAR TREK®
THE NEXT GENERATION™
STARFLEET ACADEMY™

#1: WORF'S FIRST ADVENTURE
#2: LINE OF FIRE
#3: SURVIVAL
by Peter David

#4: CAPTURE THE FLAG
by John Vornholt
(Coming in mid-May 1994)

#5: ATLANTIS STATION
by V.E. Mitchell
(Coming in mid-July 1994)

and

STAR TREK®
DEEP SPACE NINE™

#1: THE STAR GHOST
(Coming in mid-January 1994)

#2: STOWAWAYS
(Coming in mid-March 1994)
by Brad Strickland

#3: PRISONERS OF PEACE
by John Peel
(Coming in mid-September 1994)

Published by Pocket Books